D1467005

ALSO BY RELENTLESS AARON

Push

RELENTLESS
AARON

St. Martin's Paperbacks

PUSH

Copyright © 2001 by Relentless Aaron.
Excerpt from *To Live and Die in Harlem* copyright © 2005 by Relentless Aaron.

Cover photo © Herman Estevez

ISBN: 0-312-94969-3
EAN: 978-0-312-94969-3

Printed in the United States of America

Relentless Content, Inc. edition published 2001
St. Martin's Paperbacks edition / February 2007

St. Martin's Paperbacks are published by St. Martin's Press, 175 Fifth Avenue, New York, NY 10010.

10 9 8 7 6 5 4 3 2 1

To Julie
With all my heart, I love you.
I wish your family the best of all worlds.

PROLOGUE

HARLEM'S OWN REGINALD "PUSH" JACKSON was a good kid to begin with, groomed with a secure family upbringing. However, following the death of his parents, Push was left with few choices in life. From a local thug, to a ruthless killer, to a man who paid his dues and sought out a better life, Push is every young man's dream and every woman's warrior.

Still, there are some who have unfortunately crossed onto Push's list of enemies.

It is here in Harlem's underworld where the story of Push unfolds. His "stomping ground" is a much different world than others, with dark and unfriendly streets, where gangsters, thugs and hustlers are the superstars who rule.

And now Push has been compelled to handle a task that happens to be right up his alley. Push has been hired to kill.

Suddenly, Harlem's lawless encounters have a new judge and jury to balance those rights and wrongs, those beefs and scores. Push is not just a thug, he's every ounce a terror on two feet.

And you shouldn't take that personal.

WELCOME TO HARLEM . . .

CHAPTER ONE

IN LESS THAN 1 MINUTE, Roy Washington would witness a murder. He was parked on *122nd* Street, slumped down in the back seat of his glistening, jet black, wide-bodied Mercedes sedan. The car was just 3 weeks old, a testament of success, however earned. And it gave the streets a message: *this particular man came up . . . he scored, he's winning.* The streets were always watching cats like Roy Washington.

It was 9:30, early for a Friday night, when ballers, hustlers and players—Roy considered himself all of the above—were still deciding whether to live it up, or keep it on the low, play it small and intimate. This was what was on Roy's mind just now; maybe he'd take Asondra downtown to *The Five Spot* to catch something jazzy . . . he could swing across the East River and show her off at *SugarHill* in Brooklyn, or at *Manhattan Proper* in Queens . . . or he could bring her pretty-ass uptown to *Club Carib*, the swanky spot in New Rochelle. But then, of course, there was always the usual circuit here in Harlem, *The Rooftop*, *The Cotton Club*, *Perk's* or the *Lenox Lounge.* Roy let these ideas digest as he soaked into his soft, black-leather seats. There was more room to stretch out here in the back seat. And besides, the total impact of his dope hi-fi system touched him better back here. It was as if his car had become an intimate lounge in itself; a place for a man to think while he waited for his woman to get her hair done.

The Quiet Storm was pre-empted on Friday and Saturday nights so that the party music could butter up the minds of black folks, perhaps directing them to this club or that with those so-called "*live broadcasts*." The infamous "*live broadcast*"; it could be a radio personality standing in the corner of a club, 4 or 5 early birds with him, all of them making noise into a cell phone to simulate a much larger crowd. Indeed, a larger crowd would inevitably come, lured in by that very charade they heard over the radio airwaves.

The tricks they play on the radio, Roy told himself, wishing he had a piece of that scam along with those of his own. He was inspired to change the mood and reached from his relaxed position to feed a CD into the sound system. You could never go wrong with Anita Baker's Greatest Hits. And that was just the CD Roy picked. He liked how the mellow-voiced soulstress worked the scatting into the rhythm and blues.

> "Bah-bah—bah—bwee,
> bah bah—bah—bwoo,
> bah bah—bah—boo—yeah."

He found himself intoxicated by the music, (the only right thing in his wayward world), and it had him almost slipping out of consciousness. His eyelids drooped shut in an effort to stock up on some sleep so that he'd be alert for the evening. He never could tell what might cross his path: there could be a new piece of ass he'd meet, or a fresh business prospect to pass a phone number to. There might even be an old enemy lurking. It was anybody's guess what might come along. For this was Roy Washington's life: plenty of pussy, plenty of loan-sharking to do, and plenty of enemies. It went with the territory of this jack-of-all-trades . . . someone who took those high risks. He didn't care whose feet he stepped on, just as long as he got his way. Just as long as he got paid and laid, he had it made. And speaking of stepping on folks,

Damn, Asondra is taking forever up in there, thought Roy. *Up in there*, was "*Mya's Place*," where Mya Fuller operated an exclusive salon from her home. Hers was a 3-story brownstone here on 122nd Street where certain clients came to get their hair did or their nails done for the weekend. Roy had been up in *Mya's Place* a number of times in the past, for business, since she was one of his clients. But never did he have to go in there and make a scene, to reprimand Asondra for taking so long. Only now, he was swearing in his mind:

Women. Roy let out an exhaustive sigh. Such was the price of keeping a high-maintenance woman at his convenience. And Asondra was just that; keep her in diamonds, keep her going to Mya's, stick a hard dick up in her, and she'd keep her mouth shut.

Roy smiled to himself at the idea of Asondra being *his* . . . of being what he wanted: a perfect lady out in public, and an absolute slut in the bed. She was street-smart and sharp when it came to looking the part, creating that all-important illusion for the world to see. But Asondra could be a bitch, too. A devil. And that's when Roy had to put his foot down. He'd have to *check* her. It might take a good slap across her face, or he'd be extra rough with her in bed, just to remind her of who the big dog was . . . who was in charge around here. Tonight, Roy decided, as soon as Asondra came out of Mya's Place, he would let her have it. That was the problem with pretty bitches like Asondra. Let her get the best of you, even a little bit, and it was *too* far. Tomorrow she'd try to get away with something else. *Hell* no.

In his mind, Roy could see the whole picture: Asondra would hop in the passenger's seat and say, *"You like?"* All smiles and cheer casted at him.

And Roy would answer, *"Come-eer you pretty mothafucka . . ."* Asondra would quickly turn soft, her eyes half-closed in a sexy leer since he was *surely* referring to *her.* That's when Roy would flip on her, he'd grab her face and squeeze her cheeks together with his large, boney hand. Her face would be contorted with her eyes searching his. Then, while in total control, he'd say,

"Bitch, if you ever keep me waiting like that again, I'll slap the shit outta you. Got me?"

Asondra would nod as best as she could within his grip.

Then Roy would say, "...*Now put your tongue in my mouth*," just to make things all lovey-dovey again. This was how it went between Roy and Asondra. This was the way it would always be while Roy Washington, the womanizer, slash, Mack Daddy, slash, loan shark, had his way.

CHAPTER TWO

THERE WAS THE SOUND OF squeaking brakes that interrupted Anita's CD just as it was preparing for her next song. The unfriendly noise belonged to a yellow cab that stopped in close proximity to the Mercedes. All of this was captured within Roy's sleepy gaze. And furthermore, the cab was so outrageously bright against the night and the line of dark brownstones across the street.

There were no streetlights on 122nd, just another dark, dismal, haunting atmosphere that defined the reality of Harlem's mean and hungry jaws.

A man stepped out from the rear of the cab, exposing Roy to the inside, where the passenger had already paid the driver. The cab pulled away, leaving its exhaust to waft in the air, and its 6-foot-tall passenger squeezed between Roy's car and the one in front. The man's face showed itself in that fleeting instant, despite the tint of the Mercedes windshield. He had a ponytail, a mustache and goatee shadowing his red-bone skin.

Stepping onto the sidewalk, he seemed to curse himself as he looked down and wiped himself off. So Roy guessed right, that the guy got some of that snow and dirt mixture on his pants and shoes and whatnot. Roy sighed and resumed his dream.

SLEEPY HEAD WASN'T THE ONLY one out there on 122nd Street. Neither was the man who disembarked from the taxicab. Reginald "Push" Jackson was waiting, out of sight, packing an automatic firearm, carrying on with his own inner dialogue.

There he is. Raphael, the snake. Right out in the open. No time to think. Just do it. Get it over with. He'll never put his hands on my sister again. Or anyone, if Push could help it.

And just like that, it happened. Push moved like a scorching flame or a deep freeze—both of those sensations pulling at his senses as well as guiding him; creating that rush . . . that motivation. And then, of course, there was that bitter taste in his mouth from the aspirins he chewed on, the reminder that he could always turn to. A reminder that wouldn't let him forget the horrors of his past.

It took seconds for Push to launch his attack.

ROY COULDN'T BELIEVE HIS EYES. He wondered if he was seeing things and maybe the sun block tint on his passenger's side window was playing tricks on his mind.

It was as if a shadow appeared. A lean, caped shadow sweeping out from the dark belly of the brownstone; down there under the steps where garbage cans were usually kept.

Slouched low in his seat, Roy looked on with total awe as the predator shot out and faced a very surprised man. His arm swung around, gun in hand, until the weapon was pointed and locked on the taller man's forehead. There were no words between the two. Nothing to discuss. There was simply that flash fire from the weapon. The victim jerked backwards into his final fall against the snowy pavement. All of this taking place mere feet from the Mercedes and turning the iridescent white landscape into a blood-soaked Mister Frosty.

The shooter in all black, including the knitted cap and combat boots, stepped over the body and calmly pumped another bullet into the skull as if to be sure the job was done. With wickedly precise timing, after the corpse shook from the violent impact, the killer pivoted off and strolled westward on 122nd street.

"Shit!" exclaimed Roy. Looking out at the ground, then his side view mirror, then at the victim again. Roy was suddenly struck with a sense of permanence . . . of finality. His mind's eye and thumping heart were jointly reaching towards the masterful executioner who was becoming more of a memory with every westward step. Roy was already climbing into the front seat, magnetized and needing to know more about that man. *That cold killer.*

He still had time. So far as Roy could tell, the guy hadn't even reached Lenox Avenue as yet. Careful not to cause any more of a scene, he wiggled the Mercedes out of its parking space, out of the slush and eastward on 122nd, a one way street with a single lane. If he was aggressive enough he could shoot down to 5th Ave, where Mt. Morris Park was, then cut over to 121st Street and hustle up Lenox.

It wasn't like he wanted to *meet* the guy; just follow him and find out who he was. No congratulations or handshakes. If anything, Roy might manage to bump into him, (a *big* might) and he would do so as lightheartedly as he could; as though he didn't just watch this guy snuff out a man's life just minutes earlier.

Roy picked up his car phone and punched in Mya's number.

"Mya, it's Roy. Put Asondra on," he said, too wired up with too much of a blurred sense of direction to be polite or cordial.

"Sure, darling," Mya answered, likely too busy with her hands in somebody's hair to address his crass introduction. Roy heard Mya giving instructions to a subordinate and could picture the handset being passed on. It sounded as if Asondra had to take the call with her head half-under the hairdryer. Meanwhile, a radio was pumping Barry White in the atmosphere along with some hyper female radio personality.

Roy was like a fish in a fishbowl, extra-sensitive to every sight and sound. *They must be so busy they don't have a clue about what happened out in front of the brownstone.*

"Baby? I'll be another ten minutes or so. I'm drying—"

"Hey listen," Roy said, cutting Asondra's excuse short. "Something came up. I might be late gettin' over there. Keep in touch by my cell phone. Worst case, take a cab to the crib." The idea of the "cab" suddenly hit him. Hadn't he just seen what happens to folks who get out of cabs on dark streets?

"Everything alright?" Asondra asked.

"Why wouldn't it be? Talk to you in a few," Roy ended the call too abruptly to respond to Asondra's kiss. He was on 121st now, carefully approaching the stoplight at Lenox. The Mercedes crawled to a stop, close enough to the edge of the block for him to scope out the sidewalk. There were just a few pedestrians between 121st and 122nd, among them two shapely women, so bold to have their calves and thighs exposed in such frigid weather. There was a panhandler in dark, woolen clothing, with hands and fingers exposed where his mittens were ripped. Meanwhile, the proprietor of a barbershop there on Lenox, between 122nd and 123rd, was pulling down his metal gate for the night.

Roy simply waited there observing all of this while the traffic light changed a 2nd time. He eventually made the turn onto Lenox allowing the car to crawl until he recognized that same dark shadow.

It was him. Roy was sure of it. And it was a great relief to see that the killer wasn't looking his way.

Halfway between 124th and 125th streets, a taxi pulled up to the curb to let off a party of three. They scurried across the sidewalk and into the Lenox Lounge somewhat cowering from the cold. As if to read the guy's mind, Roy assumed that the killer would hop into that same cab and disappear into the night. At least, that's what *he* would've done. But that's not what he did. The man slipped in the door of the lounge right behind the others, he even helped hold open the door for them.

Roy's mind was volleying thoughts.

Just a few blocks away he took a man's life . . . smoked 'em without even blinking. And now he wants a drink?

There was no getting enough of the impression that this guy projected. How cool, calm and collected, to so casually transform himself into a clubgoer. A courteous one, nonetheless.

Spinning his steering wheel and navigating the Mercedes into a parking space close to the corner of 124th, Roy was twisted between both fear and curiosity. He had no idea why he was doing this.

Yes, he did. There was no fooling himself about something so obvious. What it was, was that Roy never had such heart. He could never be the violent beast . . . the extraordinarily smooth operator this stranger was just minutes earlier. This guy was that type of man who men such as Roy *wanted* to be like, *dreamed and craved* about it even. To just rub elbows with a man like this; maybe they would get to know each other better. Maybe some of those superpowers would change hands.

And because a man didn't mind imposing violence or shooting a gun didn't necessarily mean he had heart. It was just that certain something that a person like Roy—slickass, fast-talkin' coward that he was—was attracted to. A man with heart. A man with the courage and a strong will, who could carry out such a significant feat, And when it came to significant feats, taking another man's life was certainly a top contender.

Inhale . . . exhale . . .

Roy stuck his cell phone under the car seat and grabbed his leather pouch where he kept his black book, a 2nd cell phone and a pen. There were also some business cards in a rubber band:

ROY WASHINGTON

Under his name was his Harlem phone number (a voicemail) and there was also a dollar sign. Roy Washington, jack of all trades.

◆ ◆ ◆

THE LENOX LOUNGE WAS JUMPIN' by now, where the men had on leather jackets, bombers or sheepskin coats over t-shirts, turtlenecks and rope chains. Most men also had on dungarees or jeans, and Timberland or other fashionable work boots; basically the brand name stuff. Few wore basketball sneakers, like the latest Jordan hi-top, and perhaps a sweatshirt to match.

The women wore leather or denim skirts that barely covered their thighs, they had on stiletto-heeled booties, and maybe a full-length fur here and there. Some had on jeans which hugged their baby-makin' hips, along with the knee-length fur-lined boots. The blouses were always cut below the neckline so as to show cleavage and the strands of gold chains that hung therein.

The hairstyles ranged from finger waves, to wraps, to flip styles, to weaves that fell well beneath the shoulders. Some of the women, as well as most of the men, donned hats of some type. There were fedoras, baseball caps and a bunch of Kangols.

The blond-haired, dark-brown-skinned woman was the only one sporting a fur fedora, a brimmed hat that she kept tipped to the side and which matched her full-length pink coat. She was seated at the bar on a stool, amidst the mix of patrons. Two girls, both of them with natural blow-out hairstyles, were standing as close as they could to the blonde, as though might somehow be connected there between her legs. One of the two wore a denim mini-skirt, fishnet stockings and heels. The other had on hot pants, those paper-thin shorts that ended where the pubic hair might begin. She had muscular thighs and calves, a little more defined than her "twin," down to her strap-up shoes. The hot pants and shoes were the color of shimmering gold. Both women also had on the same tie-off blouses that left their midsections and pierced navels exposed. By the expensive makeup, the buffet of hair and the perfumed air around the three women, not to mention the way the fully dressed blonde spoke to her 2 friends, it was clear that this was a pimp of sorts, and the two standing oh so close to her were her hoes, if not merely women who provided her pleasure.

Next to the threesome was an older man with a heavy handlebar mustache and matching salt n' pepper hair that was matted back in slick waves. He was seated at the bar, with his elbows on the counter and his hands clasped over his drink. He seemed disturbed, wanting to drown his sorrows. Two men were next to him, both of them without stools, standing with their backs up against the bar. Gold jewelry glinting from here and there, accessorized with gold bracelets, watches, necklaces, and tinted eyewear, they had an arrogant way about them, with sly expressions, leering at every fine young thing that strutted past.

"Come—eer. Lemme' holla at cha'." The one with the toothpick sticking out of the side of his lips had his leg extended some so that a passing woman couldn't help but to acknowledge him. Meanwhile, his hand was down near his crotch, as if playing with himself.

Amidst this idle activity wafted an overcast of cigarette smoke that put everyone and everything into a hazy, musky atmosphere. A deejay was wedged in the corner, opposite the bar, with the speakers set carelessly on the floor, chair and table; all of this directed towards most of the 50-plus patrons.

> *"Jay-Z and Biggie Smalls*
> *make ya' shit ya' draws,*
> *Brooklyn goin' out for ya'll*
> *Bed Stuy . . . ya' don't stop . . .*
> *Brownsville . . . ya' won't stop . . ."*

The sound system in the club may have been half-assed, with the bass levels too high, and some of the music drowned out by the beats, but the songs were as familiar as sweet milk chocolate was to the tongue. The impact still had the crowd bouncing where they sat, or bobbing their heads where they stood. This was that home away from home for the men and women, the 20 & 30-somethings who gravitated to the Lenox

Lounge. It was a safe haven. Where you could get your drink on, your swerve on, and *always* your mack on. Becky, that girl who might only be familiar with green pastures and prairie dresses, would be scared to death in this joint. But for the others here, this all made perfect sense.

Roy was inside now, where it was warm. He was already welcome in his long leather jacket, knit pants and the Rolex peeking out from under his cuff. He nodded at one or two faces that were hardly familiar, and quickly stepped to the bar.

"A Bud, baby," he called out to the young, sultry, 20-something bartender with plenty of tits, ass and smiles. She was someone a stranger could immediately talk to.

Wrapping a cocktail napkin around a cold one, she popped the cap and passed the beer to Roy. He gave her a five dollar bill and said, "Keep the change." And now Roy too, was one of those idling up against the bar.

Where is this guy?

CHAPTER THREE

REGINALD PUSH JACKSON WASN'T NECESSARILY one of life's big thinkers. He just wanted the simple things. He never lived fancy or associated with many people. He didn't much go for entertainment, celebrities, big Willies, or the various lifestyles of the rich-and-famous.

"Fuck all that bling-bling shit" is what Push often told himself, since all he really wanted was to stand strong, never compromise, and live and die in Harlem. To survive and see the next day would be okay too.

When Push was just Reginald Maynard Jackson, there were those big dreams. There were those pie-in-the-sky visions of wealth and fame; no different from what other kids his age wanted, or from what danced across the TV screen. But life got the best of Reginald at an early age when his parents were killed.

It was just the four of them; Reginald, his younger sister, Crystal, and their two parents. The family lived together on Adam Clayton Powell Blvd.—also known as A.C.P.—in a 2-bedroom apartment on the top floor. It was a climb which wore you out. The only views were of rooftops to the rear of the building and Well's Restaurant across the street. The Jackson home was cramped, with little room for solitude or privacy. However, this only brought them closer together where they could learn about and from one another. The Jacksons were regulars at church, they ate at Well's once a week, and there were the family rituals that seemed to be normal: Christmas, Thanksgiving, and New Years. Beyond that, Reginald Sr.

worked for the Sanitation Department, while Mrs. Jackson was a stay-home mom.

The murders took place on an early evening. Crystal was taking dance lessons at the *Apollo Theater*. Reginald Jr. was out hustling, selling t-shirts on 125th Street. As it was detailed in police reports, Mrs. Jackson had been home alone and apparently opened the door with the chain on. Two, maybe three intruders pushed their way in, then proceeded to beat and rape Mrs. Jackson. Beaten, gagged and hog-tied to a kitchen chair, her attackers took her every entry mercilessly. Mr. Jackson arrived home in time to surprise the attackers. He tackled them as best he could, but they apparently overpowered him. Mr. & Mrs. Jackson were found just minutes after the attackers escaped, gunshot wounds to their heads, and torsos.

> . . . It is apparent that, although shot, Mr. Jackson used his last ounce of life to crawl to his wife's side . . .

So stated the police report. Reggie and Crystal Jackson, just 13 and 11 years of age, were suddenly alone in the world. Orphans. They were wise enough to avoid the city's Department of Child Welfare by sneaking off. Reginald was making enough money to rent a room and feed his sister. But eventually, he put the t-shirt hustle aside and began selling drugs. Within a month he was making $400 a day. Within 6 months he was promoted to lieutenant and afforded a 2 bedroom apartment for his sister over on 126th Street.

Within one year, Push became the block captain, overseeing 6 other lieutenants. He was "Push" now, because he was pushing more product than the others who were part of the "125th Street Crew."

A short time later, he *really* earned that nickname.

Crystal quit school when she found out she was pregnant by Turk, a local mack. The mack was more than 30 years of age (she was 13 by now) and he quickly disclaimed the child. It took a few weeks to find Turk, but Push and his wolves eventually paid the mack a visit. Turk was "invited" to a rooftop discussion, which led to an argument, which led to a smart-mouthed comment, and a one-way trip; a 6-story fall from an abandoned building on Fredrick Douglass Blvd. When Turk's body was found, it was so broken it couldn't be picked up by EMS workers. It had to be dragged onto the stretcher.

"You don't need no Turk for a baby-father," Push had said to his very frightened, very alone sister. Crystal just sat there brooding, hugging her growing belly, rocking back and forth, with no idea how to voice her rage, her helplessness or her insecurity.

Push gave Crystal $2,600, his days earnings, hoping that it might ease her pain. It did. And she said she'd name her baby Reggie.

Although nothing could replace the support of a responsible, loving father, the money helped Crystal to deal with pre-natal issues, the childbirth and early stages of young Reggie's care. Push was still doing his thing in the streets. He had been arrested a few times for possession and gun charges, but these run-ins with the law never amounted to more than 18 months in jail, and ultimately did nothing less than harden him. This miserable place, where young men and women were kept in cages, like dogs in a kennel, was where Push was left to realize his own survival skills. He quickly caught on, that you had to do one of two things: fuck or fight.

But Push was from the hard-knock streets of Harlem. Fighting was his life. So, being locked up made no difference. While Push was away, his lieutenants looked out for Crystal and her child. She never had a care or a financial worry. This was "Push's sister", and there was an understanding that required little discussion. On the other hand, if one of Push's subordinates caught a beef with the law, Push was always there to post bail, send money and take care of the children and baby-mommas left behind. Of course, money and a consistent cash flow made such conveniences possible.

Push grew more and more powerful on the streets of Harlem, nodding or shaking his head when it came to life-altering decisions. Sometimes he'd have mercy on a thief (there were *always* thieves) and he'd put a bullet in the man's leg, shooting him in such a way that there would always be a limp to remember the foul play. Push was the reason for some of the nicknames in Harlem: Crip. Hock. Left Foot. Limp Man. And now, with a few years in the game, a strong organization, and respected name to go with it, Push found himself with piles of money to manage. The cracklord Goat, who had been the boss of the 125th Street Crew, was killed. That made Push the new H.N.I.C.—the Head Nigga In Charge. Push invested tens of thousands of dollars in small businesses around town, calling it "venture capital," but never once did he draw up a contract. This was partly due to his love for Harlem, but not to mention that there was *so* much money around at times that he didn't know what to do with it.

There were beauty salons, barber shops, restaurants and small bars he invested in. Push also helped those who didn't own businesses. He heard about some of Harlem's residents who were down on their luck or out of a job, and he'd cover their rent and food for 6 months or longer, encouraging them to soldier-on and not become another dependant of the state. On another occasion, Push heard that his former residence (where the Jackson family had lived as a family of 4) was burned to the ground. He gave $20,000 to each of the residents who had lost their homes and furnishings. The relief was so instant for the 15 families that were suddenly stuck out in the streets, an act that made Push a local hero at the age of 17.

Although such good deeds don't necessarily account for the bad ones (the drug dealing and violence that went with it), Push had made quite a name for himself. But when the umpteenth Harlem Renaissance was proclaimed, a stink was made about the drugs in the community. A task force was set up and major sweeps began to strike some of the most notorious drug enterprises. Most every housing project had its resident drug gang, the most obvious targets for the feds to hit. Then came the two largest enterprises; Sugarhill and 125th Street. For Push, there were serious consequences. Of the 40 arrests, 5 became government witnesses, giving in to the heavy threats made by Drug Enforcement Agents.

"You'll never ever see the streets again if you don't testify . . ."

"Your little girl will be a grandmother before you get out of prison . . ."

"We believe your mother and your Aunt are a part of the conspiracy. We're picking them up right now unless you cooperate . . ."

And so on, and so on. There were more scare-tactics used on these young thugs than were used to topple the Mafia. It was an "anything goes" atmosphere in the war on drugs.

Unprepared for the worst, the Push organization immediately folded. Push was sentenced to 15 years in Federal prison, a less-severe sentence because of his being a first-time federal offender. Suddenly, he was 18 years young, with a new reality: under his new circumstances he couldn't expect to walk the streets of Harlem, visit his parents' tombstones, or lay down with a woman until he was close to 33 years old. And this wouldn't be an easy stretch, spent at some camp or country club where dethroned judges, shamed congressmen and former bank executives were sent to play tennis or catch a nice sun tan. Club Fed wasn't for young thugs like Push. Instead, he'd be sent to the penitentiary, behind cement walls and steel bars; where everything (except a man's breathing) was controlled by 2-way radios, handcuffs and brass keys.

Welcome to Lewisburg Federal Penitentiary—Lewisburg, Pennsylvania.

CHAPTER FOUR

GOING TO THE PEN WAS not like going to the local pokey, where everyone knew someone, or where most other detainees knew and respected a local thug with a well-earned name. Here, you had to earn that reputation all over again. And once you did, you had to *keep* earning it since there were a thousand cats from all over the world, all of them with their own thug-reps, and their stories about who they shot, robbed or killed. Every one of them claimed a rep back on the blocks where they hustled and so forth. But so what.

Within his first week, Push was the target of a convict named Popeye. Popeye was somewhat shorter than Push, and he had protruding eyeballs that were big enough to play golf with. And yet, Popeye was no slacker when it came to the weight pile, evidenced by his muscled body—an appearance that might at once seem intimidating. But Push didn't give a fuck about that. From his point of view, he had enough confidence to do battle with 3 men. And besides, Push had been forewarned that Popeye always trying to make a name for himself. And however this dude wanted to play it, Push was ready to respond.

It all began with the threatening looks and graduated to that one verbal assault:

I don't give a fuck about yo money, what you had, who you knew or the ho you got babies by . . . matter fact, I don't give a fuck about yo momma neither!

Push already had the "Fuck or fight" state of mind, something that he kept from the days back in the local lock-up, so the confrontation that Popeye asked for left Push with no other choice. Noticing how Popeye turned to one of his buddies for moral support, Push made the first move, swinging his concealed weapon—a combination lock tied to the end of a belt. He swung for the temple with a blow that busted mouth-almighty's face open. His one eye sprung out and down over his cheek. Blood squirted everywhere.

Popeye was immediately rushed to the hospital and treated for trauma—his head had to be pieced back together as well as his face and his ego. Push, on the other hand, was subjected to a disciplinary hearing. Despite his actions being an act of self-defense, he was sanctioned to spend 6 months in the hole—that building full of tiny holding cells where convicts were sent for various disciplinary reasons, or for purposes relating to an institution's safety. Escape artists, mercenaries and troublemakers (especially) were kept in the hole. But Push didn't feel like he was a discipline problem; someone who threatened the institution's safety. All he wanted was to be left alone to do his time. Popeye changed all of that.

While in the hole, Push quickly adapted. He tested himself each day. He meditated. He challenged himself to block out all of the noises that drummed on inside of the segregation unit; the cries, the cat-calls and the belligerent name calling. Despite this being the ultimate melting pot of misery, Push made the best of the circumstances. He routinely tested and strengthened his memory by using word associations to recall dates, names, numbers and faces. He also exercised relentlessly, executing 1000 push-ups, three times a day. He did just as many sit-ups and deep knee-bends to keep his midsection and legs in shape. The prison staff provided him his three square meals, showers 3 times a week, and any necessary medical attention. It was enough to survive for a man who had been stripped of everything except for his free mind. But Push didn't need much else than those mere necessities to strengthen his body and master his mind.

Dear Push,

We miss you out here. Your nephew Reggie, is doin' fine. I'm working at Perk's now as a waitress. It ain't much, but it pays the bills. I go to school part time too. I'm thinkin' about a second job at the Cotton Club—you know how I like their gospel brunches on Saturdays and Sundays. Anyhow, some of the girls around the way been asking about you. They wanna write and visit and stuff, but I told 'em you don't get down like that. I told 'em like you told me: you go hard, and you the best who ever did it.

Oh, Bernie got shot up out where you used to run the block. People told 'em to leave your spot alone, but he got a hard head.

I'm keepin' myself well, cuz ain't no man controllin' me, Push. You know how I get down! This reporter keeps callin', but if he wants to spend his money my way, it's okay by me.

I scratched up somethin' for ya'. Enclosed: $100,

Don't be a stranger.

Miss you, Love you.

Your sis, Crystal

THE 6 MONTHS IN THE hole went by fast since Push adjusted. It came to a point where he didn't care if he spent the whole 15 years there. The hole had become the only thing he knew; the only reality he woke up to and went to sleep in. Inevitably, Push rejoined the general population at Lewisburg and found that he suddenly had new friends, or at least "*pals*," since everyone knew there was no such thing as friends in prison. With all the confidence schemes, hustlers and con men, this was the best way to think; the best way to protect yourself was to go on thinking that *everyone* was out to get you. Especially, those who were the closest to you.

One of Push's pals quickly informed him that his troubles relating to Popeye were not over. Even though Popeye was now a permanent resident of the Bureau of Prisons' Springfield, Missouri, facility—a full-service hospital and psycho ward out in Missouri—the muscle-bound troublemaker had left a friend behind; a lover, in fact, who had given and taken sexual favors. Loverboy's name was Kelly, a convict who affirmed his effeminate nature with his everyday appearance: tight pants, hair pulled back in a stubby pony tail, and t-shirts tied-off at the navel. Kelly had no physical alterations (no hormone-induced breasts, yet), but the shrill voice might fool someone—surely a blind man. Kelly also had an abundance of facial bumps (the results from excessive shaving), a few front teeth were missing, and his sinewy build accommodated that ass-switching walk of his. His strut was one that could rival a fashion model's runway appearance.

"Watch out for that gump, Push. He in his feelin's about that Popeye-shit."

Push didn't lose a night sleep over the gump, Kelly. He had a 15-year sentence to serve. No time for cat & mouse games. And he wouldn't spend the time looking over his shoulder either.

"Whatever happens, happens," Push replied.

And it *did* happen.

Not 30 days after Push was released from the hole, he felt that flash of hot pain in his side. He thought it was a cramp at first, but things began to spin there in the hallway. Convicts, lights and brick walls were circling around him. The various sets of eyes all had that know-nothing, seen-nothing look about them. Kelly's face was among them, the last thing Push saw before crashing to the floor and blacking out.

"You lucky, Push," a voice said from his left. "That gump didn't know nothin' bout' usin' the steel; otherwise you'd be *done,* kid." Push suddenly realized where he was; that half-assed, makeshift prison infirmary down in the basement of the pen. He had to come through here in the very beginning of the bid to get the required physical and AIDS test. For now, however, he was handcuffed to the bed. Next to him was another convict, also handcuffed to a bed.

Push was waking now, with the anesthesia wearing off.

"Oh. You mean . . ." Push grunted at the pain ripping through his body. To himself he swore he wouldn't move again. ". . . this isn't *already* Hell I'm goin' through?"

A light flickered on the ceiling at the same time as the

neighbor replied, "No. You still alive. Hell means you already dead."

There were bandages around Push's midsection, and more wrapped around his head from the fall. *Who is this guy??* he asked himself.

"I ain't tryin' to be smart or nothin'," the guy added, "I just give it to you raw, yah-mean."

Push groaned, not really responding. And yet he found himself wondering if the dude was from the Phili-Jersey area, the "yah-mean" region of the world. He gave another look to his left, managing to do so without the pain this time.

"What happened to you?" asked Push.

"I got caught out there alone. I was comin' out the shower and them Arian brothas got me. Had to be four or five of 'em, cuz I ain't no one-on-one type a mafucka. Nair' one of them white boys got heart enough to try me alone, else they be the one up in this bed. Shit. They might transfer my ass, then I won't see no get-back."

Push had gone back to looking at the ceiling, although the neighboring convict's image stayed with him, as if the ceiling was a theater screen. The man had to be all of 6 feet and built like a brick house. Only, his leg was in a cast, as were both arms. He had bandages around his head, leaving just one eye exposed. Push wondered if the missing teeth were the Arian Brothers' work or if the dude came to the pen that way.

"My boys prob'ly checked that for me . . . . I would try to reach over and give you a pound, but . . ." He laughed. "I might fall apart. Name's Tonto."

"Sup," answered Push, then he realized that the name struck a bell. "Where you from?"

"Harlem world," a proud Tonto replied.

"Shit. You that cat, use to run beside Hollywood—"

"Yup. Sugarhill, yo."

"Ya'll use to have Sugarhill on lock!" The younger generation, one in which Push was a part of, had their own nicknames for the streets of Harlem. 145th Street was known as Sugarhill, or 45th St. 126th St. was known as 26th St., and so on. "Yo . . . my name is Push. I was . . ."

"Humph. I know you, dog. Ya'll had *twenty-fifth* on lock, word. We was *jealous* of you cats."

"Jealous?! Ya'll was makin' *dumb* money up your way. I heard when they raided Sugarhill Hollywood threw like four million in cash out the window . . . he had it snowin' Money all over that spot."

Tonto laughed. "Yeah. That still fucks me up. That's why Hollywood a legend . . . but ya'll was makin' cheese too. Plus, ya'll had the one-two-five; *Damn* prime location. Yo, lemme' tell you sump'm . . ." Tonto said, ready to divulge some inside stuff.

"Hollywood locked up fo'ever, so it don't much matter. But . . . yo, we was thinkin' bout comin' thru there. No doubt. I mean . . . don't get me wrong. You prob'ly a true-blue mafucka, but yo' money was callin' us. It was hollarin', '*come n' get it*!'"

"I'm glad you didn't do that, yo. Cuz we was holdin' ours down. Niggas tried to stick us . . . they tried and caught body bags, word. That's why I think the feds came in and swept us. We got too dangerous. Bodies was droppin' like every other day," Push said.

"Yo, man, they got Hollywood out west somewhere in deep lock where Gotti was. I'm talkin' that supa-dupa max joint . . . underground. Plus, he got triple-life."

"Imagine that. Locked up, *and* buried," said Push.

"Snitches," muttered Tonto,

"You too?"

"Man . . . you don't know the half. They didn't turn over but one dude who kicked it with us, but there was like fifteen who the feds paid. Fuckin' *paid* to testify. Like sixty of us got hit on the hill, plus they went and got girlfriends, wives, fathers . . . they arrested one dude's whole family to try and get a nigga to squeal. Only person who talked was some slick motha-fucka we use to call Flash. Skinny ma-fucka was workin' with them DEA—he really fucked us up . . ." grunted Tonto.

"Prob'ly home mackin' some girl right now," added Push. Push thought about how easy snitches and informants had it;

how their prison sentences were so minimal that they wouldn't
even be missed on the streets. Freedom and light prison sentences were incentives offered to help prosecute defendants.
"Believe me," said Push. "I know how they do. We had a few
who turned over too. I'm just lucky how I came away with
only fifteen joints. But I coulda got a life sentence for the shit
we was runnin'—*easy*."

"If you call not gettin' a L easy, then I guess I got lucky
too. I got seventeen myself. I think they was lenient because
them DEA was dead-wrong how they shot up my brother
Sonny and me . . . Sonny dead." Tonto's testimony was followed by dead silence.

Later Tonto said, "We gonna be back on the bricks at the
same time." Push imagined what that would be like for the
first time in a long time; he'd be about 32 years old. There
was no special program or extra good time which he could
qualify for since there were guns and violence connected to
his name. And it wasn't that Push got *caught* shooting anyone, it was mere rumor that Push was responsible for a few
crippled thieves who limped or hobbled along some of
Harlem's sidewalks. There was also Turk who took that "fall"
years ago. But the feds only had snitches and rumors to work
with when there was no hard evidence to tie-in such hearsay.
All they had to indicate Push's violent life were the guns involved with his case. What else made Push so dangerous (according to the law enforcement records) was the information
entered into the court proceedings by paid informants. These
weren't even people who knew Push personally, and yet they
contributed elaborate details about weapons, shootings and
homicides in Harlem, some of which Push had nothing at all
to do with. Still, all of these details were now a permanent
part of Push's files. As far as the government was concerned,
Push was just another homicidal maniac that needed to be
kept off of the streets. Locked up.

"But, I'll tell you what," said Tonto. "When I get back,
I'm on a mission. Flash is the first ma-fucka I'mma see. And
it ain't 'cause he snitched. That hot mafucka shacked-up
wit' my ex."

"Shit. You mean *after* you got knocked?"

"That coward-ass nigga snitched. He got my ex to snitch and testify against me, plus the two prob'ly layin' up right now. I used to *love* that bitch too, Push. That was my heart. Even had a baby boy by me—"

"No shit."

"Word. We was *like* that. I always use to take care a that woman like she was Queen Sheeba or some shit. She even got to keep all the money I had layin' around the house. Shit, she got diamond rings, watches, everything. Then after we got hit, she and him—" Tonto let out an angry growl. But Push couldn't tell if it was from the physical pain in his body or from the memories.

"Damn, dog. Sounds like you been through it."

"Yeah, but that day's gonna come, troop. When I get home I'm killin' everythin'. I'm talkin' bout Flash, the bitch, AND the motha-fuckin' bastard. That's my word."

"Dag, you gonna kill *your own son*?"

"I ain't *got* no son. Straight-up."

Tonto's reputation already spoke for him. He sounded too sincere, with such lethal words emerging from his lips. This was the same dude who use to sit in a 2nd floor window with an M-60 machine gun, guarding Hollywood's dynasty—the whole Sugarhill/145th Street landscape. But for Push to lay there and hear the man voice his convictions . . . just to be in Tonto's presence was the most deadly atmosphere Push had ever experienced. Yet and still, Push found himself magnetized to the older convict. They only spent 2 weeks together there in the prison infirmary, but it was a rich and rewarding two weeks. Tonto gave Push some pointers on doing time, things that would help him to avoid situations like those that got them both in this predicament in the first place.

"But, as you can see, everything doesn't always work in your favor. You gotta expect a bad day . . . a bad week now and then. Like I always say . . . it's not the time that's hard, it's the *people* who make it hard," Tonto explained. It was best to move independently. Go for *self*. Niggas respect that. But if that don't fit ya', then get with an air-tight clique . . ."

By that, Tonto was referring to a group of fellow convicts who were similar in many ways and who would watch each others backs. Tonto went on to say,

"Try and stay sucka-free . . . away from those niggas that ain't about nothin'. They ain't nothin' but trouble." Tonto and Push talked more about the good ole' days in Harlem and all the blocks, the clubs, the businesses and the personalities. They talked about the numbers runners and crack kings. Alpo. Porter. Preacher. They talked about Big Dave, Big Red and Big L., Rutgers Park, the summertime gatherings at Grant's Tomb, and how the former mayor forced so many do-good vendors off of the street corners. They remembered the *Rooftop, Wells, Sylvia's, Perk's*, the *Lenox Lounge* and *P.J.'s . . . M&G's, Nikki's, Copeland's* and also those parties that Maria Davis frequently promoted. Of course they talked about all of Harlem's forthcoming updates, such as those at the *Apollo Theater* and how the basketball great, Magic Johnson, proposed building Harlem's first major multi-cinema movie complex. Naturally, there were others that jumped on the bandwagon with their brand names: *Starbucks, Pathmark, Jimmy's*. There was the coming of former President Clinton, and the improvements at the *Schomburg Cultural Center* and the *Dance Theater of Harlem*.

All this talk about Harlem had Push to forget how Tonto intended to go home on that mission to kill. It was a complex subject to discuss, the hate and contempt that Tonto had for his baby's mother. And for Flash, the rat. Push considered another angle to reach Tonto.

"What kind of trade you goin' into? I mean, the drug thing is over, ain't it?"

"Looks like it. They got Harlem lookin' like the fuckin' Disneyworld of the ghetto. Stores and cameras and cops everywhere. But . . . I don't know. I'm pretty good wit' my hands. Maybe construction or somethin'. Always wanted one of them brownstones for my own." Listening to Tonto got Push to thinking about all the people he himself once helped; people who had been burned out of their homes, or who faced eviction. "But yo'," Tonto continued. "To be honest, I'm not on no there's-no-place-like-home trip. We gotta keep our heads right here in prison. We gotta survive this shit before anything else. A motha-fucka could get all lost in his dreams and lose sight . . . lose focus, and look what happens. We end up in here . . . in bandages 'n shit. That hope and faith and dream-shit might work in the lows—in them country club spots. But here? Cats don't wanna know shit. And Magic Johnson or Harlem ain't here to bail you out of trouble. You gotta fuck or fight."

Push understood well the importance of living in the now, however he couldn't help but to keep that torch lit in his mind. No matter how small a flame it was. He knew the difference between the convict's world and the free world; that distinction was sometimes the same as life and death and how you had to maintain your balance between the two. But then, Push hadn't been off of the streets for long, so he still had traces of hope and optimism in his mind; images of better days that were still somewhere outside of these walls. More than that, Push still had his youth. After a time, all of the hope, the optimism and the youth would slip away. During the month-long stay in the prison infirmary, Push learned to get familiar with the bitter taste of aspirin, even chewing the tablets to break them down, hoping that the contents would reach the blood stream quicker. When he was well enough, Push was transferred to another penitentiary in Allenwood, Pennsylvania. This was a newer facility then the last. However the procedures, policies and way of life were all uniform, if not identical, with the time he served in Lewisburg.

Always, next to the prison rules, there were the convict rules. The prison rules were in black and white, printed in booklets and distributed to each convict upon his arrival. If you broke these rules, the punishment could be as minimal as telephone, commissary or visitation restrictions for months or even years. It was considered the worst punishment to be sent to the hole, a period of time that is usually deducted from your "good time," making for a more extended stay in paradise. On the other hand, the convicts rules were not in writing. No booklet, lectures or orientation classes. These rules and behaviors were easy to remember: Respect the next man, keep your mouth shut, and mind your own business. *It was that simple*. Just do your time and don't cry about it. Your situation is no worse than the next man's. And besides, mommy's not here to save you. Also unlike the prison's rules, there were the consequences if you got out of line with other convicts. In most cases, that amounted to violence, or worse.

For a prison job, Push worked in the recreation department, replacing the free-weights, the bars and dumbbells at the end of the day. The rest of the day he was free to read, play a couple of hours of chess, and run around the track for 3 hours, nonstop.

When a new convict came to the pen, word spread quickly. If it happened that the guy was from Harlem, Push was immediately informed. Push and his buddies would put together a welcome package for the newcomer (toothpaste, shower shoes, hair grease, etc.) and they'd pay him a visit in his cell. On one of these occasions Push was introduced to Block.

"No . . . I ain't run with no big crew, just a few. We did small-time capers like burglaries and mom & pop heists.

"Capers? What's that?" asked Shawn. Shawn was the cream-complected member of the four Harlem homeboys. He wore circular eyeglasses and a bush afro that seemed to move a half-second after his head did.

Buck popped Shawn in the arm. "Crimes, *fool*." Then Buck shook his head and said, "Don't mind him. He was one of them special children who came to school on them little yellow buses,"

"Ya' momma," snapped Shawn. And the two posted up like they were about to thrown punches.

Push interjected, not finding the others one bit funny. In the pen, there was rarely time or place for momma jokes, not when your life could be snuffed out in seconds. Any crew that ran together had to always set an example, or else all of them might appear to be clowns underneath those masks of fearlessness.

"What, like break-ins-n-shit?" Push went on to ask.

"Yeah, basically. We use to cold bumrush bitches at their front door . . . run in and clean that mafucka out. That's how we was getting' down." Block was so heavy into trying to convince the 4 of how solid he was . . . so full of ego and that false sense of pride, that he didn't realize Push was baiting him. Push was trying to learn more about this Harlemite.

Push's body clenched when Block revealed his proud occupation in the streets. He didn't want to believe that one of his parent's murderers was sitting right here on the bunk bed, within arms reach. It was too coincidental. Push needed time to digest this. He said, "Yo, we should talk later, ya' know . . . out in the yard or something. It's a small world, *hunh*? I know we gotta know some of the same cats from around the way."

"No doubt," answered Block, already busy looking through the welcome bag.

Push and his boys stepped off, heading out of the cellblock towards the prison's law library. It was quiet there. A man could think.

"Yo, Push. You not thinkin' what I'm thinkin'," suggested Brian. "I mean, that would be a hell of a thing."

"What cha talkin' about, Bri? What thang?" asked Buck.

"Yo' dreadlocks is too fuckin' tight on yo' head, fool. Can't you see? Dude might be one of them that, well . . ." Buck was sensitive to what Push might be thinking or going through. He didn't want to press the wrong button; didn't want Push to flip-out. The man was already in deep thought.

Finally, Push put up his hands, "Ayo, we can't jump to conclusions on this. Lemme' get to know the dude better. If he *was* one of them, he's surely gonna catch it, big time. But this is my beef. Let *me* work this out. But, for now . . ." Push poked each one's chest as he said, "Keep—your mouths—shut."

• • •

3 MONTHS PASSED, AND PUSH earned more and more of Block's confidence. Block began to share things with Push; things he'd never said to another soul.

"Yeah, I miss those days of runnin' up in spots. But now that I'm in here, I wonder if it was even worth it," said Block, apparently looking for some compassion or redemption.

"Didn't you all save money?" Push worked to keep the *"you all"* in the conversation, still unaware of the whos and hows behind Block's testimonies. He wanted to know more details about the stuff they did. Egging him on, Push said, "I mean, I use to do a hit and come off with a few hundred here and there. But it sounds like ya'll were doin' it up big. Like ya'll had a method or some shit. Let a nigga know!"

"Nah. Nothin' like that."

"Well, what's the most *memorable* hit ya'll did? Like . . . what was the most satisfyin' "

Block smiled as he considered this. His eyes gleamed as though he'd just received all the answers to his high school exams in advance. Then, with an overwhelmed ego, he went on to say, "It would have to be the hit we did on the check cashing people. Either that, or the time we banged this broad up on A.C.P. I mean, we did marvelous things to this woman."

"Marvelous, huh? Let a nigga know . . . how marvelous was it?"

"Yo', I don' usually be braggin about shit like this, cuz, well, this is prison. Dudes might not like hearin' about this shit."

"What?! Abusin' women? Psssh! Ain't nothin but wannabe Macks up in here, dog. How many men up in here done beat the shit outta a woman. *P—lease*. And besides, who's gonna repeat it? Me?? What you say to me don't go no further than here, homey. Now holla at'cha *boy*," said Push, with fake enthusiasm.

Block shrugged, "I guess you right. Okay, check it . . ." Block seemed to salivate in that instant, eager to tell the story. Exactly what Push was hoping for. "Me and Alonzo and Miguel—"

"You mean, Miguel—the dude who lifts hubcaps around Lenox?"

"Oh shit! You know him? Dude ain't liftin' caps no more, Push. That nigga got a job at the jerk chicken joint up on 134th and Lenox."

"No shit. What about Alonzo?"

"He did a small-time caper on his own and got caught. He only got like six months in Rikers, though. Niggah prob'ly back living with his brother on top of Sammy's Crab Legs."

"Oh yeah? I know that spot." And Push had already committed these things to memory: the jerk chicken joint on 134th . . . Alonzo living at his brother's apartment over top of Sammy's Crab Legs.

"Lemme tell the story, son!"

"My bad, I didn't mean to interrupt. Tell it, nigga."

"So check-it. We see the door is open to the lobby, so we climb all the way to the top. Damn this spot had a lot of stairs . . . and we figured we'd break in whatever was easiest and work our way down, ya know? But we hit the jackpot on the first try. Miguel knocks and says all official-like: "I have a UPS package ma'am . . ."

Push had a stiffness in his neck, and he worked his head this way and that to loosen up; that psyched-up state of mind that a boxer might assume just as he steps into the ring. And still, he listened on, his eyes turned down to the floor so as to hide the rage that was building inside of him.

". . . And Miguel's got the UPS hat, the jacket . . . yo', son was *like that* with the bullshit disguise. So *boom!* The woman—she had to be forty—opened the door and we run up in there. But before the bitch screams, Alonzo pops her in the face. Just like that—BAMM!—she goes to the floor. She's like, '*GOD!*' Holdin' her face-n-shit, like she don't believe a niggah just hit her like that . . ."

Push cleared his throat. Again, his face turned away.

"You a'iight?" asked Block. "You need some water or somethin?"

Push coughed and hacked as he answered, "Nah, I'm good, You just got me all . . . excited. Get to the good part, yo'."

"Son, you ain't heard *shit* yet! Me and Miguel grab this bitch's arms and we twist her over a kitchen chair. Alonzo snatched her skirt off . . ."

It was them! Ma was found beaten about the face, raped, her clothes ripped off while she was tied to a kitchen chair. Push had his own inner dialogue going. Calculating things . . . enduring the pain his mom must've felt. Meanwhile, he continued to hold that stupid, phony smile on his face.

". . . So, Alonzo grabs her legs. She's tryin' to get away-n-shit, so Alonzo kicks that ho right between her legs. I'm talkin' right in the pussy!"

Push swallowed hard. It was taking all of the discipline he could find to keep from jumping on Block, to continuously pound him until he could no longer be identified.

"I think . . . I need that water." Push could hardly get the words out. If he'd said another word, breakfast might rise up from his gut. He hurried off for the water fountain at the head of the cellblock. But the water did little for him. There was a burn racing through his body that was almost unbearable. Push splashed some of the water on his face.

"Damn, son. This shit is really gettin' to you."

Push managed a deep breath. "It's all this time I got, man. It's fuckin' my head up, nah-mean? Anytime I hear about niggas gettin' pussy, I get all crazy."

"You don't look too good, son. We could do this later."

Push quickly turned towards Block, grabbing his forearm. He had to stop himself from grabbing the rapist too hard, and he did so just in time. Again, the smile and the wildly-excited eyes brightened Push's face. "No! Tell me more!" Push seethed like some mad demon.

"If you say so," said Block. Then he really poured it on. He confirmed Push's hunch. It was *definitely* them. They beat his mother; plus, each one of them penetrated one or all of her openings, including her bloodied mouth while she was hog-tied. Push imagined his mother fighting it all, maybe giving in at some point, or just being left to hope and pray she made it through. Block also mentioned a palm-sized 9millimeter, and when Push's father (Block called him "the ho's man") caught the three by surprise, he tried to tackle them to the floor. It was Miguel's gun, Block explained, as though he'd missed the opportunity to be the trigger-man. But Miguel was the one who shot both of the Jacksons. Then the three of them fled the scene, scot-free. Until now.

Push made an excuse to depart from Block's company. He found Shawn, Buck and Brian, but didn't say much. The look in Push's eyes was enough to tell the story: The four of them had to devise a plan. Block had to die for his actions.

Another month passed, with days and nights that were agonizing. There wasn't a night Push didn't re-live the events that found his parents dead and he and his sister homeless. It was especially difficult for Push to be phony in Block's presence, to continue to look into that mongrel's face knowing what he'd done. But he pulled it off, somehow finding patience and peace in what had to be done. There was so much else that he'd endured to become an adult . . . the growing pains that brought him to terms with the whos, the whats and the hows in his life. He'd tough this one out as well. As far as he was concerned, it was his destiny to avenge his parents. Nothing was gonna stop him. To spike his confidence for this mission, Push had only to think back to how he and his sister were deprived of parents, of family, of hope for the future. How they had to go on the run in order to escape D.C.W., even missing the funeral. To kill Block (and eventually, the others) felt like his reason for living; how he was captured, convicted, stabbed by a queer, transferred so that he'd later run into his co-defendants, and homeboys . . . all of these occurrences and coincidences took place so that he'd inevitably run into his parents' killer. And now, like the judge had done to him, it was up to Push to make that ultimate decision; to determine this man's fate . . . his sentence. Block would receive the death penalty.

CHAPTER FIVE

MR. RANDALL WAS THE RECREATION SUPERVISOR in charge of the weight room on weekdays, those same days when Push was responsible for putting away the weights once the gym closed. Push took time and patience in developing a relationship with the white man, who was in his mid-40s, always with the no-nonsense way about him, and usually went "by the book" when it came to policies and procedures. Push eventually worked things up to a point where they could tease one another without either being offended.

Push would say: "Randall, you prob'ly scared to death on the bricks. I bet you even wear your sunglasses at night."

Then Randall would say: "I might *look* scared, but I bet I'd have heart-enough to bust a cap in your ass right-quick."

Then Push would say: "Yeah, but you'd prob'ly miss, you and your Coke-bottle glasses and two left feet."

Randall would laugh and say: "But I'm gettin' laid with my Coke-bottle glasses and two left feet. What're *you* gettin' besides burn marks on your palms?"

And that would surely be the end of the jokes; Randall throwing that last knock-out punch. Yet Push and the others would break into roaring laughter. There was no shame between Randall and these convicts. And that's just what Push wanted; he wanted the older man to feel as though he'd gotten the best of Push. It was something of a confidence game, to soften him enough so that they could complete the task ahead. This was every bit a part of the plan.

Sean, Buck and Brian were with Push most weeknights, easily posing as volunteers to help put the weights away. Randall didn't mind a bit, as this went on for weeks. Eventually, the "pick-up crew" invited Block to come and help, hinting that he was part of the crew as well. Sometimes the guys would have 5 or 10 minutes to lift weights once the room was clear, and they'd test each other's power now and then. Again, Randall didn't so much as raise an eyebrow. Instead, theirs was a consistency and a teamwork to be admired. In the meantime, all 5 convicts were developing a routine that became as casual as personal hygiene—just another part of the day. It was only a matter of time before the right moment came along.

That moment fell on an evening when a group of outside performers, a 4-piece mambo band, visited the prison to entertain a mostly Hispanic audience in the gymnasium. Since the gymnasium was set apart from the weight room (yet under the same roof) the usual routine carried on. It was a stroke of good luck for Push. Or bad luck, for Block.

When the show in the gym ran a few minutes overtime, the additional staff on hand was utilized for keeping order and to usher convicts out of the building. Mr. Randall went to assist, nodding his approval with the atmosphere in the weight room as he turned away.

"Don't take too long fellas. I don't wanna be here all night."

"You got it boss," answered Brian, already feeling like a bona fide recreation worker. Buck, Shawn and Push all shared a knowing expression while Brian manned the hallway through which Mr. Randall disappeared. Now was the time.

"Yo', let's see if Block got a bench," announced Shawn.

"Nah, said Buck. That nigga's chest is like a birdcage. If he lifts anything over fifty pounds, somethin' might break."

Push said, "You gonna let him *punk* you like that, son?"

Block sucked his teeth as he plunked two dumbbells onto the rack in proper order.

"Man, I know what I can do. Why should I play into that shit?"

"True," answered Push. But Push also made a face with the response. Like, maybe Block *was* a punk. Block was moved to say, "Yo', you with *them* on that lame-ass challenge?" He had his hands on his hips and an expression of disbelief.

"Lame? My whole commissary limit this month says you can't lift more than a hundred pounds," said Brian from near the hallway. Everybody knew Brian's family always kept his commissary 3-figures deep. So the challenge was legit. And again, Block gazed into Push's eyes.

Push shrugged and said, "They crew, son. Whatchu expect *me* to do? If you strong like that handle yo' business. Whatchu got to lose? You know Brian's commissary *stays* pilin'. I'd go for mines if I was you." Then Push turned to the others and shouted, "My money's on the birdcage!" And the others laughed. The *birdcage* was nothing more than a dis; unless, of course, Block decided to take the challenge.

Finally, in a fit of disgust, Block tossed up a last set of dumbbells and said, "*Fuck-it!*" As if that was all the disrespect he was gonna take.

Buck and Shawn did a little dance, giving each other a pound as they bet for and against Block.

Push said, "Well I'm matchin' whatever any of ya'll are puttin' up."

"Nigga, you gonna lose all yo' money. Don't even go there," said one of his homeboys. At the same time, Block shrugged, unconcerned with all the hoopla.

"Ya'll gotta be kiddin'. I can do *ten* reps with a hundred pounds."

"Show and prove, son. I ain't neva seen you do it," said Push.

Block laid down on the bench while Shawn and Buck stood to the sides, getting the 45-pound plates onto the bar and then lifting it for Block to take himself. They all stood by watching as Block began pressing the weight up and then letting it down till it barely touched his chest. He had already completed 5 repetitions when Push turned to Brian to be sure the hallway was clear. Brian returned a thumbs-up signal. No staff in sight. Now was the time.

Push stood at the foot of the bench and nodded for Shawn and Buck to stop Block in mid-motion. He was near his 8th repetition, nearing exhaustion, as the two applied pressure to the bar, bringing the full weight down against Block's chest.

Block let out a grunt. "Yo!" he gasped—or tried to. The words barely escaped the young man's lips, with the 100-plus-pounds feeling more like 400 pounds.

With his arms folded, Push said, "Ain't nothin' up . . . *son*. We just wanna see how *really* strong you is. Add a few plates," Push commanded through clenched teeth. Buck and Shawn did as instructed, getting the weight up to 340 pounds. "You came to the right place at the right time . . . son!" Push was real close now, close enough to feel the fear in Block as his body shook there under the weight.

"See, you don't know me, but back in Harlem . . . when I was, oh, about this little . . . maybe about six years ago, I lived on A.C.P. with my moms and pops. And three wannabe motha-fuckas bumrushed her . . . they beat her and they raped her . . . then they shot her and my pops. That was you, *motha fucka*—"

"But—I . . . uhh . . ."

"What? Cat gotcha tongue? Ain't no sense in tryin' to talk, son. You already convicted y'self."

Push straddled the bench where Block was pinned down and helpless. With his gloved hands on the weight bar, Push worked it further along towards Block's neck. Before he budged from there he turned to Brian. Again, the thumbs-up.

"This is for Mrs. and Mister Jackson . . . and for me and my sister. Don't you never forget Push, motha-fucka!" And how could he forget. Push made that ugly face as he thrust the weight, causing Block's body to convulse with a rise and fall. The broken neck could be heard all the way over near where Brian stood. Block 's head was twisted to the side now—an unnatural sight, with his tongue sticking partially out of his mouth, caught between his teeth. There was a trickle of blood from the corner of his mouth and his eyes were pointed towards the wall, frozen in time, along with his life.

Push got up and all four buddies exchanged thug-hugs. Finally, the Jackson family had received some street justice. The expected storm followed Block's death. Push, Shawn, Buck and Brian were sent to the hole and held there while a complete investigation was conducted. The FBI came to the prison and interviewed the witnesses as well as Mr. Randall, who had the most explaining to do: "Why did you have convicts working the weight room who weren't assigned? Why did you leave them unsupervised?"

With Push and the others, the answers were all consistent; just as they had rehearsed: *"Yo', dude just tried some shit on his own . . ." "He should've at least asked one of us for help . . ." "Next thing I know, dude's got a weight bar against his neck with the weight all over the floor and his tongue hanging out . . ." "That's too bad. He was our homeboy. He was crew."* Although the stories were believable, federal Agents still tried to turn the homeboys against one another, making up lies, and even offering pardons for cooperation. But the four conspirators were expecting that too. They had all been down that road before. After 90 days of investigation, Push and his conspirators were released back into the general population. They quickly assumed their humble routine of doing time with that somewhat shocked look about them. It would wear-off with the passing of time.

P RISON HAD ITS MOMENTS. IT was sometimes as insulated and calm as a communal home. Sometimes it was annoying and bizarre, like a zoo. Other times it was as wild and deadly as a jungle. Block's death turned out to be just another statistic, along with the suicides, the accidental deaths and the gangland beat downs. They said you left prison in one of two ways: by bus or box.

Push continued running, even getting in as much as 4 and 5 hours straight. Running made him feel like he was as free as a bird soaring through the air. He also took some college courses and learned a lot about real estate. He learned about renovating VA foreclosures and how to bid on city-owned land. There were all the terms he had to learn, like FHA &

VA loans, amortization, balloon payments, lease options, negative and positive cash flow, and so much more. But Push never wavered from his path. It didn't matter how complex the terminology was. He attacked the studies and books the same way he attacked the track each day. He was passionate about what he wanted. He was relentless.

4 years turned to 5, and 8 years turned into 9. The holidays no longer had meaning. They were just regular days to Push; no different than any other. The only significant changes that caught Push's attention were the seasons, the faces that came and went over the months and years. The penitentiary staff came and went as well; some who did things to help Push get along; others who were more instigators and trouble makers, worse even than some convicts.

On the day of Push's release, Crystal was there to meet her brother at the gate. It had been over 14 years that they were apart. And the moment she embraced him was traumatic. She shook uncontrollably and tears of joy fell in streams. With little more than a change of clothes to his name, Push moved into Crystal's apartment, part 3 of a brownstone on 26th Street, just a block away from the landmark *Sylvia's Restaurant*.

These were bittersweet times, being in Crystals' presence. So much time had been lost between the two, so many years. It seemed impossible to catch up. Little Reggie wasn't little Reggie anymore, he was a young man now; almost 17 years old and thinking about joining the US ARMY as a means of escaping the ghetto.

"If you join the ARMY, how you gonna help me manage all the real estate I'm gonna buy?" asked Push. Reggie couldn't answer. He would just lower his head, as if that might be a pipe dream. "Tell you what," Push went on. "Gimme a little time . . . a year is all I need, and your Uncle will have somethin' nice for you. A nice salary so you can buy yourself a ride . . . somethin' to show-off to the young ladies around the way." Reggie laughed in a consensual way and Crystal overheard it all.

"Push!?" Crystal's scowl was a lighthearted one that

came with a twisted grin. But nonetheless, it was clear that
Uncle Push was making some progress with Reggie. All he
had to do now was live up to his promise.

"You know who you and I were named after?"

"I know, Uncle Push. You already told me—Reggie Jackson, the baseball player."

"But he wasn't just *any* baseball player, Reg. He was a
black ball player . . . a home run hitter . . . just about the best
who ever did it in New York. You gotta remember that, cuz
just like he did it, you and I are gonna do it. We're gonna hit
home runs in life. We're gonna win!"

And as convincing as Push sounded in front of his
nephew, he would later have doubts himself about the challenges ahead. It was a mighty task to be responsible for his
own well-being, as well as to be the surrogate father of a
growing young man. Push felt as though he owed Reggie a
future since he had killed the man who impregnated Crystal,
and since he had gone away for so long, unable to fill the
void.

IT WAS JUST TWO MONTHS after Push came home from
prison that he found Crystal in her bedroom crying into her
pillow.

"Crystal?" Push put his hand on his sister's shoulder. She
was startled by his touch and instantly turned to face him.
And that's all Push had to see: the slight black and blue
marks on Crystal's pretty face. A picture that was worth a
thousand words since Push knew Crystal was seeing
Raphael. He knew that the two were having problems, and
that Raphael was a snake—a man who lied and deceived
most of his 34 years in Harlem. Push cursed himself for
letting Crystal stay with the dude this long. But that was out
of his hands. Crystal was her own woman and needed nobody to help her make decisions. Or so she thought. The relationship with Raphael was something that started before
Push came home, so it was too late for him to impose his influence.

How could she get with a jerk like him? Push asked himself.

But this was no time to ask questions about how or why; this was time to act. His mind switched to battle-ready mode, and he immediately went to see his old friend Beck to pick up an automatic pistol.

"Whatever you can give me on a loan, Beck, I'll pay up. You know my word is good."

Beck agreed as though he had no choice. This *was* Push, despite his long absence; he was a man who said what he meant and meant what he said. The old friend went into his back room there inside of Leo's Tattoos, and emerged with a .45-caliber Ruger and enough ammunition to reload a half dozen times.

"Damn, Push. You thirty-two years old and still doin' war?

"The battle don't stop, pop. Can't let people walk all over you. You do, and you might as well go live in a cemetery. Call it quits. Don't worry about me . . . I'mma definitely be safe." And Push thanked Beck before he left the shop. Push, the hunter.

That night, Push fired more than 50 rounds from the rooftop of an abandoned building in order to refresh his memory.

And that was 2 days ago.

One dead body later, Push was inside of the busy Lenox Lounge, sitting towards the back of the establishment. The deed was done. He had his eye on the front door and anyone who happened to come through right after he did. There was a dude about 6'2", with light skin the color of a pecan nut. He had that gangsta-lean against the bar, and wore a black leather trench. Push watched as the guy smoked a cigarette held between his middle finger and ring finger. The way he did that, his hand partially covered his face when he pulled at the smoke. Push didn't stare too hard, but was aware enough to notice the goatee and mustache—just a few days growth. The way the guy looked was too cool for a cop. But then, Push knew of cool cops. This guy, whoever he was,

was drinking a beer and checking out the booty in the club. Push determined that he wasn't a threat. But then the guy went and looked back . . . back towards where Push was posted on a bar stool down the way. For a brief instant the man's eyes crossed with Push's. Push pretended not to notice, but he *did* notice, and at the same time his hand gripped the handle of the Ruger in his waistband. He wondered if the guy was pretending too, or if he himself was just being paranoid because of a mere coincidence.

I'm trippin,' Push told himself. And he took his hand off of the weapon, forcing himself to breathe easier.

CHAPTER SIX

IT WAS AS IF THE floor of the Lenox Lounge was moving up and down with the wave of heads that were bopping and bouncing in time with the music. Just about everyone was chanting along with Jay Z's lyrics. You'd think the rapper had a chorus or something.

Roy cursed himself soon after his eyes briefly met with the killer's. Had he been made? Was the killer onto him?

Damn. I shoulda minded my own business, Roy told himself. But he still managed to keep his cool, wishing for something; if only a curtain could drop out of thin air. *I wonder if he's still looking . . . I would be if I was him. It almost looks like I'm following him . . . . . . Damn! I am following him!*

Roy raised his bottle of Bud to the bartender as if she were a good friend. She smiled back, jiggling those nice tits of hers. Just like most of the patrons, the bartender was also bobbing and weaving her head, with her lips moving in synch with the lyrics. She could well have been telegraphing a message directed right into Roy's ear.

"Ain't no nigga like the one I got—"

Roy was no stranger to the song himself. You couldn't play a Jigga song that he wasn't at least familiar with. He took his cue and replied:

"No one could love you betta—"

The bartender replied, following the female's role in the:

"Sleeps around, but he gives me a lot—"

And Roy said: "Keeps you in diamonds and leather—"

Now with more attitude and her hands on both hips, the bartender followed up:

"Friends all tell me I should leave you alone—"

"H-haa . . . h-haa . . . tell them freaks to find a man of they own." And as the Jay-Z/Foxy Brown classic continued rocking the club, the bartender pursed her lips and rolled her eyes playfully. For Foxy (the bartender) to hear him over the music, Roy had to speak up some.

"What's your name, baby?" The inquiry was less of a question and more of an excuse for idle conversation.

"Whateva you want it to be, Sugar. As long as you spendin' money."

"Damn, you just as direct as you could be, ain't you?"

"Shit, Daddy, it's cold outside and I got kids to feed." While Roy found himself suddenly caught up in this woman's personal issues, his cell phone chirped from inside its carry-case.

"See if you can feed 'em with that attitude," said Roy. And just as quick as his wit, he turned his back to the bar with the cell phone glued to his ear.

"Baby, it's me," said Asondra, before Roy could get a word in. He could hear music and chatter behind Asondra.

"Hey. You ready?" Roy asked, realizing how damned excellent the timing was; that so-called curtain he wished for.

"Yeah, boo. Where you at?"

"Not far," Roy replied.

"Okay, well . . . be careful. I think there's trouble outside."

"Really?"

"Hold on." Asondra sounded as if she turned to chat with someone other than Roy. "Oh God, it *is* trouble," Asondra gasped. "They say police are out there, baby . . . something about a shooting. And the block is closed."

Roy took the deep breath of the concerned boyfriend. Meanwhile, the wheels and pistons were turning in his head. The images playing back in his mental media center. "Can you slip out the back and meet me down on Lenox?" he asked.

"I think," said Asondra.

"I'm out here now. Let's go," said Roy. And the call was over.

Roy calculated things. Asondra's call was a helpful excuse for him, considering this not so good move he made. *Lemme get out of here while I can*, he muttered as he put down the remainder of the beer in a single gulp. Then he slid the empty bottle along the bar in that single smooth motion. It was his way of telling tits-and-ass back there the bottom line: she was picking up after him; Roy, the *big dog*.

Roy tightened the belt on his coat and tugged at his brimmed hat for another fine young thing that strutted past. Then he made his way out of the front entrance, back into the winter night. It was the oddest, unjustified feeling, but Roy felt shady; as though *he* was the bad guy, or that *he* was the one making the get-away from the scene of the crime. Moments later the Mercedes was in drive. By the sound of things, as quiet as the engine purred, it was hard to tell the vehicle had been shut off at all. Casually steering the car around a double-parked car in his way, Roy glided past the Lenox Lounge, towards 125th. He ignored the rules of the road and swung a U-turn around the island dividing the 2-way traffic and he shot back to 123rd, where he expected to meet up with Asondra. There was commotion at the cross street of 122nd. A police vehicle was positioned horizontally so that no could turn onto the block. The unit's emergency lights seemed to slice through the night atmosphere, reflecting off of most every glass, metal or other shiny surface. An officer stood at the edge of the block as well, allowing no pedestrians to enter along the sidewalk. Roy hoped that wouldn't stop Asondra. He swung another U-turn, and sat the car at a curbside. With his hazard lights on, and a quick look back over his shoulder every now and again, Roy waited. He couldn't help his slight nervousness considering that certain threat was still in the lounge; or so he hoped. In the meantime, he switched CDs to one he knew Asondra would appreciate.

Harlem's wet cityscape seemed such a dreary sight beyond

the Mercedes' windshield. Most stores were closed by now. Those that *were* open included the Chinese take-out joint, a bodega grocery store and an all-night liquor store. Of course, all three businesses were the type designed for night people, with bullet-proof glass installed as a division between clerk and customer. Just another sign of the times.

The different doorways, lobbies and vestibules in between the stores were poorly illuminated, all of them leading to 2nd, 3rd and 4th-story apartments above various businesses such as Willie's Barber Shop, Lenox Avenue Taylor and Harlem Beauty, among others. There was also one of those shops that sold everything, manned by Asians who pawned umbrellas during storms, and sunglasses, t-shirts and baseball caps to cope with the summer sun. Since it was winter, there were piles of ear muffs, scarves, gloves, hats and galoshes to help brave the cold and the snow. At times it was hard to tell whether the foreigners who operated these establishments were super-intelligent to be ready with these conveniences, or if they were cunning hucksters who were taking advantage of John Q. Public's misfortunes. Or perhaps these were simply the ways and means of the average entrepreneur; plain old hard work, hustle and sacrifice. The hell if Roy would have to do any of that again. Shit, everybody needed money, so it was only common sense that told Roy what the best business in the world would be. Something everyone might need: a money store.

Roy had his hands in so many of these proprietors' pockets it was a crying shame. So many fast-food joints, restaurants, lounges, beauty salons . . . so many of these niggas strugglin' just to keep up with his high-interest payments. Roy might as well run for Mayor of Harlem—if there ever was such a thing—as many people as he had kissin' his ass just to get their due-dates extended. And the things they'd do just to get by, just to get to tomorrow.

A try at the car's door handle didn't get Roy's attention at once. However the knock at the passenger side window caused him to jump. What was he thinking, letting his mind wander like that! A dead man a half-block away, and his killer within a stones throw? He was lucky some thug didn't try and rob him. Roy looked and saw that it was Asondra. His breathing calmed.

Got to be more careful, Roy told himself.

Just as he was about to reach for the handle to let Asondra in, he caught himself; remembering that there was a convenience switch on his side of the car.

Gotta get used to these luxury-car benefits . . .

"Hey baby. Let's get outta here," said Asondra, pulling the door closed behind her. "Oh-h-*h-hoooo*, dead bodies just give me the *creeps*," she went on, not without a shiver in her voice and that exhaustive sigh.

Back into mainstream traffic, Roy ignored the lounge and focused on the night ahead. Harlem appeared to be passing outside the car like a picture show, as though it was the rest of the outside world that was moving and not the Mercedes. *Starbucks* at 125th Street was followed by *Sylvia's Restaurant* at 126th. *Kazumi's Lil' African Mart* was just past *Freddie's Fried Chicken*. Another ten blocks would be Asondra's crib, a place that Roy could just as well call his own. After all, he was paying for it.

She'd wanna go put on a dress now. Makeup. Perfume. Some of those diamonds he bought her. Roy knew her girl-routine by now. But he suddenly had other plans.

"How 'bout we stay in tonight. Enjoy each other's company for a change."

"Baby! I just got my hair done. For *nothin'*?"

"Nothin'? Girl, you got your hair done for *me,* not everybody else in Harlem . . ." Roy was about to spit some of the words he'd prepared for Asondra earlier, but they wouldn't work now. However, this bit about her hair was giving Roy more of a reason to get in her ass.

"I know, I know. It's just . . . it takes so much to sit up in the salon for all that time . . ."

"Yeah, well . . . I didn't tell you to do that. That's your own waste of time."

"But I—"

"How about no more buts. No more excuses. It's cold. It's

nasty out . . . we order some chicken and broccoli, get a movie from Blockbuster, and boom. There's the night right there."

Asondra sighed.

Roy was feeling more confident now that they were blocks away from the mess on 122nd Street. The mess he almost made in the lounge.

"I wonder who that was?" Asondra said out of nowhere.

"Who was?" Roy asked.

"The man. The one who got shot."

"How you know it was a man? Baby, tryin' to keep up with murder victims in Harlem is like tryin' to remember every Michael Jackson song. There's gotta be more to talk about than, *I wonder who died.* How's Mya's place doin'? It sounded busy."

"It was. I'm lucky I got there early."

"I bet it don't smell like nothin' but hot pussy up in there," said Roy, happy to have injected some mention of sex into the conversation, since that was what was on his mind right now. And then he made a mental note: *I gotta stop by Mya's in a few days . . . pick up that payment.*

"You nasty," said Asondra with the pretend disgust.

"And you *love* it—" Roy blurted.

"Turn it up, baby. I like this part," proclaimed Asondra as she worked her head and hands into a slow groove, her body swaying in time. Roy increased the volume. It was the least he could do to make her happy.

Asondra sang, "I got a—*nother* nasty, freaky, just-right way in mind . . . . . . tonight I'm gonna be that h*iiii*—gh score."

"Who sings that, Asondra?"

Asondra sucked her teeth and made a salty face, as if Roy had to be the biggest fool not to already know the answer.

"You know that's m'*girl,* Jilly from Philly."

"Well let *Jilly-from-Philly* sing it then. And stop fuckin' up the song." *Go on, playa, put your foot down. Let her know who's boss,* Roy told himself

Asondra pouted. "I like that song."

And Roy liked to see her surrender like this.

"Yeah, cuz she talkin' that nasty-freaky shit. *That's* why ya' like it."

"Your head is always in the gutter, Roy."

"No, my head is always in *your mouth*. I know you, Asondra. You done did every nasty thing in the book with me; so, ain't no frontin'. You a cold motha fuckin' freak, right down to your yellow bones. And the minute Jill Scott sings them words, you wanna join the chorus line. You wanna be back-up singer. I know ya!"

Asondra rolled her eyes and turned away. It was the truth, but so cold how he put it.

More of Harlem's landscape passed by: The Chicken Hut, Harlem Hosiery, the Harlem Travel Agency.

"At least I'm a lady when it matters," said Asondra. "I mean, I don't play myself out in public like some girls do."

"Oh yeah. Shit, don't get it fucked-up. You the queen of Sheeba when I take you out. Got men all starin' down your breasts-n-all. I ain't complainin'. I'm just lettin' you know that I know you ain't no goddamned angel. I know ya."

"Of course you do, Roy. Ain't you my man? You supposed to know."

"Yeah, and I know you like me talkin' dirty to you too."

"Yeah, I love that. But not *all* the time."

"Well . . . it's Friday night . . . all'a Harlem is cracklin' around us. Women out there with all kinds of tight, sexy shit on . . . smellin' good and lookin' good. The men are out there too, sniffin' it all up . . ." Asondra laughed at Roy's way with words. "There's that sex in the air," Roy went on to say. "So, ain't nothin' I want more than that nasty-*freaky* shit. *You feel me?*" Asondra's eyes turned saucy, and her lips puckered into that sensual pout. Her expression meant she was in agreement. She scooted over some on the front seat and he accommodated her, putting his arm around her shoulders.

"Who's the man."

"You are, Roy."

"Whose dick are you suckin' tonight."

"*Yooours*," Asondra answered in her meek, little-girl's voice.

"I'm gonna drop you off. Send the boy to a neighbor's or somethin', and have that ass lookin' real sexy when I get up there, you hear?"

"Mmm hmm."

"I'm gonna pick up some food and a flick," Roy said as he turned onto 135th. Then he swung through the driveway and came to a stop near the lobby doors to Asondra's building, one of Harlem's luxury high-rises. The bright, cheery, expensive-looking lobby had a doorman and was brilliant enough to be the entrance to a lavish Manhattan hotel. Asondra kissed Roy and left the Mercedes with a determined attitude and all smiles. For sure, tonight she'd be that "high score" that the diva Jill Scott sang about.

Roy changed the CD and rolled on to get those inexpensive accommodations for his night alone with Asondra. Besides the convenience of sex, he would be relieved to cuddle up with *anyone* right about now. Better to be out of sight, out of mind considering he'd just witnessed a murder and what not. As Roy parked out in front of the local Chinese fast food spot his thoughts shifted back and forth between his forthcoming night with Asondra and the events on 122nd Street. Both encounters excited him to the point of an erection.

TREVOR JENKINS WAS NOW 15 years old and content inside of his single-parent household. He had no choice, because that was all that he knew. He never knew his father except for the vague images he saw at age two. Asondra lied and told her son long ago that his father had died in a shootout, and that she was playing the roles of both mother and father. On the other hand, Roy didn't amount to much of a male role model for Trevor; he was never present or involved as a true father should be. The bottom line was that there was no one to take that responsibility; no one to fill that void, but her. Asondra helped to smooth over the absence of a father by smothering her son with love. She spoiled him rotten. He had grown up to be a son that couldn't argue much, because he never knew struggle, need or desperation. She protected him from all of that. Not only that; being agreeable with mom was both practical and it made good sense. When the newest Nike sneakers came out, he got them. When he wanted a motocross bicycle it was no problem. A skateboard, the hottest sportswear, Nintendo games . . . it was all his for the asking.

Trevor didn't know what his mother did for a living, and it didn't much matter. So long as he received his weekly allowance; so long as moms didn't get in his hair about the choices he made regarding his friends and activities. Asondra's thing was this: she wanted Trevor close to home if he wasn't in school. He was to bring home nothing but A's and B's. And he was to stay out of trouble.

"Trev? Trev? You home?"

"In the bedroom, Ma," he called out.

As Asondra went further into the apartment, she could hear the familiar beeps, crashes and other such sound effects that Trevor's video games made. *Is there more to being 15 years old than playing video games?* Asondra wondered for the 100th time.

He was in her bedroom, instead of the living room, because he liked seeing his entertainment on her large plasma screen.

"Oh . . . company??"

"Hi, Ms. Jenkins," Shatalia responded, barely looking away from the TV herself. At the moment, she and Trevor were in a head-to-head heat. Asondra thought it was so innocent how her son had a pretty 15-year-old from 2 floors down, alone in his mother's bedroom. If she thought there was anything else going on, except the obvious, she'd *kill* him! Asondra saw that Shatalia had on low-cut jeans and a Baby Phat t-shirt, no sox, and her hair was poking up into a cute ponytail. The tail bounced and danced as she worked the joystick of the video game. But the neighbor's hair wasn't the only thing bouncing and dancing, Asondra noticed. And she wondered if Trevor was so into his video game that he hadn't noticed the same thing.

Asondra was also considering dueling thoughts here: First, she would give anything to be so young again. And second, she wondered how long it would be before Trevor and Shatalia began exploring other options. Before they tried *other* things on that bed. Or for that matter, on any bed. How long could a video game hold their attention?

"Well hello to you too, Shatalia. Who's winning?"

"Your son . . . as . . . usual." It was a stretch to say that while in the heat of the moment.

"I need to talk to you, Trevor."

"Okay, Ma. In . . . . . . a *minute*."

"Now, Trevor."

"Yeah, Ma," Trevor said, not without sneering at Shatalia. "You were losing anyway."

"Was not," she replied, sucking her teeth.

"Was too!"

"Not."

Now, Trevor sucked *his* teeth. "Wait'll I get back!"

Asondra escorted Trevor from the bedroom, away from an argument that could've gone on forever. She had to remind Trevor to let the girl—*any girl*—win sometimes. Then she wanted to kick herself for thinking that way: a suggestion to help her son to win a girl over?

"Trevor, would you mind going to Grandma's for the night?"

"*Ma—!* I just went there Wednesday," Trevor argued.

"I thought you loved your grandmother?"

"Mom. Don't even try to smooth-talk me. Just tell me you want me out of the house," he replied with those squinting eyes.

"Okay. I want you *out* of the house," she finally said. Something was in his mother's eyes that he couldn't figure out, nor did he try to; the way she said that was so authoritative.

"Can I go over Shatalia's? Her mother is home and they're watchin' a Will Smith movie tonight."

"Will Ms. Brown approve?"

"Of course. She thinks I'm gonna marry Shatalia."

"God, help us all," said Asondra, rolling her eyes. More drama to come, no doubt. "I'll call. But you two better not be doin'—"

"*Ma?!*"

"I'm just sayin' . . . you know how I feel about babies havin' babies," said Asondra with her brow raised. "I'll call."

Trevor hurried off. "Shatalia, start *over*!"

While Trevor went back to the bedroom, Asondra picked up the phone to call Lola Brown, Shatalia's mom. Trevor had stayed over the Brown's home in the past, so this was routine. Asondra lived on the 18th floor, and Lola Brown, the 16th. "Lola? It's Asondra."

"Hey girl. Ya'll takin' care of my baby-girl up there? My little poo-pie?"

"Humph. Your little poo-pie is old enough to be an Essence model, Lola. But don't worry . . . I told Trevor to use a rubber on that—" Asondra cackled into the phone.

"Don't make me *read you*, heffa!"

Asondra, and eventually Lola had a hearty laugh. "Now girl, you know Shatalia can handle herself."

"Yeah, but can Trevor handle *her*," said Lola, as if to pose the challenge. And now, Lola led with the laughter. This was the way it went with these two; their private jokes about their spoiled teenagers. Asondra and Lola, sistafriends.

"Now *there* you go. I'll have you know that my son will be—"

"I know—I know . . . heard it all before, girl. The Mayor of New York. The Governor . . . the next President of the United States. I know the whole pipe-dream by now. And, oh—let me not forget . . . women will be in line by the bus-loads for a piece of him. Did that cover everything?"

"Huh . . . you just can't help hatin', can you," said Asondra, knowing that Lola was making fun of her dreams for Trevor.

Lola went on to say, "Babydoll, wake up. This is me you talkin' to. You and I both know the real deal for our black men once they come out from under their momma's protective shield. It's a cold, hungry world, baby. We all end up eventually doin' what we gotta do.

"Mmm hmm, speaking of which . . . Roy's coming over in a few minutes, so I was just wondering—"

"Now you know you ain't gotta say another word girl. Whoo-*eee!* Twice in a week! What-chu got goin' on, that nasty-freaky thing again?"

"TMI, baby. T-M-I!"

Lola was cracking up. "Listen, baby, I am not—mad—at—'chu. Do YOU, Ma. Mmm-mmm-mm, it *mus*t be nice . . . gettin' that good lovin' all convenient-like,"

Lola sighed. "Send 'em down, Lil' ole' Ms. Brown-the homebody will keep 'em safe,"

"Don't be like that, Lola."

"Oh, it's okay, Asondra, cause when it's my turn to knock boots? And IT WILL be my turn again—" Lola made an excited noise; a happy squeal. "The cops are gonna come knockin'. Be*lieve* that."

Minutes later, Asondra was alone in the apartment running around like she had no sense; cleaning up, spraying fragrance, lighting up candles and incense. She eventually jumped into the shower for a quickie; nothing but a straightforward effort to clean herself. No extensive touching herself as she did occasionally when Roy left her alone. Tonight, she wanted to leave those sensations for Roy to covet. Nothing-but-nothing was gonna come between her and this freak-session. It was about to go down.

WHILE THE SING FAMILY COOKED up the evening's fast food—*no MSG, please*—Roy stopped at Blockbuster Video, wondering what would be appropriate for a background to the most important feature of the night. That's the way it usually went down; they'd eat, there'd be small talk while they ate, then they'd make their way to the bedroom. Roy would pop the movie in while Asondra did some light clean-up, then they'd lay together and try to get into the film—*whatever* film. Next thing you know, the acrobatics would begin. There'd be very little foreplay. Roy sometimes had to remember what the hell that meant; foreplay. Asondra would inevitably get Roy excited, then he'd have her perform tricks—and she'd obey without an ounce of hesitation—before he'd finally bust-off into any or all of her openings. Roy rarely took the time to consider what would please her, because more often than not, that wasn't what was important to him. What was indeed important was his *own* satisfaction, precisely what she was there for.

Theirs had grown into such a frequent, usual activity that it wasn't so special anymore. It was merely routine; just another part of Roy's week. He knew exactly what to expect from Asondra; and mainly, that included whatever he taught her.

Why am I still with her, Roy had to sometimes ask. The answer, he knew, was that she was convenient. Nothing more, nothing less. Asondra was there when he told her to be there. She didn't give him any flack about who he was with last night, or the night before, or an hour ago. Not that he really shared all of that information with her. She just didn't ask, and that was all-the-way good. It was exactly what this man, in particular, was comfortable with.

"Roy?" A female's voice behind him in the action-adventure section of Blockbuster. He turned towards the voice, but for a second he couldn't make out the face. Was this a woman who he'd done wrong? Eventually, he did remember the face but not the name. One thing he knew for certain: he'd fucked this woman before. She had her hand on one hip as well as she cleared her throat and twisted her lips, waiting for Roy to come to his senses. There was so much that was said in a single expression.

"Nigga, you betta' *act* like you know! After all the shit I did for you? Why the fuck you ain't call me all this time?"

5 minutes later, Roy and his old flame, DeeDee, were in the back seat of the Mercedes. 7 minutes later, she was reminding Roy of the time when . . . and how he liked it when she . . .

The details were too much to recall all at once, but DeeDee

covered the highlights enough to re-open pleasurable memories for Roy. And besides, DeeDee was a woman of few words. What she couldn't express verbally, her body could physically.

9 minutes later, DeeDee and Roy were in a familiar position, with DeeDee testifying about how she loved his new car while at the same time taking him into her mouth. Soon thereafter, DeeDee managed to lift up her mini-skirt— *another one to brave that cold winter air against her legs,* Roy thought—without even taking it off. She sat ontop of Roy, riding him while Anita Baker's songs played back to back. Roy groped at DeeDee's breasts while she lay back against him, her arms folded against the roof of the car. She praised the car again, how clean it smelled and how it was so comfortable inside. All while Roy dug her out from underneath.

DeeDee eventually dismounted Roy and went back to kneeling on the floor.

"You remember how you liked me to do this? How you use to tell me to *get off and suck it, bitch*!?"

Roy chuckled. *Now* he remembered! *How . . . why . . . did I ever give this up?* he asked himself. And then he recalled that DeeDee had been strung-out on drugs. He wondered if it was still that way. It didn't seem so. But, it didn't matter either—not while she was giving herself to him. She seemed as healthy as a stallion. Or maybe a failed race horse. Whatever. *Suck it, bitch.*

DeeDee slurped and gurgled on Roy while he sat back and eventually looked at his watch. Now, he rolled his eyes. *Awwe, man. Asondra.*

"Listen. I got business. You got another one or two minutes to do what you gotta do. Then I gotta go," he said boldly.

"Damn. A nigga gets a new whip and it be like *that?*" DeeDee rolled her eyes and decided she wanted him inside of her. She mounted again.

It was this idea of her being strung-out that kept Roy from ejaculating. He couldn't get past the idea that drug fiends had been known to carry that AIDS-shit. He couldn't get excited enough. And . . . now this trick was boring him. As if to call an end to an amusement ride, Roy said, "Okay, baby. Gotta go. Business is callin'."

DeeDee moaned her discontent, but Roy went on to say, "How else am I gonna pay for my fly-ass ride you like so much?"

"You want me to clean you up?

"No . . . don't worry. I'll clean up when I get home," Roy said, fixing his pants. "And I'll call you."

"Yeah? You promise?"

"When I get around to it," Roy lied.

And DeeDee sucked her teeth, rolled her eyes and went to kiss Roy. He turned his head in time enough so that her lips grazed his cheek.

When DeeDee got out of the car, Roy said, "*Fuck.*" He forgot about the Chinese food, part of his reason for being out here. Asondra might be a little uptight by now. But no problem. This wasn't the 1st time he kept her waiting.

CHAPTER SEVEN

WHEN ASONDRA HEARD THE KEYS at the front door, she jumped. Dag, she was hungry. Maybe he wasn't that long after all.

"Hey baby . . . you like?" Asondra made a cute spin. She was dressed in an evening dress that sparkled with red sequin while wrapping her body like a second skin. The V-cut perfectly fit her full breasts, hugging them like they were someone's Christmas presents. Her cleavage was shouting out: COME AND GET ME! And yet, she still had the energy and enthusiasm of a schoolgirl ready to take on the world.

"It's nice," said Roy flatly. "You were gonna wear that tonight?"

"I *am* wearing it tonight . . . for you."

Roy smirked, a sign that she'd come to her senses. "That's better. Now you're thinking straight. I'm starved," he said. He took a last look at Asondra as she went to put the food on the kitchen table.

Asondra shrugged it off Roy's cold entry. That was just his way of doing things, how he could be a bit unfeeling now and again. It was one of the things Asondra overlooked.

"Food's ready, boo. Don't you wanna sit at the table? I lit candles."

Roy sighed, got up from the couch, and in seconds dug into the food. Sex was the last thing on his mind right now, even though it was all up in his face. It was in Asondra's eyes; those pools of desire . . . it was in her gestures and her vocal tone. Her total presence, including how her wheat-colored skin was flushed in its own unique shade of red, was a seduction that was louder than a neon sign in the dead of night.

"So where's Trevor?"

"At a friend's house." There was a dramatic pause. "Till tomorrow," she said with one of those devilish smiles. The way she said it and sucked on a juicy stalk of broccoli at the same time sent a spasm to Roy's groin. He didn't think he could get excited so soon considering that he was so damned hard just ten minutes earlier. Roy was wrong.

"I got a Will Smith movie."

"Yeah? You think we'll get to see this one?" she asked.

Roy put on a crooked smile and stuffed his mouth with chicken and rice. The answer to her question was something already promised, so Asondra said nothing.

After a time, Roy asked, "You gotta make so much noise eatin' girl? Damn." It was a lighthearted grievance; just something to say.

"I thought you liked to hear the sounds my mouth makes. Listen . . ." Asondra became more intentional, making more wet and juicy sounds with her mouth and tongue. She even had some of the broccoli juice dribbling down her chin.

Roy stared for an instant, but then he shook out of it.

"Now that's nasty," he said, but he couldn't hide the smile. And that did it. Roy was excited again. Asondra finally broke through his wall—that barrier he put up to slow her advances. He was lovin' this woman all over again for the wonderful things that she would do to him. For the convenience and satisfaction she provided.

"I guess this will be a busier night than I expected," said Roy.

"Whadda you mean?" asked Asondra.

"Nothin'. Eat 'cha food."

TEN POLICE OFFICERS STOOD AT the entrance of the Lenox Lounge in riot gear. 3 others were near the side exit where deliveries were accepted, or through which garbage was dragged out. The music was shut off and the lieutenant had a blow horn in hand.

"LADIES AND GENTLEMEN . . . I'm gonna need your undivided attention. There has been a shooting in this vicinity not thirty minutes ago. And we have reason to believe that the perpetrator of this crime is on these premises. **Quiet!** Quiet down. Now, none of yous kind people should have nothin' to worry about if you had nothing to do with it. And if you did, well . . . we're gonna find out sooner . . ." The lieutenant looked at the two girls standing near the pimp. He made a face then continued on to say, ". . . or later. Now, if you know something I suggest you come forward now before this gets messy. And I assure you . . . it *will* get messy."

More than 10 city-blocks away, there was a different awakening.

A SONDRA DIDN'T BOTHER CLEANING UP. She was crazy-horny, and her desires were building up to a point that her folds were absurdly moist. She needed satisfaction.

Who was Roy to argue? The woman said that she needed it bad. The best thing he could do for her right now was stall so that he could regain his full energy. That monster urge.

"At least let the food settle," Roy warned, as they made their way into the bedroom. Asondra picked up the videotape, but then had her second thoughts.

"I guess we could do without Will Smith tonight, hunh?" Asondra's question didn't require an answer. She was already turning her back to Roy, lifting that abundance of raven-black hair from her shoulders. It turned Roy on to see her hold it all on top of her head like that.

"Unzip me," Asondra said inside of her sigh.

All the razzle-dazzle at the beauty salon, and then dressing up, had all been for this moment. And now that was all being kicked to the curb. But, Asondra assumed, the bottom line was the packaging of her God-given gifts.

Whatever it took to make her man happy.

Roy unzipped Asondra's dress and she turned around to let her hair fall, with much of it hiding her face. She began to peel off her dress.

"Hold it. Take your time, baby. I want tonight to last." Roy, the bullshitter. "Cut on the stereo and do a little dance for me." So, Asondra licked her lips and warmed up to his demands. This was exactly what she loved about Roy, how he took complete control. Just when she was thinking one thing, there he went, deciding on something entirely different.

Y OU! WITH THE GOLD TOOTH. Yeah—you. It's your turn. Step up to the bar. Any belongings you have, put 'em here . . . spread 'em—hands on the counter. I said spread 'em!"

The patron was apprehensive, but inevitably did as he was told. The officer frisked him neckline to ankle. "Hey, LT— lookie-*here*. A pocket knife. One of those universal jobs with the screwdriver and can opener." And the flatfoot handed over the knife to his superior.

"Where'd he have it?"

"In his boot."

"Concealed weapon? Read 'im his rights and lock his ass up in the wagon with the others."

The gold-toothed patron put up a struggle, jerking his arm away from those officers holding him.

Someone in the back said, "Shit!"

"Okay, Mister shit . . . you're next. Step up!"

"Ya'll can't do this! This is harassment!"

"Yeah? Well, get my name right in your complaint."

A SONDRA WAS UP ON THE bed now. She stood tall enough to reach for the ceiling, with her legs apart, winding her head back, then around to the front so that her hair fell down over her face. Her hands and arms were positioned over her bare breasts, while her dress had fallen so that it hung off of her hips.

Between the Sheets played over the stereo while Roy laid back against the pillows, just lovin' this.

"That's it, baby . . . get into it. Start workin' that ass. Show me what I'm payin' good money for."

Asondra gradually turned around and bent over to support herself with her hands on her knees. Meanwhile, her ass was sticking out a few feet from where Roy lay.

Roy clapped. "Good shit, baby! Damn. Ain't no fuckin' way Will Smith gonna out-do this!"

Asondra smiled, totally in the moment, with the dress now sliding off of her waist.

"Pull that dress off. Show Daddy that fat ass and that furry pussy."

Roy clapped again.

Asondra wiggled out of the dress so that she was now totally nude, awaiting more directions, beckoning with her wide-apart brown eyes. "Now . . . what tricks should I have you do today? I know. Get on your hands and knees for me. Hurry up. Good," Roy growled. "Spread your legs a little . . . that's right. There she is . . . mmm, mmm, mmm. Now take your middle finger and show us where you want Daddy's hard dick . . ."

All of Asondra's goods were facing Roy now. And accordingly, she reached back between her legs and put her face down sideways on the bed. Meanwhile, she played her middle finger in, out and around her moist opening.

"You want it where?" Roy asked.

"Here, Daddy," Asondra muttered.

"I can't hear you."

"Here, Daddy," she repeated, only more affirmatively this time.

"That's right. Stick that finger in there. Show me how you like it. Pop that coochie, bitch! And I wanna hear you moan. Make some mothafuckin' noise!" And Roy reached out to smack Asondra's ass. And then, again.

IT WAS THE UGLIEST THING he ever smelled. *Disgusting.* Even the walls had that odor of thousands of unwashed men who had lived there. The hole itself might as well have been a urinal.

Never would Push forget how all of those experiences

offended his senses. Darkened his mind. In his mind it would always be there waiting to devour him and so many others like him. Prison. The Hole. Hell on earth.

This wasn't to say that he was gonna give up easy. Okay, so his mind was playing tricks on him, bringing back all those foul memories. However, Push still had sense enough to make snap decisions; to calculate and evaluate. There were only 10 or so police officers, versus his 13 bullets left in the clip, plus the one in the chamber. There was also an additional clip in his boot. Altogether, Push had enough business with him to shut this whole charade down. It was *them* who had no idea how messy things could get in here. But that job was being handled very well by the cops. They had to know damned well that this was a long-shot, something that all of Harlem would scream about by tomorrow morning. Those policemen knew it wasn't likely that the killer was here, just around the corner, waiting to be caught red-handed. But what a long shot, indeed.

Was that slim dude the po-po? Did he rat me out? So many ideas were shooting around in Push's mind, not to mention that while all of this was going on he was busy wiping his fingerprints off of the weapon. Even though he had on leather racing gloves for the entire evening, he wanted to be extra sure; that way he could sleep well at night. That is *if* he got home. When Push was sure the gun was clean, he performed the same duty with the extra clip. Then he wedged both the Ruger and the clip into a cushion of the bench where he sat, up against the back wall. Worst case scenario, he'd come back to get the equipment when this bullshit raid was over with.

There was trouble up near the front of the lounge. One of the pimp's girls, the one with the natural blow-out hair style and the gold short-shorts, had a silver nail file. The lieutenant ordered the girl locked up. But the pimp wasn't having it. The shit began to hit the fan.

"Oh no you *don't!*" exclaimed the lady-pimp, throwing down her fedora and full-length coat. Then challenged any officer who dared approach. Just then she smashed an empty Armadale bottle and threatened her contenders with the business-end of the weapon. The third woman was part of the altercation now, and the whole club full of patrons cheered them on. Push remained as low-key as possible, finishing with his stash, knowing that this would take a while.

2O MINUTES HAD PASSED, ASONDRA felt her juices getting her whole hand wet. And now that Roy had her doing both, fingering her coochie, and playing the tip of her fingernail in and out of her ass, she was too hot and horny to think. Her eyes were squeezed closed and she was moaning with sweet pleasure while Roy lay there, the palm of his bare, funky foot down there, resting against most of her face.

"Kiss it, baby. Tongue-kiss that mothafucka!" And Asondra did, licking at his foot so her wet tongue was tangy with his day's worth of odor. And this was what Roy liked; for her to suck the heel, the toes, and all in between. It didn't matter if he had walked through mud. Eventually, Asondra grew to like it too.

"I should make you do the other foot too, slut. Hit that big toe again! Suck it good, too." Asondra obeyed.

Roy was in his boxers, with his erection half in and half out of the front opening. His dick was still sticky from the bitch—*what was her name?*—back at Blockbuster Video. But it was only a matter of time before . . .

"Okay. Get over here and pull these shorts off," Roy ordered. Asondra, eyes were withdrawn and sultry with desire; her lips were pouted, partially opened and ready for instruction.

"Good girl! You know I'd have you wearing them shorts on yo' head, but you just got your hair done, wit yo pretty-ass." Asondra merely flashed Roy that devilish expression, with the one eyebrow raised and the crooked smile. Once she removed his shorts, she crawled back up to Roy's waist and took his enlarged penis in her hand. Her head lowered to take him in her mouth.

The blowjob was customary at this stage in their relationship. Something of a requirement.

Roy almost snarled as he said, "No—I didn't tell you to

suck it yet, did I? You suck it when I *tell* you to suck it."
Asondra was a little lost here, somewhat confused by Roy's
instructions as she sat with her legs folded underneath, and
her hand still holding onto his stiff organ like a loose grip on
a throttle.

This nigga is trippin', Asondra told herself.

"Now hold it with both hands," ordered Roy. "And I want
you to talk to it. Tell lil' Roy how much you treasure him.
Tell him what you wanna do with him. Go on . . . you always
talk about wantin' to be one-a-them actress-bitches. Always
sayin' you could do this better or that part better. So go
on . . . start actin'."

Asondra took a moment, but she eventually settled into
that certain submissive state of mind. She began to comply,
licking her lips and hunching over close to Lil Roy. Roy's
penis was glistening now from Asondra's mismanaged body
fluids.

"Hi baby," said Asondra, her voice as sexy as she could
make it. "You miss me? Hmmm? Mmmm . . . I miss you
too. As a matter of fact . . . I've been waiting for you for
sooo—long, and I just can't wait . . . to put you . . . in . . .
my . . . mouth. I'm gonna let my tongue . . . show you a
real . . . good . . . time."

"Yeah, bitch . . . that's right. Talk that shit. Keep on," said
Roy with the encouragement.

"I'm gonna kiss you . . . and lick you . . . and suck you
and we're gonna make beautiful music together until you
give up some of that cream I like so much . . ."

Awe—YEAH, *bitch*. Talk that *shit*!"

". . . And I have something nice . . . and wet . . . and it's
waiting for you right here between my legs. It's your little
babygirl . . . she misses you too. She wants to welcome you
home and make you nice and warm . . ."

"Good, good. Now put that dick next to your nose, baby. I
want you to smell it before you start suckin' . . . right there
at your nostrils . . . *yeah*. Now don't that smell *real good*?
Huh?" Roy seemed to have so much more to say now. The
confidence was going to his head. Plus, there was the smell

of sex in the air to serve as an aphrodisiac. Asondra did as she was told and didn't so much as hint at the sign of foreign odors. As far as she knew, the dick could've been dipped in sour milk; she was still gonna suck it. It was something so meant to be. Something so routine.

"Yeah, Daddy . . . it smells delicious," she answered.

"Then put that dick in your mouth. Now. Go on . . . oh yeah . . . I know how bad you wanna suck it. Do it like Daddy taught you." Asondra took him in her mouth, engrossed with the fumes of sex, twice-over. His taste was just another part of Asondra's day. His scent was branded on her memory. And both his taste and aroma were just another part of her dreams when he wasn't with her. Whether or not Roy washed, or had been with another woman, was simply a nonissue. Asondra was just too consumed with him to give a damn. In his presence, lust was always at the steering wheel, pushing her accelerator and changing her gears. Meanwhile, passion was often in the passenger's seat, playing back-seat driver. With so much happening at once, Asondra simply lost her mind and went along for whatever ride Roy decided on. That's just how it was all part of being Roy's girl.

IT WAS A NO-WIN SITUATION, so why fight it? The cops may have been outnumbered by bodies, but this wasn't a full-string revolt. Challenges were merely sporadic. The will and the conviction wasn't there such as it would have been back in the day. Back in the day, folks would've fought these pigs off, despite the saber-toothed dogs, the hard-hitting batons and the force of water hoses. Back then, there was unity and "Black Power." Sure, there would've been human sacrifices, but that was understood. This was home, *dammit*. Not a place for non-resident cops to test the extents of their power and authority.

So when the pimp-lady and her two hoes put up a fight, it was obvious that the experience here was felt down deep in the souls of the Lenox Lounge patrons. You could feel their crying out for help, even though they didn't budge. Sure, many of them had heart, but the reality was that they were either too old for this shit, they had commitments pending, or the bigger priority: to get out of here safe. It was that, or else they were too far removed from the struggles of the past. Too afraid. And while the group of them didn't stand up and fight, they didn't mind the ones who did. Those few patrons were challenging the outrageous, unjust acts of the man—"the man" being any force that may at any given time impose its indisputable raw power. The pimp-lady was suddenly a drum-major for justice, rebelling against something very wrong. The altercation turned into a fiasco. The pimp lady nearly got shot.

But, perhaps everything does happen for a reason since Push was afforded some much-needed time to stash his weapon. He was clean now. And after officers wrestled the pimp to the floor . . . after they tossed a few more folks with outstanding warrants into the waiting paddy wagon, Push was the next to be called. He stepped up to be searched, already familiar with the indignities of the standard pat search—other man's hands patting his body, violating his temple.

He was calm, however. And all went smoothly. He was told to move on out of the lounge (to his utmost relief) as a lucky number of others had been directed to do. He took up his wallet and keys and approached the entrance to the club.

"Excuse me. You need to step over to that squad car there," instructed an officer by the doorway. There were many more men in blue now—thanks to the pimp—all of them waiting to usher Push along. All of them waiting for his one false move. This section of the street belonged to them now—a kind of Marshal Law.

At the squad car, an officer inside lowered his passenger side window.

"I.D." he announced, simultaneously reaching his hand out into the cold. Push concealed his sigh and took out his wallet. He couldn't imagine what more they wanted— probably some silly procedure. Inside the wallet was his driver's license, one he'd received just 3 or 4 weeks earlier. He handed it over, feeling as though he'd surrendered his citizenship.

"Wait there." And the window was raised. Push could see the cop in the driver's seat tapping at a mobile computer. And now he was concerned. He thought about making a run for it. But why? Push thought about his criminal record; it had been 14 years since he'd been charged with, or convicted of any crime. He wasn't sure if something so long ago would raise a red flag or not.

These guys were probably being *extra*, checking for warrants and what-not. Come to think of it, Push didn't really have time to break the law. Well, not if you were counting the corpse around the corner.

The window lowered again.

"They call you Push?"

"Yeah," Push answered with little emotion,

"Social security number . . ." requested the cop. Push gave it to him.

"Wait there." Again the window went up.

Now, more than ever, Push wanted to run. But, no. He remained calm. It's a bluff, he told himself.

Now the car doors opened on both the driver's side and the passenger side, where Push stood. Officers also approached from behind.

"Hands on the car and spread 'em !" The words hadn't yet formed vapor in the frigid air and yet Push already felt different hands thrusting him, man-handling him. One of his hands was pulled so that his arm was stretched behind him. Then the other. Now his legs were kicked to get them further apart.

FROM BEHIND, WITH BOTH ARMS pulled back. Roy pushed his hard tool into Asondra's wet and wanton walls.

Finally, Asondra secretly exalted. And she didn't care how hard he slammed himself inside of her. It was still a relief to have that emptiness filled with something so . . . so . . .

The friction caused her to cry out with joy, the utter intensity of having her cavity filled so thoroughly . . . so forcefully.

Roy beat it up, and she liked it this way—from behind, and as rough as Roy wanted to stick it to her. Shit, Trevor came out of that space at 7 pounds, so surely she could handle whatever Roy was pushing up into her. And besides, nothing about this was painful. It was just the incredible force with which he took her again and again, his physical power driving up and against her insides.

There was nothing else that made her so breathlessly fulfilled, so much a woman. There were also Roy's words, all of them encouraging the action. It didn't matter what Roy called her, she'd be that for him. She wanted to feel used, used, used to the max. After all, that's what sex had become for her—her body needing to feel wanted, then experiencing the pressure, only to be left exhausted and spent.

"Yes! Yes!! YES!!! The pussy is yours! It's yours!"

"I'm your bitch! Yes Daddy! Fuck me . . . fuck . . . your . . . bitch!"

"Oh—h-h-*hoo*, Daddy! Oh God! Put it all in me! In me! IN ME!!!" And Asondra would scream with that hoarse-but-sensual voice.

"You like that shit, don't you! You like it when this nigga puts it up in you, you slut? Don't you? Hunh??" And Roy went on this way, bent over Asondra's back (like dogs do) so that he'd be grunting in her ear. He let her arms go as he continued pummeling her, the skin-smacking sounds filling the gaps of silence in the room.

"Who's that nigga you love? Hunh??"

"You . . . you, Roy. I . . . love *you* . . . SO—fucking—much!"

Although the action seemed to peak, Roy didn't finish this way. He pulled out his penis and told her, "Get over here and suck it. Now!" And Roy stayed there on his knees, upright on the bed, while Asondra went down on him, both her hands grabbing at something . . . a thigh, his testicles. Just to hold him temporarily filled the hole—the suspension in pleasure that he imposed by withdrawing from her. Meanwhile, Asondra's mouth and lips were messy with sex, as Roy's dick slid in and out of her lips, just as it had been between her thighs.

She took him aggressively, hungrily . . . all the while feeling that emptiness again between her own walls, hoping he'd go back in there shortly, or as soon as possible!

"Suck it, HO!" Roy knew he was stretching it by calling Asondra a ho. But that turned out to be irrelevant just now since she was too engrossed with what she was doing . . . too busy to feel the assault of his words.

And so what. Roy loved this. There was no greater pleasure. The fascination of being with what's-her-name (DeeDee) and now Asondra, back-to-back, had worn off. Now it was on with the freak session. The usual.

How many tricks can I get this bitch to do for me? Roy wondered as he hung there in the pleasure-filled moments. But, just as his mind was working, Asondra was working on him, making her muffled sucking sounds that he loved so much; causing him to throb and tweak with excitement with the sensations shooting through his entire nervous system.

Roy turned over on his back and bent his legs, while Asondra switched elbows, shifting her weight and labor to the other arm. Her mouth remained busy with his twitching muscle. Then he took a bunch of her hair in his grip and she, as usual, was loving how he overpowered her mentally and physically. Control.

Roy pulled her head up so that she only had the tip of his dick in her mouth. Then he pushed her head back down so that he was reaching down her throat.

"Right there. Don't move. Just keep it right—fucking— there. I wanna look at you like this . . ." Roy spoke exhaustively as he stilled Asondra's actions. He freeze-framed the sex just like that, experiencing his own ecstasy while he looked down at her, and his erection having disappeared between her jaws and with her lips there at his patch of pubic hair.

Roy's voice lowered, and his words dragged from his lips like a drunkard.

"That's it, I just wanna look at you . . . I want you to think about it . . . my dick in your mouth. Huh . . . you and your wise-ass mouth. All witty-n-shit. *Now* look at you." Roy wanted to say it. He wanted to tell her that he'd been with another woman just minutes before. And why shouldn't he? He could say what he wanted to Asondra. She was his.

"You're my fucking slave. Nothin' but a nasty slut. Matter fact . . ." Roy pulled Asondra's hair so that her head would follow. Her lips were off of him now, swollen from the work she put in. He looked at her for a time with that arrogant leer, then he pushed her head further down between his legs.

"Eat my fuckin' ass, bitch! And eat it till I say stop."

Asondra adjusted her body so that she could position her face—all this in order to obey Roy. An instant later, her nose, lips and chin were buried there in the crack of Roy's ass. Her hands spread his cheeks apart and she kissed his ass the way he wanted . . . the way he taught her. She'd kiss it gingerly and delicately at first, as if it was a new friend. Then, eventually, she'd progress to giving his ass loving, sensual kisses, as well as the full attention of her tongue. He no longer had to instruct her; she already knew to tongue-kiss his ass. The same as she would kiss his mouth, her tongue reached deeper, begging and panting for more. She lapped at him from top to bottom, leaving no portion unattended, until she'd finally suck on his asshole exclusively. There was one more trick he wanted tonight, since Asondra was behaving so well. One more thrill.

He ordered her to sit on him.

"Go on. Get your shit off, cuz I'm almost through with you," Roy explained selfishly. And Asondra knew exactly what that meant. She knew that the sex was about to end and that she'd have to do the rest of the work here—create her own finale to this episode—while Roy laid back and watched. She quickly mounted him. She was on her knees as she did, lowering herself onto his still-stiff tool. Heaven once again.

With her hands flat on Roy's abdominal muscles, Asondra worked her ass in circles, back and forth, and up and down, until she was bouncing on him, wincing in response to taking all of him inside.

Roy laid there with his hands behind his head. If the world could see him now. His pretty girlfriend wasn't quite so pretty after all, taking into account these ugly faces she made while she fucked him. No matter how good she looked when they weren't in bed, all of that was lost when it came to fucking. Her expressions were almost grotesque, how her face stretched and scrunched like it did. And the sounds that she uttered were primitive and inhuman, like a chimpanzee. And still, the animal she became was a turn-on.

He could sense Asondra now, wanting to blast-off into her own climax—another one. She was coming close.

"You comin'?" Roy asked.

"Almost," she struggled to say.

"Fuck that almost-shit. You're done. Get off." Asondra squealed a plea, a cry of agony that found no voice.

Roy said, "Oh, you want more?"

Asondra nodded fitfully.

"Tell you what . . . you can sit on it again. But put it in your ass this time."

Asondra's eyes grew wide, like she swallowed a bug. Afraid.

"Don't worry. I'll be easy this time. Maybe."

Asondra took Roy's words as a direct order.

WHATS THIS ABOUT?" ASKED PUSH.

"We don't owe you answers, punk. Let your probation officer explain it to you. Read 'em, Joe,"

Another voice behind Push began with the Miranda Rights.

"You have the right to remain silent . . ." And the processing began with Push surrendering to the cold hands of the law. Meanwhile, he asked the God who reigned over all ex-cons to give him the strength, courage and wisdom to deal with this latest chapter of pain and strife. His mind traveled back in time to his prison days. The hole.

He'd had incredible rage in his heart. And then he met a prison chaplain who quoted a prayer that was easy to remember. It was called "The Serenity Prayer."

Dear LORD, Please grant me the strength to cope with the things I cannot change, the courage to change the things which I can, and the wisdom to know the difference.

And with that, Push was equipped to deal with whatever challenges came his way.

CHAPTER EIGHT

THIS WAS A MOST AWKWARD feeling for Roy, to lay here beside Asondra, totally relaxed, the both of them naked and spent, with her head cuddled against his chest. He thought back to the things he'd said during the sex, how he'd called her the vilest and most humiliating names. The endless vulgarities that he'd thought up in the name of sex . . . the nastiest sexual favors he could imagine. And yet, now he felt some remorse for having been so wicked.

He had to admit that he had love for Asondra, despite how he treated her; how he cheated her; how he betrayed her trust and used her repeatedly. The two had been together, on and off, for over 15 years, and yet he didn't commit to marriage, He wouldn't move in with her. But then, if Roy was such a player, why was he feeling this uneasiness? This guilt? How ruthless a man could he *really* be? Asondra was a woman who did anything for him, and who proclaimed her unconditional love constantly. So, maybe Roy was simply comfortable with taking this woman for granted. And maybe, since this surely wasn't the first time, it probably wouldn't be the last.

Roy kissed Asondra's forehead. They had been laying there for some time now, with the candles still flickering and the incense all but burnt out. The scent of their sex still lingered along with the thin haze of smoke in the atmosphere.

"Hmmm? What's that for?" asked Asondra coming to life, snapping out of that dizzy, satisfied aftermath.

"Baby. Just wanted to let you know I appreciate you . . ." Roy wouldn't say he "loved" Asondra, since that meant weakness.

"Ummm," she replied, unable to see past Roy's front: his wooden responses. With her subtle smile, Asondra rested her face against Roy's chest.

"You don't mind me having my way with you, do you? I mean, how I call you all kinds of names."

"No, boo . . . you know I like it when you talk dirty to me."

"Yeah, I know."

"Plus, I know you just talk a lotta shit cuz you horny."

"Oh really. So if we ain't fuckin', you ain't my bitch?"

Asondra sucked her teeth. "Of course I am. And you my nigga, boo. But, I guess there's a time and place for all of that. It's not like you're smackin' me around or disrespectin' me out in public."

"Naw, baby. You ain't pushed me *that* far," Roy muttered.

At the spur of the moment, Asondra started singing, with her every word directed at Roy.

"Is it . . . the *waaay*—you *looove*—me, *bay*—*bee* . . ." And she wooed Roy into a restful state where his eyes fogged up with sleep and his mind returned to the cold killer that he'd seen out on 122nd Street. Somebody like that, with heart and courage, could be useful to someone like Roy. This guy could turn out to be the pro to protect Roy's interests. Besides that, Roy had some other concerns; some more pressing than the rest.

T HE WEEKEND WAS USUALLY HECTIC for Crystal, since she was a bartender and waitress at *Perk's Fine Cuisine* on 123rd & Manhattan Ave. So there was no way for her to know about her brother's activities.

Her job was such a relief to go to each day, to meet new people, to serve them with a smile and an attitude to brighten their day. She figured that to be her "special talent," how she gave such expert service, with a touch of personality. So, if someone happened to forget the restaurant (which

was unlikely), at least they'd remember that woman named
Crystal with the pleasant smile.

Perk's, named after the legendary Henry Perkins, had
three levels and was generally jam-packed on Friday and
Saturday nights. A fully-stocked bar was positioned adjacent
to the front entrance. On the lower levels were the restrooms,
the coat room and the pay phones. There was a sunken dining room on the 2nd level, where entrées were served until
midnight, and throughout the early evening and late into the
night, the bar attracted players, hustlers, businessmen, politicians and other such notable Harlem personalities. Spotted
amongst the rest of the establishment might be celebrities
from music and entertainment, sports, and the occasional
fashion model. Pushing up on all of the big-willies with one
proposal or another were always some of the sultriest, sexi-
est, sassiest women that money could buy. They wore the
hottest dresses, their sauciest pill-box hats, and their jewelry
could compete with their fabulous smiles and sparkling eyes.

These women knew the bottom line: that the "big dogs"
with the big dreams and the big dollars would always need
that someone special to share it all with. And Perk's had
been the spot for decades, where fish came out for the sole
purpose of being caught.

Mr. Perkins was the warm personality that brought it all
together, with his tall-bodied kindness and his stylish ability
of making everyone feel at home in *his home*. A total
stranger might suddenly receive a hug or a kiss from that
smooth, cool restaurateur, "Perk."

"Crystal-baby," the boss called out with that bellowing vi-
brato. His was the type of voice you'd expect from a man
who's lived a long and prosperous life, the essence of hard
work ethics and readiness for the day's challenges, whatever
they may be. "Give these pretty ladies a round of drinks on
me." And Perk took out a twenty dollar bill to make that grand
gesture. *Money's being spent on you baby, remember that.*

Crystal was accustomed to this, knowing that if you've
seen one pretty woman, you've seen them all. And, of course,
only another woman would easily see through the facade; the

make-up and the illusion that was almost always put on to in-spire, influence or intrigue a man. Crystal had enough experi-ence to know the deal. No matter how good looking the woman, she was but another human being who used the toi-let, who stank if she didn't wash or ate poor foods. And natu-rally, she was all too aware of "that time of the month" when things got *really* interesting: the moods, the ugly-spells and that icky discharge of blood. Of course, all of that was hidden when it came to men and women meeting in a place like *Perk's*. Men were privileged to see the pretty side of things; the make-up, the hair extensions. It was anyone's guess what the men had hidden.

But there was something else that Crystal knew well; something that she respected about Mr. Perkins. He *built* his business on pretty women such as these. So, more than just buying them drinks, he was actually investing, making the pretty-ones feel at home so that they'd come back to re-live that high-point, that warmth. It was a chemistry that Crystal witnessed over and over again, one that inevitably helped to make Perk's a legend in Harlem.

Crystal had some of her own company there tonight, Sun-day night, which was generally slower, with a less-impulsive crowd.

"So what's up, girl? Are you gonna put me down, or what?"

The solicitor at the bar was Yvette Gardner. Self-made, shapely, witty, and as fine as you could imagine without pay-ing admission.

Crystal laughed, more abruptly and louder than she in-tended. Her friend had been asking about Push for as long as she could remember, and now she finally spit it out. She fi-nally put it out there, saying exactly what was on her mind.

"You are somethin' else, Yvette. Really, somethin' else."

"Can't knock a girl who knows what she wants, Crystal. Or *who* she wants. Especially when there's a good man who, *ahem*, drops out of the sky. One who is, *ahem*, available, and who is by all accounts . . ." Yvette leaned over the bar to whisper to Crystal. ". . . A virgin."

Crystal rolled her eyes and used the painfully truthful moment to serve a Heineken to a regular being seated to the left of Yvette.

"How you doin', Crystal," the customer inquired.

"I'm good, Sam." she replied, laying the beer before him as he took a seat at the bar. "How's the book comin'?"

"Almost done. Just takin' my time, ya' know?"

"Well, don't you forget the little people, Sam."

"We're *all* little people when you look at the big picture, Crystal. But don't you worry, there'll be an autographed copy waiting for you." Crystal smiled. Sam always said the most meaningful things; like he didn't want to waste good oxygen.

When Crystal re-approached, Yvette said, "So, come *on* girl. Don't play me. Where you hidin' him? Is that most eligible bachelor stayin' at your house?"

"Maybe," Crystal replied, turning up her nose.

"Lemme find out. You know me, girl. I'll walk barefoot in the snow, from here to one-two-six if I got to. Tell me what I gotta do. I'm serious. Yvette reached out and grabbed Crystal's wrist to help drive her point home.

Meanwhile, Crystal wondered if Yvette was really serious, or if she was just horny and desperate. Crystal wasn't just gonna toss her brother out into the wind to be walked all over just because he was—as Yvette had so appreciatively put it—a virgin.

"Listen, Yvette. You know how protective I am about my brother. I love that man to death and I'd do anything for him. But the last thing I'm gonna do is have him stuck with someone who doesn't respect the total man he is."

Yvette made a face. A kind of silent outrage.

"Now wait—hold up, Yvette. I'm not sayin' that you *wouldn't* appreciate him. I'm just sayin' . . . dag, slow your role."

Yvette put her hand to her chest, relieved that her friend hadn't dropped her so easily. "Now I know you been askin' about Push for a long time, how you wanted to write and visit and all. And I *did* send him your picture before he came home. But you gotta know . . . it's deadly serious now, boo. It was one thing when he was away—I mean, he was like a legend. But now that he's home, I've been able to see Push, the grown man. He's got issues that you and I could probably never understand. Issues bigger than anyone I know, and sex just isn't one of them. That's not the most important thing to him right now."

Yvette's eyes were sad with compassion. *Poor Push . . .*

"Well, what *is* important girl??" Yvette's hand was atop of Crystal's now, squeezing it in a plea for an open door. "What can I do? No, I'm *serious*, Crystal. This isn't some pipe-dream, and I'm not a little girl with a crush. I'm thirty-two years old. I *got* a good job . . . I make *damned* good money, enough to handle me AND Push. I'm more than capable of loving that man the way, well, the way he *deserves* to be loved. You feel me, Crystal? He deserves me, just like I deserve him."

Yvette sat back on the bar stool now. She said,

". . . I'm *tired* of these half-baked, two-timin', Kentucky-fried-money negros, Crystal. I work hard for mine—too hard to be givin' coochie away. Too hard to be all pressed up against the wall of some greasy negro's fantasy." Yvette had her arms folded and her eyes were watery with some mix of pride and anxiety. Maybe she was a little *too* loud, since Sam cleared his throat and excused himself from the bar.

"Would you watch my drink for me, Crystal? I need to use the *little boy's room*." The way Sam said that was more of a submission . . . a defeat on behalf of all the men, the dreamers of the world . . . all of them squashed under Yvette's cement foot.

Crystal offered Sam a sympathetic grin as she placed a cocktail napkin over her customer's drink. And now her arms were folded too as she evaluated Yvette for a moment. She searched her friend's eyes as though she were a psychotherapist studying her patient. What she saw was sincerity and determination.

Yvette, on the other hand, felt like she was being hypnotized.

"You know . . ." Crystal took a deep breath. "It's only be-cause I believe in you that I'm doing this . . ." Crystal looked up and away. *What am I about to get my brother into.* The sparkling drinking glasses were hung up there, all arranged in so many rows and columns between Crystal and the back-bar mirrors behind her.

Yvette shivered at the assumptions left for her to con-sider, pulling at the words even before Crystal uttered them. She perched up in her seat, baited breath hanging there in her throat.

Crystal went on to say, "But I *swear*, Yvette, if you do my brother wrong . . ."

Yvette's lips quivered as she wagged her head.

". . . If I get one bad report—"

Yvette almost interrupted, she was so excited right now.

"—*I'm* gonna be the one who's locked away . . . for *woman*-slaughter, uhh, if you get my drift."

Yvette squealed with joy and her body sprung forward to hug Crystal over the counter. "Ohmigod, yes . . . I mean, no . . . oh, I don't know *what* I mean. Just . . . oh, Crystal. I won't ever let you down. Thank you so much." Yvette's eyes got wet and she sniffled as though she'd just closed the sale on her first home. "Oh, look at me! I'm falling apart here."

"You are. Go fix yourself, girl. You're a mess."

Perkins locked his doors just a little while later, and the two girlfriends took the short trip to *M&G's Diner*, one of few places that served meals around the clock. If not for Yvette and her Volvo, Crystal would've caught a ride with Mr. Perkins.

"So here's how we do this, Yvette. I'm gonna talk to him tonight. That is, if I see him. If not, then tomorrow."

"Okay," Yvette responded anxiously.

"Here's the deal. The good news is he didn't throw away your photo. I noticed it in the stuff he brought home with him—and that *stuff* was only a brown envelope. So, maybe that's a good thing. Now, the not-so-good news is, he might . . . and I stress, *might* be seeing somebody."

"Oh that's okay. I'm willing to *fight* for mine."

"Slow down, girl. It might not come to that. It's just that I haven't seen him since Friday afternoon. And it's not like he has his own place—he's only been home for a couple of months."

"So who's the bitch?" Yvette asked, her brows furrowed and her lips pursed for the challenge.

"That's just it, Yvette. I don't know. As long as he's been home, he's been busy. He's workin' on some kind of real estate contracting, something or other. But otherwise, he's been home. He talks with my son a lot. The facts of life and all that man-to-man stuff. And they play basketball together. So this is really . . . well . . . it's a *new* life for him."

"Crystal, I don't care *who* she is, or *what* she's plannin' . . . I'm ready to bring it. I'll be the LA Lakers and she'll be some no-name team from North Dakota. IT'S ON!"

Crystal sipped her coffee and chuckled at the same time.

Yvette said, "You think I'm *playin'*. But don't be surprised if in a couple of months you're callin' me your sister-in-law."

"It's not gonna be easy, child. Remember, he's a grown-assed man. He's got the weight of the world on his shoulders. He told me that doin' the time was the easy part. But a black man becoming somebody, especially in *Harlem?* That's the most difficult thing to *imagine*. I know he's putting his best foot forward, though. And if there's anyone who can do it, it's Push."

"I believe it," Yvette agreed. And for the first time that night, under the bright lights inside of *M&G's*, Yvette noticed parts of a bruise that Crystal's make-up hadn't concealed. She was about to comment, but Crystal was speaking.

"I just wanna say this, and then I'm gonna let you go for yours. That man needs compassion, affection and tender loving care. But most importantly, he needs someone to understand him . . ." Crystal leaned into her next words. "But that's just it. Understanding him means knowing that he don't—need—nobody. He's a survivor. A soldier. And I swear, it may not show in his eyes sometimes, but Push is a man who's destined to win . . . or die tryin'."

"Ooh girl, you're scarin' the shit outta me," said Yvette, after a moment of silence.

"Good. Then maybe you'll be on your best behavior. Maybe you'll be the one to ease his pain . . . to heal his wounded soul . . ." Crystal reached across to touch Yvette's cheek. ". . . and I wish you the best. I do." Yvette winced just then. It was the thought of Crystal being hit . . . assaulted. She turned her head down and away, knowing that it had to be Raphael.

"You okay, Yvette?"

"Mmm hmm." Yvette lied, thinking that she had to get Push first, *then* she'd address the blue marks on Crystal's face; the ones that she failed to hide.

Hopefully, all of that would happen very, very soon.

CHAPTER NINE

B
Y MONDAY MORNING, HARLEM WAS buzzing with commerce. So much life and energy to contradict the dark side . . . the previous weekend with its shady characters, its mischief and its self-perpetuating nocturnal dangers, all of it now laid to rest. The night was like a bat, a water bug or a burglar that couldn't operate in the daylight. It was merely sleep time, with all of the night's activities postponed until sundown. At sundown, one world went to hide, while another crept into existence.

It was now, in the broad daylight, that the weekend's consequences sunk in like a huge hangover. In many cases, the realizations of violence, of death, and of misjudgments were all crying out together:

OH LORD! WHAT HAST THOU DONE?!

Word got around about the shooting and the events at the *Lenox Lounge*. 20 of its customers had been locked up for one reason or another. That was the simple rumor. The bigger story was Raphael's murder, which grew legs and ran like so many other juicy hood tales. Gossip.

"*Gurrrl . . . did you hear about that dude, Raphael? Yeah, the one with the ponytail . . . right, the red-boned one. Well, do you know the mob had him executed on Friday night?*"

"*Chile . . . lemme' tell you, I was **there**! I didn't actually see the one who did it, you know how Mya be havin' the music*"

*bangin' and all. But they say it was that playboy . . . you know
the one . . . heard he been beatin' women . . ."*

"*Boo, you remember Raphael? He's the one who promoted those Miss Phat Booty parties they was havin' at P.J.'s.
Oh, don't even act like you don't know what I'm talkin'
'bout . . . anyhow, I heard his competitors did it . . .*"

"*That's good for his triflin' ass. I knew that freak,
wannabe-playa. Do you know we went out on a date and he
had the nerve to threaten me? Talkin' 'bout, I spent all that
money on you, and, you betta' give me some . . . what did I
do??? Girl, I got me a can of mace at ALL TIMES.*"

"*Yeah, I heard about Raphael. Heard he been goin' with
that girl Crystal, too . . . and you know that's that boy
Push's sister . . .*"

As the tales from the hood traveled on, the stone-hard
walls of the 28th precinct police station knew the truth. The
only truth. Right now, Push was the truth. The reality he
lived, wherever he went . . . that was the truth. That holding
cell in the back of the station, Saturday and Sunday night . . .
that cold, unfeeling climate where he was fed uncooked
meals and nasty tap water, while most of the 20 who were
arrested received bail and went back to their cozy homes . . .
where he did continuous workouts just to keep warm . . .
where he had only a cement slab for a bed and mice for company.

Right now, *this* was reality. *This* was the truth. And then,
of course, there was the beating they put on him. Was it 5
cops? 6?

Push was unclean and smelled of blood and sweat. His
skin was rough like a farmer's. His facial hair was a bit
thicker and his head (he had been keeping it clean-shaven
for over 10 years now) had stubble. His eyes were somewhat
withdrawn in his face like dark sockets of thought; of discipline, or rage and resentment. Still, he recorded every sight.
Every sound.

At half past 8, the nightshift filed into the station, retreat-
ing to the locker room, while the 8-to-4 shift spilled out into
their respective police vehicles, or on foot for their routine

beats. A few civilians, including a cleaning lady and an attorney, stepped past the officers to enter the police station. A dark wooden counter that stood taller than the average man was where the civilians and the attorney approached. There was a desk sergeant up there, towering over everything like a god.

"Yes. What can I do for you," the desk sergeant announced, neither confirming nor denying the civilians' right to exist.

"We're here to file a complaint about—"

"Take this clipboard. Fill out the form, and have a seat over there. Someone will be out to see you. *Next!*"

"But, excuse me . . . sir," the woman pleaded humbly. "I need to speak to someone from your Internal Affairs Department or Civilian Review Board. My complaint is about a police—"

The desk sergeant made a face and almost snatched back the clipboard as he said, "Oh . . . one of *those* complaints. You can still go over there and have a seat. Someone will be right with you."

The woman and her female companion strolled over to a rickety wooden bench as though they'd been scolded.

"Yes. What can I do for you?" It was as if the sergeant was positioned and ready to shoot down ducks. Open season on folks with complaints.

"Peter Griffin, sir. Good morning. I'm an attorney, here to—"

"EXCUSE ME! But I understand that you have my brother here . . . his name is Reginald Jackson . . ." Crystal had stormed into the station house, more or less pushing past police officers and the attorney at the head on the line. Yvette was right behind her, trying to keep some kind of control over her friend. And now, a few officers were suddenly alert in the station. They stood close by, anticipating trouble. Nothing new here, just another disgruntled customer.

Peter Griffin, attorney, might as well have been invisible, because Crystal practically trampled him.

"Miss! *First* of all! You'll need to lower your voice in my station if you expect anyone to assist you. And second of all, this gentleman here—"

"LOWER MY VOICE?? YOU DIDN'T LOWER YOUR VOICE WHEN YOU AND YOUR GOONS WENT INTO THE LENOX LOUNGE LIKE THE GODDAMNED KKK!!"

"I'm going to have to—" The desk sergeant was already decided, signaling the assistance of those officers behind the disorderly woman. Peter Griffin raised his hand.

"*PLEASE!*" He pleaded to the desk sergeant, and after hastily putting down his attaché case on the floor, he said, "*MISS!* Please . . . I'm an attorney. I'm here to help your brother. Reginald Jackson, did you say? Is *that your brother?*" Peter Griffin was pleading with everyone all at once. From the desk sergeant, he wanted mercy. From the approaching officers, he wanted a second chance before things got physical. From Crystal's friend, he wanted help. And from Crystal herself, he wanted—"You've got to stop and think about what you're doing. Think of where you *are* . . . who you're *dealing* with." Griffin was risking this girl's liberty with those inflamatory words, but at the same time he was counting on the guilt he might evoke from the desk sergeant. "Now, control yourself." Peter couldn't believe how he'd suddenly grabbed this woman's arms—this perfect stranger—and how he shook her like a disobedient child. Peter Griffin, the disciplinarian.

Yvette was there to witness all, with her hand on Crystal's shoulder and her eyes looking back, hoping for some kind of understanding from the cavalry. Somehow, Crystal calmed herself. Some sense had been shaken into her.

The desk sergeant seemed to let up, but not without saying, "One more outburst like that and I'll lock you up for disorderly conduct!" The sergeant said his piece, but it sounded more like he was antagonizing Crystal, daring her. Or . . . maybe he just wanted to have the last word. Egomaniac. In the meantime, Mr. Griffin and Yvette escorted Crystal away from the front desk, back to an isolated corner of the lobby.

"I'm sorry if I was rough, miss. But these white folks don't play. They react first and ask questions last."

Crystal instantly saw past the older man's professional presence. He looked a lot like an outspoken civil rights activist she'd seen on this or that talk show or magazine cover. She could somehow see into his soul through those spectacles of his. He seemed to care about her. He seemed to be on her side. And now, he took out a business card from the inside pocket of his suit and handed it to her.

"Now, if we do this the right way, your brother should be out today. *Maybe* within a few hours. But if we do it the wrong way, this could be messier than any of us want it to be."

Crystal's hate and rage turned to a quiet distress.

"Did you hear what these pigs did? How they went up into the Lenox—"

"I know all about it. Trust me, it was unjust. It was uncivil. It was everything that is wrong. But there are ways to answer, ways to fight back. Your way—fighting them with all the hostility—that whole riff-raff attitude is not the answer."

Crystal took a deep breath. "I got beside myself. Sorry. It's just that, Push just came out of prison. Fifteen years, and now *this*."

Peter Griffin noted the nickname, *Push*. Then he said, "Okay. Just calm yourself, young lady." Turning to Yvette, he asked, "And your name, young lady?" There was that appreciation in his eyes. *Thank you.*

"Yvette."

"Nice to meet you. Yvette, look after our friend here and allow me to take care of things at the desk. I'll be back." The attorney turned and swaggered back over to where the desk sergeant was on the phone. Griffin collected his attaché case from where he'd mindlessly left it. Then he prepared to re-address with a whole new attitude. *Diplomacy, Peter. Remember . . . diplomacy always works.*

The desk sergeant finally put down the phone.

"Now, where were we?" The sergeant asked, not necessarily thrilled at the way the attorney handled the disturbance.

"Please excuse the young lady, sir. She—"

"I'm past that. Let's get to *your* business."

"Yes, well . . . I'm here to see my client, Mister Reginald Jackson." Griffin presented his business card as he spoke. "He was picked up on Friday night and I understand you're holding him here until the Probation Department—"

"Yes-yes. I suppose you want to see your client. One moment." The sergeant took the business card and made a phone call. Griffin stepped back to say something to Crystal and Yvette. Eventually the desk sergeant announced, "Mister Griffin, you'll need to step through that door and see Officer Leffert."

The buzzer sounded and the attorney hustled through the door into the inner workings of the police station. Further on, he signed a guestbook and proceeded towards the rear of the station and its holding cells.

A S MUCH OF A SURVIVOR as Push had become over the years, and as much as he knew he could handle this sudden encounter, he knew also that this would have to end or move forward somehow, someway. There'd either have to be some kind of arraignment, he'd have to be moved to Riker's Island, something. But he couldn't be kept here, that was for certain.

They're waiting for the wounds to heal, Push decided.

The bruises were still stinging about his cheeks and under his eyes. His arms, thighs and abdominal muscles were sore as well. But he'd grown to appreciate muscle pain as a result of his daily workouts during prison, after prison, and even now, in the holding cell. So, the beating wasn't bad enough to fold Push's staying power. They didn't break any teeth, thank God, and (to the best of his knowledge) none of his bones.

Guess they thought they did something.

And the beating was for what? Was Push supposed to throw his hands up in the air and cry for mercy? Didn't they know who Push was? If anything, the cops who beat Push were lucky that they were in a group, that he was cuffed and shackled. And just maybe they wouldn't end up so lucky after all, if wishes came true for Push.

"Mister Jackson?" The voice came from out of nowhere; except it bounced off of everything. At the present moment, Push had been meditating, changing his immediate environment (in his mind) and therefore creating the warmth, the comfort and the healing thoughts that would help him to cope with the circumstances. He looked up to see a bespeckled black man with close, beady eyes, with an afro that was more wide than it was tall. He had big teeth with one missing on the upper left side, and Push wondered if the man's being black was a good sign since so much white handled him over the past 2 days. In the meantime, he didn't answer the man. He just waited for him to speak.

"I'm Peter—oh my GOD! What happened to your face? What did they do to you?"

Push still said nothing. There were still the iron bars between the two; that demarcation between good and evil. So nothing changed in Push's mind.

"Officer! Excuse me! Officer Leffert!" It took a moment, but the officer finally responded.

"What is it."

"I demand to know what happened to this man! Has he seen a doctor?"

"What happened?" asked the officer, as though he wasn't already aware. Scratching his head, the officer looked like a guilty child who got caught with his hands icky with icing from a cake he wasn't supposed to touch.

"You know damned well what I'm talking about. The bruises.

"I guess . . . I guess he fell."

"Fell? FELL?? I want a doctor here *right* away! And if I don't get one, I'm gonna sue you and *everyone* else in this

station, to the degree that you will feel worse than HIM!"
Griffin was pointing at the officer and then Push. Griffin
pulled a chair up to the bars and sat down.

"Mister Jackson . . . my name is Peter Griffin. I'm the attorney who's been hired to represent you. To get you out of
here." Griffin was more aware now of the conflicting odors
in his midst.

For the first time in days, Push was ready to speak. He
hadn't even accepted the one phone call that was offered to
him when he came in. Which was likely the reason that police officers had their way with him; thinking of him as de-
tached and disconnected from friends or family. Besides,
there was no way he was going to call Crystal, and there was
really nobody else he could look to for help. (You don't get
to scan the telephone book for old friends; no such conveniences in jail.) So, Push just figured he'd let the machine of
justice take its toll.

He'd been here before.

"Who hired you?" Push finally asked, hoping it wasn't
Crystal. She didn't have the type of money necessary to help
him out of this mess.

"Sir, that's not as important now as getting you out of
here . . . getting you some medical attention . . ."

The two, Push and Griffin, weren't more than 2 yards away
from each other. Push sat with his elbows on his knees,
hunched over like the thinking man while the lawyer sat with
his attaché case flat across his lap.

"I wanna know who hired you."

"Lets just say that . . . the *person* you're referring to is a
philanthropist. He, or . . . the person, heard about your situation and wants to help. It's quite simple." Griffin wanted to
kick himself for letting the "he" slip into his answer. Then,
as a second thought, he said, "Your sister—*Crystal, is it?*—
is out in the front lobby. She—"

"So that's it. My sister *did* hire you—"

"No sir. She didn't. I just happened to run into her a few
minutes ago . . ." And it's a good thing I did too, otherwise

she'd be back here, locked up with you. "She really cares about you, Mister Jackson."

"Call me Push."

"Wha . . . excuse me?"

"Push. My name is Push. Reginald Jackson is my government name."

"Oh. I see. Well Mister, ahh, *Push*. I'm gonna get you out of here. You just hold on, you hear me? Stay strong, brother."

"I was *built* strong, mista."

Griffin's sense of existence froze for a moment. And then he shook it off and said, "Yes. Of course you were." Griffin handed Push his business card. "I have some heads to fry out front, if you'll excuse me . . ."

Push took the card and went back to the warm spot on the concrete bench.

". . . And I'm gonna make 'em pay for how they're treating you too," Griffin said as he walked away. And he was gone.

Push thought about Crystal. Seconds later, he was recalling the Serenity Prayer.

OES THE LAW HAVE NO meaning??!! Does a man . . . does even an *animal* have any *rights*?" Griffin was outraged, standing before Captain Brock in the captain's office.

"Mister Griffin, please calm yourself. I've assured you that I'd look into the matter. I've been away since last Monday. This is the first I've heard of—"

"Captain. This is *your* house. *You're* the man in charge. Are you telling me that the minute you turn your back that *all hell breaks loose*? I've never had a client who was treated with such indignity . . . such malice and violence. And I can't imagine that such eighteenth-century torture tactics are still being used today. Of all places, here in New York! In *Harlem*, no less . . ."

"Get me Lieutenant Booker in my office please . . . I don't *care* if he just left. Get hold of him and get him in my office. *Now.*" The Captain put the phone down. "I'll get to the bottom of this, Mister Griffin. That's a promise."

Griffin was already up and out of his seat, his hand already reaching for the knob on the office door.

"I hope you do, Captain. Because if I have my way, the twenty-eighth is gonna hang for this." Griffin, civil rights activist, left to see about Jackson's release.

"No bail? I don't get it. No arraignment . . . no bail . . . police torture. Where am I, in *Asia* somewhere???"

"Sir, all we're doin' here is holding your client for the feds. They're the ones callin' the shots here, not us. We're just holding the prisoner."

"Yeah. Holding him and beating the—" Griffin had to check himself. He was out in the lobby now, dealing with the desk sergeant. Again. Plus, Crystal was within earshot, and he didn't want to get her all revved up again.

"What federal agency now has jurisdiction over Mister Jackson?" He asked sweetly.

"The United States Probation Department . . . as a matter of fact, that's the lady comin' in the door now." Griffin turned to look and his jaw could've touched the floor. It was Evelyn.

CHAPTER TEN

EVELYN WATSON WAS A USPO (United States Probation Officer) for 6 years. An aggressive, brown-skinned, woman, Evelyn managed a caseload of ex-cons that were scattered amidst the 5 boroughs of New York. And they seemed to never stop coming. There were bank robbers, phony check makers, gun-runners, tax-evaders, counterfeiters, and a never-ending army of dope dealers. Based on these so-called dregs of society, Evelyn could stake her claim of job security. Perhaps crime *did* pay in some way.

All Evelyn ever wanted to be was a counselor in school; to correct children at an early age, before it came to this. But the Board of Education wasn't paying well, and Evelyn did want to have some kind of nest egg to be proud of. Otherwise, what was all the sacrifice for? So Evelyn left P.S. 374, where there were at least 40 students crammed in each classroom, and she took the job that had been touted in the *New York Times*:

WANTED:
COUNSELORS, SOCIAL WORKERS AND TEACHERS
U.S. DEPARTMENT OF JUSTICE
GREAT PAY & GREAT BENEFITS

And here she was today, a world of training and certification tests behind her, with 40 grown-ups who (one way or another) didn't behave themselves without supervision. Many of them had been to camps, F.C.I.s and penitentiaries.

Others, many of which she could see had expert or well-paid legal representation, received suspended sentences and probation for 1 year, 3 years or 5 years.

There were fast-talkers, sly businessmen, and others who seemed to have some sort of an attention deficit disorder. There were masters of disguise, and surprisingly enough there were a few good family men. But more and more, Evelyn—"*Ms. W*" to many of her probationers—was seeing liars and pretenders multiply. She'd sense that a man was lying to her and she'd go stake out his house or apartment (secret agent–style) to find that he wasn't truly a handyman, employed by a building contractor. No, the probationer wasn't taking the bus like he stated on his monthly report. Instead, Evelyn would run the plates on a brand new BMW to find it was registered to a company which her probationer (somehow) had a link to. There'd be questions he'd have to answer at that next monthly meeting. And if he didn't come clean, chances were that he was doing dirty deeds again: all in support of his bus trip back to CLUB FED.

Even if a probationer was squeaky clean (or so it might seem) Evelyn might follow him at random. It was all in a day's pay, so what the heck.

She often wondered: *Why can't they just tell the truth? Why's it always gotta be one lie supporting the last?*

But bigger than all of that, beyond Evelyn spending her days (and some of her nights) outsmarting ex-offenders, she had her own side-hustle going; one that nobody would ever imagine. And why shouldn't she? Evelyn was a hard-working government employee. She lived with ex-offender drama every day. Not 5 days a week, but 7. There were also 10 house-arrests on her caseload nowadays which meant that the individual, be it male or female, would need to be home at all times, save for work, church or the hospital. Everything else required her approval. In other words, she constantly played phone tag. If a probationer left the house, say, to go to the local hangout with Money-B and Willie-Guns, the black box on that person's ankle would alert a computer that would in turn alert Evelyn's pager. The bottom line was,

Evelyn had no choice but to stay on-call 24 hours a day for this very taxing position. All of which came with the territory of crime-fighting. It was an experience, to say the least, that tested (to the max) her tolerance for men and their ways.

PETER WAS DIFFERENT FROM OTHER men. At least that's what Evelyn's mother said when they all gathered together on the previous Thanksgiving.

"He's a man who seems to know what he wants, dear. And how many of those can you find out there today? Lord knows I had a fit finding your father, God Bless his soul . . ." And her mother had to go and say a damned thing like that. Evelyn felt, as a matter of fact, that it was her mother who sealed the deal, endorsing things as she did. What could Evelyn say?

The attorney and the probation officer made uninhibited love that night. Their bellies were stuffed, but their minds were also full of passion. It seemed to all be bliss until Peter had to go and bring up marriage.

"What ever happened to shackin' up?" Evelyn had asked.

"*What?*" Peter thought that to be an incredible statement from a *woman*. Usually, they wanted the opposite; things like commitment & fidelity.

"Just what I said, Peter. Why is it that when I finally find a man I care for, I can't enjoy the relationship for a while. Why can't I indulge in the sports and entertainment of sex, without the dark cloud of marriage hanging over my head?"

Peter laughed. "Well, ain't *that* a bitch! And, uhh, how long was it that you expected this *sports and entertainment* to go on before you make some kind of commitment, Ms. Free n' easy?

"See what I'm saying?" Evelyn sat up some in the bed. "First of all, words like that could get you shot. A *ho* is free n' easy. I hope to *God* you're not—"

Peter cut in. "I apologize. I didn't mean it that—"

"I know what you meant. See, Peter, you want numbers. You want solid data. Baby, I deal with that at work all day long. You deal with that at work . . . in the courtroom. But these are our personal lives here; and love isn't like that. Love is about bending and molding and shaping a relationship. It's not a business with any bottom line. The judge, the jury and the Supreme Court aren't making love to me . . . they're not making me happy, either. You are, baby. So, just lay back and enjoy the ride. Stop *pressin'* me." Evelyn once heard that quote from a probationer—"*Ms. W, stop pressin' me*"—and she thought it was appropriate at the moment.

She could see that Peter was flabbergasted by the slick response since he turned away and avoided eye contact for the rest of the evening. Things were never quite the same after that night. The sex became hostile, if not infrequent. Then the phone calls and after work rendezvous dissolved. Eventually, they called it all off.

That was three months earlier, and the finality of it all still weighed heavy on Peter's heart. To him, their year-long involvement was special. And here it was November again, just a year after that horrible night in bed . . . *that sports & entertainment*. He couldn't quite get that one statement out of his head: *Whatever happened to shacking up?*

To TELL YOU THE TRUTH, Evelyn . . . I *still* need you. I've *been* needing you for the past three months, two weeks, one day, and about . . ." Peter checked his watch. "Ten hours."

"Oh, Peter. That's . . . so sweet." Evelyn's response was sheepish; her words tapering off into a soft whisper.

"I meant it, Ev. And as far as me needing you, the greatest testament that I could make . . . well, I've al*ready* made it. Last Thanksgiving, in fact."

"Don't remind me, Peter. I can't get that night out of my head. Was it me? Or was that the last time we *really* made love?"

"I think you're right. We were only together a few times after that, and, well, speaking for myself . . . there was no feeling there. No passion. More like . . . sports and entertainment."

The two laughed until they were teary-eyed in Peter's

new Audi. Evelyn's car, a half-assed government vehicle, was right there as well, double-parked just outside of the 28th precinct police station. Then, without further ado, they held each other as they hadn't in so long. Too long. There was a passionate kiss. Then there was the heavy breathing and hungry touching.

Peter was the one to pull away.

"Oh, Jesus. Evelyn, we've gotta talk," he said, realizing that a man's liberty hung in the balance while he and Evelyn were getting hot and heavy.

Evelyn smiled like a little girl and said, "We *are* talking," and she leaned in again for more of Peter.

He carefully shut her down.

"No. I mean it. We've got to talk."

"Okay. So wassup, my nigga?"

"You kill me when you talk all ghetto." Peter with the strange expression.

"I'm only around gangstas and thugs all day, Peter. Just a product of my environment. Plenty of bad taste in my blood. Now, talk to me."

"There's a man in there. His name is Reginald Jackson."

"Push," said Evelyn, waking from her dream.

"Right. And he's my client."

"Then you understand that we can't discuss him. Ethics you know."

"Are you *serious?*"

"As a heart attack." And Evelyn told Peter to call her at home before she pecked him on the cheek . . . before she left the car.

Just when he thought he had an inside connect. *Shit!*

"I'll be *damned!*" Peter exclaimed through gritted teeth. Then he eventually got out of the car too, following Evelyn like a shadow. The Audi's windows were still fogged up as the two slipped inside of the police station entrance.

INSIDE OF THE POLICE STATION, Evelyn showed the desk sergeant her credentials and was immediately buzzed in. She hadn't said more than, "Good morning."

Peter was left stranded and dumbfounded in the lobby with Crystal and Yvette. In his mind, he hadn't gotten any further than he was an hour earlier.

"Thank you, officer," Evelyn said as she made her way down the corridor of holding cells. "I'll yell if I need you."

"Yes ma'am," the officer replied respectfully.

Evelyn's heels clicked along the hard cement floor until she came to the cell where her probationer, Reginald "Push" Jackson, was assigned. After so long in her position, Evelyn grew accustomed to the filthy smells and appearances of holding cells.

"Push. *Push*?? What'd you get into a fight?" Evelyn had her hands gripping the bars as she got a closer look. The last thing she was afraid of was a man.

"Yeah," Push answered. It was easy to talk to Ms. W, since she dealt so much with ex-convicts. She was sensitive and stern whenever she needed to be. In a way, a man like Push needed a woman like Ms. W for his smooth return to society. ". . . you could say that. Of course I had cuffs and shackles on . . . and there coulda been four or five of them against one of me . . . but—uhh . . . who's gonna cry about it? Not *me*." Push showed no emotion as he said, "It is what it is."

"Oh shit, Push. How in the—" Evelyn took a deep breath and turned to pull up a chair to the bars. The compassion immediately showed on her face.

Push came closer and sat on the floor, mere feet away from where the P.O. was opening her daily organizer.

"Push. I got a call from my supervisor on Saturday morning, telling me that NYPD picked you up at . . . the Lounge?"

"Lenox Lounge."

"Okay. They say they picked you up, but they don't say why. Then there's a note here: *known criminal in the immediate vicinity of a homicide.* Now you know how these things work, Push. If you're caught anywhere *near* some kind of serious crime, and if they identify you as an ex-felon, with paper still left to your name? The rule is, ask questions later. Now, you wanna fill me in before I draw my own conclusions?"

"I was at the Lenox Lounge havin' a—uhh—orange juice . . ." Push smiled, but so did Evelyn, obviously reading between the lines and past the little white lie. ". . . And the cops just came in like gangstas. They shut the music off and started shakin' everybody down . . ." Push explained things down to the smallest detail, minus the bit about the Ruger.

"So, did they find anything on you?"

"Nope. I was clean," Push proudly replied. "They was lockin' cats up who had nail clippers, Ms. W. I was free to go, they said. But then, when I got outside another cop called me over to his car and asked for my ID. They asked me some other questions and then locked me up."

"And the bruises?"

"Miss W, I ain't cryin' about no beat-down or no police brutality. What they did to me was child's play compared to where I've been." Push lifted his shirt some to show her his scar. "Remember reading 'bout this in my records?" When he saw her close her eyes he let his shirt down and said, "I'm just tryin' to get up outta here. I need a shower."

"Not so fast, soldier. You were in the vicinity of a capital crime. Didn't you and I discuss this? Zero tolerance?"

Push showed her his defeated expression. "Of course, Ms. W, but how am I supposed to know what's goin' on outside on the streets if I'm in a club gettin' my groove on? Fourteen years, baby—"

"What did you call me??

Push cleared his throat. "I lost my head, Ms. W. I'm just sayin', if I happen to be at a coffee shop down near where some hard-ons wanna fly a plane into World Trade Center, I'm supposed to be responsible?"

"That's different."

"How? It's a crime to fly a plane into a skyscraper, ain't it?"

"Sometimes I think you're too smart for your own good, Push. Now I want you to look me in the eye and tell me you didn't have anything to do with the homicide near the *Lenox Lounge*."

CHAPTER ELEVEN

THERE WAS COMPLETE SILENCE FOR most of the ten-
minute drive home. But if you were to read minds, you'd
swear that Yvette's car was the noisiest place in Harlem.
There were so many ideas floating around like so many
clouds of incomplete thoughts; or swarms of invisible lo-
custs.

Crystal had been considering the coincidence of Push
being just a half block or so from where Raphael was slain.
Not that she cared all that much about Raphael's sudden
death. She was long past that. It was just so damned obvious; Push finding her in tears and bruised the other day,
and then Raphael being executed at the exact time Push
was there around the corner. Push wasn't even *into* clubs
and bars and crowds. But, of course, you'd have to be his
sister to know that. And it was also evident to Crystal how
far Push would go to protect her—case in point being her
baby's father taking a flight off of that 6-story abandoned
building on Fredrick Douglass. Oh yeah . . . she'd be surprised if it *wasn't* him.

Yvette, on the other hand, was more of a spectator for
the time being. She knew about Crystal and Raphael. She'd
seen the bruises. She knew about Push, the legend of 125th
Street, and how he earned his name. As far as Yvette could
tell, it was common sense: 1 + 1 = 2. It didn't take a wizard to put this together. And if that was the way street justice worked, if that was the price Raphael had to pay for

abusing her girlfriend, then so be it. One less moron on the streets.

Yvette was feeling some other things as well; there were butterflies in her stomach ever since she was driving to Crystal's apartment, and now too, as she helped cook the meal. She was finally here, just a breath away from the man of her dreams. All of her waiting had paid off, or started to. For now, Crystal & Yvette planned a hungry man's meal for Push's homecoming. And all the preparations were helping Yvette to keep her mind off of things.

Push also had quite a few thoughts occupying his mind. Yvette. He couldn't forget her face. That photograph . . . an image that had been with him for the last year of his imprisonment. All these years with her face in his presence; he felt as if he knew her personally. Although he wasn't about to let *that* show. But, at least he could finally put the face with a body. And a nice body it was.

Yvette might not have known it, but Push was indeed watching and listening to her closely. Was she offering herself to him? If so, then *why?*

Crystal. She was another issue. Push was absolutely certain she was drawing conclusions in her head. He was also sure that she was afraid for him and the type of trouble that shadowed him. But Crystal was by his side 110%, whatever his actions were. As far as Push was concerned, he was right in what he did. Raphael was dead wrong and that's all there was to it. Push was the judge and jury in the matter. Whatever consequences he had to answer to were well worth it.

Nah, Crystal won't say nothing. She'll keep quiet, Push assured himself. But, as well as things seemed to be going, with his probation officer setting him free and all, it wasn't likely that the truth would ever see the light. Push was confident that the hit on Raphael was clean. There were no witnesses. And if there were, it was too dark for anyone to identify him anyhow.

Ms. Watson was so far the only person Push had to convince. She was the *real* judge and jury, (at least in his life)

with the "*Conditions of Probation*" hanging over his head.
But now that Push had succeeded that test, all he had to do
was go on with his days—business as usual. Everything
back to the way it was.

Who was that lawyer? Push eventually wondered. *And
who was this so-called philanthropist that put up the money?*
A thought crossed Push's mind . . . the image of that man
who stepped into the Lenox Lounge after he did . . . how they
locked eyes ever so briefly. Push had this thought, and then
he let it go. Surely, Push would need to address many of
these ideas sooner or later. But for now, he headed straight to
the shower. Immediately afterward he soaked in a tub full of
hot water and Listerine to penetrate and deep-clean his pores.
After an hour of that, he filled the tub again, this time adding
menthol bath crystals and rubbing alcohol. He also applied
Vicks VapoRub and Bengay (together) to his arms, legs and
abdominal muscles. He soaked for another hour and enjoyed
the thorough sensations that the chemicals had on his pains
and sores. In the meantime, Push continuously applied hot
cloths to his face to sooth and heal the bruises under his eyes
and on his cheeks and jaw.

By 3:30 in the afternoon, Push had that shiny Snicker bar
brown scalp again, and after some extensive hygiene—the
flossing, the brushing and the toe and fingernail clipping—
he emerged from the bathroom a new man. He felt slight fa-
tigue, but a new man nonetheless.

Crystal and Yvette had cooked up king crab legs, fried
fish and shrimp, white rice and corn-on-the-cob. Yvette put
extra love into peach cobbler pie, a recipe she had memo-
rized from her grandmother down south. And there was
also a half-gallon, at least, of Push's favorite: fresh-
squeezed grapefruit juice.

Yvette put love into that too.

"Too bad you weren't here to help me with the meal
I made when he came home from prison," Crystal told
Yvette.

Yvette made a salty expression. She could've cut Crystal
for even *thinking* that, since it was Yvette that had been

soliciting herself (almost literally!) from ever since she could recall.

Thanksgiving was a few weeks away, and yet Push wasn't really feeling the corresponding holiday shows they played on TV. So, Crystal popped in an old video tape of a live concert. It was a Quincy Jones tribute with all varieties of legendary musicians who performed. Michael Jackson, Take 6, James Ingram, Jeffrey Osborne, Chaka Khan, Tamia, and a busload of other musical icons, whether dead or alive. There were also some comedians and sports stars who made guest appearances, introducing video montages and what-not. Even after the third viewing, this show was entertaining so many years later.

By 5pm, Yvette had her fill of watching and studying Push. The three of them had been sitting on a sectional couch when Yvette took one last marvel at this man from head to toe. She sighed and let her mind wander. She wasn't prepared for the shudder that romped through her body and eventually had to go in the bathroom to wipe herself. *A virgin!* she had been telling herself. A short time later, Crystal kicked Yvette out of the apartment—flaring nostrils and all—with a friendly boot in the ass.

Reginald, Crystal's son, returned from his after-school activities at 6pm—he played junior-varsity basketball—and opened the apartment door to find Push knocked-out on the living room couch with a blanket over him. He was about to go punch his uncle for standing him up and not attending his game on Sunday. But his mom was in clear view, cleaning dishes in the kitchen, putting a forefinger up to her lips to indicate that Reggie should tread lightly. Uncle Push needed his sleep.

It was no problem, though. Young Reggie was happy just to see his uncle and mentor again. It had been a whole three days that Push was away. And Reggie was clear about the streets of Harlem: anything is likely to happen during the course of one night, let alone the whole weekend.

"Let your uncle rest, Reggie," Crystal said when her son came to hug her.

"He's had a long weekend. When he wakes, tell him I'm at work if he needs to speak to me. Your dinner is waiting for you on the table." Crystal kissed her son, gathered her things, and was off and running to *Perk's*. In her heart she knew all the answers. She also realized that she and Push needed a little space just now. She wouldn't force him to say anything about what the both of them already knew. When the time came, she was sure they would discuss it. Sooner or later.

SO . . . HE'S A FREE MAN."
     "For now, at least. It's hard to tell with this woman—I mean, I can't tell what might happen beyond this. If she's gonna let him stay out, if she's gonna lock him up again . . ."

"And if you were to look into your crystal ball?"

"I would say he's in the clear. They have nothing on him. No witnesses. No evidence. No smoking gun."

"You know if he did it?"

"Can't say I do. My biggest question has nothing to do with the murder, or Push. Roy, what I wanna know is, why are *you* involved? Why are you looking out for a man you don't even know? And most importantly, why have you dragged me into this?"

"I'm paying you good money, Pete."

"Okay," Peter answered. "And I barely did a thing. So I guess I shouldn't be arguing, right?"

"Exactly."

"That still doesn't satisfy my question, Roy. Why?"

"Does he know about me?"

"Not your name. But he definitely asked."

"What'd you tell him?"

"That a philanthropist hired me."

"Good. Real good. And of course you have all his details. Address. Phone number. That kind of jazz."

"I know more about Mister Jackson than I ever cared to." Peter thought about Evelyn. *We can't discuss him . . . Ethics, you know.* Somehow he'd have to put his foot down with that woman. Some way, somehow, sometime soon.

"Okay," said Roy. "Start with the phone number. I have a pen . . ."

"Roy. I can't—"

"Don't even say what I *think* you're gonna say. Don't even!"

Peter took a deep breath. Attorney-client rules mandated that total confidence which Roy Washington was now asking Peter to break. But Peter was in a complex position since it was Roy who hired him in the first place.

Who was actually the client? Roy or Push?

"I can't do that," said Peter.

"Peter, I swear on my—!"

"*Well's.* Nine o'clock," said Peter. And then he hung up the phone. If critical data was going to be exchanged, (and he wasn't even sure yet if it would be) then there was no way Peter would incriminate himself on the telephone.

Tapes. Feds. Wire fraud. Roy would understand.

RUDOLPH EDWARDS WAS GIVEN A new assignment from Chief Mitchell, the head of the Federal Bureau of Investigation's White Collar Crimes Unit.

"His name is Fred Allen," the chief told Agent Edwards in the FBI's Foley Square offices. The chief had a nice work environment, with a large executive desk, a conference table across the room, an audio/video set up, a bookcase with a plethora of directories, guides and manuals on criminal psychology, criminal law and other such law enforcement strategies which had helped him in his position over the years. Behind the chief's desk was a 40-story grand view of the southern end of the East River and both the Brooklyn and Manhattan Bridges. To his far left was a shelf loaded with awards, plaques and trophies. Chief Mitchell, the equestrian.

Agent Edwards was right there with the chief, soaking in

the atmosphere as if it was his own office, or that it might one day be. Originally an Agent with the Drug Enforcement Agency, up until 3 years earlier, Edwards was now in his 18th year as a federal Agent. He was frequently called in to spearhead such special assignments as the need emerged. There were just so many new and innovative crimes out there, all falling under the jurisdiction of the White Collar Crime Unit, with still others going to the Secret Service and US Customs agencies. It seemed that when all else failed, when these alternative agencies couldn't handle the task, the FBI would inevitably be called in.

"He's part of an election campaign for a Mister Percy Chambers, who's running on the Republican ticket, trying to land a Congressional seat there in the 13th district." The chief picked up a folder and passed it to Agent Edwards. "But it's not the Republicans we're after, Edwards. It's not Percy Chambers, either. It's Fred Allen I want . . ."

"O—kay," said Edwards with some uncertainty.

"See, if this election is won by Chambers, Fred Allen stands to get his paws on hundreds of millions of dollars."

As Edwards flipped through the various documents and photos, he nodded. "I'm familiar with the campaign, sir."

"Good, I'm glad you said that, Edwards. Here's our focus . . ." Edwards had his pad and pen ready, taking notes as though he were preparing his weapon, cleaning it, loading a clip of ammunition . . . releasing the safety, about to fire.

"See, Mister Allen has an elaborate scheme going; he was with the Democrats last election. And there are extreme similarities in this campaign. If you look closely at the paperwork, the information shows how the Democrats took the election by that slim margin last go-round, having lobbied for a three-hundred-million-dollar Harlem Renaissance Fund. That was pretty much the juice of their campaign . . . *Vote for us and we bring all of this money into your community . . .*"

"I remember, Chief. We're gonna re-build Harlem. We're gonna fix the street lights, the abandoned buildings and the schools. We're gonna boost commerce . . . *etcetera-etcetera-etcetera.*"

"Exactly. And with these promises, and the energy that the Democrats created, the accumulative momentum took them over the top. They not only won the election, but they easily raised in excess of the monies which they lobbied for . . ."

"MMM-hmm."

"Remember Julius Anderson?"

"Sounds familiar."

"It should. We nabbed him for stealing over a half-million dollars in soft money—campaign contributions that come from private sources (or under the table) and he received ten years."

Edwards shook his head. *Now* he remembered.

"Well . . . turns out Mister Anderson doesn't want to do the whole ten years. He's offered us information about Mister Allen that has, quite frankly, sparked our interests at the bureau. We've decided to go ahead with his offer. As a matter of fact, the US Attorney's office has already given the verbal go-ahead. They're getting a judge to reduce Anderson's sentence by five years in return for a full disclosure before the Grand Jury. Anderson will be transferred from the camp he's at and they expect him to be sworn in for deposition in about . . ." Chief Mitchell checked his watch, "three hours."

"So they're sure about the information he's giving?"

"Absolutely. So here's the assignment . . . we're going to need somebody on the inside. I don't care *who* it is. I want to get tapes, photos and documents on this guy. I hear he's cocky, so he's probably got a big mouth. Use whatever resources you need. This one's big, Edwards. Big money. Big news. Big promotions."

"So chances are Fred Allen is up to his tricks again. Only now, with the Republicans," Edwards supposed.

"I have no *doubt* about it. Their campaign this time is all about some four hundred million dollars. And according to what our informant says, Allen stands to keep at least five percent of that."

"Hunh?? If he got away with five percent in the *last*

scheme, then he's *already* thirty million dollars ahead of the game . . ." Edwards with the revelation. "What would possess a man who got away with thirty million dollars to try and do it again?"

"I'll tell you why, Edwards. They're never satisfied. Greed gets 'em every time. Remember that."

Agent Edwards left Chief Mitchell's office with a million ideas. But there was just one he was absolutely sure of. And that meant going to see Flash.

Roy "Flash" Washington.

CHAPTER TWELVE

FROM WEST BROADWAY, AND ALL the way to where the old Rutger's Park sits, 145th Street belonged to Kevin "Hollywood" Evans. Hollywood was a huge man who stood 7 feet tall, with milky-white skin, colorless shoulder-length hair (as if it had been bleached or made of water), and eyes that were pink with deep red pupils. Most people who saw Hollywood for the first time were immediately startled; it wasn't merely his outrageous appearance, but also that he was the *ugliest* person you'd ever have to look at. Of course, it's always been said that *beauty is in the eye of the beholder*; but could that "beholder" hold his or her food after a good look at Hollywood?! That's the sho-nuff big money question.

Even Hollywood's nose was too damned big for his face. His lips were sculpted into a tight pucker, like he was always about to kiss somebody, and his ears were pointed like a Vulcan's, which was why he kept his hair so long—to cover *that* absurdity.

Nevertheless, wherever Hollywood might've been lacking in looks, he made up for in terms of wealth. Hollywood was the supreme leader (that's what he called himself) of "Sugarhill", another nickname for that stretch along 145th street. He organized a group known as the "One-45s", a crew that had more than 100 members, all of whom helped to control those 8 blocks (from east to west) as well as Hollywood's $10,000,000-a-month crack-cocaine operation.

The strip was usually busy during both the daytime and

nighttime shifts. The day shift was sparse because the drug trade mostly belonged to the night. But once the sun began to go down, just before the after-work rush hour, the One-45s came out and populated the strip like an army of black ants. There were many young men, fewer women, and a handful of young boys, most of whom dressed in dark clothing. Black was most popular. Black woolen hats, dark hooded sweat tops under goose-feather bombers or black leather jackets; oversized cargo pants or jeans—sometimes tucked into Timberland or Luggs combat boots. There was a sense of militancy out here, with everyone as headstrong as a band of rebels in the Congo, a honky-tonk militia from Montana, or a gung-ho battalion of trained ARMY grunts. There was that devotion; that like-mindedness and sense of duty. Esprit de corps. With the dark clothing and the curtain of darkness for atmosphere—many of the streetlights had been shot-out to maintain the gloominess—the 145s seemed almost invisible. And that was just the idea Hollywood had in mind.

145th Street was very much a commercial zone, however there were also many buildings that had 2nd floor, 3rd floor and 4th floor residences that were just above businesses such as tailors, clothing boutiques, a dozen beauty salons, half as many barber shops, bodegas, a couple of pizza shops, a florist, a few 5 & dime stores, and naturally, there were the fast food take-out joints. Many of the drab, unkempt establishments looked that way because of the consistence of loiterers who vandalized these properties over the years. The average pedestrian stood out like a jewel when they entered some store entrances, with the cracked glass doors, broken tiles as a welcome mat, and maybe the "OUT TO LUNCH" sign still in the window at 4pm—because if there wasn't enough customer support to keep the business afloat, a man had to go out and *find* him some business. Sometimes it was worth the sacrifice to keep the shop closed in order to run such errands. A trustworthy person to tend shop meant another salary, which would defeat the purpose of the so-called profitable, one-man operation.

At 145th and Lenox there were the block's only gas sta-
tions, both of them across the street from one another.
Friendly competition. Year-round basketball was played at
the old Rutger's Park on 145th and 5th Avenue. At 145th and
Adam Clayton Powell Blvd. there was the *C-Town Supermarket*. On top of C-Town was *Shiela's House of Beauty*,
with her glowing neon sign putting its signature on the night.
Across the street was a health food store, a fried chicken
franchise and some new construction. At 145th and 8th was
the famous *Willie Burgers* next to a grocery store. Across the
street was *Popeyes Fried Chicken*, more construction and another grocery store. Between 8th Ave and Amsterdam was
known as Sugarhill, where Hollywood's One-45s were heavily concentrated. This was the center of the thoroughfare
where a 36-story high-rise known as Convent Plaza towered
over Harlem. *"The Convent"* consumed an entire corner of
the 145th Street artery, its main entrance mostly facing Convent Avenue (the cross street). An oval driveway climbed a
small hill, passing under a chunk of the building itself, to
where the doorman stood inside of glass lobby doors. The
building itself had 6 elevators, with ten 2-bedroom apartments and two 1-bedroom apartments on each floor. Within
this monster, a complex that could be seen from miles away
in any direction, Hollywood occupied two floors. On the
15th floor, his crack-cocaine was broken down into dime
bags; pounds of weed were broken down into 50-sacks and
100-sacks, and Ecstasy pills were sealed in quantities of 10 &
20 per Ziploc bag.

While some rooms were used to break down and package
the various drugs, the bedrooms and apartments which had
windows facing most 145th Street activities were designated
for sentries who were armed with AK-47s, binoculars and
night-vision equipment. Six sentries kept watch over the entire operation and were on duty at all times, day and night,
tracking the activities and transactions of the One-45s. They
also maintained 2-way radio contact with a ground patrol
that was armed with weapons and night-vision equipment.
On the 36th floor, Hollywood lived in a lavish penthouse and

was known for his 10-girl sexcapades; paid-for entertainment that took place while he counted his drug profits in the wee hours of the morning. Beyond that, all he did was eat buckets of chicken and woof down Willie burgers for breakfast, lunch and dinner. By the time he finished counting his millions, he was too tired to do much else.

And this was how Hollywood lived everyday.

Agent Rudolph Edwards was only 21 back when Hollywood was crack-king. He had been with the D.E.A. just 3 years. Before becoming an Agent, Edwards served two years in the US ARMY and he completed 2 years of college. Afterwards, he followed the family tradition by becoming a fed. His father and grandfather had both been federal Agents in one agency or another. By now, Grandpa Edwards had passed away, while Rudolph's father moved from the field into the safety of behind-closed-doors forensics. When evidence, weapons or documents were sent to Washington for DNA or fingerprints, it was Rudolph's father who ran the tests and officiated the various procedures. But it was up to Rudolph, the youngest male in the Edwards clan, to carry on the tradition of engaging in such tactical, life-threatening operations that law enforcement called for. And just like the others, he had to start out as a rookie. No giving orders and no sweet desk-job. Rudolph was merely a grunt who did as he was told.

It was a cold February rush hour when Agent Edwards stood together with 80 other DEA Agents in the basement of the *C-Town Supermarket*; all of them in protective gear—bulletproof vests, padding along their arms and legs—holding automatic assault rifles, and listening closely to the special Agent in command of OPERATION HOLLYWOOD.

"So gentlemen, and ladies, we whittled it down to this . . . each block has approximately 10 members of this gang—and that's not counting their so-called ground patrol. We'll get to them in a minute . . ." They called him Custer, a name fashioned after the General who built his reputation on slaughtering Indians in the days of the wild west. Custer was shorter than the average man, with a red handlebar mustache, matching bushy brows and a clean-shaven head that was spotted with blemishes of aging along with a 3-inch scar from a bout with flying shrapnel. It was his wicked eyes, however, that distinguished Custer from most men. He had that air about him that told another story—one above and beyond those that might be subjected to anyone rules or laws. By looking at Custer you got the idea that he'd go to any extreme to reach his objective.

Custer continued with his summary for the bust:

". . . Since there are two sides of one-four-five, that brings their count to twenty, all located within . . . one . . . city . . . block." Custer was making indications on a huge diagram which detailed the entire stretch of 145th, including its cross streets, its commercial landmarks and various other red-flagged areas.

There was an informant, an inside man who helped the agency piece together the intimate details of Hollywood's operation. Edwards helped to arrest him earlier; that skinny weasel they called Flash.

"Now we feel that our primary targets are Hollywood's ground patrol. However, we have it from our informant that ground patrol communicates with the fifteenth floor sentries. Remember we discussed those yesterday? They do these check-ins every fifteen minutes or so . . . so we'll have to take out the sentries as we simultaneously neutralize the ground patrol. It won't be easy, but we've come out ahead on more difficult operations . . .

"Now each of you has been assigned to teams of six. ALPHA . . . that's Gentry, Porter, Sullivan, Dobbs, Ford and Edwards. You'll be going in as primaries on the fifteenth floor of the Convent. You'll be entering the complex . . . through the sewer system. We've checked this route and it looks like Hollywood is slipping . . ."

Custer flipped over a 2nd page and a diagram that detailed the infrastructure of the high-rise. He pointed as he spoke.

"You'll enter this elevator shaft . . . you'll intervene and

plug into the mainframe of the elevators' control box . . .
right here. Dobbs, you'll have the expertise on this one. Simple stuff to you, I'm *sure*." Dobbs flashed a slight grin.
"When the elevator comes down, you'll board—climb on top
of the car . . . take it to the sixteenth floor . . . and wham-
bam-thank you ma'am . . .

"Gentry, Porter and Sullivan, this is where your G.I. Joe
skills come in . . . we'll all be on the same frequency. On the
word go, you three will rappel down from sixteen . . . through
the windows, and we'll catch the sentries by surprise.
Dobbs, Ford, Edwards . . . you'll be kicking in the door—
these two apartments are adjoined. Dobbs, we'll be counting
on your two hundred pounds of brawn here. Now, as for
BRAVO . . ."

The BRAVO team was to neutralize the ground patrol at
Amsterdam and 145th, while the CHARLIE team was
headed for Adam Clayton Powell. The DAVID team was to
move on the ground patrol that was posted at the corner of
145th and Convent—the foot of the Convent Plaza. Similar
teams of 6 were to ready themselves along 144th and 146th
Streets, virtually sealing off any escape channels outside of
the focus point on 145th Street.

On the word go, these teams would also move in along
the various side streets, all of them pouncing on 145th at the
same time, subduing any and all of the One-45s, those dark
figures—drug pushers and runners—that meandered and
loitered along the curbs and in the streets, as well as there inside of various storefronts and foyers. In the most carefree
ways, the One-45s solicited pedestrians and drivers alike
with catcalls, whistles and gestures. All of these activities
were conducted indiscreetly as if the streets (145th in particular) were theirs to do as they pleased.

The One-45s were untouchable. Or so it seemed until
now.

"What about the penthouse, Chief?"

"Oh, we have something special in store for the penthouse. We know Hollywood's up there because he never
leaves. If I had a ten-million-dollar-a-month operation, I

wouldn't leave either. He's livin' like a fat cat up there, and we're about to take the last of his nine lives."

Supporting the DEA maneuvers was the NYPD with 30 mobile units on standby, all of them unmarked cars, at the top and bottom of 145th, as well as close to the inlets of each side street.

With all the intense manpower, and the tactical plans set forth for OPERATION HOLLYWOOD, there was little room for error. The time had come.

"Mister Flash. Are there any last minute thoughts you'd like to share before I say the word go? Before I send my men in there to do battle and risk their lives?" asked Custer. Flash was handcuffed there in the police truck, a truck that was all-brown on the outside, branded with the universally recognized **UPS** logos. Inside the truck was a bank of video monitors on one side, with various other recording devices and equipment. Against the opposite wall was a caged-in wall full of weaponry—AK-47s, submachine guns, pistols, teargas cannons, heavy caliber shotguns as well as shields, helmets, and other protective gear.

Chief Custer might've been a short man, but he was the man with all the power right now, standing before Flash with his arms folded, waiting for the insider's response. An additional Agent was posted at a short distance, his eyes pinned on Flash seated there in a swivel chair, watching the monitors like a helpless mute.

"I'd appreciate your expertise here . . . it might save one or more of my Agents' lives," Custer said with more concern than usual.

Flash deliberated. He knew Hollywood's empire inside-out. He'd already put his own life on the line by helping the feds. And the things he knew . . . the things the chief was asking for would seal Flash's coffin. If Tonto ever found out . . .

"Very well then . . ." The Chief opened the airwaves. "All units stand by . . ." Custer scanned the monitors. Video surveillance had been carefully set up to offer varying perspectives of the street and high-rise, with most of the focus on the area in front of the Convent Plaza. Custer glanced at the Agent by the rear doors of the truck, then at Flash, then back at the monitors.

"Chief," Flash said suddenly, more or less spitting the word.

"Y—*esss*?" Custer the comedian.

"Tonto."

The Chief coughed. It was something imaginary in his throat.

"Excuse me? Tonto?? Who is *Tonto?*"

"He's Hollywood's main enforcer. His right-hand man . . ."

"And?

"And . . . he's not in the building."

"So . . . where is this *Tonto?* And why can't we just pick him up later?"

"Because he's across the street . . . in the apartment above the pizza shop. He and Sonny—"

"Sonny." Custer repeated the name as he looked over at the standby Agent. The Agent shrugged. *Beats me.*

"That's his brother. They sit up in the window behind them Rambo machine guns . . ."

Custer's face was ripe with disbelief, "*Rambo* machine guns??? HOLD YOUR HORSES PEOPLE. DONT FUCK-ING BUDGE!!!" Custer took a deep breath and pulled the back of his wrist across his brow of sweat. "Ahh these *machine* guns you're talking about? They wouldn't happen to be M-60s, would they?

"I don't know no model numbers or nothin', but that sounds somethin' like—yeah. I think that's them."

The Agent witnessing this was already on his 2-way radio while Flash was still giving descriptions.

"Sure wasn't no Uzi. Them ma-fuckas was big. Like from some war movie or somethin' ."

"War movie," Custer repeated without emotion. Then he brought a handheld mic to his lips. "Johnny, get in here. The command unit. On the double." *Johnny* was Agent Johnny Santana, a big, 250-pound, barrel-chested man, clean-shaven, still with his high-and-tight haircut (a fashion which he took with him from the military), and as ready as any linebacker.

A minute later, Santana popped his head in the back door of the UPS truck-slash-command unit.

"Yessir!" he announced, as he hopped up into the vehicle.

The chief pressed a button on the console that was part of the remote-controlled video surveillance. He took hold of a joystick navigating a single camera's perspective so that its screen image shifted. A blitz of images raced across the screen before him, eventually displaying a clear shot of the pizza shop. The lens zoomed in for a closer view. "I'll be a sonofabitch," exclaimed Custer.

"What is it, Chief?" asked Santana with no clue.

"Lookie here, lookie here. On top of the pizza shop. Where the windows are tinted."

The image on the monitor showed one of three windows that were part of a semi-octagon, a bay window where there might otherwise be a pile of throw-pillows; a comfortable spot to relax and read. One of the windows was open just enough to afford a narrow portal, room enough for what Flash called *"One of them Rambo machine guns."*

"Oh shit!" Santana said after a closer inspection. "That's a barrel of a rifle!"

"He says it's one of those, well, we *think* they're holding an M-60 up there."

"Well, there's only one thing to do, Chief."

Custer and his key Agent stared at one another, saying a thousand things, and yet saying nothing at all. Santana took the silence to mean, *go*. And he shot out of the truck as quickly as he'd come in.

"What's gonna happen now?" asked Flash.

"*Ohhh*—business as usual, Mister Flash. Just you watch the little TV and consider yourself fortunate to have an exclusive view. STAND BY PEOPLE. We're about to move in."

Custer stood there, his arms partially folded as he twisted his mustache with a free hand. In the meantime, 2 fire trucks were on standby at Broadway and 145th, right in front of the McDonald's restaurant. Drug busts were known to have their share of casualties and an occasional fire. This was considered a Class A drug bust, so 4 EMS trucks were required. This might turn out to be a bit more messy than anticipated; but shit happens.

Everyone's attention turned westward as 2 hook-and-ladder engines lumbered down the hill of 145th, their screaming sirens moving eastward towards a supposed fire at 479 West 145th Street, the building next door to the pizza shop.

Hollywood's sentries up on the 15th floor were alerted, and now the 6 of them had their binoculars focused on the bright red monster trucks. Evening was beginning to set in.

"The show has begun, Agents. The show *has begun*. Are you in place, ALPHA?"

"ALPHA, in place, on standby and ready to jump, sir."

"BRAVO, CHARLIE, DAVID."

"In place, BRAVO."

"CHARLIE on standby. Looks like a party, Chief."

"DAVID, waitin' for your call, big Daddy."

"Chief, it's Santana. Denning and I are in place. The targets are in clear view." Santana held night-vision binoculars, while Agent Denning held a scoped, 30.8 caliber Remington 700 hunting rifle. He sat with his legs crossed on the floor of another UPS truck that Santana had driven into position. The truck was parked in front of the jerk chicken restaurant, some 300 yards away. The Remington barrel was resting on the ledge of the portal that had been cut into the truck metal for purposes such as these. Denning could only see silhouettes in the window above the pizza shop, but that's all he needed.

Chief Custer waited for the fire trucks to near the intersection of 145th and St. Nicholas before he began to bark orders. "Steady, Denning. Steady

The three Paratrooping Agents, Gentry, Porter and Sullivan, waited with ropes in hand and the windows of the 16th floor apartments opened to the brisk evening air, while Dobbs,

Ford and Edwards were positioned close to their mark, perched in the stairwell on the 15th floor. 2 teams were also ready in an opposite stairwell, prepared to move on the part of the operation where the drugs were broken down and packaged for street sales.

WHAT DA FUCK, TONTO. THEM fuckas is coming ova here."

"Naw. They probly goin' down the hill to ACP. The goddamn fried chicken joint probably caught fire again."

"A lotta fuckin noise, though." The two had to speak loudly just to hear each other. There was no way Tonto could hear the window break behind him, mere feet away. And he didn't even know that his brother had been struck by a .30 caliber cartridge. His head, the bull's-eye.

Now Tonto put his fingers to his face. He looked up, thinking that there was a leak in the roof, not sharp enough to remember that the roof was above the 3rd floor—not the 2nd; not quick enough to figure out that it was Sonny's blood that spit at him, not a leak.

Tonto looked at his fingers and gasped. Sonny was already falling over, collapsing to the floor with a clean hole in his head.

"Oh shit! SONNY!!!"

As Tonto rushed to try and help his brother, he too was hit by a bullet ripping into the meat of his waist. Another shot hit his shoulder, sending Tonto back to the floor.

The Chief had already announced the "**GO!**"

The Paratrooping DEA Agents climbed out of their respective windows, their ropes bound tightly indoors, and they simultaneously thrust themselves away from the building, literally flying out and descending into the night until the ropes swung them like 3 pendulums towards the 15th floor windows, where Hollywood's sentries were generally stationed.

Assault rifles at the ready, the 3 shot out the windows, subsequently crashing through and taking the sentries by surprise. 2 sentries were already down, bloodied and laying amidst shattered glass. 2 others immediately put their hands up. Another sentry who had been further back from the windows was quick enough to raise his rifle to challenge the intrusion.

Sullivan was hit in the leg and buckled to the hardwood floor. Porter and Gentry returned fire and pinned the gunman to the wall with a violent shower of bullets. His blood and guts splattered the wall like salsa sauce.

"The sixth man! Where's the SIXTH MAN!??" Agent Gentry shouted to Porter, who was down on one knee, looking to see that Sullivan was alright. Meanwhile, the entrance to the apartment imploded in time for the rest of the ALPHA team to see the 6th sentry rounding a corner in the front of the residence, his AK-47 directed towards the paratroopers. The gunman was instantly riddled with bullets.

There was mayhem in the streets. Pedestrians and drivers alike were shocked by the onslaught of sudden activity. The Chief could see it all there on the monitors as the reports came in by radio.

"ALPHA to command, ALPHA to command. The sentries on the fifteenth have been neutralized!"

"BRAVO to command, ground patrol at Amsterdam is neutralized. One man down. Another apprehended."

"Good work, BRAVO. Cuff 'em to a telephone pole and radio EMS. Make sure NYPD is notified. Then proceed to join DAVID at Convent Plaza."

"Roger that."

"CHARLIE here. We have three of their ground patrol neutralized."

"Good. Good, CHARLIE. But the show's not over. Heads-up out there."

Now, with most of Hollywood's security and lookouts apprehended, injured or dead, Agents swept in on 145th from the various side streets. The One-45s scrambled inside of commercial establishments trying to hide. They ran through the streets, climbed over cars while in motion, and others simply dropped whatever goods they held onto and tried to walk away, thinking they could blend in like any other passerby.

There were screams. Gunfire ricocheted through the atmosphere.

Rat-tat-tat-tat-tat. Rat-tat-tat-tat-tat.

Agents barreled into the apartment above the pizza shop where Tonto lay wounded and weeping over his dead brother. Other Agents smashed car windows where they saw perps dive for refuge. (You could never be sure what, if any, weapons were behind those tinted windows.)

One of Hollywood's ground patrolmen outside at the foot of the high-rise sprinted towards the building entrance, his Uzi spraying bullets at everything behind him as he made his way up the short hill, thru the underpass and up where the unsuspecting doorman stood in the lobby. The gunman was desperate now, and he took the doorman as an instant hostage, dragging his hostage back through the glass doors. Behind him, Agents were already in place.

One Agent, with his assault rifle aimed at the gunman's head, took a shot without announcement. Portions of the man's brain matter splashed onto the doorman's body, with blood painting his uniform as if a cherry pie had been thrown at him. The doorman fainted there on the lobby floor.

At the bottom of 145th, close to Adam Clayton Powell Blvd., drug runners sought refuge inside of the *Music Mart* and the *Harlem Meat Market*. All of them were immediately apprehended.

At the top of 145th, the westernmost end of the strip where Broadway intersects, one of Hollywood's Captains ducked into the busy *McDonald's* restaurant. When he realized that they were coming in after him, he leaped over the counter. The employees and customers all stood spellbound as the man raced past them, too quickly for others to move out of his way.

Heavily armed DEA Agents pursued the fleeing Captain, jumping the counter like equipment-toting track & field hurdlers. And the chase didn't last very long. There weren't very many options behind the customer service counters, with all the kitchen equipment, preparation tables and employees pointing in the direction of the fugitive. DEA Agents quickly separated, spreading out to check behind and under areas, startling workers with their pointed assault rifles. Finally, their man was found hiding in a crawlspace where french fry containers had been swept aside,

A D.E.A. CHOPPER HAD DROPPED down from the sky during all the activity, and now it was landing on top of the Convent Plaza roof. Agents hopped out of the bird and forced entry into a hatch leading down into a stairwell and the 36th floor. A half-dozen more Agents were climbing the north and south stairways, also headed for the penthouse.

The elevator had not been able to travel beyond the 35th floor. A shutoff switch, apparently, controlled its access to the penthouse and the 36th floor.

"What the hell?" Chief Custer thought he was seeing things as he gave closer attention to the monitors, still observing the operation from the comfort and safety of the command truck. "Did it start snowing already? In October??"

"Hey, Chief. That's not snow," Santana said over the 2-way. If you look real close . . . you'll see it's money."

"Money? What the—"

Flash had a wide grin as he said, "Hollywood always told us—" Another report came in over the 2-way. *"Hey Chief! It's snowing hundred dollar bills out here!"*

Flash was still saying, "—if he ever had to go—"

"Jesus, Chief!" shouted Santana. *"People are all over the streets and sidewalks. They're getting out of their cars!! It's like they hit the lottery!"*

Flash completed his point, "—that everything was going with him."

"Well, I'll be damned. Somebody alert NYPD. Seal off everything! Anybody caught with hundred dollar bills—" Even the Chief knew what he was thinking was foolish. He became frustrated. At a loss for words or solutions.

Flash looked at him, thinking he had seen it all, up until now.

"What'cha you gonna do? Arrest everyone with money?" Flash, the jokester.

"You be quiet, you fuckin' rat!" Custer spit back.

As Agents busted through Hollywood's doors, he and his girlfriends were pouring the last of the boxes out of the window. Neighboring residents cheered from their windows and fire escapes and rooftops. Many more spilled out of their apartment buildings onto the streets, complicating things even more for the various law enforcers as they scurried to pick up money from the ground or jumped up to snatch it out of the sky.

Even as Kevin "Hollywood" Evans was taken into custody, his drug money fluttered through the sky, with so many images of Benjamin Franklin falling like a sheet of heavy snow. A blizzard of money to stretch for blocks and blocks.

Giving back to the community never looked more spectacular.

CHAPTER THIRTEEN

FLASH WASN'T TOTALLY SATISFIED WITH what the US Attorney's office offered him; 4 years at a Federal Prison camp was 4 years too long. So, when Flash heard that the D.E.A. only caught 64 members of Hollywood's crew, he proposed to help them catch the rest.

"I gotta get with his girl," Flash told the agents.

"Who's girl?"

"Tonto's girl. Her name is Asondra. If I can get to her, within a couple of weeks I can help you get all of Hollywood's people. All of 'em." Flash would've turned in his own mother if he thought it could get him a get-out-of-jail-free ticket. He'd never been to prison before, and the idea of being without sex, without his friends and without his weekends of partying sent shivers up his spine.

D.E.A. Agents couldn't be sure if Flash was bluffing, or he could indeed deliver the rest of Hollywood's One-45s. In a separate discussion amongst the chief, the US Attorney and other Agents, Agent Edwards had a suggesttion.

"What could it hurt? Give the guy a few days, put him on a short leash, a body mic and an electronic monitor—"

"Who's gonna stay with this guy around the clock?" asked the US Attorney.

"Yeah, who?" asked Chief Custer.

"I will," answered Edwards.

"You'll put your job on it?"

Edwards didn't have to think long or hard. He had been

the Agent who nailed Flash in the first place. He knew how the guy ticked.

"I'll put my *life* on it," Edwards responded.

The Chief and the US Attorney agreed. This could mean another 40 indictments, ten times as many confiscations, and perhaps it would make up for how Hollywood made such a fool out of the DEA—how he tossed all that money out onto the crowded streets.

They gave Edwards two weeks.

It took Flash all of 5 days to work his way into Asondra's confidences. She let him into her residence. They ate together and talked about the circumstances relating to the bust. Flash quickly realized how desperate Asondra was. She had been dependant on Tonto for so long that folks knew her as "Tonto's girl" and not by her birth name: Asondra. She gave birth to Tonto's child, Trevor. Tonto paid her rent and other living expenses. Tonto protected her.

"Face it, baby," said Flash when he finally got with her. "That's the way the ball bounces. What happened to Tonto is one of the consequences of the game. Few succeed; others are killed, or they go to jail. That's why I got out of the game," he lied.

Asondra took offense to the things that Flash was saying about her man, but he had such a smooth way about him that she couldn't be mad. "I'm here to help you," he told her. But the truth was, he was there to help his *damned* self.

"Oh *brrrrother*," said Dobbs, as he and Edwards sat and listened, camped out in an unmarked van outside of Asondra's apartment.

"I mean," Flash continued, "I'm the man's number-one soldier. His ace boon. I'm the only one who's gonna keep it real with you. The only one who's gonna tell you the truth. I wouldn't steer you wrong, baby. Tonto is on life support, about to die. And if you go anywhere near him or try to contact him, they'll arrest you, too. An accessory . . ."

"This guy is good," said Edwards, listening closely and envisioning Flash up there with his whole dramatic performance. "Twenty dollars says he gets the pussy by Thursday night."

"You got a bet," answered Dobbs.

"And even if he *does* live," Flash went on to say, "he's lookin' at life in prison. He might as well be dead. Now what kind of life would that leave for you and your child?"

Asondra was feverishly rocking side to side, sitting back on a couch with baby Trevor in her arms. He hadn't even begun to speak yet. "You ain't got nothin' to worry about, girl," said Flash as Asondra uttered soft sobs. "I'm gonna be here for you. I'm a straight-up good man. I'll bring in the bacon. I'll make sure you're comfortable, and I'll protect you and your baby. Now, how's a man with life in prison—or *worse*; how's a man in a coffin gonna do all that for you?"

Just 18 years old, scared and unaware of what the big picture was, Asondra wept for the rest of the night. Flash knew that this meant submission, because any wise woman wouldn't have fallen for it. A wise woman—one who stood by her man. or who had close family ties—would've made endless phone calls to check on the disposition of her man. She'd find out who the lawyer was that represented her man. And above all, she'd have gone to her family for support. She'd have gone to visit her man. A wise woman would never just fall for some smooth-talker's words.

But this was Flash's angle. This weakness of Asondra's was bringing him closer and closer to his get-out-of-jail-free ticket. By Wednesday, Flash was still sleeping on the couch.

There was a knock at the window of the van in which Dobbs and Edwards camped-out. The Flash surveillance team.

Edwards slid the van's side door open, just enough for Flash to jump in.

"What're you guys sleepin' on the job?" Flash teased.

"We're not worried about you going anywhere, Mister Smooth," said Edwards, pulling the door closed behind Flash.

"Shit, I could'a snuck out the back way, took the two-train to Coney Island. And ya'll wouldn't never know it."

"Yeah," said Dobbs. "And when you got off the train in Coney Island, we'd be there waiting. Then, we'd *shoot* your ass."

"You know what? You got a point there. My bad. I forgot about how you DEA dudes operate. Shoot first, ask questions later."

"Never mind that, wise-ass. Tell us what'cha got."

"Easy-easy, DEA-man. I'm workin on it. I need some dough."

"More money? I thought you said she had money stashed somewhere."

"Yeah, but." Flash sucked his teeth and made a face. "Would you let *me* do this? I'm the playa here. Not *you*. I'm the one makin' the moves. Now, how am I gonna win her over without showin' and provin'?"

"Showin' and provin'?" Edwards repeated. "Yeah . . . we heard all of your so-called *showin' and provin'*, bubba. Just tell me something?" Edwards was now taking a fold of money from his pocket as he spoke. "How are you gonna be there for this woman? How are you gonna bring home the bacon and protect her while you're away at—" Edwards cleared his throat. ". . . *college.*"

Flash grabbed the money, then said, "I *told* you . . . let *me* do this. And don't hate the playa, hate the game." Flash uttered a sly grin, then he left the van.

"You still want to keep that bet, Edwards?"

"Every penny of it," Edwards answered as he watched Flash disappear in his rear-view mirror. "Your turn to get the coffee, comrade."

Flash made sure Asondra's refrigerator was full and that her food cabinets were stocked. He bought *Pampers* and *Enfamil* (the correct type of *Pampers* and *Enfamil*, Asondra noted) as well as toys for the baby. He even cooked what he knew how to cook—instant meals—washed dishes and helped keep the apartment tidy. Ultimately, Flash put on the performance of a lifetime, considering that his liberty was on the line. On Thursday morning, after just one week as Asondra's close friend, Flash heard baby Trevor utter his first words. It happened to be excellent timing that Flash was there at Asondra's side for the occasion, with his finger in baby Trevor's grip, pretending to be just as excited as Asondra.

"No," Asondra said. "Really. He's trying to talk."

"Ma—*ma?* Ma—*ma?*"

"You trippin'," Flash said to Asondra. Then to the infant, he said, "Tell yo' momma she trippin'."

"Dah-dah?" the baby finally cooed.

Asondra's eyes seemed about to explode in their sockets. She looked at Flash. She looked back at the baby. And somewhere within those moments, she screamed with joy.

Both Dobbs and Edwards snatched their headphones off of their ears. Asondra picked up baby Trevor and hugged him for dear life as she danced around the area in front of the crib. She kissed the baby's face all over.

"He said DAH-DAH! I can't believe it!"

Flash shrugged and said, "I guess he did."

"Oh, Flash," sighed Asondra, her eyes wet and glassy. "I'm so happy right now, but I'm so scared too."

Flash hugged Asondra and the baby together.

"I told you, baby. I'll be here for you."

"You will, Flash? You *promise?*"

"I will. I promise."

"Mmmm hmmm. Just what did I tell you! That's my MAN! Go-Flash-*Go*! The lady killer!"

That Thursday night, Dobbs handed a twenty dollar bill over to Edwards and Edwards held the money up so that he and Andrew Jackson were face-to-face. Edwards kissed the money loudly. Meanwhile, grunting and cries of passion filled the Agents' headphones. It was as if they were listening to the scrambled porn channels on cable: what their eyes couldn't see, their minds could imagine, thanks to the sound effects.

"Now *that's* the easiest twenty bucks I ever made," exclaimed Edwards, rubbing in his victory.

• • •

BUT THAT WAS OVER 15 years ago, Edwards! I'm a grown-assed man, now! I'm not even called Flash anymore. Look at a picture of me then and compare it with me today! I look totally different. Totally!"

"Okay, so you shaved your head, you've grown a few whiskers on your face and you gained a few pounds. But, you still got talent." Edwards wanted to say. But you still a lying, scheming no-good rat.

"Look at you. All business-like. What . . . you got, maybe, ten percent of Harlem kneeling to your high interest loans?"

"I don't discuss my business with strangers."

"STRANGERS?! Flash! This is ME! Agent Edwards. You not talkin to some Joe off the block. I KNOW you, FLASH. You did your little razzle-dazzle back in the day, you won the girl, you got her to help us bury Tonto, and you escaped the jaws of prison. I still don't know how you got off with just probation—a suspended sentence."

"Ten years of that bullshit," Roy argued.

"Yeah, but it sure beats three hots and a cot ANY day."

Roy was silenced.

Edwards knew that the judge had a soft spot for informants how they were putting their lives on the line. But Edwards saw things differently. *If it was up to me I'd have hung this nut.* As far as law enforcement was concerned, Roy "Flash" Washington lucked-out. Big time.

Edwards had to admit to himself that he really didn't have much to work with now, 15 years later. But then, he hadn't used all the cards up his sleeve yet.

"I need you, Flash."

"Stop calling me that. Roy. My goddamned name is ROY."

"Okay. Well, Roy. You're the man for the job. You helped us flush out Hollywood's people. You kept your word. That was some work you did. Fearless shit, man. And your life was on the line. But, with your help, we put Hollywood to bed for good. All of his other cronies are gonna be home in time enough to collect social security."

"Not all of them," Roy was quick to reply.

"Okay, well, most of them. Point is, you're my ACE. I need an ACE on my team," said Edwards, bullshitting the bullshitter.

"What's in it for me??"

Peace of mind, you snake!

"I thought you'd ask that," answered Edwards. "Let me explain what's going down, then we can talk about the benefits to you. And Edwards explained some (not all) things about Fred Allen, about the Percy Chambers campaign, and how he needed to get inside of Fred Allen's world, same as when Flash was deep into Hollywood's world years ago.

Edwards shared this information knowing that there was just one answer he'd accept. If Roy didn't go along with the plan, Edwards would have to force his hand. The election was coming up and Edwards wanted to have a strategy in place so that he could investigate Allen's embezzlement practices.

"And you want me to get close to this guy. Close enough to learn how all this money is being stolen."

"*Exactly*. Where he's hiding it, among other things—yes. Maybe wear a wire here and there. Copy some documents. Simple stuff."

"Simple." Roy said the word and it just laid there. He knew that infiltrating Fred Allen's world of politics and money couldn't be anything simple. *Who does Edwards think he's foolin'.* It took years to earn rank in Hollywood's organization. And now, Edwards wanted Roy to do the same thing overnight.

"Get to the part about the benefits," said Roy.

"Well, I figured, with Fred Allen off the street, you'd have an easier time of it in Harlem with your—ahem—business concerns. My information tells me that he's doing pretty much the same business as you are. Only he's got a lot more money to spend, and you charge higher interest rates."

Roy thought about that and was dumbfounded by how the Agent knew so much about information that was no more than street secrets. He also never considered wiping out the competition in order to take advantage of the fallout—all of Fred Allen's customers. And even so, if Roy felt any competition, (which he didn't) then why wouldn't he simply have the competition bumped off? Why should he have to work for the FBI? *For old times sake?* With an Agent who's trying, no doubt, to earn strips and medals?

"And, from one brother to another, you didn't hear me say that."

"Oh. One of those off-the-record statements."

"Something like that," said Edwards with some shame in his expression. However, Roy saw it for the act that it was. "I am a law enforcement officer," Edwards went on to say.

"Right. And I'm the Pope."

"So, whaddaya say?" The brief silence. "Brother." Edwards had to go and say that. *Brother?* He used that brother-bit one too many times. Roy didn't feel any brotherly affection towards Edwards. And just because they had the same brown skin didn't mean squat.

"I say, no deal. Not interested."

"Then I guess we have nothing further to talk about," said Edwards.

"So, can I go now?"

"Hey. Free world."

And as Roy made his way towards the door of the Agent's office, he had no choice but to overhear the phone call being placed behind him. It was meant to be overheard.

"Twenty-eighth precinct? Yes, this is Special Agent Edwards of the FBI white collar crimes unit. Yes. Who do I speak with in order to report an elaborate loan-shark operation here in your district? Yes, I'll hold."

Roy made a snap decision: the U-turn. He was now at Edward's desk with his finger on the receiver cradle. The call was instantly disconnected.

"Pressin' me, Edwards? You fuckin' pressin' *me*?"

"Then say you'll help me out."

"I can't. It would take a wizard to do what you asking."

"That, or a pretty woman," replied Edwards. And that's when Roy figured it out. He knew exactly what Edwards was after.

CHAPTER FOURTEEN

MONDAY WAS QUITE A BUSY day for everyone. It was November 10th, and New York City was all wound up, anticipating Tuesday's election. Super Tuesday, they called it. But, Roy didn't feel so super. He felt like there was a loaded shotgun poking him in the back. He felt like his life and livelihood was at risk again. He wanted nothing to do with politics, and *absolutely* nothing to do with the FBI.

But here he was again, in the thick of things. He may as well be a big clumsy pro-wrestler, up there trying to perform a high-wire act. His lifestyle had been so easy-going, so filled with luxuries and conveniences. There was more sex than Roy sometimes knew what to do with. And it was all because of his money game. Folks needed money to build their little mom & pop businesses. Maybe they were facing foreclosure, or maybe the landlord was about to call the marshals, or the telephone and electric companies were about to cut the service. It was a fact that a business needed leverage, some working capital in order to grow and compete in the world of commerce. If not, you had to struggle and teeter on the edge of bankruptcy and failure.

Roy didn't care about that. It wasn't his business to help balance the playing field. You need $10k? $25k? $50k? Come and see Roy Washington. He'll have that money there, in cash, before you can blink. And it's not a free service. Roy wasn't a public benefactor. He wasn't anything like Peter Griffin so wrongfully stated: "a philanthropist." No. Roy Washington charged high rates. The highest. And, if you didn't pay on time, the warning would be painful. A brick might suddenly find its way through the plate-glass window of your store. Or there might be a band of thugs to come holla at ya. Maybe there'd be a small fire. Oh, and if none of that kept the payments rolling in on time, you might just end up like Wendy—of Wendy's Bakery on 135th and ACP. Or it could be worse, like Charlotte—of Charlotte's Hair Salon on Lenox and 129th. Wendy's shop suddenly burnt down to the ground. And Roy Washington was there to receive his portion of the insurance money. And Charlotte's business had that terrible tragedy to cope with when a rented pick-up truck skipped the curb and sidewalk to smash through the front of the shop. A woman and child were killed, and the driver (the dope fiend driver), went to jail for vehicular homicide. Roy took a loss on that mess, but it was all part of the game. A lesson for others to learn by.

> You'd better pay Roy Washington,
> and you'd better pay on time.

Roy arrived at *Well's* as instructed to meet Peter Griffin. But now, he found himself wondering why. The earlier meeting at the FBI offices had flipped his priorities upside-down. What he once thought was important, now didn't seem that important at all. He was *supposed* to have the Mercedes washed and waxed. He was *supposed* to stop by Mya's for money as well as *Stringfellows Nightclub, Joyce B Hair* and a couple of nail salons. Plus, there was this chic named Nina who wanted $15,000 for her jerk chicken restaurant. Roy liked loaning money to the women business owners. He found them easier to persuade and manipulate. And besides, here and there, a blowjob just might get a "late payment fee" erased.

However, all of those business concerns were now set aside, postponed for the time being, while he figured out how to work this plan of his. Roy parked across the street from *Well's Restaurant*, double-parked in front of *PJ's*, yet another nightspot owned and operated by a black woman.

Gotta see her at a later time, noted Roy.

There were cars lining the streets, back-to-back and double-parked on both sides (the uptown side and the downtown side) of Adam Clayton Powell Blvd. Roy wondered what all the congestion was about, and *why did Peter invite me here?*

He shrugged it off and started across the street, tying off the belt of his trench coat as he did. He made it across the southbound lanes and waited on the narrow island that divided the road. Once the traffic allowed, Roy shot across, passing between other parked cars to get to the sidewalk and, eventually, into the restaurant. A light dust of snow was beginning to fall. At the crowded entrance of *Well's*, there were balloons affixed to the glass door—an amateur's work. Black folks, most of whom were up in their years, were filing indoors ahead of Roy. With how they were dressed in their Sunday-best, Roy swore that church was in session.

He heard applause once he finally crossed the threshold to where it was warm and busy with conversations. He had been here a few times before and liked their tasty fried chicken, collard greens and rice. The cornbread was delicious too. And another thing; the atmosphere inside of *Well's* spoke of Harlem's rich history. You could feel the ghosts here: Malcolm X, Adam Clayton Powell, Cab Calloway, Lena Horne and Duke Ellington. You got a sense that all the many decades of joys and sorrows, the celebrations and struggles, were all captured in the stained woodwork, the wall paper and vintage lighting fixtures. This was 1920 construction preserved at its best.

There was a long stain-wood bar to the left, all of its high-chairs filled with bodies. Behind the bar was a woman as pretty as any *Essence* model. In fact, if Roy wasn't on an in-and-out mission, he'd be sitting there at the bar, talking shit to her until her heart shuddered and her eyelashes fluttered. For now, he simply smiled at the thought as he negotiated his way across the tiled floor towards the dining area where most of the activity was concentrated. The applause kicked-in again as Roy got closer to the dining room, and at once he realized that this was a political rally. *Oh brother . . .*

A woman was speaking about Harlem infrastructure and how it could be improved. She had a large diagram up on an easel and used a ballpoint pen as a pointer. Roy was able to see this, though he had to raise up onto his toes to get a better look.

Where the fuck is that lawyer?

Just then, Roy heard Peter's voice right there in his ear. The attorney had been standing just inside of the dining room, up against the wall. Peter gestured for Roy to step closer and he moved over some to make room. In the meantime, from his blazer pocket emerged a slip of paper. He put it in Roy hand as though they were both secret Agents.

"What's this?" Roy asked in a low tone so that he wasn't interrupting the speaker up front.

"It's a rally for Percy Chambers," answered Peter.

"No," Roy said, still with the hushed voice, and looking at the note. "I mean *this*. What's this?" And now Roy answered his own question, opening up the note to see the name, phone number and address written there.

"It's a rally," the lawyer said again, ignoring Roy's obvious concern. "That's the new Congressman right there."

Roy could see the tall, dapper-looking man with thinned-out facial hair—a shadow of grey that matched the wavy hair up top. He also wore spectacles.

"You mean, Chambers?"

"Yeah. There in the tweed suit. Glasses."

"I can see that. But I thought the election was tomorrow."

Peter smirked. "You have a lot to learn about politics, Roy . . ."

I could care less about politics, fool.

"The election is already won. This is a landslide victory. A no brainer."

"Oh. So that means, you keeping hope alive," said Roy. At the same time, the crowd applauded the speaker at the podium.

"So without further ado, I like to introduce the campaign manager . . . your friend and mine, Mister Fred Allen!"

A riotous applause swelled in the intimate dining room. The capacity crowd was overjoyed and zealous, wearing **GO HARLEM!** hats and blowing noisemakers.

"Sorry I had to bring you out here, but I had plans already—"

"Shhh, I'm trying to hear," said Roy, very out of character.

Peter looked at Roy with a peculiar expression.

"THANK YOU. THANK YOU! LADIES AND GENTLEMEN. Please . . . I know what you're thinking already and I don't even need a crystal ball. So before I say another word, how about a big round of applause—" The speaker left a dramatic silence that haunted the dining room, as if a celebrity might be in attendance; one that hadn't yet been discovered. "—for, NEXT CONGRESSMAN! PERCY CHAMBERS!!"

The crowd jumped to its feet with explosive applause, whistles and foot stomping.

"GO HARLEM! GO PERCY!!! GO HARLEM! GO PERCY!!! GO HARLEM! GO PERCY!!!"

"OKAY-OKAY. Let's get down to business," Fred Allen announced, backing off of the mic and the loud squelch he caused by trying to speak over the crowd. He took a moment to let the noise settle.

That's him, Fred Allen, Roy told himself, as he looked, listened, and considered the task ahead of him. *Gotta take this guy down and get this monkey off my back.*

"That's the man right there. He's bringing four hundred million to the party!" an excited audience member shouted. Another followed with, "Fred, you go, boy. You gonna bring Harlem back to life!"

"TAKE US OUT THE RED, FRED! TAKE US OUT THE RED! TAKE US OUT THE RED, FRED! TAKE US OUT THE RED!!"

The crowd began chanting again. It went on for a good 30 seconds.

"Now-now! Now-now!!" Again, the waiting for everyone to settle. "This isn't my party. I'm just here to help push the cart. It's *this* man who we're here to take to the throne. It's *this* man—" Fred was pointing at Percy for each emphasis. "—who's going to see that Harlem's new Empowerment Fund serves each and every one of you. He's gonna get our dark, abandoned blocks back to life . . ."

"Yeah!"

"Alright now!"

"Amen to that!"

"He's gonna see that our understaffed, undernourished, underrated schools are well-staffed with well-paid teachers. He's gonna see that they're painted and fixed and cleaned where need be, and once again our schools will breed tomorrow's leaders, tomorrow's scholars, and tomorrow's heroes of Harlem!"

"Alright!"

"GOD BLESS HARLEM!"

"AMEN! AMEN! AMEN!" cried one woman.

"GO PERCY! GO HARLEM!! GO PERCY! GO HARLEM!!" The room became an instant choir of call and response between the left and right sides of the floor.

"I think I'm gonna be sick," mumbled Roy. But in the meantime, he was clapping, smiling and pretending to agree with everyone else. "What I wanna know is, what are *you* doing here? Don't tell me you're on some campaign committee."

"Roy, this party—I'm speaking about the Republican Party, in case you didn't know, is responsible for bringing four hundred million to this town. A whole lotta lawyerin' is gonna be needed, if you catch my drift."

Roy's smile finally turned genuine. "Oh, so Mister Lawbooks doesn't have his head in the sand afterall."

"Don't let the image fool ya', Roy. I do what I gotta do, when I gotta do it."

Roy chuckled. Then he turned back to Fred Allen. So many Fred Allens had come through Harlem, all of them promising this and that, staking claims and launching pie-in-the-sky campaigns. Roy wasn't hating on Fred, but if there was a big chunk of money coming to town, he'd be damned if he wasn't gonna get in on the action. *Fred Allen, I got your hero of Harlem, alright.*

"I'll be right back, Peter." Roy made his way around those crowded bodies and found some quiet in the bathroom. He pulled out his cell phone and dialed Asondra. "It's me. I want you to get dressed. Put on one of them tight dresses— that red one you wore the other night, that'll work. No— don't make no excuses. I don't wanna hear it. Just get in the dress, do what you gotta do to your hair, and jump in a cab. Be at Well's in twenty minutes . . . yes, *Well's.* That's only six blocks away, so don't have me waiting. Well, then leave *without* the bath. Use a washcloth and some hot water." Roy thought quick and then said, "Tell you what . . . the rent's due tomorrow, isn't it? No, I didn't forget. I've been busy. I got your rent money, money for food, everything you got comin' is here in my pocket. So get your ass down here in twenty minutes. And I mean twenty minutes."

Once Roy shut his cell phone he realized he wasn't alone. A woman who looked to be in her late 50s, grey-haired and hunched over, stepped out of the bathroom's only stall and she made a face at Roy. As if to skin him alive.

"Excuse me," she sneered, with an attitude bigger than that of an angry boxer. She stepped past Roy to use the sink and mirror. Roy chuckled under his breath and excused himself quickly from the co-ed restroom. It was 9:20 when a seat freed up at the bar, and Roy hurried to it before anyone else could. Everything, it seemed, was about competing for available resources.

There she was. The bartender was attracting Roy's attention again. He got a closer look now. She had to be all of 5'8", with the whites of her eyes sparkling in contrast to her chocolate chip-brown complexion. Roy was always comparing a woman to some kind of food. Asondra was the color of oatmeal. Mya was peanut butter. The bartender here, she was a chocolate chip. She had a wide, beautiful smile, a sincerity about herself, a sculpted nose and cheeks, black hair that bounced with large, spunky curls, and she projected that certain open-mindedness. In black slacks and a long-sleeved white shirt that was unbuttoned to just below the collarbone, there was nothing to suggest that she intended to lure or seduce, and yet Roy found himself imagining her well-kept, lanky body underneath his, her curves rising and falling with his manpower.

"What can I get you, Sugar?"

"Whatever you're havin', puddin'." Roy would've called her chocolate-chip, but the food references were reserved as pet names. Maybe, if he played his cards right.

"Oh-h-h-h-ho . . . alright. A playa in the house, huh? Since you're treatin', how 'bout a Harvey's?"

"I'm with it," Roy replied.

As she fixed the two drinks, Roy could see out of the corner of his eye that she was checking him out; his reflection in the mirror there along the back bar where all the liquor was displayed. Pretending not to notice, Roy went on posing with his best Mack Daddy vibe. He thought it was cute, sly even, how she used the mirror to investigate Roy with her back turned. Why didn't she just face him and let her eyes wander? Would that be too honest? Too obvious?

When the bartender returned, the two toasted to nothing in particular. She made sure to take up Roy's money. And that seemed sort of sly too; the business before the pleasure.

"So, what's your name, sweety?"

"Maria. And you?"

"I'm Roy," he said, and there was that coincidental applause erupting in the other room. Great timing.

"You from around these parts? I know your face looks familiar."

And Roy said, "I lay my head here, ya know. But I'm in Jersey, here, there. Back and forth. I'm always on the move," Roy lied. "What about you?"

"I got three jobs, baby, plus I promote parties. So I get very little sleep. But Harlem is pretty much my home these days." Maria took out a card that was a little bigger than an index card. Roy immediately knew it as a tool that promoters used to advertise their various parties and concerts, passing them out at the exits of hot spots around the city.

"You might be too old to come to my hip hop functions, but I have a big singles mixer going on just before Christmas."

"Too old? Just how old do you think I am?"

Maria shrugged. "Maybe forty. Forty-two, the most."

Roy laughed out loud and that too corresponded with the applause in the next room. "GO PERCY! GO HARLEM!! GO PERCY! GO HARLEM!!"

"You got me all twisted, girl. Off by ten years." Roy lied, observing the advertisement that she handed him. "But you definitely got the single part correct."

Roy was offering plenty of hints, with his eyes looking directly into hers. *I like you already, boo.*

"M.A.D. Productions. I've heard of that name before."

"I hope you would, all the work I've done promoting my events. M.A.D. is the initials of my name: Maria A. Davis. That my company. We done *MAD Wednesdays* for years. *Sweetwaters, Honeysuckle West. The Country Club. ESSOs*.

"Okay. Yeah, I heard of you. So what's the A stand for?" Roy asked this while he made an obvious glance at Maria's ass.

Maria's eyes grabbed at Roy as if by a chokehold. She said,

"Aggressive."

"Mmm. A business-only mind, hunh? I know quite a few of them. You ever have a need for extra capital? Maybe something to take your company to the next level?"

"Depends on what kind of money you talkin'. Like a regular bank loan? Or one of them loan-shark deals?"

Hmmm, this one's slicker than I thought.

Maria went on to say, "'Cause I got three children to feed, baby. And I can't afford to be pissin' money in the wind. School clothes, food, the rent. Life ain't something I take for granted. Especially when it comes to finances." Maria said this and excused herself to tend to another customer. Roy, in the meantime, felt a thousand pounds lift off of his shoulders. This was a rarity for Roy; a woman that wasn't so hungry and desperate that she'd accept any ole' kind of money.

When Maria came back, she asked Roy, "So tell me more about this money you offerin'."

"Oh, I was just askin', sweety. Speculatin', ya'know? I have this friend that's in the money lendin business. Not me.

"I see," said Maria. And now the applause worked in her favor.

Maria studied Roy at that instant.

Roy eventually said, "You might not be interested in his type of money, I mean, with your three kids n all."

"Mmm-hmm," Maria responded with the raised eyebrow. Her eyes seemed to look right through Roy, and she said, "Well, thanks for the drink. Hope you make it to my mixer. Bring a friend."

And just like that, Maria turned the Roy switch off. He immediately changed his mind about her body underneath his own, her curves rising and falling, and so on. All the ideas of sex disappeared.

Maria was obviously not a woman like the others he'd dealt with. She couldn't be manipulated or easily persuaded.

Roy brushed it off and checked his watch.

It was 9:45 when Asondra hurried thru the entrance of Well's. She had a wool scarf wrapped over her head and face, and she was sucked inside of that full-length, black mink that Roy bought her 2 birthdays ago. "Sorry, boo. The traffic is a mess."

"You still late," Roy scolded her as he helped her get the fur off.

Now he told her, "Go check your hair. Bathroom's over there."

"What's all this about?"

"Never mind. Do what I told you. I have someone I want you to meet. Now, get." Roy popped Asondra lightly against the ass with his upturned palm. As Roy folded the mink over his arm he kept an eye on Asondra's strut as well as Maria at the other end of the bar. He got up from the stool, left a tip (despite the brush-off he'd gotten), and he made his way towards the underpass to the dining room a moment later.

"Okay," Asondra chirped with a new attitude. "All freshened up." Roy took her hand and worked his way through the crowd of chanting supporters, with their GO HARLEM! hats. He felt like it took a hundred "excuse me's" to get back to where Peter Griffin was standing. Again, the attorney made room for Roy while clapping in concert with everyone else. Peter nodded his greeting to Asondra.

". . . AND SO . . . it's every one of you who have made this election a dream-come-true for me. Some folks say that this has been all about money . . . that money is what has won us this election according to the various polls in the *NEWS*, the *POST*, the *AMSTERDAM*, etcetera-etcetera. But I'm here to tell you that this election is NOT about money. It's about PEOPLE! It's about HARLEM!" Applause and cheers agreed with the politician. "This election, if you care to know the truth, isn't even about me. Harlem was here before Percy Chambers, and it will surely be here *after* Percy Chambers. But the one most important element that will always be here is the consciousness of the people—the residents and business owners of Harlem. GOD BLESS HARLEM!!!"

The audience rocked the atmosphere with "GOD BLESS HARLEM! GOD BLESS PERCY CHAMBERS!" The chant continued for a time while Roy pointed out Fred Allen to Asondra.

"Yes," Asondra said. "I see him."

"I want you to go up and introduce yourself. And after you do, I want you to tell him you've admired his way with words for quite a while now. Repeat that for me,"

"What?" Asondra's lip twisted up at the corner while her eyes dug into Roy.

"Just repeat it. I've admired . . . your way with words . . . for quite a while now."

Asondra was apprehensive at first but she repeated what Roy said.

"Now, he's probably gonna be all-smiles, all up in your

face. But that's what we want, so get real bashful with him. You know how you women do: actin' all shy, like a little girl."

Asondra took some air in, contemplating Roy's instructions.

"Then I want you to get real close to him, like I am with you right now. Get in his ear and tell him, I wonder if you have a good woman in your life.

"Roy!"

"Shhh. I'll explain it all to you later. But for now, think sexy. BE sexy. Now repeat what I said so I can be sure you got it right."

Asondra let out an exhaustive sigh. "Do you have a good—"

"No. Listen carefully, Asondra. I want you to get in his ear. I want you to be sexy. *I wonder if you have a good woman in your life.*" Finally, Asondra did as Roy asked.

"See? Now that wasn't so bad, was it?"

"With you, no it's not. But with him? A stranger? That stiff up there? I know this *better* be good."

"Later, I'll explain later. Just turn on the smile and the beamers, and shine. If he wants to set up a date or somethin', then accept."

"Roy!"

"Shhh!" someone nearby exclaimed.

"Here," Roy said. He tore off a piece of the folded note that Peter had passed to him. Then he turned and took a pen out of Peter's shirt pocket. He jotted down Asondra's phone number and gave the pen back to Peter. Peter was so heavy into Percy Chambers' speech that Roy's activities were all irrelevant to him.

"When you take his hand, when he shakes your hand, slip this to him."

Asondra searched Roy eyes for some explanation, oblivious to all the attention that she drew with her red sequined dress, her abundant cleavage, and how her luxurious black hair played softly against her "oatmeal" complexion. All the while, Asondra felt sucked-into some ongoing plan. Something devised by Roy. And circumstances being what they were between them, she had no choice but to adhere and follow instructions. She took the folded note,

"Now, what are you going to tell him after you introduce yourself?" Roy asked for a final rehearsal.

Asondra felt as though she was approaching the Vice President of the United States or something, with all those suited men up there at the head of the dining room. The speeches were over now and the room was filled with chatter amongst many of the evening attendees lining up for the meet-and-greet with Mr. Chambers. There were less people trying to reach Fred Allen, which only made Asondra tremble with every approaching step. She was intimidated, to say the least, by the man's overall image; clean-cut, an afro everywhere but for his receding hairline, the tweed suit, and the cheesy smile. Asondra would never meet or associate with this category of individual in her day-to-day existence. It was new and frightening.

But she was determined to grin and bear the man's looks. As far as she was concerned, he wasn't the winner of the ugly contest, but he wasn't the loser either. A step closer, and there was his cologne. Plus, some white woman suddenly pulled up beside the man.

"Hello, Mister Allen. I'm Asondra Jenkins."

"Well, it's nice to meet you young lady . . ." He already took Asondra's hand. *This isn't right. I can't just slip him the note, now.*

"Have we met before?"

"No, but . . . I've been admiring your way with words for some time now."

"Is that so? Are you with the party?"

"Well . . . I'm kind of just passing through. New to the whole political bit."

"Really?" Fred eyes briefly reached into Asondra cleavage. *He still holding my hand. Maybe now . . .*

Asondra took a deep breath and pulled herself closer to Fred Allen. She whispered in his ear just as Roy instructed. At the same time, she pressed the note into the palm of his hand. Asondra, the secret Agent.

"Well . . . I, uh . . . have you met my assistant?" Fred didn't give an answer to Asondra's question. He just went on with his practiced diplomacy. "This is Sara Godfrey. Sara . . . meet Miss . . . Jenkins, was it?"

Asondra noticed the hand (with her note) disappear into his pocket.

"Yes. Miss Jenkins."

Sara said, "Nice to meet you. Are you with the party?" *Again, with the party question.* And just then, Asondra felt it. While she shook Sara's hand; the cold reception and phony smile. Asondra suddenly felt like the ultimate intruder. Like she was there in the middle, interfering with something. "I was telling Mister Allen that I new to this."

"Oh? Well perhaps I can introduce you to Mrs.—"

"Not so fast, Sara. I don't know that the young lady here wants to dive right in. We don't want to force anything on her, do we?" There was a "thank you," that Asondra implied through her smile.

"Well, it really was nice meeting you, Mister Allen."

"Oh, I'm sure we'll see one another again, ma'am."

Asondra turned away with a bashful expression as she let the next person pass. Roy was waiting over in the same spot, his eyes reaching for her.

"Excuse me?" said a woman's voice behind Asondra. It was Sara again, this time with an abrupt tone.

"Y-yes. Oh . . . hi."

"Right. Hi to you, too," said Sara as she came real close to Asondra's ear. Her face was turned away in the meantime, with her phony smile gleaming in the event anyone was watching. But there was nothing pleasant about the woman's tone. She said, "I don't know who you think you are, all up on Fred like that with your red dress and tits, but that's *my* man. So forget what you got in mind." Sara stepped back, flashed her Pollyanna smile at Asondra once more, and she turned to walk away.

Asondra had come to know jealous women in the past, but never had it come to this. And NEVER EVER from a *white* woman. She had never seen a white woman turn so ghetto so suddenly. *Who does this flat-ass Harry Potter look-alike think she is??? She's lucky I don't smack the shit outta her. Four-eyed bitch!*

When Asondra got back to Roy, she didn't want to hear shit. She reached for the fur coat on his arm, then the scarf.

"Take me home!" she demanded, and immediately strutted off, hardly excusing herself as she worked her way through the older smiling faces with their GO HARLEM! hats.

Roy wondered what went wrong. He saw Fred Allen's eyes follow Asondra as she stepped away, not even paying attention to the person before to him. *Must'a worked. He's hooked. But what happened? What did that white woman say to Asondra?*

"Peter, I'll kick it with you later," said Roy.

Peter pretended to give a damn, but Roy knew better. He was still too caught up in the mania so thick in the dining room.

Back in the car, Asondra punched Roy in his shoulder a little harder than playfully. She said, "Why did I just do that? What was that about?"

"I said I'd explain," Roy replied, hardly affected by the punch. "What was that with the white woman?"

"Huh! Miss Harry Potter? Asondra noticed that Roy was unfamiliar. "Well, of course you wouldn't know. You don't have your own kids." Asondra with the verbal stab. "Anyway, that bitch had the nerve to step to me, talkin' about *who do I think I am with my red dress and tits,* and *that's my man.* Roy, I didn't ask for this shit . . . to rush out of the house, in the snow, to have some short white *bitch* all in my face who I don't even know."

"Easy, Asondra."

"EASY?? That HO don't know ME! I'll beat her ass till she IS black." Roy thought that this was hilarious, how Asondra was flipping like this. She looked mighty sexy when she was angry, too. It was a sight he hadn't seen but once before, when she argued with a woman at her apartment building. Something about the other woman hogging all the driers down in the laundry room.

"You hungry?" Roy asked out of the blue, right in the middle of Asondra's ranting and raving.

"I . . . I . . . guess," Asondra stopped to say, with the idea of food having its own way of neutralizing anger.

"Good. Since you all dressed up, we go by Perk's for dinner. I'll tell you what I have in mind when we get there."

Perk's Fine Cuisine was about 10 blocks away. Too far, where Asondra was concerned. She couldn't wait to hear this.

"I hope you set it up so I get to see that bitch again, so I can have a few words with her."

Roy finally let his laugh go.

CHAPTER FIFTEEN

IT WAS COMING DOWN HEAVIER now, the snow building up on the windshield of the Mercedes, where the wipers couldn't reach. The streets themselves were wet, with accumulations of snow where tires didn't tread. The snow somehow made the dark, mysterious streets acceptable. It sort of subdued things with that effervescent glow. The window sills, rooftops, the branches of trees . . . the gates, the staircases and stoops . . . the pedestrians. Nothing and nobody was immune to where or how the snow could make its impact. It was one of those great balancers in life, how everything seemed to surrender to the raw, indisputable power of nature. Whether it was snow, rain, or even the incredible heat of the sun, everyone and everything had to cope with and succumb to nature's fury.

Roy *did* have that money in his pocket.

Asondra had asked him for $3,000 this week. Last week it was only $1,500. Next week she'd expect about $3,000 as well, so that she could begin her Christmas shopping. All of this, however, the asking and receiving, was routine since the relationship between Asondra and Roy had grown to be heavily dependant upon sex and money. It was this way ever since the day Roy began working his way into Asondra's confidence. When Tonto was shipped off to prison; when Roy received that sweet suspended sentence from the judge; since Trevor began to talk, then walk, then need clothes, then go to school. From day one this was *all* about sex and money.

There was never a time that Asondra had to have a job, or go on welfare or hook on the streets. She didn't have to do any of that since Roy was there to take care of everything. Early on, Roy was small-time, concocting small-time scams to help make ends meet. He had been living with her on 144th street, where Asondra was forced to venture out as an independent woman. She had long since left that safe haven that was her mother's world; that single family household where she spent her childhood, and she filled the voids of family, friends and familiarity with the conveniences offered by Tonto, a drug dealer. Tonto's successor, Roy, went from his small scams into more complex ones . . . more profitable ones. And he eventually moved Asondra and Trevor to 135th street, where she now lived. He rarely stayed at the new apartment and visited only when it was convenient for him. Yes, there was the sex, but even a playa needs companionship and sense of belonging.

Asondra didn't mind how Roy operated, and she suspected that he did his share of fooling around on the side. But she didn't argue these circumstances since Roy always took care of her without much of a hassle. It was the only practical decision, as far as she could see. Asondra had no specific trade, and the only things she knew how to do best . . . the only skills that came natural to her were those which made Roy happy. That meant doing as she was told, being his freak when he demanded, and never complaining. So long as she did these things, in her mind she'd never need to bust her ass like so many other single moms. She'd never be homeless or poor. And she'd always have the money she required. Poor Asondra never considered what life would become if Roy were to leave, or worse, disappear. And the little money that she managed to squirrel-away would never compensate for any insecurity, the cost of living, or the want for compassion.

ROY FOUND EASY PARKING JUST outside of *Perk's*, and he stepped around to open the passenger side door for Asondra. Roy, the gentleman. The two crossed the sidewalk quickly enough to avoid any substantial amount of the falling snow while a bow-tied man held the front door open for them. Soon, they were warm and comfortable at a table for two.

A waitress took their orders and Roy began his soft-sell.

"I don't ask you for much, Asondra. And when I do, it's because there's something important that I need." While the explanation went on, Asondra thought back to some things Roy had asked of her. There was the time he asked her to mention his money-lending business to Mya. That was many months ago. Then the hint was also dropped to Charlotte and Joyce B. They all quickly became clients. There were times when she opened up bank accounts, depositing checks for him. There were a bunch of times she made cash withdrawals from credit cards that were not hers; all of them were in other women's names, and required Asondra's use of false identification. Yes. There had indeed been a number of things that Roy asked of her, not to mention how she went up onto the witness stand to testify against her baby's father and then-boyfriend, Tonto. Asondra still had no idea how Roy got her to do *that*. And yet, she had to admit to herself that she didn't mind doing those things for Roy. It helped to make him successful, and he always gave her the things she wanted.

Somehow, this latest involvement seemed so much different; why, she didn't know.

". . . And right now, Asondra, what I need is *extremely* important. That man you met tonight is gonna call you.

"Me? Why??"

"Because you asked him to . . . tonight, when you gave him your phone number," Roy said after a sip of wine.

"Roy!? That's what you wrote on that paper?"

"Listen to me, and listen good." Roy said this and took out a pound of his money at the same time. It easily amounted to over $10,000 in hundred dollar bills. And as usual, it captured Asondra's attention, with her nostrils opened wide.

"See, baby, that man is gonna make me a very rich man, very soon. And he's gonna do that because of your help—"

"Me? I ain't nobody." Now Asondra took in some of the

wine. It was more of a swallow than a sip, something to wash down her disbelief. But, she had an idea that what Roy was selling her required a much stronger drink than the one she was having now.

"Oh, But you *are* somebody. You're Asondra: sexy, easy to talk to . . . and a *nice* ass. Men like Fred Allen are attracted to women like you. *Why*? Because you're out of their reach. You're someone who he wouldn't run into on an average day. I make that dude out to be one of those ugly ducklings back in school, the one who couldn't get the girl for one reason or another. And now, because of his status, a girl like you drops out of the sky. You're like a gift from God, baby."

"So *that's* what that was all about. *'I wonder if you have a good woman in your life'.*"

"*Exaaaactly.*"

"But Roy, what happens when he calls? You don't expect me to—"

"Oh, but Asondra, I *do* expect you to. You're gonna get him excited. You're gonna turn him on. You're gonna smile and giggle and seduce him until his eyeballs do hoola-hoops around his head." As Roy said these things, he was peeling hundred dollar bills off of his money roll. Asondra's eyes volleyed between Roy's face and the money. Now, he was placing the money out on the table before her, as though the bills were playing cards. But, more than the money, Asondra saw her rent being paid, clothes for her son, food.

"Think of him as just another boyfriend, and I'm giving you permission to date him."

Asondra's apprehensions softened and her voice turned faint. "But baby, the man is as ugly as I don't know what."

"I know, I know. But his money is so damned pretty. You see that brick wall over there?"

"Where the mirror is?"

"Yes, but the wall, minus the mirror."

"Well, yeah."

"I want you to look at that wall as if it was a movie screen. The movie that's showing is called Roy, Asondra and

Trevor. You and I are the stars, and we're laying on a beach in the Caribbean . . . Trevor's out there with us. He's sitting on the sand, playing the latest *Nintendo* game. Whassername is with him too."

"Shatalia?"

"Right. Shatalia is there too. It's a warm, clear, sunny day, and there's not a care in the world. You've got that sexy bathing suit on, but instead of wearing it at nasty ole' Jones Beach, you're sunbathing on that Caribbean beach . . .

"Hey look! The images are changing, we're on a safari now. We're standing up in one of those *Hummer* jeeps with binoculars. Trevor got a video camera, too—thinks he's Jacques Jenkins or somethin'. "

Asondra giggled at the idea. "You so stupid, Roy."

"Hey! Look there! A giraffe! And, oh-wow . . . a gorilla over there. And a lion. Now there's you and me again. We're riding a horse, butt naked, through the desert."

Roy and Asondra were still facing the brick wall, leaning into one another and imagining the sights and sounds. Asondra stopped laughing and said,

"I look a hot mess, sweating like a pig out there in the sun."

"See? That's my girl. It's all in your imagination." Roy was facing her now. No more movie. He took Asondra's face in both hands until their eyes were locked and searching each other's souls.

"Let me be serious with you Asondra. Fuck the beach, the African safari and all that. You and I are going to have the snazziest penthouse in Harlem. Everybody's gonna be able to look up and say: *Asondra really made it big*. You'll go out on the town with me, a big diamond ring on your finger . . ."

Asondra blushed. All the pictures Roy painted were swirling around in her mind; everything bright, colorful and exotic.

". . . an expensive diamond necklace and diamond-studded brassiere . . . you'll have the best that money can buy. The world will be at your fingertips. And all you have to do is exactly what I tell you."

"Okay. You got me all hot and dreamy, Roy. Tell me what I need to do." Asondra couldn't get the words out fast enough. And just as she said it, the waitress was standing over the two with their food.

It had to look awkward, Asondra having said those words, with all that money laying on the table in front of her.

"I'm sorry to interrupt. I can come back if you like," the waitress said in a withdrawn tone. Roy stacked the money neatly on Asondra's side of the table.

"No—no," said Roy. "Please go right ahead. We're starved."

"O—kay," the waitress said, expressing some of that awkwardness. "We have our roast chicken on white rice. And for you, the red snapper. And here are your side dishes. If you'll need anything else, my name is Crystal. I'll be close by. Enjoy."

That word might have had many meanings. *Enjoy.*

Roy explained things more as the two ate. He wanted Asondra to seduce Fred Allen, and yet Roy used the words: "become friends." He wanted her to play cat and mouse with Fred, and yet Roy used the word: "tease." He wanted her to blow Fred's mind, and yet Roy used the words: "stroke his ego."

"But you didn't answer my question, Roy. You're not saying I have to fuck him, *are you*?"

"Now, Asondra, lets be adults about this. He's just a man . . ."

"He's a man with money . . ."

"And??"

"And . . . we'll cross that bridge when we get to it. Of course you don't expect the man to want so much from a little date. Now . . . didn't you need a little more money?" Roy took out his bills again. He peeled off $500 more; a bonus so that she'd let the issue go. "I want you to buy yourself a new dress tomorrow. Go by Mya's place and get all done up. You and I are gonna have a little party tomorrow night. A little celebration. After all, there's a mission for you to accomplish, baby."

Roy handed Asondra the cash and said, "Stick that between your tits. I want the waitress to see that the deal's complete."

Asondra chuckled as a willing conspirator and stuffed the bills right there so that there'd be no doubt.

THE PLAYA WHO FED THOSE hundred dollar bills to the cutie in the red dress weighed heavy on Crystal's mind for a time. She wondered if the girl was a whore and if he was her pimp. She wondered if he was her sugar Daddy, and she was his willing nymph. The girl was too sensible, it seemed, to be anyone's pushover.

Crystal couldn't help wondering what that lifestyle was like—someone just handing you a pile of money because of your looks. If that was the case, if that had ever been the way Crystal decided to go, she thought proudly, *I'd make a killing. But, no. It's the hard-knock life for me. I'm gonna stick it out and make life happen for me. I'm gonna win with hard work, and I'm gonna keep my pussy for a man who deserves it. No more Mack Daddies.*

And that thought brought Crystal to thinking about her brother.

I love you so . . . I don't ever want you to go back to prison.

CHAPTER SIXTEEN

PUSH WAS WIDE AWAKE AND waiting for Crystal when she stepped through the door at 2am. It was a busier night than usual, it being the eve of the election and all. Add to that, how folks ambled in out of the snow for warm conversation.

The snow had stopped by now and the city's salt spreading trucks could be heard outside with their tire chains grinding and slapping the pavement. But for sure, mother nature or the city's clean-up crews had no control over things that needed to be said between Crystal and Push. It was time to clear the air.

"Long night?"

"A little. Election eve and all. I had some guy throwin' money at his date, like he had a money tree or somethin'."

"Pimp?"

"I guess. Or somethin'." Crystal had her coat off now and she shook her hair free from the scarf. It felt good to be home, out of the cold. "Push, I gotta talk to you." *Before my shower, my sleep . . . before anything.*

"Mmm-hmmm . . . I thought you would. Reggie's fast asleep. Come on over and talk to your big brother."

Crystal went to sit on the couch, a foot away from Push. There was a single lamp that illuminated the living room with a dim glow. It was the only light on in the apartment for now.

"Push." Crystal turned her head down. She didn't know where or how to start.

"Let me," Push said, his hand on Crystal's knee. "You already know, so there's no sense in beating around the bush. As long as I'm alive, Crystal, ain't no man never gonna beat on you like that. Never. Matter fact, I'm still mad enough to go spit on that snake's grave."

A chill zipped through Crystal's body. There it was. His admission. It made things so much easier, but left her at a definite loss for words.

"What if he killed you, Crystal? What if—"

With her eyes wet, Crystal said, "Alright, Push. Alright." Crystal's words came out like a dying plea, "Let's not talk about it no more. She wiped her eyes. "What's done is done. But Push, I can't go on walkin' on eggshells, afraid to date a man, with you—"

"As long as a man don't put his hands on you, he a'iight with me. But I can't sit here and lie to you . . . I can't tell you I wouldn't do the same thing again. I can't. Because the fact is, I would do it again. That's just me."

"But Push. I can't have you going back to prison. And that's just me. For almost fifteen years I've had to survive out here without my brother. For a little longer, I've had to survive without a mother and father. Crystal's tears ran in constant streams now. "I'm tired of losin' family, Push. You're the only family I have left; you and Reggie. Please think about me when you're out there doin' what you do. Be a man, sure. I'll never take that from you. You're the strongest man I know—brother or not. But dear God, please don't leave me out here alone again." Crystal fell against his chest now. "*Please,*" she muttered.

Crystal's mention of their mother and father opened up another door, and Push couldn't help what needed to be said.

"In prison I ran across one of our parents' killers."

"PUSH!" Crystal's high-pitched response was full of shock. "You didn't!"

"Yes. There were three of them, sis. And one of them, the one I met, told me everything. He's no longer with us."

"Oh my G—" Crystal gasped at the realization.

"There's two more. They're in Harlem. They don't even

know who I am . . . who you are. They won't even know I'm coming."

Crystal was wide-eyed for a time, and she couldn't breathe a word. Eventually, she said, "But how—how do you know they're here?"

"I've been home two months, sis. I've seen them. They're still alive and kickin'. They don't even know I was peepin' them."

"We should call the police, Push." Crystal had her hand against Push's chest, the other against her own.

"Crystal, be serious. It's been almost twenty years, baby-girl. Them police *been* dropped that case. I bet if I walked down to the police station in the morning and said I was the one who did it, they wouldn't be able to find the file. NO, sis. This is somethin' *I* gotta do. For you and me. For mom and dad."

Crystal said nothing. She put her head back against Push. She knew as well as he did that their parents died a horrible death and that so much had been taken from them as children.

"But you don't need to worry, Crystal. I won't ever leave you out here alone again. Thats my word." Push wet his lips and stared ahead at nothing in particular.

"I'm not worried, Push. God's on your side. I'm sure he is."

THEY FINALLY ARRIVED HOME. SO much election-eve fever. Nonsense. Meeting all those helpless, hopeless pawns who pushed the campaign day and night; passing out fliers, driving up and down the streets of this decrepit city— GO HARLEM! HA!—with loudspeakers blasting from their cars and vans; their little stickers and posters dressing their vehicles with no discretion whatsoever.

"Why do we even deal with these niggers?" asked Sara, taking off her coat and hat. She and Fred had just stepped in the door of Fred's town house on Striver's Row—the vanity name for 138th street. It was 2am.

"It's part of the game, baby. It is part—of—the—game."

Fred lifted all 5 feet and 4 inches of Sara into the air, there in the entry hall, and she squealed like a teenager in love. When he let her down, she lifted up on her toes and draped as much of her arms as she could (her wrists) around Fred's neck.

"Just think about it. In less than twenty-four hours we'll own the world. And in a few more weeks, we'll be richer than anybody in Harlem! GO HARLEM!"

"FUCK Harlem," exclaimed Sara with a sneer.

"Fuck New York too, baby. We're leavin' outta this hell-hole as soon as the first year is up. Get the money and go . . . let Chambers deal with the mess we leave behind. We'll go to Africa and live."

Sara sucked her teeth. "Africa?? More niggers, Fred? That's something that I don't need. More goddamned, stank-ass niggers. I don't even want a nigger for a butler."

"Hey!" Fred made an angry face. "Thass *mah* people you talkin' 'bout miss Sara!" From the angry face, Fred quickly flashed a broad smile. Then he said, "But you're RIGHT! We'll go to Europe instead!" Fred laughed at his own performance and tossed Sara in the air again. When he let her down they shared a moment-long, sensual kiss, with their tongues wrestling like fiends, until Sara abruptly stopped.

"Wait a minute. Put me down." And when Fred did as she asked, Sara asked, "Who was the bitch, Fred?" Sara had her hands on her wide hips. Her eyes were cutting in like sharp tools.

"Who?? There were so many!" Fred said that like he had just left his own private dreamworld where he had so many fantasies to choose from. Sara immediately reached up and smacked Fred's left cheek. The sound was sent across the marble floor and down the dark hall of the residence.

"Damn!"

"You fucking well know which one I mean, niggah. The red dress. The tits. The whisper in your ear while you held her hand. You think I'm a fool, don't you."

"Oh . . ." Fred was still holding his hand against his stinging cheek. ". . . that one. *Honestly,* babe. I just met her."

"Is THAT so."

"You have nothing to be worried about, snookums. Really. You know I don't fuck around with black girls. She looked like a whore . . . a fucking prostitute in that dress."

"Well, alright then. Thats my niggah talkin'. Did I mess up my baby's make-up?" Sara served up a compassionate pout as she petted Fred's cheek.

"Damn, you got a helluva swing there."

"Pick me up and carry me upstairs. I promise I'll make it all better."

Upstairs in the bathroom the two shared the space, stripping and then stepping into the shower together. Fred undid Sara's ponytail and washed her straight brown hair. Sara told Fred to get down on his knees while she shampooed his short, receding afro. Meanwhile, Fred soaped Sara's breasts that sagged off to the sides. Still on his knees, Fred also scrubbed her pubic area, the thin brown hairs between her legs, and those that sprouted from the area around her asshole. Sara washed Fred's hairy chest, his hairy underarms, and his nappy pile of pubic hairs that smothered his testicles and which trailed up and around his ass.

"You need to do some more walking and jogging," Sara told Fred as she tended to his details. "You're gonna have to get rid of this gut if you expect to be any kind of decent politician."

When the shower was done, the two went into the bedroom dripping wet, and they immediately indulged in an hour's worth of sucking—his face between Sara's legs, and her face between his—which ended with both of them sloppy and exhausted. They kissed and fell asleep in each others arms. And this, to them, was love.

ROY HAD WORK TO DO. The Republicans won the election as expected, and Percy Chambers was elected as Congressman, Harlem's new leader. To Roy, this meant pay dirt. It would only be a matter of time. He easily found out where Fred Allen lived—in an expensive townhouse on Striver's Row, a home that almost blended in nicely with so many other brownstones along the block. The home would've been uniform, except for Fred's exquisite taste. He was different than other black men and he didn't mind letting others know with his refurbished colonial exterior. The home was just as clean and immaculately kept as most others on Striver's Row, except that Fred Allen's property seemed more stately. More prestigious, like a white diamond among other yellow ones. An older man pushed a bright yellow cleaning cart up and down both sides of the street, maybe a few times a day, cleaning up sidewalks and curbs. If there was dog mess, gum wrappers or other miscellaneous trash, his job was to clean it up.

Roy noted the activities on Striver's Row; the late model cars that were parked here, and the variety of deliveries—from newspapers to groceries—that came throughout the day. He noted Fred Allen's comings and goings; how he usually had that short white woman with him. But, rarely was he alone except to drop a bag of trash outside, or to take in some fresh air.

There were also his morning walks at 8am.

Using different cars during his investigation so that his Mercedes wouldn't be so familiar, Roy tailed Fred a few times as the man went off to work, when he attended the dozen or so post-election events, and when he had intimate dinners at the *Cotton Club*, *Sylia's* or *Perk's*. The man got around. And as he did, it seemed that everyone knew him. So far, Roy didn't notice Fred visiting any clients; something (in Roy's experience) a loan shark might do in his daily routine.

How can he operate his money lending business without so much as visiting his clients? This was one thing that Roy just couldn't figure out. After all, this was one of the things that most interested Roy about this venture. Agent Edwards had told him: "*He's doing pretty much the same business as you are.*" But now, Roy wondered about that. How does this man collect? And if a client was late or past due, how did he handle that?

Clearly, Roy had a lot to learn.

Deciding to take the Mercedes out for a morning drive, Roy hoped to see Fred Allen face-to-face. He was thinking that, perhaps, something would work out. He could be impressive to the politician, and maybe win over his good graces. Accordingly, he double-parked at the western tip of 138th street, where he knew Fred to turn the corner everyday at approximately 8:30am.

As far as Roy could tell, there were no FBI Agents watching, so he took a stab at it.

"Hey, Fred! Hey! FRED ALLEN." Roy had the passengers' side window lowered as he persuaded Fred to approach the car.

"Hi there," answered Fred, in his best phony voice. "Do I know you?"

"If you don't you sure need to. I was there a couple of weeks ago when you gave that terrific speech at Well's. Get in, please. Love to chat with you for just a moment."

Fred deliberated briefly, then said, "Well . . . not too long. Gotta be at the office in a bit." Once he was in the car, he said, "Nice ride you have here . . . "

"Thanks. Whaddo *you* drive?"

"Oh, me?" Fred's proud expression seemed hard to conceal.

"Just a Caddie . . . ya'know. A little somethin'. But of course, I don't do the driving these days."

Go ahead, it. Say you have a driver, so I can act like I surprised.

"So . . . what brings you this way? You live around here?"

"Born and raised in Harlem," Roy answered in an effort to side-step the specifics Fred was asking for. "In fact, we probably know a lot of the same people. Name Roy. Roy Washington."

The two finally shook hands.

"Really."

"Actually, you and I are in somewhat of the same business. See . . . I help. See . . . I help small business owners. I lend them money."

"Yeah? That's strange. I can't say I know the name. What's your company?"

Roy sidestepped the man again saying,

"Oh, I'm more of an independent investor."

"Okay."

"And you with your empowerment fund. You *also* loan money to small businesses."

"Yes, we do."

"So . . . I was thinking . . . what if I could set something up where you can push some money to my clients."

"All they'd need to do is come by the Harlem State Office building and fill out some applications."

"Yes. Well. I was hoping for something a little more exclusive. Maybe I can be a representative."

"You mean, a middleman?"

"Something like that. Your money . . . my legwork. I have close to sixty small business that could use your low-interest capital."

"You know what? As a matter of fact, I *have* heard of you. Roy Washington. You're a loan shark aren't you."

"Well, I wouldn't say it quite that way."

"They never do. But when it comes down to it, that's what you do. High interest, arm-twisting, all that jazz."

"Fred . . . *everybody's* got a hustle."

Fred got out of the car. Then he leaned into the open window.

"You see that clean-up man there?"

Roy looked across the street. The older man in the bright blue uniform and cap was pushing the yellow push cart with all manners of cleaning supplies, brooms, a rake and shovel.

"Yeah, sure."

"Well, I put that man, and hundreds like him, to work. That's what the Empowerment Fund is about. It's not about raping folks of their hard earned money."

"Like I said, Fred, everybody's got their hustle." Roy said this as though he knew something he shouldn't . . . as if he had a secret. Then he added, "Isn't the taxpayer's money considered hard earned?"

"I'm done here. Any further inquiries, please contact my

office. Otherwise, I don't indulge in under-the-table business deals." Fred backed up from the Mercedes. "GOOD MORNING, TITUS!" He put on a brilliant smile and waved to the clean-up man across the street as he pivoted off to go home.

Roy didn't want to pose a threat like some stalker, so he took off. There were other ways to deal with Fred Allen.

By 9am Roy was stressed, with so many thoughts cramming his brain. He cruised down St. Nicholas Ave, remembering that he had to stop and see Mya about her weekly payment. He figured that the incident on 122nd St. was forgotten by now, as if it never happened. With the comings and goings of snowfalls, the blood had likely disappeared from the sidewalk like a bad dream. Roy was sure, however, that his memory wouldn't fail him. He'd never forget how that man was snuffed out. It was as heartless and cold as what he'd seen the D.E.A. do to Tonto's brother, Sonny, back in the day. Only, the D.E.A. had the *license* to kill. This guy, Push, only had his own heart and the dark Harlem night to protect him.

"Mya, it's Roy." Roy was on his car phone, making a left onto west 122nd St., moving eastward towards Lenox Ave.

"Oh, hey. Your girl's not here, love."

"I'm not looking for my girl. You know what I want."

"Weren't you coming next week?"

"Was, but didn't. I got a lot of late payments that kept me busy. One woman got a smart mouth and I had to—well . . . I'll save you the gory details. What'cha got for me," asked Roy, with less of a question than it was a demand.

"I . . . can you come by on the weekend? Like, Sunday? It's been hard, with Thanksgiving and all. Plus, Christmas is around the corner—

"Funny thing is, I don't believe in Thanksgiving or Christmas. I believe in getting paid now . . ."

"Roy, I . . ."

"You what?" Roy was in front of Mya's now, little did she know. He brought the Mercedes to ease into a double-parked position.

"Will you take half?" she asked.

"And the other half?"

"The end of the week. For sure . . ."

"I'll think about it," Roy said. Not a second passed before he said, "Okay. I thought about it . . . Bring the money down now."

"Now? Roy, I'm doing a perm . . ." Mya with no lack for excuses.

"Now." Roy hung up on Mya. He dialed Asondra as soon as he got a tone. "Hey it's me." As Roy looked out to the street, the memory of the murder—the darkness, the dark figure jumping out from under the brownstone—seemed to be all but erased by the morning light.

"Oh. Hey, boo," Asondra said in a happy mood. "He called again . . ."

"Really . . . What's that? Five times?"

"Six. Last night, after you left, we talked for about an hour. He wants to see me. He says he wants to have dinner up in Westchester. Something about needing to get away from Harlem for a while."

"I bet," he said as he watched Mya skip down the steps.

"What should I do?"

"Hold on." Roy put his hand over the mouthpiece of the car phone. He unlocked the door to let Mya in. He often did business in the car, so Mya saw this as usual.

Mya said, "Hey. Why are you pushin' me, Mister?" The words came out affectionately. "I'm doin' the best I can. I'm not *that* late. Here's six hundred. It's all I have."

"It's not enough," Roy said as he took the money from Mya's hands. She had on thin rubber gloves still, from the perm she had been giving to a customer. She even smelled of relaxer chemicals.

Roy pretended to be angry.

"Roy," Mya pleaded. "Don't be cruel. I'll pay."

"Yeah, you're right. You'll pay . . . and you'll pay interest. Right now." Roy had the phone pressed against his thigh all the while, to keep Asondra from hearing. With his free hand, he depressed a button so that his seat eased backwards. More and more, there was space growing between Roy's body and the steering wheel.

"You are trippin' mista. Fo' real. I'm inside doin' a perm, and you want what?" Mya made a salty face and said, "You gonna hafta stop this *bullshit*, Roy." Mya was about to disembark from the car.

"Tell you what . . . don't give me no more money. Whatever you owe me, the slate is clear."

"Hunh?? Now, I know you trippin'. I owe you over five grand. Just come back in—"

Roy cut Mya's words short by grabbing her wrist. "I said, you keep the money. You gonna need it, bitch, by the time I get through with you."

Whining, Mya said, "Please, Roy. I'm sorry. I'll pay you, I promise—"

"Yeah, well it's too late for the pleas. I want interest . . . *now*. Now, handle yo' goddamned business before I make the call and send Mya's Place up in flames," Roy demanded.

Reconsidering, Mya asked, "Can't I come back in a few minutes?" She put her hand on Roy's leg as she asked this. And this was just how Roy liked his clients. Nothing like a woman begging for mercy; it made his dick hard, how he instilled such a fear in this woman.

"Perm, or no perm, you'll pay interest, now." Roy pulled his zipper down, adjusted himself in the driver's seat, and pulled out his sudden erection. As if to encourage Mya, Roy said, "Hurry up, so you can get back to your customer." Mya was about to argue, but Roy put his forefinger to his lips. A silent shhhh, as he went back to his phone call. Meanwhile, he pointed down at his exposed penis. Nothing new for Mya, who'd been late before. "As you were saying?" Roy said into the phone.

"Everything alright?" Asondra asked.

"It is now, so . . . you think you ready to see him?" Roy was experiencing pleasure and trying to keep his train of thought at the same time, "Will you . . . be able to . . . handle yourself?"

Mya was angrily pulling and pushing on Roy's foreskin, trying to get this over with as quick as possible.

"I think so. You told me every—*what's that?*"

"What's *what??*" Roy replied.

"The noise, Roy? Sounds like you're havin' a Slurpee."

Roy chuckled a bit under his breath at how Asondra hit the nail right on the head. "No. I'm getting the car washed," he lied.

"Oh. I'm so stupid. Anyway . . . I can handle it. I don't think he'll make any crazy moves on the first date."

"I doubt it. See you around ten."

"Ten?"

Roy looked down at the back of Mya's neck and head bobbing in his lap. He said, "You better make that ten-thirty."

CHAPTER SEVENTEEN

THANKSGIVING WAS EVENTFUL FOR PUSH, and that had nothing to do with pilgrims, family gatherings, or lavish turkey dinners. It had everything to do with Yvette Gardner, Crystal's friend.

She had invited Push to her Riverside Drive apartment—a refurbished pre-war duplex with very tall ceilings, carved wood moldings along the borders of walls, door jambs and window sills. Yvette wanted to go all-out, to cook up a hellifying turkey dinner that would satisfy any man's appetite. But Push said that he wasn't into the holidays, and none of the rituals that went with them. However, he did want to explore this possibility of Yvette being that first woman he'd lay with in more than 15 years. Crystal had forced the issue.

"Push, I wouldn't set you up with some chicken-head from around the way. And Lord knows, we got our fair share of them. Yvette is different. She's a self-made woman, like me. And, before you make jokes about that . . . this girl's got a lot on the ball. A lot of class."

"I gotta be careful sis. I ain't got no bugs, no diseases. I'm clean as a newborn baby."

"Mmm hmm . . . I know you are. And so does she." There was a thought that crossed Crystal's mind that her brother was attractive, available, and a hell of a catch. All the things she wanted for herself. The thought was fleeting, and she brushed it off with a sigh. "Yvette has been keeping herself that way, too. Trust me, I been listening to her carry on about this for long enough to know."

Push took Crystal's word for it, which landed him in Yvette's duplex on Thanksgiving night.

"So if you don't want the whole turkey-spread I planned, what do you want?"

"How about a turkey burger?"

"A turkey burger," Yvette said flatly, with her mouth still partially opened.

"Something wrong with turkey burgers?"

"No—I. No," Yvette answered, somewhat defeated. The burgers were easy to make and they disappeared as quickly. It was a meal that left a lot of spare time for the two to get better acquainted.

Yvette would swear that she dreamed and imagined and fantasized about this moment over and over again. She and Push, alone in her apartment. But suddenly, after the meal, she was stuck . . . at a loss for words. Too much distance between them in terms of experience, age, and understanding.

Push, on the other hand, already knew that Yvette was a wanton woman. Thanks to Crystal, he was knowledgeable— maybe too knowledgeable—about Yvette and her thoughts and intentions.

"A little nervous?" Push asked.

"Is that a guess?"

"I hope I'm not jumping out there, but it's your body language. A picture is worth a thousand words."

"So . . . what does my picture tell you?" Yvette was there on the couch, a few feet away from Push. Her knees were close together, with her hands in her lap. She looked straight ahead at the crackling fireplace.

"How about we not screw this up with too many words," Push said. "Just as long as you know that I'm out of practice for—"

"I know. You don't have to bring it up."

"I want to. You should know about me . . . that I'm what you call, hardened. A little insensitive. I just don't want you to take things the wrong way . . . whatever happens."

Happens? Lord, help me . . . what is it exactly that's gonna happen? Yvette's mind raced.

"Wanna come closer?" asked Push.

What a question! I'm too scared to come closer! And if I say no, I guess you'll kill me too? Yvette said nothing. She just scooted over on the couch, more obediently than anything else.

"Can we start with a hug? A little thank you for the turkeyburger?"

Yvette smiled at Push's suggestion. It seemed childish, a thank you hug. But that was probably . . . or *exactly* what was needed right now.

The warmth of Push's body excited Yvette and frightened her at the same time. She could feel her nipples harden, and a stirring below her belly. His scent was like an aphrodisiac, drawing her in, taking her senses by storm.

She turned her head to kiss him. It was lacking something at first, but she stayed with it, learning his mouth as well as teaching him with her own. Her breasts were against his chest, her heart pounding with his.

Push had to force himself to take it slow. His mind was moving faster than he could bear as Yvette hands explored him, stripping his shirt away. She nibbled at his neck and torso until the taste of him drove her wild with lust and passion and desire. She wanted to do everything for him . . . anything. She wanted to feed herself to him . . . to possibly fill that void he'd lived with for too long. Too long, indeed!

It was crazy, how many thoughts were running around in Yvette's head: *If I go down on him, will he think of me as a whore? And if I don't, would I not be doing enough? Would I be a prude? I want every inch of him inside of me. I want to give him every inch of me.* Yvette's thoughts turned to words.

"This might sound crazy to you, but . . . I need to say it . . ." said Yvette, trying to express herself, despite the stirring of her emotions. "I'm no slut, Push. I mean . . . I can be whatever you want. Whatever. But I want us to last. I want—"

Push put his whole hand over Yvette's mouth. He didn't want to talk his way through this; he didn't want her to, either. He just wanted nature to take its course. She was a woman, and he a man. They were attracted to one another. What else was there to discuss?

Push sucked Yvette's supple breasts until she moaned with joy and pain—he couldn't tell which. His hands went everywhere, handling her sides, her curves, her back and her legs. While he kissed the undersides of her breasts, Yvette maneuvered herself aggressively so that her face was between his legs. She took his engorged penis in her mouth and enjoyed the meat of him on her tongue and between her gums. She wanted nothing more than this for now, or for as long as he wanted. To her, this was satisfying, how she was satisfying him.

Push grunted, succumbing to an anxiety that gripped him in so many ways. Yvette was also gripping him, his erection filling her hands and mouth so that no flesh whatsoever went unattended. She was gentle. She was intense. She experimented. She knew too much and too little at once. She was devoted. She fawned. She was innocent and naive, like a teenager; but then she balanced that with motherly love. The activity became too much to bear without letting himself go. Push had that powerful urge to explode, but he restrained himself. He too, wanted this to last.

It felt natural to meet Yvette face-to-face, in that missionary position; an embrace that both of them equally enjoyed. He repositioned Yvette, manhandling her so that she was on her back, on the carpet of her living room. Her legs naturally clasped behind Push's back and pulled him closer. Her walls were wet and silky as he eased inside. The disbelief of this all finally catching up with him, Push squeezed his eyes closed. So many years . . . so many lonely nights . . . so many dreams gone unrealized; so many nightmares and feelings of abandonment. So many thoughts of exile . . . of emptiness. So much pain and anguish. So many imaginary tears.

Yvette was crying now, with tears silently streaming down her temples and into her hair. These were joyful tears as much as they were painful ones. Push was a mammoth inside of her. Not that he was too much for her—he wasn't.

But the force was overwhelming. She could feel all of the years of imprisonment with each thrust. His hard muscles on her body felt good, but they also told a story . . . many stories. Push didn't need to say a word, and yet Yvette was engrossed with all of his life experiences filling her continuously, over and over. His moans were answered by her sighs. His power and strength were met by her willingness and submission. She was a participant, and yet she was a humble servant as well.

Finally, Push was so provoked by Yvette's sounds that he took hold of her ass and leaned over top of her, like a wrestler pinning his opponent's upper back to the floor for a three-count. His head was just beside Yvette, his face burrowing into her head of hair as she shrieked under him. Her responses were deafening, and still appreciative.

Both Yvette and Push spilled secret tears as they lay spent in each other's arms. At some point, Yvette smiled with utter joy, petting Push's head, while Push wallowed in a weightless frenzy. Now, he was truly a free man. A new man. And it wasn't only the sexual healing, the release, or the woman. It was that Yvette was somehow now a part of his life. As if she now took part in his struggle.

Push drifted off into a whirlwind dream, recounting the events of his life and how he took control of cause and effect. It had been three times now that he'd taken someone's life. Not that he was counting, but he now had that athletic sense of knowing . . . those certain references that one could call up at any time to affirm that raw capability. Those who accomplished most any great feat, those who could do it again and again, would know this same sense of energy. Their belief systems would stay jammed in that comfort zone: I did it before, and therefore I can always do it again. And just as it was with basketball, baseball and tennis; just as it was with track and field, and swimming and mountain climbing, so too was this the mentality of a successful killer. Like it or lump it, right or wrong, evil or just, Push was indeed a killer. And now that the latest endeavor (Raphael) was behind him, there were other priorities to consider. First and foremost, he had to protect Crystal and Trevor, the only family he knew. Second, was to reach his objectives in the real estate game so that he would inevitably become financial secure.

Push wanted to rehab and refurbish a few of Harlem's abandoned buildings before it was too late and they were all bought up by the smart investors. He'd settle for one brownstone right now, even if it took working for a contractor, builder or developer at a construction site. He'd take it just to get his feet wet. Just to earn a living until things came together. For now, his cost of living was minimal. He didn't need anything but food and shelter, and maybe a cab fare to visit Yvette once in a while.

The third priority, after the family's security, one that was as important as family security and money, was something of a family concern as well. Push couldn't get the words out of his head: "Miguel—that nigga got a job at the jerk chicken joint up on 134th and Lenox . . . Alonzo—nigga probably back livin' with his brother on top of Sammy's Crab Legs.

If it was the last thing he'd do, his last dying breath would be spent repaying Miguel and Alonzo for what they'd done to his parents. By now they had likely forgotten the horrors they inflicted on the Jackson family. But Push would never forget.

It was 2 days after Thanksgiving—and that delicious turkey burger—when Push was home watching the 6 o'clock news: the usual razzle-dazzle about the state of the world, according to New York. Most of the stories seemed to be linked somehow to the election turnout: *will the new politicians keep their promises?*

Push became alert when the broadcast showed Congressman Percy Chambers and how he'd have a $400,000,000 Empowerment Fund that would help to bring Harlem back to life. Accompanying the story were images of abandoned buildings, dark and dangerous streets, and playgrounds which needed fixing. And then it dawned on Push: *Of course! This is where the money's at. These people can help me with my goals, and I can help them with theirs. My labor—their money.*" Push decided that he'd meet with this Percy Chambers soon. And soon wouldn't be soon enough. But first there were the loose ends to see to.

The telephone rang in Crystal's apartment and Reginald popped in the door at the same time.

"Hey, Uncle Push."

"Hello?" Push was speaking into the telephone as he waved to his nephew.

Now, the voice on the other end of the phone said, "Hey. What's happenin', Reggie? Or should I call you Push?"

"Depends. Who is this?"

"Call me a friend, your friend."

"Listen. If this is a prank call of some kind, you called the wrong number. And I'm definitely the wrong person."

"Come on, dog . . . is that any way to treat the man who helped you out of jail?"

Push straightened up on the couch. *The philanthropist.*

"Hold on," said Push. He cupped his hand over the phone and turned to Reginald. "Reg, there's food for you in the oven."

"Thanks, Uncle Push."

"So it was you. The philanthropist."

"No biggie. I'm always looking out for a brother in need."

"Yeah, but how'd you get this number? Where do I know you from? And how do you know me?"

"Oh. My bad . . . I guess it's a little mysterious, hunh? I meant to call earlier, but us, ahh . . . philanthropists are busy people. But to answer all of your questions, let's just say that I know your work."

"My work. What, you know me from back in the day?"

"I heard of you. But more recently . . . *very* recently."

Push allowed a dead silence, then the caller went on to say, ". . . and I thought I'd reach out to you . . . maybe we can work out an arrangement. I need a man like you. A man with, I'll call it *talent.*"

Wheels were turning in Push's head. Who was this dude? What work was he referring to? Recently?

"Why don't we cut to the chase. I'm not with all this beatin' around the bush. Where you know me from, dude? Cuz if you knew me for real, you'd know I don't play no cat-and-mouse shit."

"One twenty-second Street. You heard of that crew?"

The silence again. Push's wheels were turning much faster now. *It was him! The slick lookin' dude who came into the lounge after me. Shit! Why didn't I check that nigga when I had the chance? FUCK! It was supposed to be no witnesses!*

Push's conclusions were more or less final when he said, "I don't think it's a good idea to talk on the phone. Maybe we should meet. How about down at the lounge?" Push suggested this while he continued to narrow things down in his mind. There was no such thing as *the 122nd street crew*. The caller couldn't have dropped a more telling hint. Push was suddenly left with another dilemma. He had to do something to fix this loose end, a loose end that could very well turn his whole life around.

"For now, knowing what I do about you, I don't think that would be a wise decision, wouldn't you agree? I mean, I wouldn't wanna end up like . . . like our friend who got out of the taxi."

Silence.

"So then," the caller continued, "we understand one another. Good. I've left you something. A bag. It's taped to the bottom of a chair at the lounge."

"A chair," Push repeated. "At the lounge."

"Just have a look around. I don't think you'll have a problem finding the package. It starts to get busy around this hour, so you need to hurry down there. Do a little searching."

"What's in the bag? A bomb? Extortion note?"

"Nothing like that, Mister Jackson. I told you . . . I need your services. Your talent. I wouldn't dare hurt you . . ."

Push responded to that in his mind. *You can't hurt me, fool.*

"You'd better get goin'. We wouldn't want anyone else to get hold of it." After those words, the line was disconnected.

"Shit," Push exclaimed, in a low enough tone so that his nephew wouldn't hear. Then, so that he would, "Reg, I'm steppin' out. Be back in a few."

"Okay, Uncle Push. Just remember . . . the Knicks are gonna slam the Sixers tonight."

Push forced himself to laugh, then said, "No way, Jose."

"By the time you get back, they'll be dead, buried and fossilized."

"Sure," Push said as he grabbed his coat and cap. Seconds later, he was skipping steps to make it down to the lobby, then out into the cold night.

The sun had just set and the wind made the cold air bite and sting. For all that life burdened Push with, this was a pleasure. The cold and the wind symbolized the struggle; a constant life or death challenge. It could be bitter enough for your fingers to freeze and break off. It could bring fevers and flus and pneumonia that could whisk away a baby's life, or slay the most powerful stallion. The winter was just brutal, depending on one's ability to cope. That's what Push found himself facing all the time, taking on the brutal challenges in life. It's all he knew since he was young: his parents, prison, the hole, the stabbing, the police brutality. That was the world according to Push. So what would another challenge mean? What was the bitter cold, but a welcome visitor.

This would make it 6 times that Push stopped into the Lenox Lounge since he came home from prison. There were the 3 times before Raphael, (that's how he saw things lately: *before* Raphael, and *after* Raphael), then there was the night of the arrest, then that next Tuesday, following his release when he went back to retrieve the Ruger. And now this.

Push moved swiftly along 126th street, feeling like somewhat of a puppet—how this guy made him jump just like that. *That's my fault,* he mumbled as he crossed the street and turned down 125th, towards Lenox. At all times, he wondered whether or not he was being watched, and he cursed himself for not thinking about that before. It was strange knowing that someone had watched him murder a man in cold blood, and yet, the guy hadn't called the police. Whoever he was, he had allowed the trail to grow colder still.

I wonder where he was? In an apartment across the street? In a nearby car? Or maybe he was waiting for Raphael all the while, already peeping out of a window for him. Push conjured all of these thoughts as he went from 125th to 124th, from 124th to 123rd, to 122nd.

The trail can't be too cold; there's no statute of limitations for murder. They can pick me up again in thirty years if they want to. If they have evidence or a witness. It'll always be there—a cloud hanging over my head. Shit! What does this guy want!? And why is he bringing me back to the vicinity of the crime? These thoughts weighed heavy on Push's mind as he considered the last few steps.

Just as Push made his way back into the Lenox Lounge, he concluded, *Fuck it. If it's a trap, it's a trap. I'll blast my way out.*

The venue wasn't busy this evening, as it had been on Friday night. There were a couple at a table by the window. No deejay on Tuesday nights. The same foxy bartender as always. Hips, tits and lips. Push went to the bar, purchased a bottle of Guiness Stout, and he strolled to the back where he had stashed the gun 2 weeks earlier. There were chairs and tables neatly arranged—none of them occupied—and Push took his time to check each one whenever the bartender had her back turned. There were no strangers to straggle into the club after him. Not this time, anyway.

So far, no bag.

It's taped to the bottom of a chair. You know where, the caller had said. *How would he know what I know?* Push wondered. *Unless he was watching, of course.*

Switching seats from the chair by the wall, Push went to the edge of the bar. This was where the two had met each other's gaze for that brief moment. Push and his many assumptions.

"Excuse me sweetheart."

"Hey sugar, 'nother beer?"

Push shook his head and said, "I don't know if you remember me, but I was here a few days ago when the police came with the paddy wagon."

"Baby, I'm so upset about them fools . . . you have no idea."

"Okay. Think back to that night. Over there, in the center of the bar, there was a guy in here; before the police came. He was a slick-lookin' dude with a brimmed hat and tinted glasses. Light brown skin and a trench coat. He was talkin' to you . . . pushin' up on you, I think . . ."

"Baby, you just described every wannabe-mack in Harlem. And, not to brag, but at least half of them have pushed up on me. I honestly don't know who you mean. But there was some guy that came here today, call himself tryin' to be a mack. I think he was here that night."

"Really."

"Mmm hmm. He bought me a drink and tried his ole' silky-smooth talk on me. But . . . it was strange. When I went to get a drink for another customer, he disappeared."

"Okay," said Push, not interested in too many specifics. "Now this is very important. Where did he sit?"

"Right there where you at . . . don't tell me he's some kinda stalker or some shit."

Push wagged his head and went on with the small talk.

"No, I was just hoping to see him again. I'm looking to do business with him. You don't know his name, do you?"

"No, sugar. He didn't say. They never do. I guess that's that big secret these macks keep to themselves."

All the while that foxy was blabbing, Push had his hands under the seat of the high chair, feeling around for . . . there it was. It was a paper bag. Small, like it had a half-box of chocolates in it, and about as heavy as a brick.

"Excuse me, baby. Gotta earn my tips," said foxy. And she strutted off to tend to another customer who had just come in the lounge. Push slipped the thin, brown paper bag, complete with the loose strips of tape, inside of his coat, wedged underneath his armpit. Moments later, he too snuck away from the bar and thru the entrance. The package secure under his arm, Push headed back up Lenox. He gave a side-long glance down 122nd, and then across Lenox, wondering still if he was being watched. There seemed to be no sign of a tail, but Push had to at least imagine that there was.

Changing directions, Push dipped down into the stairwell leading to the underground subway station at 125th St. If anyone was following him by car, that was a dead issue now.

He paid for a token, then inserted it in order to pass through the turnstile. With his mind's eye, Push knew there were eyes on him, behind the doors where transit cops spied, plotting on fare-beaters. Push stayed alert. The **4, 5,** or **6** train would be coming through anytime now. He found a bench far enough away from the token booth, and close enough to see if he'd been followed. Finally, he opened the bag. Inside was a cell phone, the ultra-slim type, and the indicator light was on. The light was green, to show that the power was on. There was a "roam" signal as well, since cell phones and underground subways don't usually work hand in hand. And matching the cell phone's length, width and mass were two neatly wrapped stacks of money. They each had money wrappers such as banks use. Both pink wrappers had $10,000 printed on them. There was also a photo.

Push immediately covered everything and looked across the tracks to the southbound side. There was a bag lady, a couple kissing and carrying on, and nobody paying any particular attention to him. On the northbound side, where Push was, things were the same. It was a gloomy atmosphere; isolated. And nobody had come down the stairs after him. The token clerk, a heavyset woman with a purple weave in her hair, was bopping her head to music that was loud enough for outsiders to hear. *Watch out for the big girls! Watch out for the big girls!*

Push opened the bag again and counted twenty thousand dollars. He put his thumb against the side of the bills and flipped them back, only to let them go. He did this as a casino dealer would do with a deck of cards. And the money, he found, was real. Push wondered what the phone was for.

And now the phone rang.

Push almost dropped everything at the sound. Shit was getting spooky. Wouldn't whoever this guy was have to have followed Push to know he now had possession of the phone? To know exactly *when* to call him? Push decided not to answer it and checked the vicinity again.

Let the motha fucka sweat.

The 4 train was coming. Push had wanted to head back home, but now, since he knew he'd been followed (or at least watched) he cut off the ringer sound on the phone. He stuffed the phone and the money inside of his coat and boarded the train. It didn't matter where the train was headed. Even if it never stopped, that would be okay too. Push needed to get away. He needed to think.

CHAPTER EIGHTEEN

PUSH GOT OFF THE TRAIN at 161st street, where Yankee Stadium was located, and he walked along the side of the stadium—a behemoth of a presence in comparison to Push, just a man; mortal and unimportant in the overall scheme of things.

Across the street from the stadium was an infinite row of stores, or so it seemed, with all of their galvanized gates drawn down, forming what might otherwise be one giant-sized washboard. The subway tracks were overhead, supported by such incredibly tall steel pillars at various intervals. Push ignored the graffiti scrawled on the storefronts across the street, the pillars, and the stadium's exterior; he was oblivious to the odors that were hanging in the midst, the aftermath of beer-guzzlers—probably hundreds and hundreds of them—who have left a game at some time or another, only to empty their bladders against these walls. There was also the clatter and noisy rattling from the trains passing above—like a hundred metal garbage cans being dragged down the street at once.

The sights, the odors and the violent noise pollution were all enough to drive a person's senses wild. However, Push was unaffected by his surroundings. He might as well have been in Siberia, with all that he had on his mind.

It was past 7pm and the sky was darker, a grey color with no sign of the moon. But Push knew the moon was there; it was always there. It was always full. He came upon a few abandoned cars and a string of stray dogs passed by, all of them with their tails erect. It was a chase, with the female out in front. Eventually she gave up the chase, and all of the others would have a go at her. Push took this to be another example of how this was but a dog-eat-dog world.

There was an opening in the fence that served as a perimeter to the stadium's vast parking lot. Push climbed through . . . intending to camp out in the center of the lot. There was no baseball in November, and yet portions of the blacktop were clear of snow. Push saw this as the middle of nowhere, just another deserted spot in the Bronx, and as good a place as any for a man to think. He swaggered out to a comfortable distance, so that there was nothing but the darkening sky above. There was the stadium behind him, the Major Deegan Thruway to his right, and he was seated in such a direction so that Harlem was out there in front of him. The ground was cold underneath him for a time, until it warmed from his body's heat. His full length black wool coat was crumpled there in the area around him, and he had his knees pulled into his chest with his arms wrapped around his legs. The black knit cap was pulled down to his eyebrows.

There was an unquestionable focus right now. Push could think and imagine and have a true understanding of his existence and what it meant in the whole scheme of things. He could see and imagine so much life out there in the distance . . . all of those lights inside of all those tiny apartments . . . all of those buildings. Push focused on much of this and none of this at the same time. He made himself lose that focus, to the point that his vision was foggy and everything blurred. He was here, but then, he *wasn't* here. It was all so surreal now, how he was currently sitting out in this wide open space, and yet he wasn't free. He was imprisoned again. There were still imaginary, (but very real) handcuffs, chains and shackles restraining him. And to revisit this sense of imprisonment was not difficult at all. He didn't reject it or brood about it. It was almost as if it was natural to be a captive. A caged animal.

Was I ever free? Was I ever without a burden? Without some heavy issues on my shoulders?

The cell phone vibrated again. When Push depressed the switch earlier to disable the familiar electronic chirp, he wasn't aware that he didn't cut it off all the way. What he actually did was activate the "vibrate" option.

So the so-called philanthropist hadn't given up after all. Obviously. Push couldn't help but to be curious. He depressed the button marked TALK and raised the phone to his ear.

"What?" Push uttered in a low voice, his lips barely moving.

"*Whew!* Jesus, man . . . I thought I just pissed away twenty gees."

"Mmmm and what if you did?"

"Listen . . . I don't *want* you to do this, but right now, if you want to, if you don't feel I'm being sincere, you can take my money and disappear. Hang up, and I promise I'll never call you back. Toss the phone."

"Money ain't a thing, hunh?"

"I'm not saying this to brag or anything but the minute I wake up, I've already spent twice the amount of money I gave you."

Push said nothing for a time. "So, when I take your money, you ain't gonna do nothin' but turn me in. You think I'm stupid?"

"Man, I'm tellin' you . . . I need you. You shouldn't look at me as an enemy . . . as a man who would betray you."

"How do I know that? That you can be trusted? How do I know this ain't no setup?"

"Easy. Hang up. Take the money and—"

"You're repeating yourself."

"But I'm keepin' it real. How else can I prove that I need you? I have a job for you. It involves . . . well . . . your skills. Now would any cop pay you hard cash to do something like that? To erase a problem?"

"Maybe. Depends on who you really are. I read books. I ain't no fool. This could be some crazy CIA shit. You know, how they use a man who's expendable to do a job—like a fall guy."

"You're lookin' too hard at this, man. I'm tellin' you. You're makin' something big out of something small."

Push said nothing.

"It's just . . . I got lucky seeing you . . . well, to see what I saw. You were like a work of art. No muss-no, no-fuss. Just, one, two, three. CIA? Me? Man, if anything, I'm your number one fan."

"You sound rehearsed."

"You're mistaken."

Push suddenly changed the subject and said, "The photo."

"That's the job. Easy work."

"What's it to you? What's the big deal? You got family problems? Beef with this person? Why don't you go see a counselor?"

"This is bigger than a family matter. Bigger than a simple business competitor. The job means a whole lot of money to someone like me. A whole lot . . ."

"So that's it. The twenty gees. This is about money . . ."

"Make no mistake about it, Push. Twenty large is twenty large. I just thought it was enough to handle the job. Plus, I never paid for any thing like this before."

Push took out the photo and deliberated.

"What's this, the address?" he asked, looking at the back of the photo.

"I told you. Easy as one-two-three. Case it for yourself and you'll see."

"Case it? What 'chu do in yo' spare time, watch Mod Squad reruns on TV LAND?"

A SUDDEN CHARGE OF ADRENALINE overcame Push as he sat there, negotiating the particulars with the financier. The man wanted someone killed for whatever reason. He paid up front, and even provided the address of the proposed victim. It didn't seem hard at all.

And yet, that wasn't the immediate issue.

The electricity running through Push's veins was a reaction

to the 3 figures that suddenly drew near to him. No warning, they just crept up on Push like predators. And that's how he took them, as a threat. Then he popped two aspirins in his mouth and began to chew.

There were four of them in all. Tron was the short, stocky one, the leader. His cousin, Slim, and Ajay were of the same state of mind as Tron: troublemaking, aimless and experienced stick-up kids. Black was the newest member of the crew, and it was actually Black that spotted the wanderer first, the moment he stepped through the fence and into the Yankee Stadium parking lot.

The 4 thugs had been hanging out up on the subway platform, waiting to catch a passenger alone . . . waiting for someone with some indication of money, jewelry, whatever. Something to make the night a worthwhile one. In the meantime, they passed around a 40oz. bottle of Malt liquor and got high on weed—preparation for the evening's activities.

It was a slow week, thanks to the weather. But maybe tonight . . . "He got a cell phone," said Tron. "That must mean somethin'."

"Could be. Or it could be one of them hook-ups. Then what we got?" Ajay said.

"Shit, then I guess we gonna have us a few free calls." Slim joined in on the laughter. The stick-up was a "go."

Tron set forth a quick and simple plan. They'd ease up on the stranger, and Black would come from the opposite direction as the element of surprise. Tron was the only one carrying pain—a Saturday Night Special that he frequently fired from certain Bronx rooftops where pigeons, subway cars and US mail trucks were his usual targets.

Slim had a switchblade and Ajay had on brass knuckles over his leather gloves. Black, who wanted so bad to be the quartet's enforcer, carried a wooden baseball bat that he'd already beaten a pitbull to death with.

"Listen . . . you better call me back," said Push. Then without another word, he flipped the cell phone closed and started to put it away.

"No sense in doin' that . . . I need to make a call."

"Oh yeah? You couldn't find a payphone?" asked Push.

"Nigga, if I wanted to use a payphone, I wouldn't need *your* shit. Now hand the mothafucka o'va."

Tron already had his parka coat unzipped, but now he pulled the flaps open further, sticking his thumbs in the waistband of his dungerees. The pose was so that the stranger would see the gun stuck there behind Tron's beltbuckle.

"Yeah," added Ajay. " 'Fore we have to rearrange your teeth." Ajay was pounding his brass knuckled fist into the palm of his other hand.

"Yo', I don't want no problems. Here." Push handed over the cell phone, and he did it in such a way as to seem easy; a pushover. He suddenly realized that there were four of them, not three.

"What else you got?" asked the leader.

"How bout' money?" Push said, his mouth still bitter from aspirin.

"Watch it ma-fucka!" The leader pulled the gun and pointed it at Push.

"Easy-easy. The money's in my coat."

"Anti-up then. Real slow-like, nigga."

Push took his time and pulled out $10,000. "It's your lucky day. No shit. I told you, I don't want no trouble," Push said, and he pulled the money apart so that a few bills fell free onto the ground. He passed the rest of the $10,000 to the leader.

"Slim, get them bills, man. Them is Benjamins."

"Goddamn Christmas up in this be—atch," exclaimed the one with the brass knuckles. And now, he too was bending down for money. The phone chirped.

"You should let me get that," said Push. "So I can tell her I'm okay. My girl gets all crazy sometimes . . . thinks I'm seein' somebody else." The leader laughed. Then he said,

"Maybe we should invite her down . . . have a little party." He tried to figure out which button to press to answer the call. At the same time, he tried to manage the money and his gun.

"Hello, Suckers-are-us," the leader said into the phone.

As he did, one of his buddies passed him the money that had fallen.

Push saw this as his opportunity. His hand eased under his arm where the Ruger was in a shoulder holster. Without warning he pulled it out and shot the short, stocky dude in the mouth. Push rolled away from his seat just in time to avoid being hit by the bat.

The big black dude had taken the swing, and now that he committed to nothing but air, he fell off balance. It was the cue for Push to shoot him in the calf, causing the injured man to let out a perilous cry.

Money was everywhere now, since the leader of the coup toppled to the pavement, holding his face, yelling "MY MOUTH! MY MOUTH!" Only the words were too slurred to understand.

Someone tried to pick up the gun.

"If you move another step, you catch the next one, slim." Push was standing now, looking around to be certain that there were only these three thugs to cope with. As though he'd studied an instruction booklet on this sort of thing, Push stepped over to the one that swung the bat. He was holding his leg for dear life, the vapors accompanying his hollars in the cold night air. Ignoring him, Push checked his body for any firearms.

"You two, lay down. Do it!"

Immediately, the two others complied.

Push stepped over them now. No guns, but he found the switchblade. "Stupid motha-fuckas. Now look what happened to your buddy here. He done went unconscious."

The one who Push shot in the mouth had indeed fallen and hit his head on the pavement. The bullet had passed through both cheeks, leaving his mouth bloodied with broken teeth.

Push went to pick up the cell phone.

"YO," he said into the mouthpiece.

"DAMN, PUSH! WHAT THE FUCK!!"

"Don't sweat it Just a stick-up attempt . . ." Push had the switchblade opened as he said this. He sliced open the cargo pants, dungarees and coats of the 3 fuck-ups so that their skin would be exposed to the cold air. When he was done, they looked no worse than stand-ins for a castaway audition.

"Now ya'll carry your friend here to the hospital. And next time you try and rob somebody? Use a little more smarts."

Push took the money that was still in a bunch and left whatever else that was loose and laying about the lot. He continued his phone conversation, strolling away the same as he'd come.

"Still there?"

"Ahh . . . y-yeah. Are you okay?"

"Sure. But I have some bad news for you."

"Huh?"

"The price just went up. I want another thirty thousand. Tomorrow." There was some hesitation, but the philanthropist agreed. Now it was Push who was in control. He had passed the point of sensitivity issues and easily assumed that necessary indifference towards life. It was such a God-less state of mind to be in, but so legitimate a feeling when Push thought about how cold and cruel the world was. When it came down to it, the bottom line was this: the earth would continue to spin and the sun would continue to shine. Once *that* show was over, so too would everything else be over. Everything else was unimportant. Everything.

"You are not to call my home again. And in case we ever have a problem you're gonna need to give me a number to a beeper . . ." Push gave instructions on where to leave the balance—the $30,000 he demanded—and he anticipated that the job would be done before the year was out. A little over 30 days.

When Push concluded his phone call, he realized that he had a new profession. It was something he knew how to do and, so far, was successful at. And it might not necessarily mean he was successful at killing, per se, as much as he was good at making calculations and sound decisions. It might be that he was a person who was disciplined and that he could make up his mind and see something through to completion. Timing had to be precise, for timing was indeed everything. Killing another person required all of these elements.

Push considered this new profession (if he could call it that) the next level in his life, where morality and ethics were irrelevant against intentions and actions, just as they would if he had been fighting a war. And so here he was once again: Push against the world.

CHAPTER NINETEEN

WINNING THE ELECTION WAS THE easy part. The generous smile, the handsome image and the way with words were all of the essentials to seduce the housewives. And the housewives ultimately did the rest, persuading their husbands to join their way of thinking by whatever means necessary. They might make that special meal, they might make things more comfortable in the home, and they even used sex to get their point across

And they said it was *a man's world*.

This was Fred Allen's philosophy: Win over the women by showing sensitivity to their issues: equal rights, health care, and all things relevant to children. Any good-looking politician could follow this routine and, according to Fred, they'd win an election hands-down.

It worked this time around. It was a matter of logic. And now that the Honorable Percy Chambers would have an office there in the Harlem State Office Building, that goliath of a presence on 125th Street, one that took up nearly an entire floor and that was paid for with tax dollars, the stage was finally set for his staff to serve as an inlet for the concerns of citizens of Harlem, business owners of Harlem, community groups, special interest groups, religious organizations and others who were Harlem-based.

They needed an advocate to speak and lobby and act on their behalf. Someone who could argue for and against, who would assure their receipt of those funds . . . that money which would contribute to the growth and well-being of the

Harlem community. On the other hand, the Percy Chambers office would also serve as a part of the grander scale; the big puzzle of democracy . . . of government. Since Harlem was recognized as a "minority community", it was a plus for the President's Committee on Banking, Housing and Urban Affairs to "contribute" to Harlem issues. The records would reflect 1) the Diversity that which the committee devotes its efforts and such acts of righteousness would 2) Substantiate the purpose of the committee, its offices, its staff and the budget which feeds it all.

If the committee on Public Works and Transportation contributed to the renovation of the 125th Street subway platforms, this would show again that apportionment of funds reached into most urban areas and that such uses of tax dollars were justified. This was also a plus. Congressional committees and their Chairpersons, as well as dozens of other administrative offices and departments were all required to produce quarterly and/or annual reports detailing their affairs and use of resources. If the powers that be so decided that an office, a committee or its chairperson was useless, that element could be extinguished without so much as a vote to keep it alive. Thus, the system was a landscape of backscratchers. You scratch my back, I scratch yours.

This is all to say that Percy Chambers now had his work cut out for him. All of the networking he had done throughout his political years, all of the many relationships that he had with this chairperson or that ranking community leader, all of the lobbying he had done before Senate Committees, Congressional Committees, Bureaus, State Officials, the Governor, the Mayor . . . all of his favors—it was now time to cash in on all of the connections, all of the various irons in all the various fires.

Bigger than the 8-figure conveniences he'd enjoy, come January 3rd the Congressman's 6-year term would begin, and he'd be that man in the hot seat whom many would come to address. They'd come to his office, there'd be small talk, and ultimately a check would be cut on behalf of The Harlem Empowerment Fund. The Congressman would do this over and over and over again until his goal was achieved. He already had the verbal commitments (something he'd worked on for about 2 years) which added up to the $400,000,000 he promised during the election campaign. But now was the time for everyone to put their money (or their budgets) where their mouths were.

Fred Allen would merely take a back-seat at this stage of the show. There was a Committee to oversee the Fund and Sara Godfrey was the Chairperson in charge. She appointed the treasurer, the secretary, the vice-chair, and others who ultimately saw her point of view. The Committee took in proposals from all the many organizations, community leaders, small businesses and others who wanted grants or loans from the Fund. They met and discussed these proposals. Decisions were made, allocations were arranged, and rejection letters were mailed.

By now, because this was the 2nd time that Fred and Sara went through such dynamics, it was easy for a "phantom" proposal to find its way on the conference table, and for the proposal to win approval from the committee.

The previous Empowerment Fund which Fred and Sara set up (for the Democratic Party), found a proposal on the table for Acquisition of Air Rights. The proposal suggested that an office be set up and a marketing plan installed in an effort to sell the air rights above Harlem to cell phone and communications corporations. Air rights have been known to earn a community as much as $50,000,000 so that wireless communications and satellite antennas could be established in a certain area, city or state. So, it seemed logical for a half million dollars to be invested so that the opportunity for such financial gains could be pursued.

Because there was no one person or agency to confirm such expenditure or to question how or where the money would be spent, it was quite simple for that money to find its way into the "Fred and Sara fund." This too was something that was done over and over again. Phantom proposals were nothing but schemes to appropriate, or "find" venture capital. A misuse of taxpayers' money.

"Fred, I'm thinking of cutting the donations this time around. I mean, since this will be our last go at it. We might a well take what we can." Sara had a handful of paperwork that the Committee would need to address—the various community programs which would benefit from donations and grants. Fred was eating a Caesar salad, reading the *Journal*. Fred shrugged and said, "Well . . . at least give a little somethin' away. Maybe to that woman who deals with the crack babies."

"The little bastards. We've been payin' good money out for that shit for far *too long*, Fred. You'd think the problem would've died off already."

"That problem ain't never gonna go away, Sara. As long as I'm black."

"Well, shit, Fred. You oughtta hurry up and bleach yourself. Either that or we gotta set up a new phantom. I can see it now: PROPOSAL TO KILL OFF ALL CRACKHEADS." Sara turned to go back to the study.

"And you'd probably approve that proposal too."

"Me? Why Fred . . . you know we have a committee to handle the Fund. It's not just *me*." There was obvious cynicism in Sara's eyes. She had the devilish smile, too.

"Yeah," Fred chuckled. "You, your cousin . . . your second cousin, and the housekeeper who takes care of your parents." Fred was aware of all the tricks Sara instituted; after all, it was he who showed her the ropes.

In response, Sara stuck a friendly, yet intentional middle finger up at Fred. Just for that slick comment, she'd make him lick her ass tonight. And she'd be sure to keep it extra tasty for him, too. Back in the study, she made a list of organizations and community groups who would receive letters of denial. It would amount to another 2 million that she and Fred would take with them to Europe at the end of the year. And besides that, there would be some extra money for her cousin to close the sale on his new house.

• • •

SARA, BEING AS BUSY AS she was with the new committee and the concerns relating to the Fund, allowed Fred the freedom to explore the dark side of his life. He was already a frequent patron of a handful of nightclubs that featured adult entertainment. Because of his exposure as a politician, it was important that he keep his thrill seeking outside of the Harlem's vicinity. So he often took the Cadillac to Queens and dipped into DREAMS on Sutphin Blvd. or JOHNNY JAY's on Astoria, or FICKLE FILLY on Linden Blvd. Sometimes he'd go out to Westchester and stop by *SUE'S RENDEZVOUS*, or he'd go further upstate to the *GOLD CLUB*.

Fred spent thousands of dollars during these outings, sometimes renting out the club's private rooms and buying up enough champagne to accommodate one or two business associates and the 10 or so exotic dancers that entertained them. The girls were many, and the names seemed so familiar from club to club. It was clear that these women didn't mind leading double lives and using fantasy names like Passion, Moet, Ecstasy, Cinnamon, Fantasia, Foxy, and Juicy and so on, to conceal their true identities. Maybe they worked as a court stenographer during the day, or as a nurse at one of the area hospitals. Maybe a kindergarten teacher or an executive assistant at Bear Sterns. Either way, it didn't matter much to Fred. All that mattered was that he and his associates were kept happy, and many times, satisfied.

And then there was this Asondra Jenkins chick.

Wow, was she ever a breath of fresh air to Fred's senses. Attractive beyond his wildest imagination, Asondra's looks surpassed Sara's by a landslide. Plus, the girl had to be at least 9 or 10 years younger, with the energy and physique of a high school cheerleader. *Those breasts! Those lips!!*

And she *had* to go and whisper in his ear like that.

*Hell no, I don't have a good woman in my life! Not as good
as you!*

Fred called Asondra that 1st night, not a week after they
met at Well's Restaurant, and he found her to be very open.
And open was what Fred liked. He appreciated a woman
who recognized a man of many means and resources (such
as Fred Allen was), and who didn't present much of a challenge. A bit of teasing here and there was okay, but a smart-
mouthed woman, a woman who was too "independent" for
her own good, was a burden he could do without. He was at
that stage in his life where he had the money and power. Respect was something (as far as Fred was concerned) that
should be practiced without question. And Asondra seemed
to have that balance; she was submissive and naive where it
counted, and she was street smart and witty the way Fred
liked it.

He could see that this young woman hadn't spent a day of
her life outside of the city, which spoke to her lack of experience, and that suited Fred just fine. He wouldn't mind
teaching her a thing or two; after all, he was more than 15
years older ... and didn't most of these young women—
those from broken or dysfunctional families—need a father
figure in their lives?

Fred intended on filling that void.

The phone calls became more frequent; certainly more
than what mere political discussions called for. Then, Fred
found himself masturbating, or at least touching himself,
during these calls. Eventually, he decided that he had to see
her. And after that, (maybe as soon as possible) he intended
on staking claims on her diamond mine.

ASONDRA WAS A NERVOUS WRECK. No matter how much
coaching Roy had given her, she was still afraid. She had
already towel-dried her armpits and pubic area 3 times in
anticipation of tonight's date, the 1st date, when she'd be
alone with Fred Allen.

Why am I so scared?

Despite the intimate discussions on the phone, seeing him in person was a much more taxing experience. The man said all the right things to Asondra, and even made her laugh (genuinely) during the calls. She found herself admiring him after one of the conversations, in awe of all the places he'd traveled, the important people he said he knew personally, and all the power he seemed to have.

"I'm in control of over four hundred million dollars," he told her.

And now it was time for the next level—was this considered 2nd base?—where she'd have to be face-to-face with him for hours. She sure hoped it wouldn't be longer than that.

The doorbell rang there in her apartment. She couldn't imagine who that would be. All visitors had to be announced by the doorman in the lobby, per building policy. And Trevor was over Shatalia's.

Please don't let it be Fred.

Fred told Asondra he'd be there (in his limo) by 7:30, and it was only 7:15. Too early!

Asondra pulled at her dress and smoothed it along her curves. She had on a burgundy form-fitting backless dress that reached as far down as her thighs and had a single spaghetti string that held it up to her cleavage. She didn't yet have on the matching strappy heels to complete her look, but her hair was done, swept up to the crown in a ponytail of natural free-flowing curls. This appearance took at least 25 minutes of standing in front of the full-length mirror, wondering if she had too much skin showing, with her neckline, cleavage and most of her legs uncovered. But this was what Roy said to wear.

Asondra looked through the peephole and was immediately relieved. She unchained the door and threw back the deadbolt before she let Roy in. "What happened to your key?" Asondra asked.

Roy stood there staring for a moment. He had to admit that Asondra was a bombshell, and he took the pleasure of reviewing her from head to toe.

"I just wanted to make you sweat," Roy said as he stepped inside. "I knew you'd think it was *him* at the door," he snickered.

"It's not funny, Roy. I'm as nervous as a virgin."

"That's because you ARE supposed to be a vigin. At least, you're supposed to *seem* like a virgin. So . . . you ready?"

Asondra took a grueling, deep breath, finally closing the door. Now, she stood with her back against the door.

"Roy, I haven't been on a first date ever in my life. Before . . . well, before *him* (she meant Tonto), it was just the fooling around with the boys on the block. But with him, I guess I was just young and stupid. I saw he had money and a shiny car, and I was immediately glued. And you . . . well, uh . . . you just walked into my life out of nowhere and *took* what you wanted." Asondra had her hands on her hips, charging Roy with theft. There was a pretend disgust on her face.

How right you are, woman.

"Look. This is real easy, girl. Just follow your emotions. Do what you would do with anyone else. Forget he has money. Just be you. If he says something funny, then laugh. If he says something deep and romantic, then act like those were the most wonderful words you ever heard. I told you, Asondra. I want you to *turn him on.*" Roy was close to her now. "This is that time to be the actress you always wanted to be. Do your thing, momma, and most importantly, don't be afraid."

"I'm not," Asondra said doubtfully as she looked into Roy's eyes, trying to make him proud.

"Good. Now, what've you got, ten minutes before he gets here?"

"Mmm hmm."

"So I say this is a good-enough time as any . . . maybe a little boost for your confidence." Roy was in her ear now.

Asondra didn't understand at first. But then Roy closed in for a kiss. It wasn't much, just a warm-up to say what he wanted. Roy's hands roamed her body and cupped her ass and breasts. Then he turned Asondra around and pulled up her dress so that it was gathered around her waist. There was no time lost here.

Taking down her panties so that they stretched around her lower hips, Roy had her with her hands flat on the door, her ass poking out, naked and accessible.

"Roy, you're gonna get me all nasty before the date."

Roy didn't answer, too busy unzipping his pants and readying himself to enter her. He pushed Asondra so that one cheek was against the door and so that her back was bent ever so much.

Already wet with perspiration, Asondra's folds allowed for Roy's slick entry.

He smacked her ass as though he were riding a horse. Meanwhile, he slid in and out of her slippery pussy, provoking her laborious breathing, and building up momentum enough so that Asondra had to press harder against the door, imposing that natural resistance. In the meantime, one of her hands gripped the doorknob to help her endure Roy's force. "You're gonna handle this . . . little job . . . like . . . we talked about . . . AREN'T you!" Roy grunted these words as he drove his hammer into Asondra's tool shed.

"Y—y-yes," Asondra shuddered in response.

"And you're . . . gonna be as . . . sexy as you . . . can be . . . AREN'T you!"

"O—Oooh—baby, yes!"

"What's the goal . . . WHAT . . . IS . . . THE . . . GOAL!"

"To . . . uhhh! To get . . . m-money . . . Oh ROY!"

Roy continued to bang her from behind as he exclaimed, "Get money! Get money! Get motha—fuckin' money!" And he dug into Asondra as fast and as thoroughly as he could manage, without breaking down the door of the apartment, until he finally ejaculated inside of her.

Asondra let out a blistering cry, meeting Roy's orgasm with her own. She sighed with such uncompromising belief, how all of this was perfectly acceptable to her; all of it just what she liked, how she liked it, with Roy actually playing his part of a give and take . . . not just him being selfish. She couldn't count the amount of times that it was her making *him* happy. But events such as this made it all worthwhile. This was both satisfying and uncomfortable, to be standing there with her lower half naked, Roy's semen already streaming down her thighs. At the same time, she was still enjoying the end of her climax, a high that she didn't want to come down from.

Asondra was somewhat weakened when Roy pull out. Then he man-handled her, turning her to face him, before somewhat forcing her to her knees.

"Roy?" Asondra softly cried. He was messing up a wonderful moment for her. "I'm gonna be a *mess*," Asondra argued as her body surrendered, lowering to that familiar kneeling position.

"Good. It'll be something more for him to look at."

"Well . . . at least let my hair stay in," she asked. Then she took Roy's limp, slimy penis into her mouth.

The buzzer sounded.

"Mmmm mmm mmm," Roy muttered. "Let 'em buzz a few times. You're busy right now."

With him inside of her mouth, Asondra still managed to say, "A *little*!" Meanwhile, Roy had his hand clutching the ponytail of hers so that she'd continue to service him at the pace he so desired.

Again the buzzer.

"Yeah, baby . . . those lips of yours need to be *insured*. Shit! Suck that mothafucka."

Asondra did as she was told. Seconds later, Roy picked up the wall phone and stretched its cord so that Asondra could finally answer it. And finally, she took a break from the pleasure she provided.

"Melvin?" she said, and then listened. "Okay, could you tell him to hold on? I'll be right down . . . thank you, sweetheart." Asondra, the expert multi-tasker.

Roy took the phone, replaced it, and with his other hand, he once again pulled Asondra's head to his groin. Not a second was wasted. "Now I want you to listen to me. No—don't stop, just listen. When we're done here, you're gonna pull your panties up, fix your dress, and take your ass downstairs . . ." Roy cuddled her head as he spoke. In the meantime, Asondra engrossed herself in her work, creating noises that sounded desperate and wanton. "The first thing I want you to do when you get in that limo is pucker up and kiss that motha-fucka . . . and I'm talkin,' a big fat juicy tongue kiss. You got me?"

"Mmm hmm," Asondra murmured, with Roy's penis still sliding along her tongue.

"Make it a good kiss too . . . like a promise is being given. I want that motha-fucka to TASTE MY DICK. You got that?"

"Mmmhmm . . ."

"Okay," said Roy, finding it hard to put an end to this. "Get up. It's time to get money." Roy helped Asondra to her feet. She turned her eyes down as she wiggled back into her panties.

"Roy, I'm *leaking*," Asondra whined.

Roy pulled out a handkerchief from his pants pocket and folded it two times. "There."

"What's this for?"

"Hold it right there. I'll show you," Roy said. Then he bent down to swab his fore and middle fingers along Asondra's gooey thigh. Erect again, he whispered into her ear.

Asondra rolled her eyes, figuring right: that Roy had to be up to something weird, or nasty, at least. Then, as instructed, she took his two fingers into her mouth and sucked them. She had her eyes closed, as if this were a dark and taboo exercise.

In the meantime, Roy took the handkerchief to wipe himself off. "Open your eyes baby. Show me how much you love this shit," Asondra's hopeless gaze was less than sultry, but she managed to make the man happy anyway. "Now he'll *really* have something to remember me by."

"What about the dripping, Roy?"

"It'll be okay. Tell 'im you got all wet waitin' for him. He should explode when he hears that."

"Roy!" Asondra said, but didn't put up much of a fight

about it. She suddenly just wanted to get on with this, wherever it was going. Soon thereafter, she left.

"Thank you, Melvin," Asondra said as she strutted through the lobby with nothing but the burgundy dress, the soiled panties and a matching purse.

She immediately noticed the limo, so long that it stretched the entire length of the entrance. It had rounded edges and sparkled there under the outdoor lighting of the high-rise. A female chauffeur, blonde, tall and lanky, winked at Asondra as she came around to open the door.

Music could be heard from inside the limo, even before she stepped in. Fred Allen was sitting there in the rear seat, his back to the furthest corner and his leg slightly folded in front of him.

"My-my-my . . . don't we look INCREDIBLE tonight!"

Asondra smiled as she approached and eventually sat there beside him. Fred did not disappoint Roy, since he immediately pursued that first kiss. Asondra hid her inner thoughts. *Okay, buddy. You asked for it.* She turned her head to meet his, her lips partially opened. She would've rather given him a less-intimate kiss . . . something simple and friendly. However, Fred overindulged. And besides, this is what Roy wanted—why, she had no idea.

Fred tilted his head into the kiss, offering as much of his lips as possible without being too aggressive. In the end, Asondra gave him exactly what he (and Roy) asked for.

During the half-hour trip to Westchester and that little Japanese restaurant that Fred had visited once or twice before (with this or that exotic dancer) he and Asondra made small talk about TV, sports stars and music. Fred made the poor choice of expressing his interests in jazz: John Coltrane, Sirius Chestnut and Miles Davis.

"You're so old-school," Asondra said.

And that made Fred mention, "I also like Regina Bell, Phyllis Hyman and Anita Baker. That girl, Jill Scott is nice, too."

"Okay . . . now you're comin' down to my level, a little, anyway."

"What about you? Who do you like?" asked Fred.

"I like Jill, Alicia Keys, and Maxwell. I still like R. Kelly."

"You're kidding. Even with him pissing on the young girls?"

"I don't think the music has anything to do with the sex crimes."

"True. Maybe the music inspired the sex crimes though, ya' think?"

"Maybe. But I still like the music."

Fred could see that they didn't see eye-to-eye on music. Not exactly. So he changed the subject.

Later, over dinner, Fred asked Asondra about her upbringing.

"My mom was basically my mother AND my father. She did both jobs, so I didn't really miss a father at all."

Fred quickly realized that Asondra had a void in her life, only she was in denial about it. He made that a mental note: looking for a father figure.

"Besides that, I'm really just a homebody. That's why I'm always home when you call . . ."

Fred thought about the bold statement Asondra made when he first met her: *I wonder if you have a good woman in your life.*

He never forgot that. It had been bugging him since she first mentioned it. Ever since that day he found himself asking the ceiling over his bed: *Is Sara really a good woman?* And, *What's so special about Asondra? What am I missing?* And most importantly, *What does she see in me?*

All of these questions had haunted Fred, and now the answer was right here in his company.

"I been meaning to ask you something, Asondra . . ."

"I'm all ears," she said with a sexy expression.

"What does a pretty young woman like you see in a man like me? I mean, you can go anywhere and have any man you want . . . maybe even a basketball player or a rapper, even."

"Well to be honest with you, Freddy, I'm not really looking for a man. Or at least, I wasn't until *you* came along. I've recently experienced a terrible breakup with my son's father, and . . . well, I'm really tired of men who don't know what they want in life . . ." Asondra the aspiring actress. It even surprised her to hear such things from her own lips. Following thru with the act, Asondra reached across the cocktail table and laid her hand atop of Fred's.

"And Fred, you are truly a man who knows what he wants in life."

"I am," Fred confirmed.

"You are," Asondra repeated. "And a man like you really deserves to have a woman who will bend over backwards to make him happy . . . to encourage him . . . so he can be even more successful."

"Yes. YES. You are one hundred percent right." Fred could hardly contain himself.

"I'm sayin', just to support how important a man you are, a woman should agree with anything you want . . . anything you ask for . . ."

"Anything," Fred repeated, with that dumb expression across his face, as if he'd used his last breath. She had him mesmerized by her directness, her deep gaze and her sensual tone of voice.

"That's right, Fred. I mean . . . just say for instance that I was your woman . . ."

"Okay." The word couldn't reach the air fast enough.

"Well . . . I wouldn't even mind if you wanted—oh, I'm being too open."

"NO! No . . ." Fred nearly shouted, but caught himself in time to lower his voice. "No . . . please. Go on."

"Well . . . I was just thinking how a man like you needs all the attention he desires. And, well . . . I wouldn't even mind, that is . . . if I were your woman, I wouldn't mind if you wanted more than one woman. Cuz, you deserve it, Fred."

"I . . . *deserve* it," with his mouth agape.

"Yes. You do. You should be treated like a king. The king of Harlem."

"Right. The king of Harlem," he repeated, still dumb-struck by what she was saying.

By the end of the night, Asondra had Fred eating out of

her palm. He couldn't take his eyes off of her. He might've even forgotten that he was involved with a woman named Sara. And that's when he remembered that Sara might not even be around for long. Who was to say that she wouldn't meet with some untimely accident? She could get hit by a car, or catch a heart attack . . . anything could happen.

"Fred?"

"Yes, Asondra?"

"I've been thinking. I'm having these first-date jitters. A big issue is bouncing around in my head, maybe you can help."

"Please. By all means . . . share."

"I . . ." Asondra lowered her head and swallowed. "I'm feeling something special tonight . . ."

"Yeah? Me too."

"I'm feeling this strong desire . . . deep down under my belly."

"Really."

Asondra squeezed Fred's hand tightly.

"Fred, I want you more than you could possibly know."

"Oh, Asondra. You've read my mind I want—"

"But, I'm struggling inside, Fred."

"Struggling? Why??"

"Well . . . it's like my mother always told me; if you lay right away, he'll never stay."

"She said that?"

"She did. So I'm really struggling here, because I want you somethin' awful. I mean, you've got me bubbling inside, to the point that . . ." Asondra put her hand up to put a stop on time. She winced and squealed simultaneously. Then, so that Fred could see, she reached her hand down between her legs and into her panties. She was still wet. Seconds later, she brought her hand up and held Fred's hand, wetting him with her (and Roy's) juices.

"Don't you see? Nobody has ever done this to me Fred. Nobody."

Fred was frozen, screaming inside: **SHE DIDN'T JUST DO THAT**!

"Jesus. Asondra, I . . ." He lost his voice, turning into a thirsty, hungry, fiendish addict, desperate to inhale every breath to come from Asondra lips.

"Fred, I . . . I wouldn't know how to act if you and I . . . if we were to be alone together. I can see myself losing my mind." Asondra's eyes closed partially as she licked her lips, squirming in her seat as if she had a craving that was too intense to bear.

"Oh, Asondra!" Fred growled the words under his breath. It wasn't the volume, but the power in his words that came across. He seemed to want to lunge across the table, and then Asondra put her hand out, placing it on his chest. Asondra, the linebacker.

"But remember what my mom said."

"Of course, of course," Fred said with frustration pulling at his face.

"You wouldn't want me to go against my mother, now would you?"

Fred scratched the area of his head that was follically challenged, highly aggravated about this predicament. His eyes turned down with discouragement.

"But . . . don't you feel bad, Freddy, cuz Asondra's gonna make your dreams come true."

"She is? I mean, you are?" Fred Allen, the bitch.

"Mmmhmm."

A ND THEN WHAT DID YOU say?!"
"I told him I wanted our next date to be real special. I said I'd fix him a nice home-cooked meal . . . at his house. I did just like you told me, Roy. And he did just like you said he would. He hesitated. He got all fidgety, and he made one excuse after another about his house . . . something about renovations being done."

"Then what'd you say?"

Asondra chuckled. "I told him we could do it on the floor, in the sawdust."

Roy laughed hard, with his hand to his chest, so that it seemed painful. He was lying there on the bed while Asondra brushed her teeth in the adjoining bathroom. She had just taken a shower and now wore a sheer nightgown as she performed some last minute hygiene.

"You are a trip! In the SAWDUST!" Roy broke out in roaring laughter, tossing about on the bed.

Asondra went on to say, "The man is in love with me, Roy. He actually said that three times in three different ways. '*I love you so much I could cry. I don't know why I ever loved anyone else . . . If I could spend the rest of my life loving you, I wouldn't need another thing in this world . . .*"

Roy said, "Mmm mmm mmm. I think I've built a monster."

"Lil' ole' me?" Asondra said after a final mouthwash. She cut off the bathroom light.

"Come eer, girl," Roy demanded. "Drop that goddamned gown, too." Asondra obeyed. Then she climbed onto the bed to snuggle up beside Roy.

"You proud of me?"

"Am I? Girl . . . do you know what you did tonight? You didn't just make Daddy proud, you made Daddy very, very rich."

"Yeah?" replied Asondra with the wide smile and girlish voice.

"Yeah. So for a reward I'm gonna give you something real special tonight. REAL special."

And Roy went to finish where he left off before Asondra's date with Mr. Fred Allen. It was his turn to service her. A not too frequent show of his gratitude.

CHAPTER TWENTY

MORE AND MORE, ASONDRA BECAME comfortable with her role playing. She already knew that she was considered the "other woman" in Fred Allen's life, and that he had to creep in order to make a phone call, or to arrange a date.

Most importantly, Asondra was always on alert for any sudden attack from Sara the jealous girlfriend.

On their 2nd date, Fred took Asondra to New Jersey—her 1st time ever traveling so far from Harlem—and again they had dinner.

Asondra took a firm stand halfway through the date.

"Fred if you expect me to kiss you like I *wanna* kiss you, you're gonna have to get your teeth cleaned. That yellow color really looks gross." Asondra and her nerve.

Fred's expression turned sour, something Roy said she should expect. And then Asondra said, "Would you do it for me, Freddy? Then I can really show you how I like to play."

His face lit up again, complete with his yellow-tooth smile. It was clear to Asondra that she was gaining some control over this man's actions. She didn't know how or why, all she knew was what Roy was telling her all along. And she followed those instructions to the tee.

By the end of the night, Fred finally got up enough heart to ask Asondra if she'd like to spend the night with him at a hotel. He offered to pay for the most lavish suite in the most expensive hotel in New Jersey.

Asondra blushed some, but then she closed her eyes as if

to consider her answer, even though she and Roy had already discussed what her answer would be.

"Fred?"

"Yes, Asondra?" Fred was on the edge of his seat.

"I'd love to be with you . . ." Asondra turned her head away for a pause that was premeditated. Then, just when Fred was about to explode with joy, Asondra put her hand over her face and began to cry.

"Asondra? What is it? What's wrong?"

She went on for some time with the crying. And since dinner was over, Fred quickly escorted her out to the limousine.

That's when Asondra let it all go.

"Please, Asondra. Please tell me what's wrong!" Fred was hysterical and crazed with concern.

"I . . ."Asondra was full of sniffles, even gagging. "I didn't think you . . . saw me that way. I . . . I'm not a . . . a whore." Asondra let off a loud shriek and turned her face into the soft leather seats of the limo. Fred immediately reached to console her. He went out of his way, apologizing as repetitively as a broken record.

When Asondra ran out of tears, she said, "Just take me home." And there was nothing else to say.

The next day, a van pulled up into the oval driveway of the high-rise where Asondra lived. Two men in coveralls hopped out and began unloading numerous bouquets of flowers, all of them heading for Asondra Jenkins's apartment. Each flower arrangement had a different note attached, each of them claiming how sorry Fred Allen was.

Asondra immediately called Roy, and the two laughed about this latest development over the phone.

Next, she called Lola, Shatalia's mom, and had her come and take half of the flowers to beautify her own apartment. "Who is F. Allen?" Lola asked.

Asondra snatched the "sorry" note from Lola, and then took them from the other bouquets as well.

"It's a little inside thing me and Roy got goin'."

"Oh? And would you mind explaining the limo picking you up last night? And last week?"

Asondra looked up to the ceiling. She said, "Is it just me? Or are there eyes watchin me?"

Lola rolled her eyes. "See. And I thought you was my girl."

"I AM your girl, Lola. But certain things ain't for everybody."

"Ex—CUUUSE me," Lola exclaimed with some saltiness. "I didn't think you and I rolled like that."

"Don't be silly, Lola, I'm just playin'. I'll tell you all the nitty-gritty details . . . soon." *Soon as the job is finished.*

"Well, go on wit' yo' bad self," Lola said. And the two friends scooped up bunches of flowers before heading down to Lola's place.

Asondra ignored Fred's calls for almost 2 weeks. On December 20th, she finally picked up the phone instead of allowing the answering machine to do it.

"Asondra??"

"Yes. It's me."

"Oh, ASONDRA! Please don't hang up. Please. Just hear me out, would you?"

Asondra sighed, "I guess."

Then Fred rambled on about underestimating her and expecting too much too soon, and blah-blah-blah. Asondra pulled the phone away from her ear for most of the conversation.

"I don't know what I was thinking . . . I just need a second chance. Please. I'd give anything for that . . . Asondra? Are you still there?" Asondra had her hand cupped tightly over the mouthpiece as she and Roy listened and laughed.

"Yes, Fred. Is that all you have to tell me?"

Roy smiled at Asondra's quick reply, giving her the A-okay gesture.

"Just tell me you'll see me again, Asondra. Tell me it's not over between you and I."

There was silence on the phone while Roy whispered into Asondra's ear.

"Asondra??"

Asondra made wild eyes at Roy. His instructions were crazy, as usual. "Say it!" Roy's lips moved without the sound escaping.

"Fred?"

"Yes?"

"I'll see you again . . ." Although she could neither see nor hear Fred's reaction, she could sense the jubilant expression on his face and the quickening heartbeat.

Asondra wondered: *How much of this teasing could the man withstand before he busts? Before he wants to . . .*

"But Fred?"

"Y-yes. Yes, Asondra??"

Roy knew right away that Fred loved saying Asondra's name, and that it was like ice cream slipping off of his tongue.

"I don't want to just *see* you, Fred. I want to come to your house. I want to stay the night. I want you to make me feel like a woman. And, Fred?"

"Yes?"

"I want it *all* on Christmas Eve."

THIS WAS INDEED TOO MUCH to handle. Why in the world did she demand this for Christmas Eve? *Whatever. It doesn't matter. I'll just have to make it happen,* Fred told himself, figuring that he had about 4 days to do it.

"First things first," he said to nobody in particular.

The good news was that Sara expected to visit her mother and father for Chanukah. Her parents lived in Long Island, and her visits were customarily both business and pleasure. Her cousin, Josh, her 2nd cousin, Beth-Anne, and the housekeeper, Marge, who looked after Sara's folks, all played critical parts in the maintenance of The Empowerment Fund. So whether it was Rosh Hashanah, the Sabbath, or a bar mitzvah for some young boy in the Godfrey clan, the occasion always served as an appropriate time for a committee meeting. Otherwise there were no routine meetings held. Of course, such meetings were supposed to be in Harlem, in Percy Chambers's offices. But who was going to complain about something over which Sara and the Godfreys had complete control?

Sara was expecting to leave for Long Island on December 23rd. The thing was, Sara told Fred that afterwards she expected to spend their holiday vacation—the 6 days between Christmas and New Years Day—in Tokyo, Japan. And she wanted this to be the two of them alone and without interruption.

It was back in July when they spun a model of the globe and blindly stopped it. Sara's finger rested closest to Japan, and so they had been anticipating this vacation for months now. At least Sara was. Now that Fred had suddenly committed to other plans (Asondra), he had to find a way out of the trip to Tokyo. It didn't matter about the money already spent on the tickets, or the hotel reservations, or anything else for that matter. Being with Asondra meant more than all of that. Therefore, Fred had to concoct something fast.

On December 22nd, Fred came back from his morning walk and found Sara at the front door waiting.

"You're just in time baby. It's your Aunt Carol."

Fred hurried in the door, saying "Wow. I haven't heard from her in ages! Is everything okay?"

"I don't know. We didn't really get a chance to speak when you pulled up to the . . . Fred?"

"Yes?"

"I don't think I've ever met your Aunt Carol."

"Hunh? Well . . . I guess you're right. But face it, pumpkin, you haven't met *most* of my family. After that disaster with my father, you didn't want *anything* to do with them. Remember?"

"True."

"Lemme see what she wants," Fred said as he kissed Sara and rushed to the telephone. Sara followed him.

"Auntie Carol? Hey! How's everybody? And Uncle Johnny? The cousins?" Fred listened as he pulled Sara to his side, stroking her hair. "WOW! Well, how is he?? You don't say . . . you don't . . . say." Sara silently sought hints relating to the conversation.

What's going on?

"OH MY GOD! How terrible!" Fred did his best to shake and shiver. If he did it enough he figured, perhaps he could provoke his own perspiration.

Sara could see Fred shaking and took on a concerned expression. She stroked Fred's back as he continued with the call.

"Auntie Carol, I don't . . . know what to say. Sure, I . . . I'll do whatever I can. Do you mind if I call you back with a firm answer? Okay . . . be strong Auntie . . . for Uncle Johnny's sake."

Fred hung up and was immediately sad. He brought his hand up to his face, covering an unfolding performance of distress and suffering.

"Fred!" Sara ducked to look up under his hand, patting his chest to have him snap out of it. "What's wrong, baby??" Sara was almost as distraught as Fred appeared to be.

"It's my uncle. There was a terrible car accident. They say he may not make it . . ."

"Oh my . . ."

Sara did her best to sound hurt, but deep down she was relieved. *Whew! I thought it was something serious. His uncle? As far as I'm concerned, all of his relatives can go straight to hell. Lazy, no-good niggers!*

"I'm sorry to hear that, Fred." Sara thought back to Fred's statement: *"Do you mind if I call you back with . . ."*

"Fred? What was it you had to call Carol back about? *What* firm answers were you talking about?"

Fred worked up the courage to say, "Uncle Johnny needs a blood donor. My blood and his blood are the same type—it's something we always knew, in case of an accident they'd know who to call. Anyhow, he's on the operating table now, and they need to do a blood transfusion. I wanted to discuss it with you first before I made the commitment. I know how much you were looking forward to Tokyo."

"Okay. So . . . you go to—where are they?" Sara was ready with a solution. Ready and willing to troubleshoot, Sara assumed the attitude of a general in the middle of a battle.

"They're down in Phoenix," answered Fred.

"Phoenix?? As in, ARIZONA??"

No you dumb bitch . . . in Portugal! Fred's true thoughts did not reflect his answer.

"Yes . . . half of the family lives out west, on my mother's side."

Well at least it's not his father's side of the family, Sara was thinking. *That fat, freckle-faced fool.*

"So . . ." Sara's mind cranked out solutions, still. She thought about their plane leaving for Tokyo on Christmas morning. "Will you be able to go down and come back before the flight?"

"I'm afraid not. That's why I needed to talk it over with you. They say it would take a day to get me prepared for the transfusion, and then . . . well, not only would I be weak after the blood is taken, but it might not be nice to just up and leave the family—"

"You don't have to explain. I understand, baby."

"I mean, if you say no, then it's no. It's up to you, cupcake. We planned Tokyo for so long. And I wanted to get away so bad."

"Oh don't be silly. This is someone's life we're talkin' about here. Tokyo can wait. You go ahead. Your family is important . . ."

To you it is. Shit! Why can't they find a cow to get blood from?

"Maybe we'll re-schedule after the New Year."

"What about you? How will you spend the holidays?"

"Oh, I'll be fine. I'll just spend some extra time with the family. You know how I hate to stay in Harlem alone."

And did he ever.

F RED PACKED UP THE MOMENT Sara agreed. Sara wanted a last-minute send-off, a quickie up against the wall. But time wouldn't allow. By noon on the day before Christmas Eve, Fred had the limousine out in front of the townhouse, ready to sweep Sara off to Long Island. They kissed like it was their last and the limo pulled off. Fred could've jumped for joy right there on the sidewalk. Instead, he fulfilled his urge to shout.

"TITUS! YOU'RE DOIN' A FANTASTIC JOB, OLE' BOY! As a matter of fact . . ." Roy approached the street cleaner and reached into his pocket at the same time. "Here's a little bonus. Treat your family *real* special this Christmas. And give your wife my love!"

Titus had to look twice at the two hundred dollar bills that Mr. Allen gave him.

"You're too generous, sir. Happy holidays to you and yours as well."

As happy as Fred was, he might've given Titus $1,000 without feeling the sting. He couldn't wait to call Asondra to confirm their date—the home-cooked meal, the intimacy . . . her words were virtually written on the walls in his head: *"I don't want to just see you . . . I want to come to your house. I want to stay the night. I want you to make me feel like a woman."*

Fred was so excited, in fact, that he couldn't wait for Asondra. With the house all to himself, he went into the study where the miniature model of Harlem was situated on a roundtable. An architect to build the model, complete with street signs, traffic lights, and landmarks such as the *Apollo Theater*, *Grant's Tomb*, and *Mt. Morris Park*.

Right there in the study, with the bookshelves full of Harlem memorabilia, walls graced with portraits of Supreme Court Justices Clarence Thomas and Thurgood Marshall, and that tricked-out appearance of other lavish furnishings, Fred pulled up a chair to the roundtable. He stood on its seat and he shouted: "I'M ALL YOURS ASONDRA-BABY!" Meanwhile, Fred pulled out his limp penis, and eventually . . . eventually . . . brought himself to erection.

His eyes were closed as he pictured Asondra and Sara together, there with him in his study, nearly scratching each other's eyes out in a senseless, violent fight over who would suck him off.

There was music playing in his mind too. It was Ella Fitzgerald who was scatting and singing while Fred whacked at his hard muscle.

"Like the first embrace when the night is tight . . ."

Fred experienced that first twitch that had him brace himself for more of the same.

"You hit the spot, like a pipe and slippers by the fireside . . ."

With his knees giving a bit, Fred still managed to keep himself upright. His legs were slightly bent, and his head turned up as he squeezed his eyelids tighter and jerked his erection harder and faster.

Asondra smacked Sara (at least, in Fred's mind she did), sending the short white woman back into the bookcase, the model of the globe falling to the floor by her side. Asondra didn't let up. She charged at Sara, kicking her between the legs. Sara screamed with pain. Fred grunted from the sensation (Sara's pain, as well as his orgasm) that shot through him. Then, all of those sounds somehow died off.

Ella again:

"Matter of fact, I don't know what it is that you've got, But baby, you hit the spot!"

Fred's semen spit out of his hard penis, hosing down the miniature city, as if some tiny buckets of cream had fallen from the sky.

So weak and spent was Fred that he had to lower himself carefully in the chair so that he wouldn't fall. Meanwhile, he witnessed a mess that he never intended to explain to anyone. Ever.

Once he relaxed, Fred told himself, "Now it's time to get my teeth cleaned."

CHAPTER TWENTY-ONE

SARA ATE MATZO CRACKERS, BAGELS, lox and cream cheese until it was coming out of her pores. This was her way of answering the anxiety she harbored . . . the tension she was experiencing inside.

Call it a woman's intuition, but something felt very wrong about this. As the Godfreys celebrated the lighting of the 4th candle on the menorah, Sara decided to follow her heart. She crept away from the festivities and found a telephone in the guest room of her parent's Long Island home.

"Information? Yes. Can you give me the phone number for a Mrs. Fred Allen?"

Sara's investigation had begun.

AGENT EDWARDS ARRANGED A 2ND meeting with Roy Washington. This time, Edwards took the trip uptown, and the two occupied a table towards the back wall of SHOWMAN'S, the jazz club on St. Nicholas, just off of 125th street.

"What made you wanna meet here?" asked Roy.

"I know how you like classic soul n' all . . . or, at least, you proclaim to like it."

"You get older and you start to appreciate some of the finer things in life—but . . . how do *you* know what music I like?"

"You'd be surprised how much I know about you, Roy Washington." Roy suddenly hated Edwards even more. The idea that he had been studied annoyed him. And there was nothing he could do about it.

"Actually . . . that's why we're here today . . ."

"You and the two Agents across the room. Who's the woman? Agent ninety-nine? You think she can take ten inches?" Roy asked with a certain cynicism.

Edwards chuckled to himself. His back-up, exposed.

"You're a lot wiser these days too, Roy. I'm impressed. But . . . I'm also impressed on the work you're doin' with whassername . . . ?" Edwards looked at his pad. "Asondra Jenkins?"

"What about her?" Roy said with an air of concern.

"Well . . . congratulations are in order, are they not? I mean, limos . . . flowers . . . you really did your thing, Washington. We're all, ahh . . . proud of you down at the office."

"And that's what you came here to tell me?"

"No. Not only that. I just figured you might want to update us. Since we last spoke, so much has happened . . . the Republicans won, as expected. You've got your girl in place . . . the target probably inundating her with phone calls and gifts . . ."

So they tapped her phone. This motha-fucka.

"No, Mister FBI-man. I don't have anything for you. When I do, I'll call you. Are we through here?" Roy was abrupt, ready to get up from his seat. He noticed the back-up Agents peeking over, as though their presence was still a secret.

"Not so fast, Washington. I just wanted you to know that we're in your corner. If you need anything, you know where to get me."

"Cut the bullshit, Edwards. You asked me to do something. As a matter of fact, you're *forcing* me to do something. And just to make you happy, I'm doing it. So let me do my thing . . . you do yours. And every thing will work out in the end. Cuz, you wanna know something? You and I really do the same thing."

"How's that?"

"We both use deceit to get what we want. We both tryin' to come-up . . . to gain off of others' misfortunes. I make another few dollars . . . you get a promotion. What's the difference, really? There is none. We're both slimy mothafuckas,

Edwards. Face it. Only thing is, I'm on *this* side of the table, and you on *that* side. So let's stop bullshitting each other and finish this job. Cuz after this is done, I done. *Done*."

Roy got up to leave, but Edwards grabbed his wrist, about to say something. He said nothing and let Roy go.

He came thru once. He'll come thru again.

CHAPTER TWENTY-TWO

ROY & ASONDRA WEREN'T THE only ones handling their business. Push had become quite active since the night he received the $20,000 . . . the same night he took the trip to Yankee Stadium and pumped a couple of slugs in a couple of thugs.

He sometimes had to laugh at the idea of how he left those four, with their clothes all shredded, freezing out there in the bitter cold. They'd never forget that experience ever in their lives (and neither would he) until they grew old and stiff.

That brief, violent run-in with the thugs, and then his picking up the balance of the $50,000, had him anxious to soldier on. The next few weeks would be busy ones.

Push stopped by Leo's tattoo shop again to pay Beck for the Ruger he loaned him, and also to pick up a 2nd one to match it. He also purchased a double-holster that would criss-cross his chest, allowing him to conceal both weapons under his arms.

As a backup pistol, Beck sold Push a 3rd gun, a palm-sized 9millimeter and a leather holster that would attach it to his ankle. Besides the weapons and holsters, Push bought enough ammunition to refill clips more than 6 times each. That was probably 60 rounds more than he needed for what he had to do, but better to be safe than sorry. Besides, now he could afford such conveniences.

Speaking of money, Push had to stay away from putting his money in the bank. Any substantial deposit would have to be reported to "Ms. W" on that disclosure form that Push had to fill out each month when he visited her, so for the time being, he kept it on his person, along with both weapons. When that seemed too risky, considering how cops could do what they wanted these days (DWB-Driving While Black; WWB-Walking While Black; BWB-Breathing While Black) Push paid an unexpected visit to Yvette.

He didn't have a problem stopping by her place, considering how she treated him like a king n' all. He was, however, concerned that she might think he needed her. He didn't want that crutch. There was too much on his mind these days; hardly the time and patience for loving someone.

The visit now was more of a necessity than an act of devotion or desire. Sure, Push got entangled with her again—the tongue tossing, the body bending and so on—but there was a greater purpose here. He couldn't leave all of that money, or the weapons, over Crystal's place. Since that was also his residence (according to the Probation Department) Ms. W had the license to drop in anytime she wanted, and without warning. She could check inside of cabinets, behind doors and in drawers if she so felt the need.

Ms. W had already come through twice, and Push was relieved that she did so during the daytime, when Reggie was at school. It would annoy him to have to see his nephew exposed to such procedures and government Agents. Ms. W was generally nice about the whole thing, respectful of Crystal's privacy, and as professional as she could be. And Push was cool about it all, too. After all, Ms. W did spring him from the lockup. And Push realized also that she just had to do what she had to do. Whatever made her happy. But, at the same time, there was no way Push would endanger his sister and her son with so much money or weapons piled up in her crib. It was just the principle of it.

Yvette was another story. She had the attitude that she was down for her man. "*A down-assed Bitch*," they called it nowadays. In fact, she was making every indication that Push *was* her man. So it didn't seem so hard to use her place to stash his "resources." He actually felt that they were safer there. And he would've explained things to Yvette, but he thought better of it. It wasn't like she was his partner in crime—*and wasn't killing a crime?*—so it was best that he kept his mouth shut.

The night Push brought his stash over, after an extended engagement of hot sex, he left Yvette's bed and quietly crept into the living room on the 1st floor of her duplex. He lifted part of her sectional couch onto its back and cut an opening in its underside. Here was where he put $48,000 in cash. He kept just under $1,000 in his pocket. He also stashed the additional ammo in the couch before he set it back in place.

What were the odds that Yvette would lift up the couch and find this stuff?

The next afternoon, Push left Yvette's place, his mind relaxed and set on a mission. Two loaded Ruger automatic pistols were concealed under his leather jacket and the Jerk Chicken joint on 134th and Lenox was fresh on his mind like basement rent-parties and hot buttered popcorn.

MIGUEL CARDONA WASN'T A COLD-BLOODED killer by any stretch of the imagination. He was just a snake, a person who lived the life of Peter Pan: he thought he was above and beyond it all. He thought that an ordinary life was not good enough for him. He didn't have the capacity for complex thinking, commitment, or stable relationships. The only thing (he thought) he had going for him was his job at the Jerk Chicken Joint, his knowledge of the latest movies, what actress was screwing who, and which hip hop mogul made the most money. Miguel also swore he was the best looking, and today—his mischievous life behind him—he did little else but work, collect girls' phone numbers, and hang out at clubs.

And this was one of the three who killed the Jackson parents?

"You should really let me manage this place, Ms. G. With all of my connections, I could bring you so much business you'll have to get a bigger place, buy more chicken . . . you might even need a farm, you'd be sellin' so much chicken."

Ms. G. made a face. *Likely story.*

"Miguel, if I could cash-in on your mouth, I'd be a millionaire. Now get your coat on and take this order over the Schomburg Center. I'm sure Mister Carter is hungry."

Ms. G. was the proprietor of The Jerk Chicken Joint, an establishment which her late husband opened years and years ago. These days it was just she and her two daughters to operate the business. Miguel and Reese were the only two male employees. While Reese did most of the heavy cleaning of pots and pans, Miguel mostly swept the front lobby where customers stood and ordered food, and he was used for a few other chores such as window cleaning, taking out the garbage and delivering food to established clients. In the end, Miguel was the most expendable of any employee Ms. G hired, far and away from any such "management position."

Miguel took his goose feather coat, the order for Mr. Carter, and he headed off to the Schomburg.

It was close to 8pm when Miguel crossed 134th street towards Lenox. He had on his headphones and an old-school tape blasting EPMD in his ears.

> *"I produce and get loose*
> *when it's time to perform,*
> *wax a sucka like Mop n' Glow,*
> *that's word is bond."*

Miguel was moving along the sidewalk in a half-dance, half-walk. His arms, hands and head wiggled, bobbed and gestured to the rhythm of the song. He wasn't performing, but you couldn't tell otherwise, as much as he was emulating the values in the rap lyrics.

> *"Lay down,*
> *because you might get shot!"*

A man had crossed the street up ahead, and now he was on the sidewalk, soon to pass by Miguel. He had on all black, and moved swiftly, as though he had somewhere important to go.

Miguel didn't pay him any attention. Just another nigga on the street.

Miguel rapped louder, just to show the stranger how much he was up on his old-school lyrics.

> *"Lay down,*
> *because you might get shot!"*

Miguel played a pitbull's grit across his lips and an un-friendly stare in his eyes. But only Miguel and God knew that he was as phony as a 3-cent coin.

PUSH SWORE HE HEARD THE guy exclaim something about "Lay down, because you might get shot!" And he at once remembered the line from the old-school rap group, EPMD. But then he realized that the asshole's music was so loud that he couldn't hear himself. He had no idea how loud he was, being heard from as far as across the street.

That's Miguel. No doubt about it.

Push had already been in the Jerk Chicken Joint twice, noticing the twerp Miguel's name being called out loud by the proprietor, some woman named Ms. G. Tonight was a lucky night. He just happened to be in the establishment at a time when the proprietor asked Miguel to make a delivery to the Schomburg.

Now, more than ten minutes later, Push was about to see Miguel eye-to-eye. He popped two aspirins and began chewing.

> *"Now I'm known to be a master*
> *in the emcee field,*
> *no respect in eighty-seven,*
> *eighty-eight ya kneel . . ."*

There was no traffic on 134th Street, where the two were about to pass one another—Miguel from the east and Push from the west—and the only light was that of porch lamps and the moon above. Parked cars aligned both sides of the ONE WAY Street.

Push noticed two pedestrians on the same block; both of them crossed the street before he got a look at their faces. By now, one of them was inside shaking off the evening's chill. The other pedestrian was a woman far behind Miguel. She seemed to be moving slow. *Probably an older woman.* But there was no stopping now. Push was too close to the mark. His mind already made up, the bitter aspirins creating a gritty taste in his mouth.

Just as Miguel was about to pass, Push moved on him.

He thrust the man so that he fell back onto the staircase of a brownstone. The big bag of food broke open and Mr. Carter's hot jerk chicken and rice sent vapors wafting in the air. At the same time, Miguel's headphones slid off of his head.

"What the fuck, man." Miguel was suffocated with disbelief.

"You Miguel, ain't you," Push asked, already knowing the answer

"Well, shit . . . did I fuck up your order or somethin'?"

Push pulled open his jacket and crossed his arms to reach for both pistols.

He pulled them both out and aimed them at Miguel's head and torso.

"Oh—SHIT!" Miguel shouted. NO! PLEASE!!" he pleaded.

Push squeezed off the first shot, striking Miguel in a knee. There was a blistering shriek. The 2nd shot hit Miguel in the groin, provoking a louder cry. Push enjoyed how this was going . . . slow torture, just like Miguel and his friends did to his mother. But this was already taking too long, jeopardizing Push's escape plan. Every second felt like ten. He squeezed the automatic weapons continuously until Miguel's blood seeped from so many gooey cavities. His body jerked around on the steps as if some powerful electrical current had possessed him. His face was now unrecognizable, bloodied meat.

Satisfied, Push put away the weapons and realized that the elderly woman had stopped in her tracks just 30 or so feet away. Quickly spinning off, he took long strides towards Lenox Ave. His heart drummed violently in his chest as he wondered who might be looking this time. Meanwhile, he tugged at his knit cap so that it covered almost all of his eyes. All he needed to see was the ground in front of him.

With his heavy breathing overwhelming his ear canals, Push finally reached Lenox in time to catch a downtown bus. On the bus he occupied the seat closest to the front door. Across the aisle a little girl was sitting aside of her mother. She hugged her mother as suddenly as Push looked her way. Meanwhile, Push prayed that the bus would move faster. He put his head down in his lap, half wanting to disappear and half nauseated from having committed his 4th murder. When he let his head up, the little girl and her mother were gone and the bus was pulling to a stop at 110th Street—the edge of Central Park. Push got off and walked until he found a coffee shop on 96th Street and Amsterdam Ave. He wasn't a coffee drinker, but he needed something to settle his nerves, as well as he needed a place to be isolated.

Still, adrenaline possessed his body as he sat alone. The coffee was already working (or perhaps that was all in his mind), even washing down the acidic taste the aspirin left on his tongue. He couldn't help but to recount the event, despite how much he wanted to banish it all from his mind. There was a man who had almost passed Push just before he crossed the street. There was the older woman who was far behind Miguel and who stopped when she heard the gunfire. There was the gunfire itself—the sounds that still popped in his head. 16 shots in all. POP . . . POP, pop, pop . . . he had emptied two clips into his victim, plus whatever single shots were in each chamber.

More than the sounds of gunshots and Miguel yelling . . . more than the slight echo that all the noise returned, there was the odor of sulfur still hanging in his nostrils. He could still feel the kick of the pistols that he had unloaded.

Push already experienced these feelings of recounting the

act back in November, when he executed Raphael. He went through these same feelings of unease and second-guessing and wonder and concern and insecurity and . . . and now they were all back again. He was reliving these feelings. But now, although he couldn't live the experience down, for some reason which he could not explain, he was feeling better about it. In a way, he was feeling rather Godly, but didn't want that sliver of cockiness to go to his head. He knew better.

Stay humble, Push. Come back down to earth.

The personal part of Push's activities was partially satisfied. Of course, there was one more face to see, the last of his parents' killers, but that would eventually be addressed. It might even be handled as easily—learning Miguel's schedule only took one day—but now there was business to handle. A commitment he intended to fulfill. Push still didn't have a name for the guy who was commissioning him for this job, and that irked him some. But that, so far, was something he could live with. For now, the philanthropist was simply "*the man*," and there was a $50,000-contract to carry out. This "hit" that he was paid to do was an entirely different kind of work than what he'd just finished. This meant studying the address that was given—the one written on the back of the photo. A sort of investigation. He'd have to rent a van, a van with one of those bubble windows in the back, so that he could park across the street from the address and spy without being seen himself.

An hour and 2 coffees after Miguel's rendezvous with death, Push hailed a livery cab and headed back to Yvette's place. There was a sense of warmth there. There was even safety (although he knew that was not smart to assume) within her embrace. And now that a part of his intentions was complete, he could at least absorb himself in the love she gave him. He would at least try to reciprocate.

CHAPTER TWENTY-THREE

IT TOOK HALF A DAY to find the van he needed. Some older fellow who parked along Morningside Drive and passed out **YOU NEED JESUS** brochures eventually had no choice but to loan Push the van. He accepted $700 in cash and a $1,000 deposit, to be returned when the van was brought back. But Push had no intentions of returning the vehicle. So far as he was concerned, he just purchased a van for $1,700. When he was done, the van would be driven into New Jersey and burned.

For one week—the week preceding Christmas—Push parked the **YOU NEED JESUS** van somewhere along 138th street, always within viewing distance of the address. It was a building that matched the size of most others on the block, only this one stood out. It had a white exterior where many others were brick faced. There were even 2 columns and wrought-iron gates out front, as if the President lived here in Harlem.

Push noticed that the block had its own clean-up man, maybe in his 50s, who pushed a cart, picked up trash and swept here and there. He'd even taken out a couple of trash cans from the underbellies of the brownstones where folks had either forgotten to move them to curbside, or otherwise away on vacation.

"TITUS" was the name embroidered on the man's blue coveralls . . . something Push noticed as the guy passed the YOU NEED JESUS van everyday, 2 times a day. And "Titus" never gave the van a 2nd look. He turned in at 4pm and emerged again the next morning.

Harmless.

Push wondered why people called this street, otherwise known as Striver's Row, a place where "ditty-folks" lived. As far as he could see, the caliber of people who lived here was no different than anyone else. They had routines, left for work every morning, came home after rush hour, and some went out to walk a dog or take a run. If anything, there were a few later model cars on the block. But nothing outrageous so as to make this "rich folk's land". The sidewalks weren't diamond-studded. Day and night came and went just as they did on any other block. Putting things into proper perspective made Push shrug. And he remained focused on his target. One thing, however . . .

There was a point when Push felt apprehensive about executing this woman. Especially a white woman.

Didn't they hang blacks for killing whites?

But naturally, that was only the case (if that was indeed the case) for someone caught in the act. Not to mention, he'd have to be tried and convicted. It was another idea that Push shrugged off. He'd never be subject to those circumstances. Not that he was untouchable, because the incident at the Lenox Lounge proved that he wasn't. It was just that Push was becoming a professional at this. 4 murders and no convictions.

Yet, this thing about killing a woman had to be overlooked. Push had to see this for what it was: a job. It was a job that would (he guessed) be done by someone, if not him. So then, *why not* him? And if he was supposed to be so good at this, so professional, then the idea of a female target . . . a white female target . . . then that wasn't supposed to matter. A killer was supposed to be insensitive when it came to the "*who*" and the "*why*" behind the task.

And so the right and left sides of his mind came to a decision. He wouldn't take the money and run. He would handle the task and fulfill his end of the contract. Sure, there was that contradiction bumming deep inside Push, to want success in his own life, and to take away lives at the same time. But he was still a man of his word. That had to count for something. He'd have to somehow desensitize his thinking. Push noted how the woman (his target) accompanied a black man into his parked Cadillac, and sometimes they were ushered off into a waiting limousine.

Obviously, he's hitting that.

There were times that the woman went out and came back alone, or went to take a few suits down the block to 8th avenue, where FDR DRY CLEANING was situated on the corner.

That the woman spent the night at this home, that she was always with that man, and that she was taking his suits to the cleaners, told Push that he was *definitely* hittin' it. Meanwhile, he decided to use the fever of the holidays to his advantage. Since he pretty much figured out how he'd accomplish this, Push backed off of his minor investigation, intending to leave some breathing room before showtime. However, before he did another thing, Push took Yvette on a day-long shopping spree where the two shopped for Crystal, Reggie, and they also purchased gifts for one another.

"I wanna make one thing clear to you, Yvette . . . this has nothing to do with Christmas whatsoever," said Push. "I just know that traditions are hard to break." So his "giving" was simply to bring joy to his family at a time of the year when joy was thick in the air.

Push bought a fur coat for Crystal, 3 sweat suits for Reggie, and an $800 dinner dress for Yvette.

"Push . . . It's . . . it's beautiful. Absolutely, beautiful. But where did you get all this money?"

Push saw that Yvette was excited as well as concerned, and that she was only looking out for his best interests, not trying to sound like a Probation Officer. He already had one of those.

"Just something I had stashed away. You'll keep it between you and me, won't you?"

Yvette made a strange face and said, "Now you know I'd

break down walls for you, Push. Just don't put me out there. And don't compromise your freedom . . ." Yvette had eased up to Push there in the shopping mall, and now she had her arms around him. ". . . Because I'd be losing part of myself if you did."

With more than $5,000 in gifts, the two headed back uptown. Yvette was already wearing her fur he'd purchased, and it went well with the bright green dress she had on underneath. As they carried the packages to the doorway of Crystal's building, a woman's voice crept up from behind.

"What's happening, Mister Jackson." The woman's voice caught them just before they entered the building.

Push turned abruptly to find Ms. Watson. And she wasn't alone. Standing alongside of her was a white man with pointed facial features—the nose, the jawline and the hairstyle. He was about her height, he wore a tweed blazer over a white shirt and printed tie. His wool overcoat could've swallowed him, it was so big. And the cold weather caused his face to redden—either that, or he was embarrassed from staring at Yvette.

"Oh. Uh . . . hi Ms. W . . ."

"Looks like you all need some help here," the P.O. suggested.

"We're fine," answered Yvette, who was automatically defensive.

Push could automatically feel the tension and intervened.

"Oh, ahh . . . Yvette? This is Ms. Watson . . . my *Probation* Officer." Push emphasized who the woman was so that Yvette would ease up.

"And, Ms. Watson, this is Yvette, a friend of my sister. I was just helping her carry her Christmas gifts in. Would you like to come up?" Evelyn made a snap appraisal of things. This looked innocent enough, and she was in too much of a good mood to get into it with this chick on the side.

I wonder if he's fucking her, thought Watson. *I'll have to ask you some questions next time you stop by my office. I'm privileged to know that information too, ya know.* Ms. Watson's curiosity was hidden under the diplomacy.

"Well, I was just stopping by, Mister Jackson. No big deal. You go on and have a nice holiday. And you do the same . . . Yvette, is it?"

"Yes." Yvette offered an apologetic smile, but it wasn't all that sincere.

Inside of the building's entrance, Push felt a load had been lifted from his shoulders. He escaped the woman's wrath once again.

CHAPTER TWENTY-FOUR

A MOMENT LATER, PUSH ASSUMED the worst. You couldn't convince him that bad luck hadn't come his way once more. He was full of conclusions to jump to. Maybe someone knew about Miguel and somehow found out it was Push who killed him. Somehow they contacted Ms. W, she had gone and grabbed a fellow Probation Officer . . . and they came out to make the easy arrest. *Hi, Jackson . . . you're gonna need to come with us.*

And then Ms. Watson would pull open her jacket where there was probably a fully loaded .357 Magnum. But all of this was mere afterthought by now, since she was (as she said) *just stopping by.*

And there was no way Yvette could know just how relieved Push was right now. Or *did* she?

Once they were inside the entrance, with the front door locked, Yvette said, "*My* Christmas presents, *hunh?*" The comment was made with that twisted grin, how Yvette might guess exactly what was going on. But Push was okay with that. Maybe he had more of a partner than he initially denied.

"Listen, Yvette, take these presents up to Crystal and Reggie. Give 'em my love. I gotta tend to some business." Push didn't wait for a response. His kiss left Yvette in a stupor, and he made a dash towards the back of the hallway, through a rear exit.

"Yes, sir!" Yvette said, with a cute salute.

This was as good opportunity as any for Push to make his

move. While his P.O. was out in the front of the building, no
doubt getting back into her car with her co-worker, probably
jotting down a note or two in her little book. Watson was the
one concern that haunted Push. He knew that it was her duty
to follow him to find out small details of his life, and to ver-
ify them. A marked police cruiser . . . an unmarked police
car . . . a detective? Those types were easy to spot from a
mile away. But, Ms. Watson was unpredictable. There was
no telling when or where she'd show up.

So now that he had her pinned down, sort of, there was no
way she could be in two places at once.

Push needed to accomplish a couple of things. First he
had to stop by Leo's Tattoo Parlor again. Beck had a couple
of silencers for the Rugers, attachments that Push requested
after the hit on Miguel. Push had the **YOU NEED JESUS**
van parked on 127th Street. He shot out of the back entrance,
through an alley, and into the van. All the while he was pac-
ing Ms. W. A moment later he was in the driver's seat, moving west on 127th. Five minutes later he was in the front of
Leo's Tattoo Parlor.

"Too much noise," Push had explained.

"Well why didn't you say so?" Beck asked. And it wasn't
until now that Push recognized Beck as more than a gun
supplier—less of a tattoo parlor proprietor. There was an unspoken loyalty here. "See me sometime tomorrow," Beck
had said.

The next stop would be 138th Street.

S ARA GODFREY MET FRED ALLEN once upon a time, 9 years
ago. He had been interviewing candidates who could vol-
unteer their time for the Democratic race. There were 45
volunteers selected, and all of them took on various respon-
sibilities for the big Democratic Convention that was held at
New York's Madison Square Garden.

There were mostly young women volunteers, with just 12
men, and they all performed mundane duties such as passing
out convention paraphernalia, manning telephones, inflating
red, white, and blue balloons. And of course, there was the

biggest job of all: decorating the indoor stadium so that it was a Democratic paradise for anyone present, and especially the large television audience. Mr. Allen, one of the campaign managers in charge of the rally, admired Sara's diligence to carry out her assignments, and so he asked if she would join his own staff as an office intern. She was just 21 years of age at the time. And from an intern, Sara graduated to office manager. Later, when Mr. Allen saw that it would make life even more convenient, he had Sara as his personal assistant. That meant everything from scheduling his appointments, to helping him balance his bank account, to doing his laundry.

It was when Sara was eavesdropping on Mr. Allen's phone conversation with a man named Julius Anderson (the same man who would later receive a 10-year sentence for stealing over $500,000 in campaign contributions and subsequently seek a deal with the US Attorney's office) that she discovered Fred Allen's nefarious activities. But instead of keeping what she knew a secret, Sara approached him about it. This was a bold gesture on her part. However, there were *many* things that Fred Allen didn't know, but would quickly find out, about Sara Godfrey.

"Fred?" Sara used his first name for the first time, which was a shock to her boss. It was as if all respect and salutations had been tossed by the wayside. The study of Fred's residence had a depressing lamp-light that only further haunted the scene Sara was making. Fred was silent, waiting for what Sara had to say—this young white girl who did everything for him except kiss his ass.

"You need me," Sara said.

"What are you talking about, young lady? And what happened to our understanding about your addressing me as *Mister Allen* at all times?" Fred admonished Sara with his tone, but it didn't seem to take effect, her with folded arms and that cocky pose.

"Huh. You're kidding, right?" Sara twisted her face as she said this.

"No. I'm not *kidding*."

"*Oh yes you are.* As long as you're setting up dummy

companies, phony committees and stealing money from the
Harlem Renaissance Fund . . . *Oh, yes indeedy,* you're kidding. And you know what I think? I think we outta *re*—
arrange our relationship a little. As in, me, Sara . . . your
partner . . . and *you*, Fred, the man who's gonna give me
everything I'll ever want in this lifetime."

"This is extortion, Sara. And it won't work."

Sara sucked her teeth as she circled the desk there in the
study. The miniature model of Harlem was there to the left
of them, as if a million tiny people might be watching these
new revelations unfold. "Now, Freddy . . . we don't have to
use such extreme measures, do we? I mean, I'm a grown
woman. You're a grown man. We both have talents, intelli-
gence and other—how should I say it?—*resources,* that
could benefit the both of us. So why don't we just look at
this as a simple partnership." Sara managed to sit on the
desk in front of Fred. He was there in his leather executive
chair, just a few feet away, looking up at her like a demon
had just entered the room.

"Partnership," he repeated in a defeated tone.

"Sure. I'm a Yale graduate, Mister. I played your little
internship game . . . passed out your little campaign hats,
noisemakers, nametags . . . I've done everything a housekeeper would do for you. But guess what, Fred. The game is
over. Sara's not going to be used anymore. Sara's the one
who's gonna be doing the using . . . Sara wants to make
some money, too. And she wants to make it with you."

"Are we talking about a raise?" Fred asked.

Sara let out a wicked laugh; something like a witch on
laughing gas would do.

"Ohhhh Freddy . . . you have so much to learn about me. *So*
much . . . Let me educate you about Miss—Sara—Godfrey.
Some things I didn't divulge to you and your *simple* screening
process . . .

"I come from a shrewd Jewish family, Fred. My mother
was the type to shut up and do as my father told her. And
maybe that's what attracted me to dear old Dad. Call me a
Daddy's girl, but that's where I picked up my sledgehammer

attitude. If I don't like something? Or if I don't get my way?" Sara carefully slipped off her shoe and placed her stockinged foot against Fred's groin. "I start *destroying* shit." It was another first—the cursing in front of Fred. He was being shown the REAL Sara Godfrey. And frankly, to him, this was one crazy bitch. "Ask my father why he's in a wheelchair, Fred. He'll never tell you the truth. But I'll tell it. Because I want you to realize what a *serious* woman you have on your hands."

Sara explained how her father abused her as a child, and how he made it seem like it was "God's will for her to *do as Daddy says*." And Daddy said so many things, from Sara's 5th birthday until she was 15 years of age and smart enough to say "no." But by then it was too late, Sara's father had impregnated her. She went to have an abortion and, at the same time, a hysterectomy. She'd never have children in this lifetime.

"So I became bitter, Fred. I made my father put me through college. I made him buy me a car. And he's given me more gifts than I could bear to look at. But I've made a ritual out of burning his gifts, Fred. I remember every April 7th, the day I had the operations, I would light a small bonfire in the backyard at our Long Island house. I've burned clothes, fine art, and sometimes furniture. OH YEAH! And my mother is practically brain-dead, Fred. So all she did was sit there in the house and watch me through the window. *What's she gonna say?* Well, if you ask me, it's too late to say much of anything. Mmm hmm, just ask Pop why he's in a wheelchair. He won't tell you how I snuck in his bedroom at twenty years old and used a pair of hedge-cutters to snip his dick off!"

Fred swallowed hard when Sara said this. She was growing into more of a monster every passing second. And his own penis had now shriveled up underneath her foot.

Sara applied some pressure with her heel.

"SO the bottom line is . . . I'm gonna get what I want, Fred. You can ask the boys in college who tried to fuck me over . . . or the teacher whose brakes suddenly malfunctioned . . . or you can go and have a talk with Daddy. *DAMN, I got Daddy good*. And he couldn't call the police or anybody else for that matter. He belonged to me."

"W—what do you want, Sara?" Sara with that wicked laugh again.

"Let's start with you and I, Fred. I notice how you look at me when I'm around I know you want to fuck me. So, this way . . . MY way, you'll get to have your cake and eat it too. Now let's go upstairs and celebrate our new relationship."

"Celebrate?"

"Mmm hmm. Upstairs in your bedroom."

And so, against Fred's will, the two had become lovers. The relationship was all about politics, sex and money. It was about power. But it was always Sara who told Fred what to do, ever since that day she overheard the call. Sara Godfrey, in the right place at the right time.

Fred had no choice but to learn to enjoy this. And that's what he did. And now, 9 years later, Sara suspected that Fred was doing the very thing she had been watching for. She suspected that he was seeing somebody else.

While the relatives gathered in the Godfrey home, most of them trying to make the disabled parents feel like more than just vegetables; and while the children played with their toys on the floor, Sara dipped away to the den where a telephone and computer were stationed at her father's desk. Sara had never heard of an Aunt Carol or an Uncle Johnny before, these people who Fred claimed were on his mother's side of the family. So this was the perfect opportunity to do a little checking. Sure, it was getting late . . . tomorrow would be Christmas Eve, and there probably weren't any offices open where a small army of Percy Chambers's staff were always helpful if Sara needed them. However the Internet was a 24-hour personal assistant, librarian, research department, and around-the-clock database for intimate details about most anybody.

Thanking the God who created technology, Sara did a name search on Fred Allen, Johnny Allen, Carol Allen, and just about any other Allen family member Sara could recall meeting or hearing about. She came up with 3 dozen possibilities, personal web pages and websites that were not related to either business or politics. Sara wanted grass-roots details. And one by one she began to eliminate irrelevant information. Eventually Sara struck pay dirt when she stumbled on a little girl named Wednesday Allen who had her own website. It was designed as sort of a hobby and called "WEDNESDAY'S FAMILY TREE." Wednesday's photo was there on the home-page, with the cute pigtails and the ribbons in her hair. She was 9 years old, and her hobby was tracing the Allen family's roots.

Sara said, "I'll be damned," as she reviewed the site, Then she picked up the telephone and called the information operator. "Yes. Can you give me the number for a Mrs. Carol Allen in . . . ?"

So Fred does have an Aunt Carol, after all. I must've been mistaken. I'll just drop her a line and offer my sympathy and well-wishes for Uncle Johnny. How could I have been so wrong about Fred? He never betrays me, because he knows damned well what I'd do if . . .

"Thank YOU," Sara said. She ended one call and started the next. In the meantime she adjusted her attitude from that of the jealous bitch to the compassionate maiden.

"Hi. Is this the Allen residence?"

CHAPTER TWENTY-FIVE

WITH HER FULL LIPS, HEALTHY tits and shapely hips, walking with a confident strut in a sheer olive peasant top, an exposed midsection and a green patchwork skirt with sequins; you couldn't tell Asondra that she looked anything but incredible. She was, as they say, *the shit*, with those knee-high boots, the fur jacket, the gold hoop earrings, and the funky-fresh hairdo done up in cornrows that swept up and back into a long braided tail. She had a huge red bow at the back of her head, affixed to the hair before the braid snaked down and over her shoulder.

Clearly, Asondra was made up to be someone's Christmas present, and here it was Christmas Eve.

Fred was waiting there on the landing as Asondra climbed the short case of stairs. He winked at the chauffeur, acknowledging a job well done, and then focused specifically on his visitor. As his dinner guest approached, Fred felt his face scrunch up in an expression of confusion or pain; and yet it was merely an ugly face he made in response to how DAMNED FINE! this woman was. How utterly overwhelmed he was . . . stifled by her appearance. He could bust with how he was bubbling with so much excitement. "Merry Christmas, Fred." Asondra had come within arm's distance of him, but she didn't stop there. She pressed up to him slightly and kissed his cheek, her warm breath caressing his ear as she did.

She continued her strut over the threshold and into the townhouse.

Fred looked at his watch. 7pm. The nightfall hadn't exactly

set in yet, so, if any neighbors wanted to, it wasn't hard to be nosey . . . to catch an eyeful of his dinner—dinner-guest, that is. But as inviting as Asondra looked . . . with her whole "Merry Christmas Fred" appeal goin on, who gave a *fuck* about the neighbors and what they thought.

"Where should I put my bag, baby?"

Fred closed the door, telling himself that this was not a dream, and he helped Asondra with her waist-length fur coat.

"I'll take it," Fred declared most possessively. Then he said, "I like the bow. It almost makes you, well . . . you look like you've been gift-wrapped."

Asondra turned to face Fred with a slight chuckle. She draped her wrists around his neck.

"I AM gift-wrapped, Fred," she said with the sensual pout. "And I can't wait for you to *un*-wrap me."

Fred quivered and his erection grew amazingly stiff. Asondra made it a point to look down dramatically at his embarrassment.

"There's something else, Fred . . ."

"Yes?" he stammered.

Asondra's hand slid down the front of Fred's body until it felt his throbbing muscle.

"I'm not wearing any panties," she said, including that devilish grin. And then she walked away from him . . . left him right there while she went to explore his home for the first time.

A half hour later, Asondra had made herself at home in the kitchen. Fred had followed her instructions and purchased two small Cornish hens, as well as other groceries in order so that she could put her cook game down. Asondra seasoned the hens and let them bake in the oven while she made candied yams, stuffing, white rice and corn on the cob. This was no different than the attention and love she gave to Trevor's holiday meals. There was also cranberry sauce, mushroom & onion gravy, and cornbread. Dinner was about to be served when Asondra buckled there at the kitchen counter. Her hands went to her belly and she bent over some, wincing as she did.

"OH GOD! Asondra! What is it?"

"Ooooh . . ." She let out a soft cry. Fred went to help her, his hands at her waist, "It's okay . . . I'm fine," she managed to say.

"You sure?"

"Just a little cramp. No biggie."

"Why don't you sit . . . take a break."

"No really . . . It's nothin'," Asondra replied. She was erect again, as if nothing had happened. "It's best that I work it off, ya know?" Asondra gave Fred a sweet peck on the chin. "You're a dear. Maybe you can help me work it off after dinner."

Fred didn't know if he should smile or just be relieved. He tried but it felt unsure on his lips.

The bell rang, sounding like an idea popped up in someone's mind. It was only the Cornish hens, however. They were ready.

"Okie-doakie," Asondra said in a sing-song, high-low pitch. And as she bent over to open the oven door, she buckled again. This time, her soft cry was more intense, more like a moan.

Fred was there to catch her. She fell weakly in his arms. He swept her off of her feet and out of the kitchen, placing her on the living room couch.

"I'm calling a *doctor*," Fred demanded.

"N-no . . . uhh . . . no doctor."

"Asondra?! You're in pain!"

"It's just my cramps. I get them real bad around this time . . . it's like a warning. I just need water. It'll be okay after the meal. I promise."

Fred took an exhaustive breath. He didn't know what to think. After all, she should know her own body.

"The hens, Fred. Take them out of the oven."

Fred hesitated, but inevitably hurried back into the kitchen as Asondra asked. When he returned, he was shocked to see blood. Asondra had a handful of his KLEENEX tissues in her hand and on a nearby low table.

"I'm sorry about your table . . . your couch. I . . ."

Fred immediately understood, noticing her hand was down under her skirt. He turned away to be respectful. "It's my period. I didn't think it would come till tomorrow. That's why I wanted to see you on Christmas Eve. I wanted this to be special . . ." Asondra managed to tear up some.

"No-no, I understand. No need to explain. I can get you a towel."

"That would be nice," Asondra replied. And when Fred left the room she sat up and tried to clean herself. This was messier than she expected, but it was perfect timing. She couldn't have been happier.

THERE WAS VERY LITTLE TRAFFIC getting back into the city. Much of the traffic, especially on Christmas Eve, was headed *out* of the city. All those residents who spent their days and nights holed-up and warehoused in so many of the city's high-rises couldn't wait to get away. Whether they were headed to their relatives out in suburbia, or on some kind of vacation, the bulk of traffic was always like this around the 11th hour of most holidays.

This suited Sara fine. She wanted to get back to Harlem and she wanted to get back there FAST. She could almost *smell* Fred's blood even before it was shed. She could already see the gash (the gashes) that breached his skin before she inflicted the wounds. She could feel the penetration of the GINSU kitchen knife, how it's long blade sunk into Fred's muscle tissue provoking his screams and cries for mercy. Sara was experiencing these feelings there in the back of the taxi as it glided down the Meadowbrook Parkway, towards the city.

And the woman. *Whoever* it was who caused Fred to lie like this and (*of all things*!) put on an act, fabricating news of his dying Uncle Johnny, when in fact his uncle was as fit and healthy as any athlete. *Whoever that woman was had to die.*

Maybe I'll slash Fred's face . . . or I'll just tie him up, cut off a finger . . . but I'm still gonna kill the bitch that's with him . . . maybe I'll cut her head off and put it in his lap.

There were so many options for Sara to consider, and most of them sounded crazy.

But crazy is as crazy does.

PUSH WAS PARKED IN THE **YOU NEED JESUS** van for most of the afternoon. He watched through the tinted porthole window of the van as residents of 138th street arrived home with Christmas trees, Christmas presents, and bottles of cheer for at least two ongoing holiday parties.

By 7pm, the activity died down and everyone seemed to be snug in their warm homes, with their merry gatherings.

The radio said that the snow was expected to start soon, promising a white Christmas, like they did every year. Meanwhile, a black limo pulled up. A pretty light-skinned sista with a braid down her back, a big red bow, a fur jacket, a skirt and heels, stepped out of the vehicle and went to kiss the man on his cheek . . . the man that was waiting up on the stoop . . . the same man who Push observed in past days, always accompanying the target, that woman in the photo. The woman who Push was hired to kill.

This was strange. Was this pretty woman the man's daughter? Sister?

Is this some freaky interracial threesome-shit? Push couldn't figure it out. And, really, it didn't make much of a difference. He was focused on one objective. One person.

He already considered how he'd carry this out.

In studying his victim he saw that 1) she was easily identifiable. She looked like that little boy on the videotape back at Crystal's place. Harry Potter and the sorcerer, something like that. Only, the woman wasn't a little boy. She was, well . . . a woman. She just had the boy's face, the glasses, the puny eyes and pointed nose, and the long hair. 2) She usually came out of that house a half dozen times during the day, whether by the man's side, or on her own to take out a bag of trash. If not tonight, then she'd definitely show her face in the morning. As usual, she'd step out on the front porch to stretch and take in a couple of seconds of fresh air.

Then she'd bring in the *New York Times* that had been tossed in its plastic bag early in the wee hours of the day.

As far as Push knew, this was the routine. So, it was only a matter of time. And patience was his middle name.

It was 8 o'clock.

S ARA PAID THE CABBIE AND stepped out onto the sidewalk. The taxi pulled off behind her as she stood for a moment and lit a cigarette. She stared up at the townhouse, more or less contemplating the full extents of the violence she was about to unleash. The devil was with her.

There was a stockpile of past events that she could pull up from her memory. Enough to empower her with courage and the necessary malice aforethought to do this. Another drag from the cigarette, then she ceremoniously flicked it at the townhouse as she went to climb the stairs. She reached in her purse and took out the keys for the front door as well as the kitchen knife, with its ten-inch blade catching the moon's glow for a fleeting second.

She knew the security system was disabled, because the tiny red indicator light was off next to the doorbell.

Seeing *that* only served as further confirmation, and Sara fumed even more.

Phoenix, Arizona, MY ASS!

The instant Sara reached the porch, she heard the voice behind her.

"Turn around."

Sara's eyes smarted and her face contorted in disbelief. She turned, too curious about who in the hell had the nerve to speak to *her* like that.

P USH IMMEDIATELY SAW THE KNIFE. It wasn't expected, and it wasn't a threat. But it did support the moment— how he was in a "zone" and committed to seeing this through. It was as if he had entered the end zone of a football field, where, out of nowhere, an opponent was challenging his easy score.

And that was what the client—or philanthropist—had promised. *In and out . . . easy as one, two, three.* But now there was a knife. Not necessarily the greatest competition facing a loaded automatic pistol, but that wasn't the point. The point was that she was ready with the knife, as if she might be expecting this. Who carried a big kitchen knife out in the open like this?

But then again, this *was* night . . . dangerous . . . Harlem, was it not?

Before the woman could open her mouth to scream, Push climbed 2 of the stairs and leveled the Ruger so that it was pointed at her upper body. He hadn't yet practiced shooting with the silencer on—which he'd already admitted to himself was stupid—but the feel of this was still familiar, like the aspirin he was now chewing.

The sounds were familiar, as well: like a compressed cough.

Eckhh! Eckhh! Eckhh!

Three shots sent the woman falling back onto the porch with the widest white eyes Push ever saw.

Still concerned with the noise his weapons made, even if it was only paranoia, Push hurried, climbing the rest of the way up the steps until he was standing over the body.

The woman was sprawled there with gunshot wounds to her abdomen, her left breast and collarbone. She was still alive . . . still fighting to breathe . . . to survive this.

The knife was on the steps and of no help to the dying woman. Interested only in finishing the job, Push squeezed off more shots.

Eckhh! Eckhh! Eckhh!

The forehead. The cheek under the left eye. The mouth. Three new gaping cavities.

It was done.

Push stuffed the gun back under his jacket, in its holster,

then he traipsed back to the street and climbed into the YOU NEED JESUS van. A one minute endeavor.

The snow was coming down a bit harder now, enough to sprinkle the pavement and melt the moment it did.

Push wasn't sure if anyone witnessed this, however he *was* sure that nobody was near enough to get a look at him. And that's really all that mattered here.

The van easily started up and Push followed the route he had practiced once already: south on Adam Clayton Powell to 126th street; then westward to the up-ramp of the West Side Highway. The snow was brilliant along Harlem's landscape, making it hard to see. And that was perfectly fine with Push. This time, the weatherman was telling the truth after all.

He took the West Side Highway until it transformed into the Henry Hudson Parkway. There was the sign: *LAST EXIT BEFORE TOLL*, and he used it. This plan was a new one; Push decided against New Jersey, and the toll. Blocks and blocks of tenements appeared as soon as he left the parkway, this dark and dismal neighborhood, where Push could see that at least one other vehicle had been torched.

This would be a cinch.

Push had two cans of gasoline in the back of the van; one to douse the front and rear interior, the other set to explode once it caught fire. He knew that the number 2 train could be caught 3 blocks east of here—a perfect escape.

Before he even reached the end of the block, he heard the incredibly loud explosion behind him. So much for needing Jesus.

CHAPTER TWENTY-SIX

ASONDRA TOLD HERSELF AT LEAST a dozen times:
If Roy could see me now.
  Her performance, if you asked her, was superb. The melodramatic agony she displayed in response to the cramps . . . the blood she managed to make a mess with, appropriately enough (and just in time) for Fred to see and feel embarrassed about seeing.

And now there was her performance at the dinner table.

"You're not eating, Asondra . . . and the food is downright delicious . . ."

"I don't know what it is," Asondra replied, her fork fiddling with the candied yams. "I mean . . . I'm hungry as I don't know what, but just not for food. You wanna know something?"

Fred almost choked on a chunk of hen he was chewing, but still managed to say, "Yes?"

Asondra waited a second, took a deep breath, and then laid down her fork.

What? What?? Say it girl! Tell me you want me to climb over the table and fuck your pretty young ass until it rains chocolate covered cherries!

"I'm getting sick just looking at the food. I'm sorry," Asondra said, and then she got up from the table in a huff. Fred scrambled after her.

"Is everything okay?" he asked, sneaking up behind her. His hands massaged her neck and shoulders as they both stood there in the living room looking out of the picture window at the snow-brushed landscape.

"You might not understand if I told you. It's kind of a woman-thing."

"Why don't you try me, baby. I'm all ears. You can keep it real with me."

Asondra did an about-face and Fred's hand fell to her arms now. "Keep it real? Once a month I gotta deal with this . . . woman-thing . . . and it sometimes comes a day early . . ." Asondra put her hands to her face and wept. "Why did it have to be *today*?"

Fred pulled Asondra into his chest and attempted to embrace her, even with her hands to her face and her arms wedged between their bodies. "It's alright, Asondra. Don't sweat the small stuff."

Fred tried to kiss her, but she rejected.

"I'm sorry. I . . . ." Asondra with the phony shiver. "I just don't feel up to it, baby."

Fred hugged her again and took an aggravated breath. It was all she would allow.

"Can you send me home?"

"Can't you stay the night? Maybe you'll feel better later."

"I only brought one tampon . . . I'm afraid—"

"No sweat. I can have the chauffeur go and pick up what you need." Fred with all the answers.

Don't you get the fuckin' point? You asshole?

"It's not just that, Freddy. My doctor prescribed pills for me to take for my condition. Whenever things get this bad, I'm supposed to—"

"Didn't you bring any?" Fred asked, hiding his disgust.

Asondra put on the discouraged expression, wagging her head. Fred said, "Well maybe I can—" Asondra put her two fingers flat against Fred's lips. *Okay, stupid. You asked for it.*

"Fred? Send me home . . . *now*." And Asondra smoothed her palm against Fred's cheek to help soothe the blow she just delivered. Then she went to collect her things.

A moment later, Fred had gotten off of the phone with the

chauffeur (having practically begged the driver to drop what she was doing) and went to prepare some of the food for Asondra to take home.

"Oh, you're so sweet, Freddy. Why couldn't things go our way tonight? I so looked forward to—"

Fred interrupted, saying, "It's no biggie, baby. It's the thought that counts. Maybe we'll get together again real soon."

"You can count on it Freddy-boo. I never met a man like you. So kind and considerate. And even after such an upsetting evening . . ."

Fred wagged his head, trying to shake the truth away. It was the most frustrating feeling to have her here in front of him . . . talking to him . . . still alluring in that shy way. All of this right there in his face, and yet he couldn't touch it—not the way he wanted to.

"I feel so guilty . . . like, I . . . I should *do* something for you." Asondra approached Fred apprehensively. "Just . . . just tell me what you want, Freddy. Force me, if you have to."

Fred couldn't believe he was hearing this.

She feels that bad that she wants me to punish her? That she wants me to take what I want? Who is this woman?

"Please, Asondra. Don't even take it there. I would never make you do something you don't want to do. NEVER."

"Oh, Fred. I promise you . . . I'll be worth the wait."

"The best things always are, baby."

How long before the taxi comes?"

"Taxi? Come on, Asondra. I wouldn't treat you like that. Is that the way fellas have been treating you all the while? You goin' home the same way you came."

"I asked because . . . I wanted to know if I had time to . . . this might sound silly to you, but I just wanted to see your bedroom. I mean at least I can go home and have something to *dream* about. Am I crazy?"

"Nooo . . . not at all. Of course you can see the bedroom. I think you have a few minutes before the limo gets here . . ."

Fred led Asondra, hand in hand, up the stairs to the 2nd floor and his master bedroom.

"Wow. This is like nothing I ever dreamed about . . . out of a fairytale. You mind if I try out the bed?"

So I can tease you some more?!

Fred stuttered but easily agreed. This was a dream for him too, to see what she looked like on his bed. It was as if it was already goin down: him on top of her on top of him . . . riding . . . screaming. Asondra crawled onto the bed so that Fred got an eyeful of her ass, then she softly fell onto her back and moaned at the luxury of it all. "It's so soft, Fred. So . . . are you sure you won't come and take what you want?"

Fred turned his head away, restraining his urge. He wanted to do just what she was asking for, but he was smart enough to know that it would be a first and last time. And Lord knows he'd had his fill of those. The gesture was more important.

Asondra took no more chances. She scooted from the bed and onto her feet. Just then, the horn blew outside. But it wasn't just a BEEP BEEP.

BEEP-BEEP-BEEP-BEEP-BEEEEEEEEEEEEEEEP!

No sooner than Asondra stepped out of the townhouse did she let out a hell-raising scream. The shriek had to ricochet off of every exterior of every home for blocks.

"OHMIGOD!   OHMIGOD!   OHHHHHHH . . . OOOOOOOH." This was no act.

Asondra kept bouncing with her feet flattening the snow in that same spot there on the front porch.

"My God," Fred exclaimed, finally taking in the sight himself. The chauffeur got out of the limo once the door to the townhouse opened, and now she was just as startled as they were up on the landing, standing by with a fixation on the bloody horror on the steps. With that emergency technician's state of mind, Fred said, "Come on, Asondra, lemme get you to the car. You don't need to see this." Fred encouraged Asondra with his arm around her, turning her head into his chest.

"OH, no-no-no-no-no . . ." Asondra whimpered erratically. "I can't go THAT way!"

Fred acted quickly. "The basement. Come on." And the two hurried into a U-turn, back into the house, towards the

cellar door and downstairs. Meanwhile, Asondra felt as if
she'd been sucked into a tornado. The victim out on the porch
wasn't identifiable, with the face and body so bloodied. The
face was also inflamed where the bullets had entered. It was a
sight that tore at Asondra's heart. She was suddenly afraid and
shaken; an absolute response that overcame her state of mind
to the degree that she needed physical and mental guidance.

Fred tried to console her in both ways, holding her as
they went to the limo, talking to her as if all was going to be
okay. "It's okay. Just don't look up there," said Fred as he escorted her through the basement door.

The chauffeur was still standing outside of the limo, now
on the car phone, surely contacting 911-emergency.

"Charlie, take Asondra home please. Get her out of here
now. I don't want her involved. Okay?"

"Yes, boss. Do you need me back here?"

"Not at all. I suppose we're done for the day."

But Sara's done for good.

Charlie closed Asondra in the back of the car and she circled around to the driver's seat. She also traded glances with
Fred before the limo took off down 138th street.

It was just he and Sara's dead body now. But in a few
minutes the area would be flooded with nosy neighbors,
emergency vehicles, and every sort of street-level authority.
But before all of that, Fred was able to put on one great big
satisfied smile.

AGENTS EDWARDS AND FOGARTY HAD called it a night the
moment they watched Asondra kiss Fred Allen and
slither into his home. Kim Fogarty was the Agent who
Roy spotted that evening when Edwards called for the pow-
wow at Showman's. Kim Fogarty, as Agent 99. Fogarty
wasn't the pushover one might expect, considering her
dumb-blonde act, and how she poured on the naivete and
flirtatiousness. But tonight, she went for the sucker-bet.

Edwards was still laughing about it now, an hour later. He
had bet Fogarty $20 that Asondra would step to the plate,
that is, allow herself to be manipulated and puppeteer by

Roy Washington, even to the degree of giving her body for the cause.

Fogarty gave the woman more credit than that. She didn't think any woman would surrender her jewels so easily, simply because a man told her to. Sucker-bet.

But now, Edwards was being paged by Captain Brock of NYPD's 28th Precinct. And bigger than that, the readout was coded with a 911. Edwards had just taken off his coat to join Patrice, his wife, in a bit of last-minute gift wrapping for tomorrow morning. This would be the 2nd Christmas for Jon, their son, the 3rd Christmas for Egypt, their daughter, and the 4th Christmas that he and Patrice spent together as husband and wife.

"Captain? Agent Edwards. You called me?"

"Yes, Agent Edwards. You know why we cooperate with you boys in the feds? Because when it all comes down to it . . . the bottom line to all of this is that we're supposed to be on the same team . . . but I'm NOT going to sit back while you all allow women to be executed on my streets. Not me!"

"Captain—what's happening? What woman? Who was executed?"

"Oh. You mean you don't know?? Now, pray-tell . . . however did *that* happen? You asked me to have my men lay back from 138th street so that you all could go on with your investigation . . . we did what you asked. And you're telling me that you didn't see this??"

"Captain, honestly . . . I have no idea what you're talking about."

"Well I think you need to come and see for yourself. A woman named Sara Godfrey was just gunned down in cold blood on the porch of your politician-friend, Fred Allen."

Edwards didn't need to hear another word. He kissed Patrice and called Agent Fogarty. Then he headed back to Harlem.

"I don't get it," said Captain Brock. "How could your Agents miss *this one?* I thought you were keeping an around-the-clock surveillance?"

Edwards was still stunned by the sight of the woman,

bludgeoned with multiple bullet wounds, then left to chill for an hour in the falling snow.

"Agent Edwards?"

"Y-yes. Uh . . . well, we didn't quite have the 24-hour surveillance going on. It's Christmas Eve n' all . . . we assumed that the two were in for the night."

"*What* two?"

"Well . . . Fred Allen and his visitor, Asondra Jenkins."

"Hmmm . . ." The Captain considered this and then gestured to his lieutenant.

The crime scene was more like a Hollywood movie set now, with halogen lamps illuminating Fred Allen's home with the blinding light of 2 suns. The street had been blocked off at both ends, and a small army of police officers were interviewing residents, all of this finding the evening's festivities and warmth rudely interrupted.

"I'm sorry, ma'am; my Christmas Eve is ruined too. Now if you'll just answer one more question . . ."

Police photographers snapped final shots of the murder scene, and outside of the **POLICE LINE: DO NOT CROSS**, the press corps had just begun to record their spin on the tragedy.

"A BRUTAL CHRITMAS EVE . . . NEWS AT ELEVEN."

"L.T., you interviewed Mister Fred Allen, yes?"

"Indeed, I did sir."

"Did he mention a guest for the evening?"

"A guest? No, he said that he was home alone."

Okay. The first lie.

Then Captain Brock said, "Think we oughtta have another talk with Mister Allen."

YOU HAD TO SEE THIS, Roy . . ." Asondra was at home now, explaining the evening, its highs and lows. She still hadn't left the horrific details alone. "Holes all over her *body*. The bloodiest thing I've ever seen. And she was just laying there in the snow with that look on her face . . ."

"Asondra, I got that part. She's dead. Okay. Get to the

part about the police. Did they question you? Did they ask you about your relationship with Fred Allen?"

"I never saw any police, Roy. The man just rushed me into the limo. It was already waiting out in front."

"So, you're out of it. Good."

"Good? More like, great. I don't wanna be part of any— hey, Roy . . . do you know this is the second shooting that came so close to me within two months? This one was too close . . . like the harm is comin' closer to me."

"I doubt it, doll. It's just coincidence, Trust me. You just need . . . a little . . . relaxation . . ." Roy had stepped behind Asondra and his hands were roaming her body, massaging and comforting her at the same time.

"You would've been real proud of me, Roy . . ." She reached her hand back and pulled Roy's head closer to the back of her neck. He kissed her. "I mean . . . it was just like you said . . . he was like a marshmallow, ready to do whatever I said . . ."

He continued kissing her neck as she spoke.

"And my period. It couldn't have come at a better time. I didn't have to fake too much . . . maybe the part about the cramps, but aside of that, it all worked out beautifully."

Roy hiked up Asondra's dress now, his hands smooth along her naked hips.

"And you should've seen his face when I told him I didn't have panties on . . ." Asondra laughed out loud. Roy's hands caused her to quiver and the laughing turned into a hearty moan. "Roy, you ain't nothin nice," she responded to his touch.

"I'm just finishing where you all left off. And when I'm done with that, I'm gonna eat me a good ole' Christmas Eve dinner." Both Asondra and Roy laughed as they worked up a love fever. The telephone rang.

"I wonder who that could be?"

"Let the answering machine get it, baby. You and me are about to bring in Christmas with a bang . . ." Roy had undressed Asondra, and she lay there on the bed like eye candy while Roy took his time with his own clothes.

"Bang! Bang! Bang!" Roy with the pelvic thrusts.

"Asondra? Are you there? Asondra?" Fred's mechanical voice beckoned.

"It's him," Asondra said inaudibly, as if the caller would be able to hear her.

"Asondra, we've got a little problem over here . . . uh . . . the police want to speak—"

"*We have to*," a 2nd voice explained in the background. There were also other faint discussions on the call. "Sure. Ahh . . . the police *have to* speak with you about . . . well, you know. Are you there?"

"If she don't cooperate, we'll go pay her a visit," the 2nd voice said behind Fred.

Now Roy said, "Go on . . . answer it."

Asondra made a face. Her pleasure-filled moment interrupted.

"It's okay, baby. It's nothin. They're gonna ask you questions that's all. Shit, just tell em' what you saw. No big deal. Actually . . . this works perfectly with my plan. I'll explain later. But just pick up the phone and see what they want. Relax. I promise it'll be fine."

Asondra pulled up a sheet to wrap her naked body—as if the caller would see her—and she picked up the phone.

"Fred?"

"Asondra," he said with an exhaustive breath to carry the name. "I was . . . I fell asleep. The cramps," Asondra lied.

"I know, I know. There's a little problem here. The police just want to ask you some questions. Ahh . . . they say they can do it here or over your place. I explained about your . . . uh . . . condition."

"You want me to take a taxi over?" asked Asondra, repeating what Roy said in her ear.

"I'll send the limo. She can't be that far away," Fred said,

"Okay. I'll be dressed," Asondra said, again with Roy's words coming from her mouth.

After the call, Asondra wagged her head. It was just the tragedy of it all still fresh on her mind.

"Roy, I . . . I just can't face all that mess back there. It's—"

"Asondra, listen to me . . ." Roy sat on the bed and stroked her temple. "The mess you're talkin' about? Trust me, they already cleaned that up. The body's probably in some station wagon by now. You're gonna answer a couple of questions . . . *How do you know Fred Allen? What was your business with him? Why did you leave the scene of the crime?* Simple shit, Asondra. All you gotta do is tell the truth, But guess what? Because of this . . . all this trouble you gotta go through with the police interrogation? That man is gonna feel like he owes you *big time.* And that's just what he's gonna do, *pay big time.*"

"I hope you're right, Roy."

"I'm always right, baby." Roy kissed her forehead, then told her, "Get dressed. The limo will be here soon."

"Roy, will we spend Christmas together? You, me and Trevor?"

"Sure. Why not, you deserve it."

Asondra thought hard about Roy's reply for just a moment. But too much was going on in her own head to grow conscious all of a sudden. *You deserve it.*

CHAPTER TWENTY-SEVEN

PUSH NEEDED TO SETTLE DOWN. This was such an overwhelming feeling . . . a sensation even, to be able to take a life and get away with it. But his right thinking was saying *Don't let it go to your head, Push.* So to relax was a must.

There were a few things that relaxed Push these days. A good workout. Some focused meditation. Sex with Yvette. Push got off the 2-train at 96th street and walked to Riverside Drive.

I hope she's home.

WHILE PUSH WAS EXPERIENCING THAT exhilaration, Fred Allen was issuing final apologies to the Lieutenant, the Captain, and some other officers who stood by. He said that he was thinking of Asondra's health, and didn't want to upset her anymore than she was. But, he mentioned, at the same time he didn't intend to obstruct justice and that he was all for cooperating with authorities.

They all shrugged it off, knowing that there was a larger concern here, how the FBI was investigating Fred Allen and his multi-million-dollar scheme. It was already complicated exposing Allen's lie. They even had to ask themselves some questions: Will he wonder about the suits (the FBI) among us? How can we do this without divulging sensitive details about the Agents who had been watching him? And could that be kept as secretive as possible? If there was one thing for certain, one thing that couldn't be questioned, it's that there is more of a reason to watch Fred Allen now than there ever was before. And still, questions remained. *Who killed Sara Godfrey and why? What did her death have to do with the millions of dollars Allen was stealing?*

By midnight, the police and most of the press had gone. Charlie had returned from bringing Asondra home again. Charlie: that Covergirl presence stayed with her day and night. Blonde hair, sparkling eyes, a shapely build and a sense of duty.

"Thanks for putting up with all of this back and forth stuff, Charlie. I owe you."

"I guess," she replied, now with a smaller chip on her shoulder.

"I'll have to give you a bonus for—"

Charlie sucked her teeth. "It isn't *about* a bonus or money, F.A. I do have a girlfriend I need to answer to . . . Christmas Eve n' all."

"Tell you what," Fred said after a moment of thought. "Why don't we go pick up your girlfriend and make a night of it. Maybe we'll go to FOXWOODS or down to Atlantic City."

"All you have to do is say the word, boss."

"Charlie, this is a leisure trip, not business. For tonight, you can drop the chauffeur routine and let's go out and have some fun."

Yvette didn't make it home until eleven that night. When she did, she found Push sitting against the railing by her front door. "Baby!? How long have you been out here?" Yvette asked, disapproving of Push being out in the falling snow.

"Nothin' but a minute," he lied.

Yvette sucked her teeth and said, "Come in, Push."

Jesus. Will this man go to any extreme?

Before Yvette took off her own coat, she took off his. Then his trademark black knit cap and gloves.

"Your sister is hoping to see you for Christmas."

"She knows I'm not into that."

"But still, Push. For Reggie, at least."

"They get the gifts?"

"Of course. They haven't opened them yet, but . . ."

"Stupid traditions."

"Will you go, Push?"

"Yeah, I'll go. But I needed to see you tonight."

"YOU . . . needed me? Has the sky fallen, and I missed something?" Yvette had her hands on her hips as she said this.

"You know I don't do much talking Yvette."

"I know—"

Yvette barely got the words out before Push was up on her, his lips against hers. She didn't know how to take this, but she *sure* wouldn't reject it. She ignored the taste of aspirin on his tongue and accepted the advance like always.

Push immersed himself in Yvette's embrace, her kisses and her carnal sighs. On one hand, he enjoyed this. He *wanted* to enjoy this . . . how she touched him, excited him and gave him pleasure.

On the other hand, there was relief here. An escape. There was tension, unrest and opposing thoughts that were all pulling at him . . . at his senses. There was still the pent-up rage of a lost teenage life, of lost liberties and, still, some unfinished business.

Bigger than all of that, there were the memories and images. The bullets that penetrated the bodies of those perfect strangers. Their faces stayed with Push, those very faces just before and just after they met their demise. Push had all of these images, memories and the horrors that went with them . . . it was all a part of him, a complicated mosaic of gross references. And now that Push was alone with Yvette, all of that seemed to melt away. She was actually providing therapy, however temporary, by merely loving him. Their being naked together felt like the answer to all of his imbalances. A cure-all. The sex itself was complex and indefinable, how a part of it was romance and passion, and yet another part was an unconscious attack . . . anger and frustration. It could even be considered as violent. Yvette was so much into the act . . . so thoroughly overcome by Push and his power, that it satisfied her again and again. She cried and she rejoiced, both.

Life as she knew it had changed forever. Just as it had after the last time they made love. Or the time before that.

WAKE UP TROOPER." PUSH NUDGED Reggie at 7 o'clock Christmas morning, more excited than his nephew was about the sweatsuits he'd bought. Push had to give Reggie a little tickle to get an acceptable response.

"Okay-okay-okay," Reggie groaned his irritation.

It felt funny to play with his nephew like he did, considering that Reggie was now 17, with a thin mustache and his own adult challenges to conquer. But for Push, Reggie was still young and in need of leadership . . . a father figure. This was one of the conflicts of interest in his life, how he was suddenly involved with incidents which would threaten his liberty, and yet, he knew that his presence was necessary in the lives of both Reggie and his mom.

Crystal woke to find her brother and her son fighting it out on the Playstation's adaptation of an NBA championship. It was a sight to behold, their first Christmas together. Still, Crystal intended to speak with Push about all these gifts.

If he thinks I fell for Yvette's claim, how she had paid for the gifts, he's underestimating me.

THE NEW YEAR CAME IN uneventfully, except for the small party that Crystal threw at home.

Yvette brought along her brother, Solomon, (calling herself trying to play Cupid), and Reggie invited Tasha, a girl he hoped to one day call his own.

Friday, the 2nd of January, would've been the first business day of the new year, but Push figured everyone would use that day for everything *but* work. So he put his business intentions aside until Monday, the 5th, when he'd wear one of his suits. That's the day he went to Congressman Percy Chambers's office at the Harlem State Office Building.

Things were so busy there, with nobody knowing exactly how certain protocols (appointments, inquiries, proposals, and such) were to be handled, that Push found it easy to see the Congressman informally. They shook hands, and Chambers was as cordial as could be, but the bottom line was that any proposals relating to the Harlem Empowerment Fund had to be handled by Fred Allen and the Committee Chairperson. "And who is the Committee Chairperson, sir?" Push was respectful, anticipating at least some kind of runaround, but aware that the Congressman meant well. Push had his pen and pad at the ready. Loaded.

The Congressman stuttered at first, as though he'd been caught off guard with the $20,000 question.

"Uh . . . I . . ." He cleared his throat. "I believe Mister Allen will be able to help you with that."

"And is he here?"

"No. He's . . . attending a funeral. I'm sorry. You can leave a message at the front desk if you like, and I will surely tell him that I spoke with you myself."

"Thank you. It's been a pleasure meeting with you, sir . . . I hope you'll be able to help me repair some of the homes in Harlem . . ."

"I can't see why not. With enterprising young people like you, we should be able to help one another."

"Thanks again," said Push, having no idea that he had killed the woman whom he came to see.

FRED SPENT $30,000 ON SARA Godfrey's funeral. He made certain that the Godfrey family was accommodated with enough comfort that the ceremony would appear and feel as though a president had died. The wake as well as the burial was attended by just 12 members of Sara's family. Fred even paid to have special accommodations for Sara's father, the invalid.

Nobody could understand the strange smile on Mr. Godfrey's face, how he looked so satisfied in a time of such loss. And the entire endeavor was executed with a closed casket, until Sara was laid to rest in a special limestone mausoleum. Fred quietly brooded over the cost of the tomb while a Rabbi conducted the ceremony.

Twenty-five thousand for this fuckin' gloomy room. I swear,

I'm gonna come back here and jerk off on her grave when this is all said and done. Bitch. Understandably, Fred was happy to be rid of Sara. Now, he was free to handle the Committee as he saw fit. *One by one, I'm gonna get rid of them Godfreys. You're fired! Ha, ha, ha, ha . . . patience, Fred. Patience.*

For now, Fred was thinking of the void left in his life. He needed a new assistant to help him with the business affairs and menial housework. Who could he have fill Sara's shoes? What woman?

The thought brought a huge smile to Fred's face. Asondra.

Fred already arranged for a 3-week vacation, to be alone . . . to mourn Sara's death. So now, he'd use that time to *personally* train his new assistant.

"There's no more fakin, Roy. He wants to see me tonight. He says he has a proposal for me. Somethin' about an opening on his staff."

"But that's exactly what we've been banking on, Asondra. We're *this* close to pay dirt."

"Roy, I can't fake anymore. I ran out of excuses. I—"

Roy and Asondra were in the Mercedes, stopped by a red light along Lenox Avenue. He'd just picked her up from Mya's, where she spent half the day having her hair microbraided. From a distance, her hair appeared to be relaxed.

Roy had reached out to casually touch his fingers to Asondra's lips. "Shhhh . . . baby, don't lose focus here. Get over the emotions and anxiety of it all. You need to change your thinking about this. I mean . . . look how far you've come with this dude. He's eatin' out of your fuckin' palm. Not just *any* woman could do somethin' like that. He fell for *you*. You are fierce, girl. FIERCE. He couldn't beat you mentally and he won't beat you physically."

Asondra wanted to see things Roy's way. She tried. But it was so hard. Even impossible, she thought. He actually wanted her to go all the way with this!

"I don't wanna fuck him, Roy. I DON'T WANT TO!" Asondra folded her arms and looked out of the passenger's side window.

Why won't he get the message?

Roy pulled over to the first empty space along the side of the street. He also turned off the radio and its newscast about the unsolved murder on Striver's Row.

"Look at me, Asondra. Asondra?"

She turned her head swiftly, but her eyes were unwilling to give in.

"We didn't come all this way to turn back. Put yourself in my shoes. Okay . . . so you needed me to seduce some woman so that she could sign over the deed to the apartment building you live in. So I wine and dine her. I get her all hot and worked up. She'll do just about anything for me. Only thing is, the woman is sixty years old, and I have to fuck her to make her fall in love with me . . ."

"That's different."

"Let me *finish*! You want me to fuck this wrinkled pussy that Lord knows how many men have been in . . . who knows? Maybe she don't even keep good hygiene down there. I mean, the bitch just makes my stomach turn . . . and I really don't wanna fuck her."

"So now what?" Asondra's face changed for the better. It was clear that she put the shoe on the other foot, so to speak.

"Now what? Now . . . I think about you . . . what you want—because I love you. I want what you want. I don't want her. I'm doin' this FOR YOU.

"I'm gonna throw on a goddamned rubber and give her a hard dick all night long if she wants . . . until she screams for mercy. But the fact of the matter is, I'm doin' it because I love you. Because you asked me to. Then, BOOM . . . you have seventy families payin' YOU rent every month. MO' MONEY, MO' MONEY, MO' MONEY!"

"You're trippin."

"No. I'm keepin' it real. And you wanna know the difference between seventy rent checks and Fred Allen?"

Asondra rolled her eyes, wanting him to get to the point. "Hundreds of millions of dollars, thats what the difference is. Now . . . would you look at that man over there?"

"Where?"

"Comin' out of the bodega."

"Okay. What about him?"

"Would you fuck that guy for, say, ten million dollars cash?"

"Is that a trick question? And if I say yes, then I'm a whore?"

"Forget about me, Asondra. I don't exist. Just give me an answer. If it would put ten million cash in your hand within ten minutes, would you do it?"

"I . . . yes. Alright? You satisfied? Yes, I'd fuck him," Asondra said in a hasty tone.

"Okay. So then, try and think that way about our friend. He's just a man. Just another swingin' dick. Make him put a rubber on . . . sike yourself up for the occasion . . . and BOOM. We're in like Flynn. And guess what? You and Trevor can have all the money. All of it. Just let me come over and rub your feet now and then . . ."

The comment made Asondra smirk.

"Can a poor man do that? Can I come and suck your toes? Maybe kiss your ass now and then?"

Asondra finally let out a genuine laugh, and Roy knew he had her.

"See? That's my girl. Come-eer." Roy pulled Asondra to him and gave her a wet, sloppy kiss. "You already made me proud. Now let's see if you can blow my mind."

S HE LOOKED LIKE AN ABSOLUTE vamp that night. Her lips had a high gloss. Her mascara fine-tuned her sultry eyes. Underneath the fox fur she wore a white camisole that accentuated her already abundant bust, plus a matching skirt that left most of her legs naked down to the bone—white leather booties.

Asondra immediately felt a deja-vu as she stepped out of the limousine, climbing the stairs to where Fred was waiting on the porch.

The same porch.

As far as Asondra could imagine, the woman was still there, spread out in the snow with her blood too cold to ooze anymore. Asondra forced the memory away.

Just think about the money.

And now it was all gone. The snow had cleared and the pavement was ashy like un-lotioned skin. Now it was up to her to be strong. To carry this out to the end.

He's just another swingin' dick. Hundreds of millions of dollars.

At least his teeth were white now, Asondra told herself, rationalizing as she replayed the performance of Christmas Eve.

"Hi, baby," said Fred with that smug look about him.

And why shouldn't he be a pimp about it? He already knows I'm gonna give up the pussy.

Asondra went through with the tender kiss, the hug and the warm breath in his ear. This would open that same pleasure center like before.

Next, she stepped inside the house, feeling more like she just ventured into the deep end of a pool, she being the beginner with no life preserver around her neck.

The door was closed now, and just as Fred went to throw the deadbolt, Asondra reached for his hand. In her mind, she saw Roy, not Fred.

"Fred?"

"Yes, baby. Talk to me." Fred with the confident smile.

Ohhh . . . so you ARE the pimp now.

"Put your arms around me, Fred. Tell me you'll be gentle and kind to me tonight."

Fred took Asondra into his arms. "Baby . . . I'm gonna treat you like a queen tonight. I'm gonna change your life forever. And I expect that you're gonna do the same for me."

Asondra closed her eyes and, as if to take a plunge, she kissed Fred more sensually . . . more passionately than she ever had since.

The night had begun.

PUSH DIDN'T WANT TO WAIT 3 weeks to see this guy Fred Allen. Life didn't wait for anyone; it just kept on moving, like it or lump it. If you didn't move with it, it would pass you by.

And Push didn't want to merely be a "mover" with life. He wanted to be ahead of the game, like a squirrel gathering nuts for a long winter. The first thing that Push did was discuss his intentions with Yvette. "I need to set up a corporation, Yvette. I'll be the head of its board of directors—the one to make the decisions and all—while you can be my vice president. In other words, you'll be in charge of the business and its affairs. Like a manager."

Yvette listened closely and didn't object.

"We're gonna need to open a bank account. We're gonna need an accountant. And we're gonna need to file our company with the State of New York."

"I know about the filing part. They do that downtown, in the building where I work, on Center Street."

"Good."

"But one thing, Push. Where are you gonna get the money to open the account? And to hire an accountant?"

Push said, "Get up."

Yvette thought he was gonna smack her for asking something too personal. But she got up anyhow.

Yvette actually liked taking direction from Push. *Such a General you are.*

Push turned Yvette's couch onto its back while she stood there wide-eyed with her mouth opened as if for a dentist.

She watched as Push pulled out bunches of money and stacked them one at a time on the low table next to the couch.

"Turn around," Push said. And when she did, he took out the pistols and stuck them in his waistband, under his shirt so that she wouldn't see.

Push turned the couch back to normal and had Yvette to sit again. "Now . . . here's forty-five thousand. Five thousand is for you. It's just a little something to start with, but there's more where that came from. Eventually, both you and I will be on the payroll of the new corporation. We'll call it MELRAH."

"MELRAH? What's that?"

"HARLEM, spelled backwards."

"I like it already," said Yvette. She wanted to ask Push

about all the money, but instead, she asked "How do you come up with all of this business sense all of a sudden?"

"What you think, I was sleeping all those years in prison? I took up real estate courses. I spoke to many men who were in the real estate game . . . even in politics. There's more wealth in prison, behind those walls, than you could ever imagine."

Is that where you got the money? From your friends in prison?

"Now, you might be concerned about the money . . . like, will the bank ask questions, etcetera. Well . . . what you'll do is deposit this money over a short period of time. Four thousand here . . . six thousand there. Banks don't care too much about those numbers, unless they know for sure that there's illegal activity going on. But the numbers we're dealing with . . . they get that kind of play every day. They're more interested in taking your money than interrogating you about where you got it from."

"I'm with you. I know a lot about what you're saying, Push. My girlfriend opened up a flower shop downtown. She explained a lot of this to me."

"Good. So then you're not a virgin."

"Not exactly," Yvette batted her eyes at Push and flashed a crooked grin at him.

Push went on to discuss a few properties that he had his eye on over the past months. A couple of them were abandoned. Another simply needed some handiwork. Push wanted to obtain that property first. "We'll make an offer to the owner. We'll offer him ten percent more than the property is worth. That means we'll need an M.A.I. appraisal."

"M.A.I. Never heard of that."

"It's just a standard that banks look at. The appraisers are what they call certified. Their appraisals are legitimate. So let's say the appraisal came in at a hundred grand. We'll offer the owner a hundred and ten . . . maybe a hundred and twenty."

Push went on to explain and put his hand up to clear the air. Yvette immediately went silent.

"First of all, the owner can even get a buyer at eighty thousand. Why? Because the property looks the pits. But me? I see it for what it *could be*. I envision it in five years from now, after I put love into it."

"I get it. So the equity will go up and the property will be worth, what?"

"Maybe one thirty. One forty. Maybe more. In the meantime, the owner and I will work out the terms on low-interest payments for the money I'll owe him."

"Wow."

"And to begin with, I going to lease the property from him, fix it up, then refinance it."

"So the bank will give you money for it? While you lease?"

"Not exactly. They actually are going to give the loan to the owner. But because of our side agreement, the owner is loaning *me* the money to fix up the property and so on."

"That's brilliant, Push. I have never known you to be a real estate guru."

Push worked out some notes on a pad when Yvette asked, "What if the owner won't go for the deal?"

"This is the only way I'll do the deal. Otherwise, we keep it movin'. Pick another property. There are hundreds and thousands of properties that are in need of help. It's because of *my energy* that the property will be improved . . . it will be worth money to a bank, whereas now, it isn't worth the land it sits on."

Yvette nodded and shook her head at the same time. He was amazing. She found herself wanting to embrace him, but instead, she merely sat by and marveled. Push, the real estate tycoon.

"By this time next week, I expect to have six accepted offers."

"Six?? But I thought you only had your eye on one."

"Underestimating me again?"

Yvette with the wide eyes. *Who is this man??*

CHAPTER TWENTY-EIGHT

AT TEN P.M. SHARP, ROY Washington wasn't just a loan shark and a snake anymore. Now, he was a trespasser.

Asondra did it. Just as they had planned. Somehow, she diverted Fred Allen's attention so that the front door would be left unlocked for Roy's easy entry.

Also according to the plan, she was to be busy with Fred at precisely 10pm, so that Roy would be able to go through Fred's home office. Asondra had already told Roy about the office, its file cabinets and home computer. So Roy was prepared to be a while. And if Roy knew Asondra, she would definitely keep Fred busy.

Roy and Asondra discussed one more important subject:

"What if he gets out of the bed?"

"Make a loud sound of some kind. Scream if you have to."

"Like maybe I saw a mouse?"

"Right. And you said that you were amateur at this?"

But that idea was no good anymore. Roy could see that—or rather, he could *hear* that—as soon as he began picking through Fred's files . . .

"NO! OH FRED!" Then the screams.

What the fuck is he doing? Killing her??

Roy was both concerned and curious. He left the study and crept through the dark townhouse, up the steps to the 2nd floor, and down a hallway towards Asondra's shrieks. He didn't have a gun, but he figured he sized up Fred pretty good, assuming he could take him on if worse came to worse.

And come to think of it, that still might not ruin the work that Asondra put in . . .

"OH GOD! OH FRED!! FRED!! FRED!!"

Roy might be observed as a burglar, in no way associated with—

JESUS! The smell of sex was strong where Roy was standing at the threshold of the bedroom. The door was wide open, also according to plan, and a lamp illuminated the limbs and curves of both Fred and Asondra in an ongoing bout of aggressive penetration. Roy immediately grew an erection as he caught Asondra's eye—the both of them sharing a determined look. The thing is, Roy couldn't tell if she was pretending, or if this was a genuine expression of how she was accepting this guy.

Her shadow was cast against the wall nearest to the bed as she bounced up and down on Fred. She had a blindfold covering Fred's eyes and he was spread-eagle on his back, a broad smile across his face. Roy could hear the wet skin-slapping sounds that Asondra's ass was making against Fred's groin. And he knew that there was no way she could fake THAT.

Now Asondra turned up one hand to Roy, wondering if he got what he came for yet. Roy wagged his head, seeing it was okay for him to come into the room so long as he kept quiet.

"Awe baby! You are the ONE GOOD FUCK!" Fred exclaimed.

Asondra rolled her eyes as if this was boring her. And now Roy was close enough to whisper in her ear. She stopped the bouncing and went on with a slow grind; it was the only way she could steady herself to hear what Roy was saying. "I'm still looking. Keep up the good work . . ."

"OH! YOU'RE KILLING ME BABY OOOOOH . . . WORK THAT THING! MOMMA! WORK IT!!!"

"You see the shit I'm going through for you?" Asondra whispered.

"You don't seem to be having such a hard time . . . *work it, baby*," Roy whispered back, trying to be funny.

But Asondra didn't think it was ONE BIT FUNNY. And in spite of Roy's sarcasm, she began bouncing again. Fred was still as hard as a 2×4, empowered by the *Viagra* pills he'd taken earlier. Asondra was more aggressive now, her hands on the bed, supporting herself . . . banging her ass up and down and making her own animal cries for Roy AND Fred to hear.

"You like that, Freddy? Hunh??" Asondra spoke to both men at the same time, eyeing Roy as she did.

Roy swallowed, frozen at the idea of his woman intentionally fucking another man right there in front of him. He almost forgot his purpose here . . . he even thought about whipping his dick out right now . . . he'd have her suck it while she fucked the blinded politician.

No. I gotta get back to business.

Roy lifted the camera that had been hanging around his neck and quickly snapped a flash photo. And he broadcast an evil smile.

"HEY!" Asondra yelled.

"Yes, baby!? OH YES BA-BY!" cried Fred.

Roy put his middle finger up at Asondra and left the bedroom, returning downstairs to the study. He had to hurry . . . no telling how long this would go on.

As he left he could still hear Asondra. "Nothin', lover. Just keep it hard for me. I'm coming to suck it in just a minute."

Roy snickered under his breath as he made his way down the hall. *She's joking . . . sayin' that shit to spite me.*

MAYBE THIS WASN'T SO BAD after all, Asondra thought as she carried on with her performance.

He seems to be healthy. He's a self-made million-aire, and he treats me like a queen. Roy was never like this. What has it been? Fifteen years that I've been with Roy? And what has he been to me except a demanding bastard? Sure, he put some cash on the table every now and then . . . But with Fred, money would never be a problem.

So many thoughts pushed through Asondra's mind, all while she was feeling this man's throbbing beast inside of her . . . encouraging her to imagine things as they could be, instead of as they were now. Asondra recalled Roy's words:

"Would you fuck that guy for, say, ten million?"

"We're in like Flynn . . . you can have all the money . . ."

"Hundreds of millions of dollars, baby . . ."

And then there were Fred's words:

"I'm gonna treat you like a queen . . ."

"I'm gonna change your life forever . . ."

Asondra turned around now, still with Fred fully inside of her. His hands had been grabbing her ass, and now that she was half lying astride of him, he fondled her breasts. Asondra pictured Roy downstairs, going through piles of papers. Maybe he would find something. Maybe he wouldn't.

"You're so beautiful, Asondra. I could love you like this forever."

Asondra took off Fred's blindfold as the two continued to grind. She wanted to see his eyes . . . to know that what he said was sincere.

"How do I know that? How do I know about forever, Fred? How can I trust you?"

Asondra noticed that there was wetness around Fred's eyes, and now that the blindfold had been removed—*was he crying?*

"Just tell me what you want and you've got it. *Whatever.*" Fred let out a moan and Asondra felt a shudder within her nether regions. Of all things, *she* was actually coming. An occurrence that she thought would never take place.

"Oh God," Asondra cried. And this time it was for real. She sighed and bent forward to hold Fred, her naked body against his. She held onto him like a lover, not an actress. She sought harmony here. Comfort. Meanwhile a river felt its way through her being. It was a rush that she hadn't experienced in ages. Like the first time she fell in love, or thought that she had.

She held Fred tighter now. He was security and tenderness.

And now that she thought about it, he really *did* belong to her.

There was a sudden crash downstairs, and Fred heard it loud and clear.

"What's that?" he spat.

And now was when Asondra was to say, *"Oh, don't be silly. You're hearing things."* And then, as a last resort, she was supposed to suck his dick. And that was only in case of an emergency like this . . . something to surely cause Fred to see things her way.

Roy had joked: *"He might even have a heart attack."* But Asondra didn't want to follow the plan. Not now.

"It sounds like a burglar, Fred. Do you have a gun?"

"Shit. DO I? Baby, this is Harlem." And Fred reached down under the night table for his firearm. "Stay here. I gonna go down. Call nine-one-one," Fred said as he rolled out of the bed for his robe.

S HIT!" ROY EXCLAIMED IN A hushed tone. He had knocked the lamp to the floor.

Clumsy motha-fucka!

After he cursed himself, Roy remained still. There was no sound in the house. He shrugged it off, assuming the worst—the worst being Asondra's mouth filled with that creep's aged dick.

Oh well. She ain't shit but a freak, anyway. Go on . . . suck it.

Roy told himself that it could've been a lot worse and he tried to find his way around in the dark. Eventually, he found the light switch. "Good," he muttered once he realized it was a dimmer dial and not just a switch. He turned it enough so that he would see where the hell he was going next time.

The curtains were closed, so nobody would see him from the street, and Asondra was busy upstairs, blowing the home-owner's mind—at least, in theory. So, as far as Roy could see, he was good for another 5 minutes. Roy returned to his investigation.

• • •

T'S YOU! THE JERK I met last—**HOLD IT RIGHT THERE! DON'T FUCKIN MOVE**. What the *fuck* are you doin in my house?"

Instinctively, Roy had his hands partially raised. "Don't shoot, man. Listen . . . the FBI is investigating you. They're usin' me to get to you. I'm stuck between a rock and a hard place . . . you've gotta believe me. They're using me."

"Investigating me for what?"

"Something about your Empowerment Fund. A snitch . . . one of your old partners, dropped a dime. He's going for a reduced sentence. He told them all about you . . . how you own a piece of the Fund. YO, MAN! They know *all about you!*"

"So, what does that have to do with you trespassing in my house? Why would they need *you* to break into my place?"

"They wanted me to get inside. They forced me man . . . they want me to find documents . . . evidence."

"Did they wire you too?"

"No. But they wanted to. And they wanted me to plant bugs in your house, too."

"Take off your jacket."

"What?"

Fred raised the gun higher. It was a .38 Special. "I said, take it off."

Roy said, "OKAY! EASY!"

"Now the shirt."

Roy made a face, but did as he was told.

"Turn around . . . lemme see . . ."

"I told you, man. I'm not wired."

"Honey? What is it? Ohmygod! You caught him!"

"Stay back, love. Did you call nine-one-one?"

"They should be here shortly," Asondra said.

Just then, Roy swung around and said, "YOU FUCKIN BITCH!"

• • •

FRED SNAPPED. ROY'S WORDS PUSHED a panic button in his head and his finger tugged at the trigger. The .38 Special went off, with one shot hitting Roy just above the heart. He fired again, and the next bullet hit his right shoulder, spinning him back into the architect's bespunked toy model of Harlem.

Asondra screamed, then fainted.

Fred heard sirens in the distance and he considered the situation. He approached the trespasser, leveling the weapon at his head.

"P-please. They m-made me . . . I . . ." The intruder tried to catch his breath.

"I don't negotiate with burglars," said Fred. "And one more thing . . . she is NOT a bitch." Fred pulled the trigger once more, hitting Roy Washington somewhere about the left eye.

Oh my. Did I do that?

Quickly now, Fred went to the drawer of his desk and took out a box big enough to hold a dozen Cuban cigars. Inside, there was a palm-sized 9millimeter pistol. He used a handkerchief to wipe the weapon clean and bent down to put it into the dead man's hand. He had to fold the fingers over to create a strong enough hold on the weapon. Next, Fred took the camera that the intruder brought with him and he went to hide it.

If Fred didn't say so himself, he was quite the perfectionist.

CHAPTER TWENTY-NINE

TWO MURDERS WITHIN WEEKS OF each other, both right under the noses of F.B.I. Agents. It was unfathomable how Agents Edwards and Fogarty were there that night, parked in a dark blue sedan, just a couple of brownstones to the east of Fred Allen's home. They noticed Asondra Jenkins go in after sundown, and then Roy Washington, at 10pm. Edwards was left to assume that his "inside man" was getting the job done, as usual, by any means necessary.

After all, it was Edwards who more or less urged Roy into this line of work years ago, when the feds took down Hollywood, and now, as they plotted on Fred Allen.

This time, however, Edwards was wrong. *Dead* wrong.

It was just an hour later when sirens descended on Striver's Row. Edwards and Fogarty were completely taken by surprise. *Again?* And again the blizzard of emergency vehicles returned to 138th Street as if they were here only yesterday. Then Captain Brock showed up in his unmarked car, a jade Chevy Corvette.

Still keeping with their, so-called, undercover surveillance, the two FBI Agents sat and speculated.

"What the hell is going on now?"

Then came the knock at the driver's side window.

When Agent Edwards lowered the window, a police officer announced, "Captain Brock says he'd like to see you two."

The Agents went along without question, and quickly found themselves ushered into the center of a murder scene.

Shocked and amazed, they looked down at Roy Washington's corpse. Roy Washington, loan shark-turned-philanthropist-turned-dead trespasser.

"The woman there says she watched the whole thing. The victim trespassed, pulled a gun, and your buddy over there on the couch shot him full of holes . . . but either I'm dreaming, or this makes two killings that took place right under your noses."

Edwards started to say something.

"Right." Captain Brock cut Edwards off before he could get a word in edgewise. "I know . . . you went home for the night . . . the last time. But, hey . . . I'm not complaining. I'm not blaming anybody. I'm just wondering if I should assign a coroner to this specific address . . . if it might interrupt your little . . . uh . . . *investigation*. Or *is there* even an investigation anymore?"

Edwards was at a loss for words, still stunned by how this took place while they were parked outside. He knew, however, that he'd have to come up with answers somewhere along the way. So far, the best answer he could think up was that he had no answers.

How was I supposed to know the man was a burglar? It's not my job to protect the man's house from thieves.

These were Edwards's only thoughts, short and sweet. The more complex he made this, the more trouble he could be in. So he played stupid. So did Fogarty. The old blue wall of silence lived on.

Now that the plan to undermine Fred Allen had backfired, there was no way to produce evidence for Fred's boss, Chief Mitchell, the US Attorney's office, or for the support of the allegations of the imprisoned Julius Anderson.

Chief Mitchell, head of the FBI's White Collar Crimes Unit, decided to pursue the federal complaint against Fred Allen anyway, despite the lack of evidence. However, the grand jury would not likely hand down an indictment. The complaint would be handed back unpursued, on account of unsubstantiated information.

Back to the drawing board.

Fred Allen saw the investigation as a plot . . . an attempt to tarnish his good name. But he found it laughable that the FBI charged him with the stealing, when Sara was the one in control of the Committee's activities regarding the Empowerment Fund. If worse came to worse, he could always lay the blame on Sara.

For now, Fred was enjoying his new friend, Asondra.

PUSH WAS READY WITH HIS closet full of business suits, his corporation, business cards for MELRAH, and an agenda. There came a point that he wondered what to do with the cell phone. Indeed, he finished the job. *Do I keep it?*

He had been in the shower after day-long prospecting of gutted brownstones and abandoned buildings that were crumbling from years of neglect. He found that 50% or more of the properties within 2 square miles were in poor shape and had been claimed by the city for nonpayment of taxes. Other properties were owned privately, used as tax write-offs.

"Push," Yvette called out.

"Whassup?" he hollered back from the shower.

Yvette came closer to the bathroom so that they could hear one another without shouting.

"Baby, there's a cell phone ringing somewhere. But I can't seem to find out where it's coming from.

Push stepped out of the shower and wrapped a towel around himself. He still had water and suds dripping about his skin as he hurried past Yvette.

"Well, exCUSE me," said Yvette, backing out of his way against the wall to avoid getting wet herself.

Push grabbed the cell phone out of a leather bag he kept. "Yeah," he answered.

"Damn. I thought you disappeared on me. I mean, I wouldn't blame you."

"What is it now?" Push asked.

"Oh . . . hey . . . easy, trooper. I just wanted to congratulate you on a job well done. That's all. Rest easy, dog."

"Listen, man. Stop callin' me dog. I'm not your dog."

"Just a figure of speech. My bad. Besides . . . you're a professional now, aren't you?"

Push didn't respond. Yvette was nearby, enough so that Push could feel her presence. He would have to be careful about what he said.

"Anyway, Push . . . I'm just calling to say thanks a million. And, well . . . what if I need you again?"

"There is no again. It's over."

Yvette came over to Push now. He didn't consider the opportunity here: himself standing naked except for the towel. "That means I'm tossing this as soon as you hang up."

"That's a pity. We could make money together. We're a good team."

"I don't need that kind of money," Push replied, wanting to call it *blood money*. Yvette was reaching around Push, smoothing her hands about his chest. Eventually she circled him, biting the corner of her lower lip in that I-want-you way. Then she sat down on the couch, positioning Push so that he stood between her legs. She parted the towel and took hold of him. Yvette, with the tongue and cheek.

"Suit yourself. Well . . . I guess that's it," said the caller.

"I guess it is," said Push, "Nice doin' business with you." Push turned off the phone and removed its battery so that it would never ring again.

Less than a week later, Push was following his agenda, introducing himself as a real estate developer, although from a small businessman perspective. He didn't want to be mistaken for an upscale buyer—no sense in letting everyone know his long-term goals.

He met with the Greater Harlem Chamber of Commerce, a former President of the United States, various real estate Agents, a former Housing Commissioner, the President of Carver Bank, the largest African-American–owned bank in the country, civic leaders, a few pastors, and also other property owners. Eventually, Push met George Murphy, a well-known and controversial Harlem slumlord who used many of Harlem's run-down properties for tax-shelters. Murphy could care less about the revitalization of the Harlem community and was mainly concerned about the bottom line: positive cash flow.

"I noticed all of the properties along West One Twenty-eighth Street belong to you."

"Most of them do. About thirty. But then, who's counting?" Murphy laughed at his own joke. Short, balding and bespeckled, the white man's belly stuck out as if he were pregnant. In his own mind, Push immediately named him Pot Belly.

"Well, I'm here to make you a proposal, Mister Murphy. I'm interested in renovating all of them."

"Whoa . . . there-there, young man. Are you sure you know what you getting into? I've never heard of—what is it?—MELRAH?? What have you all done?"

"My corporation is new, sir. But my proposition is a proven strategy. See, I'm looking to put my sweat and hard work and finances into making those properties profitable . . . instead of thousand dollar-a-month tax shelters . . ."

"Why wouldn't I do that?" asked Murphy. "Why wouldn't I put my own hard work and finances into making more money?"

Because you're probably a lazy, no-good . . . Push caught himself digressing. Then he said, "I guess you could, if you really set your mind to it. But *me?* I believe I can pump some vitality back into the community. It just seems like for years Harlem has been coming up with the short end of the stick. I want to help bring this place back to the way it was in the 30's and 40's . . .

"How old ARE you?"

"I almost thirty-five now. But—I know what you're getting at—see, I read. I know this community's history. Back in the day, people believed that Harlem was the center of the universe."

"I see. Well, young man. To be frank with you, I don't believe you can give me what my properties are worth. On a good day I could sell that entire block for a few million bucks. At least."

Push already knew the facts. He knew the man was lying.

He studied the city's records on the property values, taxes in arrears, etc. He had spoken to businessmen who were aware of Murphy's schemes, how he worked around the city's rent stabilization rules, even forcing tenants out of their homes on occasions when he found he could charge a higher rent.

"I guess I underestimated things," Push lied. "I figured I could pay you one and a half times the amount you're writing off each month . . . maybe even two times." Push was at least truthful about the profits he could make and what he could pay Murphy. Push went on to say, "But you obviously have better deals happening. So . . . sorry to waste your time . . ."

"Now, not so fast, young man. Not so fast. Did you say *twice* the amount I'm writing off?"

"Sure did."

"Can you guarantee that somehow?"

"I believe I can," Push affirmed.

"Well, get me a written offer and have documentation on the guarantees. We just might be able to do business."

Push shook Murphy's clammy hand, immediately sensing a trace of insincerity. This was a notorious slumlord, and Push would have to be careful.

A RE YOU READY, SWEETHEART?" YVETTE asked from where she stood in front of the bathroom mirror.

"I don't know if I can ever get use to these ties," said Push, still fiddling with the knot.

Yvette came to the rescue and faced Push to fix his collar and tie until it was sharp.

"Thanks," said Push with a defeated smile. And then he said,

"You sure look the part."

"I'm just a reflection of my man. His other half."

"Hmmm . . . you say all the right things," said Push.

"That's because you DO all the right things . . ."

Push put on his wheat-colored blazer and they both went

out to Yvette's car. In less than 15 minutes they expected to be at Congressman Chambers's officer where Yvette had made an appointment to speak with Fred Allen.

ABOUT A MONTH PASSED SINCE Roy Washington was shot and killed. Fred Allen was now back in his own office, next to the Congressman's. Many saw Fred as the hero who faced the mad gunman. The office was quite orderly these days. The staff was settled, handling their respective duties to keep the political machine running smoothly.

The Congressman had been addressing leaders of every sort, and representatives of government who had committed money for the 400-million-dollar Harlem Empowerment Fund.

Meanwhile, Fred Allen, who had been the Congressman's campaign manager, was now the Chairman in charge of the Fund. He was also the treasurer, the secretary, the Vice-Chair, and every other title that controlled the Committee.

Of course this was temporary for him to have 100% control over the fund, but things had to be reorganized since Sara's sudden death. And now that Fred Allen was sure that the feds were investigating him, he had to do a massive house cleaning. He spent hours shredding documents, phantom proposals and other records that might incriminate him. Fred was suddenly a different person. He had gotten away with his self-defense alibi, when in fact he killed Roy Washington in cold blood—just because he posed a threat . . . just because he gave Fred the perfect excuse to kill.

Bigger than all of that, Fred was liberated, and now he had the woman of his dreams. She was young, sexy, and she turned him on at every instant. Asondra could do no wrong. Eventually, he decided, she and her son would move to Striver's Row and they'd be a family. And to hell with what the neighbors thought, how Fred left no breathing room between one woman and the next. For now, Fred walked the straight and narrow. He constantly reminded himself of how blessed he was to 1) be alive, and 2) to be free of the feds, prosecution and possibly jail.

Fred kept Asondra close by his side during these times, training her to fill Sara's shoes. It was a big task, he had to admit, but in time Asondra would know just as much as Sara did, and more.

"Your ten o'clock appointment is here, baby."

"Asondra . . . I love you bigger than the sun and the moon, but we have to have some office ethics. I know it's easy to forget, but I can't have the rest of the staff calling me *baby*, if you know what I mean."

"I do. Sorry . . . ahh, *Mister* Allen."

"No need to be sorry, *Ms.* Jenkins. And I'll be happy to see my appointment now, *Ms.* Jenkins." Fred with the smile.

Asondra and her business outfit went out to escort Yvette Gardner and Reginald Jackson into Fred's office. This was the 1st time Push was to meet Fred, but it wasn't the 1st time they spoke with one another. It took a minute, but Push remembered seeing this man as the companion to the woman . . . he was the man who stood outside on the porch of the townhouse that night.

And now that Push thought about it, the woman who ushered him into Fred Allen's office also looked familiar. Push replayed Christmas Eve on his mind's movie screen . . . he had been camping out on 138th St., in the back of the YOU NEED JESUS van, watching the woman climb the stairs of the brownstone to plant a kiss on Fred Allen's cheek. The images became as clear as if they were taking place right now, before his very eyes.

His various concerns kicked in now . . . how this was too close for comfort . . . how he needed the backing of the Fund for his West 128th Street proposal . . . how he had murdered someone who these folks knew personally. All of these thoughts were swirling around in his head until he finally heard the voice.

"Good morning. Nice to meet you," Fred said as he shook the hands of his two visitors.

• • •

NOW IT WAS FRED WHO felt the chill.

The presence of his visitors didn't bother him whatsoever until they introduced themselves.

"I'm Yvette Gardner, President of MELRAH Corporation, and this is my partner, Reginald Jackson . . ."

The name drummed around inside of Fred's head much like 20 basketballs bouncing all at once, all of them out of synch, pounding that wooden floor of his consciousness.

Reginald Jackson. Oh SHIT! This is PUSH!?

Fred felt his eyes water some, and he tried his best to stop the trembling. To help shield his falling apart, he began a sudden uncontrollable cough. He excused himself and stepped over to a cabinet, his back to his visitors, as he poured himself a drink. He threw the drink down and took on a gruff voice, one Push wouldn't recognize.

Or so he thought.

"Can I offer you a drink?" Fred asked, his back still turned to them.

I've gotta keep the deep voice. That's the only way he knows . . . the voice. Shit! It's probably too late.

Fred thought back to how he hired Push to kill Sara. It was important to keep his identity a secret, so the cell phone came in handy. The money was nothing to him . . . it was simply the price he had to pay to free himself. He hoped that during all of their conversations that he never said anything foul.

But then, Fred had only just called Push to thank him for a job well-done. So, was it really necessary to be scared to death? Had he even recognized Fred? Fred asked that question of himself out of paranoia, but of course the answer was obvious: Push was the only link between Fred and a well thought out murder.

No . . . he wouldn't do anything to me . . . he's just as much at risk as I am.

Still petrified, Fred spoke very little and allowed this woman, Yvette, to present her proposal. They had a decent plan. Unlike others who came in his office with something-for-nothing pipe dreams, this couple wanted to put up some

of their own money, and merely needed matching funds to
guarantee their monthly payments to the seller.

Fred was listening, but then again, it was all such a blur.
All the while, he tried to keep from any lengthy eye contact
with Push.

Shit! He's actually right here in my face!

"What's wrong, Push?"

"Nothin'," he lied, as he and Yvette boarded one of 10
elevators in the Harlem State Office Building. They were
alone now, the car dropping downwards to the basement,
where an underground passage led to an adjacent parking
garage.

"And you expect me to believe that?"

"Okay. Ready for the bad news?"

"Hit me," Yvette said.

"I don't think they'll go for the proposal."

"Why? It's a win-win proposal. You said it yourself. The
Fund won't feel the risk . . . we'll be able to begin work on
the properties . . . move the tenants in . . ."

Push wagged his head.

"It has nothing to do with that," Push said. "Absolutely
nothing," he muttered.

"Then what?"

"Call it my gut feeling."

Yvette and Push didn't wait for their proposal to be ap-
proved. They went ahead and made an offer on just two of
the properties. 440 and 441 West 128th street. The lease payments would be $4,000 a month, with 50% of the money go-
ing towards the full purchase price of the property. Murphy
gave his oral agreement of $100,000 per lot. The two prop-
erties they chose required less work and less capital to renovate, however the clock began ticking the moment George
Murphy accepted the offer, and issued MELRAH's contract.
The property would be purchased in full within 2 years, time
enough to renovate, assign residents, and build substantial
equity. Push's intentions were to turn each brownstone into 3
separate residences, since there were already 3 floors. Each
floor would bring in at least $1,500 rent per month. He also

expected that the renovations wouldn't take more than 2 months. So the labor began.

Push leased a van and made continuous trips back and forth to Home Depot for the various fixtures, tools, paint, lumber, sheetrock, nails and screws, electrical supplies and paneling. Installing toilets, sinks and full baths was the most complex work to be done. Then came the electrical wiring. Beyond that, most everything else was a cinch. Push had his vocational training (from prison) to guide him every step of the way. And he overestimated the time it would take to complete the job. With Reggie to assist him, and Yvette lending a hand now and again—such a tomboy—in her construction boots, jeans and scarf to wrap her hair—Push finished the work on the 1st brownstone within one month. The 2nd property was finished by March 1st. By the first day of spring, 5 of the residences were rented. Push moved into the 6th space so that he'd have a place of his own as well as a "home office" for MELRAH. Ms. Watson visited Push while he was hard at work, banging away so that he didn't hear her creep in the door.

"Oh! Shit, you scared me to death," Push lied.

"Sorry about that. I knocked."

"No biggie."

"So this is the dynasty, hunh?"

"This is it. I either get rich like Donald Trump, or I sink like the *Titanic*."

"Mind if I have a look around?"

"No. Not at all. Be my guest."

And Ms. Watson wandered for 10 minutes or so.

"Don't let me stop you. I just wanted to see your work. I'll let myself out."

"Okay. I guess . . . I'll see you at your office."

"As usual . . ."

Push didn't look forward to the monthly visits, and hoped to hire a lawyer soon so that his probation term would be reduced on account of his good adjustment. Yvette passed Ms. Watson as she came through the door and greeted the Probation Officer more sincerely than she had in the past. Push told Yvette that she should change the way she looked at the woman since they'd likely be seeing so much of her . . . when they least expected it.

"Hey, baby." Yvette came and kissed his cheek. She had a picnic basket with lunch for two, and encouraged Push to take a break.

"I made your favorite: Chicken Caesar salad."

"With the chunky blue cheese?"

"Mmm hmm!"

"I'd show you how grateful I am, but—" Push indicated how dusty he looked.

"Oh, don't worry. I'll be looking forward to some of that gratification later," said Yvette.

"Any mail come to the P.O. box? Voice mails for MEL-RAH?"

"Nothing from the Congressman, if that's what you mean. It's been almost three months now. I'm beginning to think you're right about the whole thing."

"You should know about my gut feelings by now . . . they're as sure as my taste in women."

Yvette smiled. *Men and their egos. What makes him think that it was him to have the taste . . . to do the choosing?*

T HE FILE FOR THE MELRAH proposal was still lying on Fred Allen's desk, in a pile with others that were not yet decided upon.

Asondra was in Fred's office alone, organizing his desk while he was in a conference with the Congressman. She noticed the file and how far back it was dated. By now, a decision should've been made for or against the proposal. Asondra made it a point to bring it to Fred's attention. She had a good feeling about the two who presented the MEL-RAH plan. They made a cute couple in her eyes, and she envied them, how they were young like her. Not that she had a problem with Fred being older. After all, he did do as he said he would: he changed her life and treated her like a queen.

But Asondra couldn't help thinking . . . wondering how much better things might be if Fred was a little younger . . . like Ms. Yvette Gardner's man. Fred came out of his conference that day and looked through his messages. The one he knew he'd be getting sooner or later said, "From Dorothy." And the message was simple: *"There's no place like home."* There was a question mark after the message; Asondra, in need of an explanation. Fred faked a yawn. He went to lock his office door and then lifted the cushion of his couch. He pulled out the thin attaché case which had been waiting there for "Dorothy's" call.

Fred let down the cushion, put on his fisherman's hat, sunglasses and the tan trench coat. Although spring was here and there was a breeze out there, one which never ceased to prey on a person who didn't dress appropriately, Fred wasn't merely dressed for the weather. This was his sorry excuse for a disguise.

As he was leaving the office, Asondra was coming in with a handful of papers.

"Babe . . . er . . . *Mister* Allen, you mind if I have a minute of your time? Before you disappear on one of your day-long errands?" Asondra literally backed Fred into his office, un-willing to let him pass

"Sweetheart, I—"

"Eh-eh-eh . . . remember our office ethics."

"Okay, Ms. Jenkins. I promise you I'll be back in an hour, and we'll leave work early. Maybe a bite to eat at *Sylvia's?*"

"And we'll have time to talk?"

"Yes. We'll have time to talk, Asondra. I promise—already. Now, if I don't hurry and get to my appointment, Harlem gonna fall apart at the seams."

Asondra twisted her lips and stepped aside.

"There's no place like home." Might've been a quote from the big movie *The Wizard of Oz*, but for Fred it was the code for *"Meet me at Grant's Tomb. 12 noon."* Not to mention that it took more than two months for this meeting; a time when Fred & "Dorothy" could be sure that the heat had cooled down.

They knew about the FBI investigation, and they knew about it for months. Before Roy Washington knew about it. Even before Agent Rudolph Edwards knew about it.

That was then:

A matter of being in the right place at the right time. *The right place* happened to be the cafeteria inside of the Manhattan Federal Courthouse; a cafeteria where the privileged few were permitted to eat—Federal Law Enforcement Agents, U.S. Attorneys and their assistants, Judges and their clerks, as well as Parole, Probation, and other officers of the court.

The "*right time*" was months earlier, when the US Attorney was discussing politics with one of his assistants, as well as Chief Mitchell of the FBI's White Collar Crimes Unit. The discussions turned into a hot debate about soft money— under the table campaign contributions and how money was more important than a candidate's message.

"*Then we need to go after people like Percy Chambers. He's pushing this heavy number around every time, I read the paper or hear the radio . . . four hundred million-this, four hundred million-that . . . why isn't anyone asking where he's getting this four hundred million? Or how he's spending it?*"

"*He's right you know. In corporate America the S.E.C. and the I.R.S. account for such huge amounts of money. But in politics? It's like these fast talkers with their gift of gab have all the freedom in the world. They create frivolous committees, foundations, funds . . . it never ends.*"

"*But I don't think Chambers is being deceitful.*"

"*Maybe not. But his campaign manager is another story. Fred Allen is his name. He's a scam-artist. I can feel it in my bones.*"

"*Mitchell, can we put some pressure on their little monopoly?*" asked the US Attorney.

Mitchell had replied, "*I can do a number of things. And I have just the Agent for the job. All I need is your go-ahead . . . because now its politics. But when it comes my way, it's criminal.*"

Little did they know that their discussion was overheard.

The name Percy Chambers raised a red flag. But the name Fred Allen ignited fireworks.

And this was now:

FRED SPOTTED HER ON A park bench close to the historic landmark. He circled the block one time to be extra sure he wasn't being followed, then he pulled his Cadillac up to an easy stop. She climbed in and Fred drove away, hooking around the park once again, until he found a place to set the car on busy Riverside Drive.

"Did you bring it?"

"Of course. What'd you think? I spent it?"

Fred reached into the back of the car and took the attaché case from the floor. He handed it to her.

"What are you gonna do with all that money, Evelyn?"

"Oh . . . my god." She needed to catch her breath. Finally, part 1 of 1.3 million dollars.

"Well?"

Evelyn sighed. "Fix up my mom's house . . . hell, I might just go *buy* her one!" She laughed until the shivering set in again. The seriousness of it all. "I need a house of my own. And a snazzy car like yours wouldn't hurt."

"Sure it would. Government employees don't make the kind of money that affords Cadillacs or big homes."

"Well, maybe I don't need to be a government employee then. Maybe I'm in the wrong business."

Fred wagged his head.

"Don't change anything Evelyn. Not for a while. You'll compromise both of us."

"You're right. As usual. Maybe I'll just get a *Toyota*. A compact one." Evelyn smiled and looked back into the suitcase. It was lined with stacks of neatly bound, crisp, one hundred dollar bills.

Inhale . . . exhale . . .

She closed the lid.

"You got those boys real frustrated, Fred. Shootin'

their inside man like you did. I was worried about you."

"Had to be done. I had no choice. You were right about them being onto us. The guy confirmed it before I shot him."

"I heard you do that well too. Shooting, ahem . . . armed burglars. Made sure he was nice n' dead, hunh?" Evelyn made a face.

Fred shrugged his shoulders. "He was the only thing standing in the way. A lot of money on the line, ya' know?"

"Oh-h-h-ho . . . I know alright." Evelyn patted the attaché case.

"By the way . . . you'll never guess who I ran into a little while ago."

"Who?"

"Your street thug. Push. He came into my office with his girlfriend, looking for matching funds to secure his investment in some brownstones." Evelyn, with the wide-eyed stare.

"You kidding. Did he know? How could he know? He never saw your face."

"But, I slipped. Before I found out his name, he heard my voice. And my voice was the only thing he had to go on. I can't be one hundred percent sure, but I think he made me."

"Shit," Evelyn said. "This was supposed to be clean, Fred. No strings."

"It's still no strings, Evelyn. It's kind of strange, but I think he sort of respects me. At least, that's the impression I get. Otherwise, I'd probably be dead by now."

"And I'd probably agree with you: That man ain't no joke, Fred. I watched him move like a panther in the night. Took out his victims—"

"I know, I know, you told me." *You should've seen him, Fred. He was a work of art No muss-no fuss. One, two, three, I've seen cons at work, but this guy? He's a master.*

"Then you know not to ever get on his bad side," Evelyn warned. Fred thought about the man's proposal that was buried somewhere on his desk.

"Hmmm, a good thing you mentioned that," said Fred.

"And the next time you work up a scam like this, I want

in. You never know what kind of resource a person like me could be."

"I'll keep that in mind, too," said Fred.

Evelyn got out of the Cadillac. But before she closed the door, she said, "By the way, nice girlfriend, Fred."

Fred made a strange face. He already knew that to be a truth. But how did she know about Asondra?

Evelyn read his mind and said, "My last name ain't Watson for nothing, *Sherlock.*"

And while Fred laughed, Evelyn closed the door. Attaché case in hand, she crossed the street, flagging down a taxi as she did

Later, Dorothy.

CONCLUSION

THE DAY AFTER VALENTINE'S DAY, Yvette and Crystal virtually killed themselves trying to get around the various building supplies that lay about the floor of the 3rd brownstone where Reggie and Push were busy at work.

This third property, 442 West 128th street that MELRAH went into contract on was identical to the 1st and 2nd properties.

"PUSH! Where are you!?" Yvette called out.

"In the kitchen. Watch your step!"

Crystal forged ahead of Yvette, unable to wait. This was truly *exciting news*.

In the kitchen Push was under the sink, with his upper body hidden. Reggie was close by, affixing a plate over the light switch.

"Hi, Mom."

"Ooooohhh . . . my big handsome son, the handyman."

Crystal gave her son a quick kiss and turned to Push. He was on his feet now.

"What's all the excitement about?" He said this as he brushed himself off. Both he and his nephew had on denim coveralls.

"Ta-DAH!" Yvette sang out, holding up a letter.

"Let me do the honors, Ms. President," said Crystal.

"Surely." Yvette and Crystal being silly.

Now Crystal cleared her throat.

From the office of Congressman Percy Chambers . . . it is

with my pleasure that I hereby wish to inform you . . . my office has discussed your 128th Street proposal . . . and we agree that it is an excellent opportunity for us to commit whatever financing you feel is necessary to complete your project . . . ramble, ramble, ramble . . . please contact my office at your earliest convenience so that we may support your efforts . . . sincerely . . . Percy Chambers."

Crystal squealed as she handed Push the letter and jumped into his arms, teary-eyed.

"I'm all dirty, Crystal," Push said.

"Oh, who cares! You are the most amazing man . . . the most wonderful brother a girl could ever have."

Push returned Crystal's hug and the two swiveled this way and that. "Well . . . ahem. Can I be part of the celebration?"

Push turned to embrace Yvette and Crystal ran her hand through her son's hair. It was a truly glorious time for all.

PUSH'S PROBATION VISITS WERE ALWAYS on the 4th Friday of the month. It was a pitiful routine, but it had to be done. This whole area in lower Manhattan, with courthouse, the string of law enforcement agencies and all other forms of government, was an intimidating circle of institutions to have to visit, even for killer. The visits with Ms. Watson didn't usually take long—5 to 10 minutes. It was always the same questions.

How's work? Any problems with police? Or any other agencies of the law? You're staying out of trouble, yes??

All the while, Ms. Watson would look over the form that Push would need to fill out before stepping into her office. The form asked the same basic questions, but also for a more detailed outline of his personal business: debts owed, money in savings or checking accounts, gifts received, and every other piece of nitty-gritty detail to enable the Probation Officer to assess his day-to-day activities. Push knew that this was mere procedure and that it was just as easy to lie as it was to tell the truth. He had little to hide, but then of course, there were some things he'd *rather not* talk about. "Okay,

Push. Now that the routine stuff is done with, I need to have a heart-to-heart talk with you."

Push considered Ms. W's words and how she grew so accustomed to calling him by his nickname. *Please don't tell me this is gonna get sexual. Heart-to-heart? Does that include some kind of touching?* He wondered if he misjudged Watson. He couldn't imagine what she wanted outside of their routine chat. Then she came from behind her desk and pulled up a chair. She was a few feet away once she sat down and studied Push.

"I needed to make myself real clear here, so that there's no misunderstanding. I've watched you closely these past months . . . how you've set your foot down into society to stake your claim . . . and I have to say that I'm really impressed. But, as with all things, everything ain't always what it seems. I have plenty of people on probation that lie to me right in my face. And you know what? I pay it no mind. I just let them have enough rope to hang themselves. I don't know exactly what you're into out there, Push. Of course I've seen your handy work with the brownstones and you've got a devoted woman by your side . . . and there's your sister and her son who you've been a father to. What I mean to say is . . ."

You're a killer. Be careful, man. Just like I followed you, others can too.

"Whatever you do out there, Push, be careful. Don't take life for granted. Don't throw it all away for any nonsense . . ."

I hope you don't go after Fred Allen. That's really what I want to tell you. That and so much more that you don't know.

"What, are you leavin' town, Ms. W?"

"Maybe. Maybe not."

"Yes you are. And that white dude is takin' your caseload, isn't he."

"You're real observant, Push. Maybe, like I said before, too smart for your own good. But just remember what I said. You have a good thing goin' out here. I wanna see you become successful. Not another statistic."

"No problem, Ms. W."

Can I go home now?

"You're dismissed."

Evelyn found herself amused by all of the unspoken truths—thick as 12-year-old funk—that hung in the air between her and Push. He was in the dark when it came to Evelyn's knowledge of (or involvement in) his actions during the past 12 months, ever since he stepped out into the free world.

He'd die laughing, or crying, if he knew I was following him that night on 122nd Street, and how I needed to spring him from the jaws of the 28th precinct—he was the solution to the problem Fred & I had with Sara . . . I know about his gun supplier, about his girlfriend's address, job and bank accounts . . . about Miguel, the YOU NEED JESUS van, and the last of the 3 stick-up thugs who murdered his mom and dad.

Sometimes Evelyn thought that she was too adventurous . . . that she knew a little bit too much. Enough even to endanger her own life. But for now, she was just concerned for Push.

"Be careful, buddy. If you underestimate me, who else are you underestimating?"

Push had to pass through the waiting area to reach the corridor and elevators. A handful of probationers were still out here where he had been. Three men and two women. One woman looked to be in her early 20s, while a man with glasses and grey hair could've been someone's grandfather.

Halfway through the waiting room, Push was stopped in his tracks. There was an extremely pale black man, with skin ashy like frosted sourdough bread, seated by the wall, falling asleep with his mouth partially opened. His hair was short, black like smog, and matted down over a grossly balding spot.

His half-closed, beady white eyes seemed to be sunk into their sockets and (Push couldn't help but to look twice) he had all but two teeth missing.

Damn this man looks like he's dead.

"Tonto?"

The man jerked back into consciousness.

"Huh? Who? Oh . . ." He wiped his watery eyes.

"Shit. Tonto, it's me . . . Push. From One-two-five . . . we met up in Lewisburg."

"Hey Puchhh . . ." The way the name came out, it was missing everything but the P. "Lon kime . . . huh?"

Push guessed that Tonto meant: *"long time . . ."* Only, it took a second to read between the lines.

"Yeah. It has been a long time. When did you get home?"

"Lachh wee—"

Damn . . . he just got home and he looks sick as a dog. What did they do to him in prison?

"You gonna be a'iight?"

Just then, the receptionist called a name.

"Tha—me," Tonto said. Push saw the man needed help getting up and he assisted. Once Tonto was on his feet, with a cane to support himself, Push quickly slipped a 100-dollar bill in his old friend's pocket.

"Take care, Tonto."

Tonto gave a wave as he struggled towards the door that Push had just left out of. *Hunched back, hair fallin' out, and he can hardly walk. That man is dead.*

Push wagged his head and left the building. He'd been here in this miserable setting for long enough. Maybe too long. He was reminded that he had to find a lawyer to get his probation period reduced. And then he thought about things Evelyn said. She always seemed to see right through him . . . like she knew something more than she was entitled to. More than Push ever knew.

Push shook the thought. *She's bluffin'.*

I T WOULD BE SUMMERTIME SOON, when more folks were outdoors after sundown. That would complicate things for the task he had to complete. *Alonzo . . . brother's apartment . . . on top of Sammy's Crab Legs.* Between overseeing the massive effort to rehabilitate West 128th Street and his newfound social life with Yvette, there was barely room to breathe.

Push would have to make time. After all when it came

down to it, it seemed as though everyone else's fate was in his hands.

"You can never tell what's in a man's mind. And if he's from Harlem, there's no use in even tryin' . . .
From *Harlem Blues*

A Message From The Author:

I wrote this novel from the bowels of society; from the darkest, loneliest, most secluded place a man could possibly exist. From start, to finish, this novel took all of two weeks to write. Charge that to my passion, my devotion and my discipline.

I want to also say that there are so many Asondras in the world . . . so many Crystals . . . and so many Yvettes. The she-ro in this story is modeled after you, but she also succeeds for you, so that you may have a template to learn from. Women make both good and bad choices in life, as do men. But, it is here that I make clear my understanding how much harder it is for our sisters and mothers.

There are many taboo words, definitions and slangs which I use in my stories, and which readers may feel are "excessive" or uncalled for. However, it is the truth. It is a certain reality. It's how many of us live; it is how many of us speak; it is a way of life for generations of our people. Whether we accept it or deny it is irrelevant. It was simply necessary for me to create truth and reality in my characters.

I expect that you will take from these pages both the good and the bad of how we interact with one another. Buy 5 copies and give them as gifts to the "un-aware," so that they too may know the pitfalls and possiblities of life.

Sincerely,
Relentless Aaron

You can e-mail Relentless Aaron at:
relentless166@aol.com
or visit the website:
www.relentlessaaron.com

Peace

READ ON FOR AN EXCERPT FROM

To Live and Die in Harlem

BY RELENTLESS AARON

COMING SOON FROM ST. MARTIN'S PAPERBACKS

MELRAH WAS HARLEM, SPELLED BACKWARDS, an idea that Push conceived for a business name. Yvette, Push's girlfriend from the time he left prison, had assumed the role of Vice President, while Crystal, his sister, was also on the Board of Directors as a silent partner. And most importantly, every unit was occupied.

MELRAH's office was on the ground floor of 440, complete with its own entrance there by the underbelly of the front staircase. Just above the office, on the 2nd level, lived Horace Silvers, the proprietor of SILVER WEAR, a large clothing store on 125th Street. Above Mr. Silvers, on the top floor, lived Denise Cosby and Sheryl Roberts. Push originally had a problem with renting to the two lovers, figuring that their *"way of life"* didn't follow nature's own laws (that whole boy-meets-girl activity) and so, he figured, they probably had some cards missing from their decks. And if that was the case, how responsible could they be where it came to maintaining a household . . . or paying the rent?

But there were other standards—issues that Push looked at as *complications*. And yet, such things actually helped to widen Push's one-way perspective. For one thing there was THE FAIR HOUSING ACT that prohibited such discrimination. Just because Push *assumed* that Denise and Sheryl might not be perfect tenants didn't justify a rejection of their application for the residence.

Naturally, Push didn't want to commit any "prohibited" acts. Furthermore, Yvette was right there to witness this . . .

the women coming to the office . . . their convictions about being lesbians, and also how they were otherwise fine prospects for tenants.

And Yvette said to him, "I think we should let them have it, Push. One is a doctor and the other is the manager over at Magic Johnson Theaters."

"Listen, I don't have no ill feelings towards them. I just wondered if they'll be drama, that's all. You know, cat fights n'whatnot. And . . . okay, so what if I did have my own personal issues about them. In time, maybe I'll understand how or why they are the way they are. But in the meantime, I just want good tenants who will pay on time and take care of what I put sweat and tears into renovating."

"I agree, Push. We've had our fill of the nonsense. So . . . what if I kept an eye on things? I mean, isn't that my job anyhow?"

"I guess."

"Okay then. Let me do my job," said Yvette. She kissed Push on the forehead and that was the last of it. The girl-girl activity was a firm GO.

Next door, at 441 West 128th, Francine Oliver, who stood out in the short line of Black record company executives, lived on the 1st floor. Above Francine was empty, except Francine leased the 2nd floor on behalf of PGD, her employer. That residence had a 5-year lease, and she had it all decked out like it was Elvis Presley's 2nd home—appropriate for any guest that the record company ushered in from out of town. Lastly, there was the Wallace family—one of the latest headaches: the rent was late again.

With all of the rentals filled, Push was able to cover the monthly payments without delay or pressure. His tenants paid him, and he paid George Murphy. It was a simple and routine arrangement. Furthermore, as agreed, 50% of MEL-RAH's payments were to be applied towards the total purchase price after 2 years.

But here was another headache. Time had run out on the 2-year agreement. It was time for MELRAH to fulfill its end of the lease-option. Furthermore, there was a larger deal waiting in the wings. Murphy had agreed to sweeten things for MELRAH, considering how well the business arrangement was going. Since there were 34 properties in all—mostly abandoned brownstones—which Murphy owned, he offered the whole block of properties for a paltry thousand dollars each—a total of $34,000 per month, so long as MELRAH could close on half of the properties within 2 years.

Push took the time to discuss the deal with Yvette, figuring all the labor they'd employ, the supplies required, and other expenses that were necessary for such a large venture.

"Baby, we *could* do this," Yvette said in a most encouraging overture. "Except this time you won't have to break your back to get the work done. We'll hire contractors, handymen, and get it finished in half the time."

"It's a lot of work, Yvette. Do you realize we'd be overseeing thirty-four properties? And if we're purchasing them at a hundred thousand each, the whole deal is worth three million dollars."

Yvette shook her head, unwavering from her position—the motivator.

Push said, "Not only that, Murphy wants us to close the deal on half . . . half of the properties, Yvette. What's that? Over one point seven million dollars? *Have you forgotten the color of our skin?* We ain't supposed to have money like that. I'd feel more comfortable with doing, like, four or five properties at a time. Build my way up to that many houses. What you're talking about is a lot of work to be done in a very short period of time. Think about it. I don't think I wanna carry that much pressure on my back if it's not necessary."

Yvette approached Push, hands on hips, and took a stance, like she couldn't believe her eyes.

"Is this the man I've devoted my all to? A wuss?" And there it was. She had to go and say a damned thing like that.

A wuss? Has she lost her fuckin' mind?

"Now just a minute woman."

Yvette stuck her hand in the air, as if to officially tell her man to *talk to the hand.*

"No. *You* wait a minute, Push. Didn't you once tell me that you wouldn't be the one to always make the decisions? That you would—*what was the word you used—surrender* things for me to handle? Because, why? Because, as you say, *you have faith in me*? Well where's the faith, Push? *Hunh?* Where's it?"

Push still had his foot stuck in the quicksand of being called *a wuss*, but also, he couldn't deny Yvette's personal power or her convictions. The woman was sharp. She had it goin' on upstairs, outside, inside, and down there. And this latest confrontation only showed him that, yes, he chosen a helluva woman to stand by his side. The old heads use to say it in prison: "*You need a woman who's a lady by day, who cooks and cleans for you, and turns into a slut in the bedroom.*" Push always saw that as an outrageous thing to say, especially in this day and age, and especially since he had a grown-assed sister who had her hard times with this Mack and that. But, in the end, his personal choice was to have all of Yvette—whatever that turned out to be—and if he were lucky enough, she'd compliment him with her right hand high and Ruger by her side.

For now, with how she was speaking to him so sassy . . . that spicy " *'bout it-'bout it*" way of addressing him, with the sex appeal going in her favor, how could he ever disregard her? This was Yvette, in all of her ghetto fabulousness, and she had every bit of his attention, however she had to get it.

"All I need from you, sir, is your blessing. Because we are *going* to make this happen. And yes, there's work to be done, but no more than we've *been* doing. The biggest change, as far as I can see, is with the paperwork. And that's *my* department. And besides, we can always turn to the Empowerment Fund, Push. So we might as well make the most of this. Think bigger, because baby . . . we've already *been* thinkin big."

Eventually, Push kept his own promise. He surrendered to his woman. Maybe not a wuss after all, he told himself.

"I'll go with whatever you say, babe. You ain't let me down yet, Miss Donald Trump." Caught in the sparkle of her own eyes, Push went on to say, "Just keep me informed. Any complications, I wanna know." Yvette brushed up against Push like the prize catch she was.

"Can I show you some of that appreciation I'm so good at?"

"Tryin to mix business with pleasure again, Yvette?"

Push's accusation fell on deaf ears; Yvette already had her blouse stretching over her head. She enjoyed doing this for him—unwrapping herself spontaneously, and for his eyes only. In a matter of seconds she'd be tasting his flesh, another peak moment in her life.

From the emerging master of urban fiction comes another gritty, shockingly true-to-life suspense ride—a sweeping tale that takes readers from the streets of Harlem to the Brazilian jungle where the drug wars are being fought...to the death.

DON'T MISS RELENTLESS AARON'S NEXT NOVEL

The Last Kingpin

ISBN: 0-312-94967-7

COMING IN JUNE 2007
FROM ST. MARTIN'S PAPERBACKS

. . . AND LOOK FOR

Extra Marital Affairs

ISBN: 0-312-35935-7

NOW AVAILABLE IN TRADE PAPERBACK
FROM ST. MARTIN'S GRIFFIN